THE SWEETEST THING

by

Cathy Woodman

Magna Large Print Books
Long Preston, North Yorkshire,
BD23 4ND, England.

British Library Cataloguing in Publication Data.

Woodman, Cathy
    The sweetest thing.

    A catalogue record of this book is
    available from the British Library

    ISBN   978-0-7505-3568-7

First published in Great Britain in 2011 by Arrow Books

Copyright © Cathy Woodman, 2011

Cover illustration © Rachel Ross by arrangement with
Random House Group Ltd.

Cathy Woodman has asserted her right under the Copyright, Designs
and Patents Act, 1988 to be identified as the author of this work

Published in Large Print 2012 by arrangement with
Arrow, one of the publishers in the Random House Group Ltd.

Magna Large Print is an imprint of Library Magna Books Ltd.

Printed and bound in Great Britain by
T.J. (International) Ltd., Cornwall, PL28 8RW

THE SWEETEST THING

Jennie Copeland thought she knew the recipe for a happy life: marriage to her university sweetheart, a nice house in the suburbs and three beautiful children. But when her husband leaves her, she is forced to find a different recipe. And she thinks she's found just what she needs: a ramshackle house on the outskirts of the beautiful Talyton St George, a new cake-baking business, a dog, a horse, chickens... But life in the country is not quite as idyllic as she'd hoped, and Jennie can't help wondering whether neighbouring farmer Guy Barnes is the missing ingredient.

THE SWEETEST THING

To Tamsin and Will

Chapter One

Chocolate Brownies

After that, the life-changing event that was the big D, I swore I'd never fall in love again. I resolved to harden my heart and steer well clear of emotional commitment, yet here I am, completely besotted – and before you say anything, I'm not talking about a man but what has to be the most beautiful house in the world.

Nestled part-way up the hillside which rises from the valley where the River Taly meanders down towards the sea is Uphill House, a longhouse dating all the way back to the sixteenth century. It has diamond-leaded windows set deep into thick walls of cob, painted the palest pink, and a hat of golden thatch. It sits in four acres of land on the outskirts of the East Devon market town of Talyton St George. The house hints of security, comfort and forever-ness, if there is such a word, and I can only hope that after all the heartbreak my family's been through, this relationship will be permanent.

Having left the car at the front, I make my way through the rickety picket gate and beat a path through grass and flowering mallow up to my waist, to the porch that consists of half-height walls and worn upright timbers which support a tiled roof. Ducking beneath a tangle of faded

11

wisteria, pink and yellow climbing roses and honeysuckle, I reach the front door.

I lift the edge of the mat which lies on the stone step, pick up the envelope beneath and open it up to find a note and a key. I scan the note. It's very brief and hardly welcoming, which isn't surprising considering the way the writer of the note has behaved over the sale. Buying Uphill House has been what you might call an uphill struggle, but then – I smile to myself – when has attaining the object of one's desires ever been easy?

To J. Copeland. Have oiled lock. G. Barnes.

G. Barnes has communicated to me through estate agent and solicitor so far. I still have no idea what the 'G' stands for or what 'G' looks like, although I have been told that he's the farmer who lives in the house next door. When I say 'next door', the farmhouse is a good thirty metres or so further along the drive, and on the opposite side. The handwriting on the note is a scrawl suggestive of a character with few manners and poor social skills, although I suppose that splashing oil over half the door and the step could be interpreted as a thoughtful gesture on his part.

Taking care not to get oil on my green embroidered tunic and black cropped trousers, I slide the key into the latch, jiggle and twist it until it turns. I push the door open. It creaks on its hinges, whether in welcome or protest at our arrival, I'm not sure. Its rather dilapidated condition suggests that it has been left in peace for some while.

Inside at last. It's quite a shock, stepping from the glaring sunshine and intense heat of the hottest day of summer so far, into the cool, dark hallway. I pause and breathe in the scent of the house, a rural perfume of rose petals, damp timbers and farmyard. I let my gaze travel along the hall that is lined with dark oak panels, to the grimy glass window at the end, through which I can see a slightly distorted view of the back garden with the paddock that slopes up to the copse beyond, and my pulse thrills with joy and anticipation.

Finding myself single again at forty after fourteen years of marriage was the last thing I'd expected, but now that I've got through the divorce, I'm going to grab this opportunity – new home, new business, new life – with both hands. I can't wait to get into the kitchen and get started.

However, there is the small matter of a lorry full of possessions to unload, the unpacking to do, and the children to settle before I can begin to master the Aga. I turn to my three offspring who have followed on behind me, clutching various bits and pieces they've brought with them from the car: headphones, iPods, a teddy bear and the cool bag. They are unusually quiet; apprehensive and overwhelmed by the sight of the new house, perhaps. It's been a stressful few days.

'Well, what do you think?' I ask brightly. It's the first time they've seen it, apart from the virtual tour on the agent's website which was filmed in soft focus to disguise the cracks in the walls and all-enveloping brown dust. I did bring them with me the first few times I came house-hunting, but they were soon bored with the whole idea and in the end it was easier for me to come to Devon alone while they were spending their allotted weekends with their father. I look at my eldest in his bright orange Hollister T-shirt and jeans down around his thighs so you can see his boxers. Adam's fourteen going on twenty-four, taller than me now, and lanky with an unruly mop of brown hair, grey eyes and a smattering of teenage spots. He's growing up so fast, growing away from me. I can feel, with a pang of regret, a dull ache in the centre of my chest, that Adam doesn't want to think of himself as my little boy any more.

'Well?' I go on.

He shrugs.

'It's okay, but I don't know why you care what I think now when it's too late to change our minds and go back home.'

'Adam, I thought you were cool with it,' I say. 'That's what you said.'

'That was ages ago and before I saw this dump.' I can hear the bitterness rising in his voice.

'We'll make it our own,' I say, suppressing a flicker of worry over his state of mind. 'We'll decorate your room how you want it, and of course there's plenty of space for the dog.'

We don't have a dog yet, but Adam's always wanted one, and I can see from the way his expression softens that he's feeling a little better about the move already. It'll be all right, I tell myself. He'll soon settle. He'll have to because there's no going back. This move has to work for all of us. The children might not appreciate it yet, but what I've done, I've done for them.

'What do you think, Georgia?' I ask, turning to my middle child who takes after me, being petite and brunette. She has her hair tied back in a ponytail and wears a thin black cardigan over a white vest and blue jeggings. She's ten next birthday and very much a tomboy.

'You didn't say it was falling down, Mummy,' she says, keeping her hand tucked into her sleeve as she points towards the sloping lintel of the doorway that leads through into what the estate agent called the drawing room. The whole house slopes in all directions, floors, walls and ceilings, but that's part of its charm.

'I think it's always been like that.' I feel my youngest reach out for my hand and link her small, slightly sweaty fingers through mine. 'What do you think, Sophie?' I look down, awaiting her answer while she looks around, her blonde curls bobbing around her shoulders, her eyes wide and blue, and her rosebud lips pursed in thought. She's eight and far more girlie than her sister – she's wearing a pink summer dress and has a smear of my mother's lippy on her cheek.

'It's a witch's house.' She shudders. 'I don't like it.'

'Oh, I'm sorry,' I say, disappointed and slightly panicky that none of the children share my enthusiasm for our new home. It's been a wrench for them, leaving London, but I'd hoped they'd love Uphill House when they saw it. I wish that they could see its potential, like the estate agent who'd showed me round several months ago.

'Mum, can I have something to eat?' Adam says from beside me.

'I thought you might run off to explore,' I say, hopeful of having the house to myself for a few minutes, time to gather my thoughts before my parents and the removal people turn up.

15

'I need food first,' Adam insists.

'There's food in the cool bag,' I say. 'Georgia, can you pass the bag to Adam, please?'

Georgia drops it at her brother's feet, size nines in skate shoes with fluorescent laces, and Adam rifles through, coming out with the tub of chocolate brownies I baked last night when we were over at my parents', keeping out of the way of the removal people who were packing the last of our things into boxes and crates. When the going gets tough, the tough get going – whereas I just get baking.

'Not those,' I say quickly. 'They're for later.'

'But I'm starving.' Adam examines a second container. 'What about the cherry cake? Don't tell me you're saving that too...'

I was, but I'm feeling guilty for dragging him away from his friends and the skate park so I give in.

'Just make sure you save a piece for Granddad then.' Unfortunately for my dad, the baking gene skipped a generation. My mum's mum baked and so do I, but Mum gave up trying years ago, her rock buns turning out like granite and her coconut cones collapsing into what our family folklore calls coconut flatties, rather than rising up perkily like Madonna's bras in the eighties.

'I wanna piece of cake else it's not fair,' says Sophie from behind me, the very arbiter of fairness. 'Adam, pass the box over.'

'I don't want any, thank you,' says Georgia politely, and I smile to myself.

They're so different yet I love each of them unconditionally even after three hours on the road,

16

and that's saying something. There can be no harsher test of a mother's love than a one-hundred-and-fifty-mile car journey on a hot summer's day.

Georgia is the quiet, sensible one whereas Sophie takes after her father's side of the family: outgoing and self-righteous. Adam's personality lies somewhere between the two. He wasn't planned, but he was the best mistake I ever made. Georgia came along a little later than intended, and Sophie was conceived on impulse. Her arrival should have been the icing on the cake, but was more like the jam through a Victoria sponge, sticking the layers of our marriage back together after one of David's affairs. It didn't last, which is how we ended up here, I suppose.

It's too late for regrets though. The deal is done. The money – David's divorce settlement was generous as it should have been, since he didn't show much in the way of remorse for what happened – has changed hands and there's no going back. Today, I locked the door on my old life and left it all behind ... all of it apart from the children, of course, and the car, and the removal lorry. Oh, and my parents who followed on behind in their own car. They've insisted on coming along to help with the move and I'm grateful because I don't think I could have got this far without them.

'Jennie, we're here!' My mother joins us in the hall, greeting me with a hug as she always does, as if she hasn't seen me for weeks. She's sixty-six but could easily pass for ten years younger. Her hair is short and sculpted, and she tells the children that she irons her face to keep the wrinkles at

17

bay. She's wearing cropped trousers, a cotton top and flat sandals, and Adam towers above her.

'How's my gorgeous grandson?' Mum grins as Adam retreats rapidly out of touching distance. 'It's all right. I shan't kiss you. And you and Sophie?' she adds, turning to Georgia.

'I was sick in the car,' Georgia says.

'I expect it was because of those wiggly lanes,' Mum says.

'Yes, what kept you?' I say.

'We took the scenic route.' Mum rests her hands on her hips and tips her head to one side. 'Actually, your granddad got lost. But you know what he's like. He won't admit it.'

'Neither will Mum,' Adam mutters.

'Mummy was in such a hurry to get here that she ran straight into a tractor,' says Sophie, wiping sticky crumbs from her face with the back of her hand.

'Almost ran into a tractor,' Georgia corrects her as Mum raises one eyebrow.

It's true. I was whizzing along, a bit miffed because the SatNav had lost the signal and stopped speaking to me, and wondering how one tree could look so much like another, which only goes to show how out of touch I am with the natural world, something I intend to change very soon. That's right. I wasn't concentrating, which is why the tractor came upon me more quickly than I expected as I negotiated a sharp right-hand bend.

Unsure I was going to stop in time, I screamed, 'Hold on tight!', slammed on the brakes and waited for the bump.

18

'We were this far–' Georgia holds up her hand, demonstrating a gap of about a centimetre between her finger and thumb '–from this great big–' she struggles to find words adequate to describe the monstrous machine '–huge tractor.'

'It was enormous,' I agree, smiling.

'And it was blue,' says Sophie. 'And Mummy went very red.'

'I don't know about that.' All I know is that it was the first time in ages that my heart's beaten faster. I lowered the window as the driver jumped down and approached.

'I think that man wants to speak to you,' Sophie said, somewhat unnecessarily.

I wasn't so sure I wanted to speak to him, I thought, when this face appeared, an unfriendly face, the forehead furrowed, the eyes cool grey-blue and staring, and the mouth set in a stubborn line. My first thought was that it could be a handsome face in a rugged kind of way, the complexion tanned, the jaw-line square, but then its owner began to speak in a voice as deep and dark as burned sugar.

'What do you think you're doing? This isn't a bloody racetrack.'

'I know ... I'm sorry,' I mumbled. I was speeding. I admit it.

'You could have been killed. And your children.'

His eyes drilled into mine. I looked away, the irresponsible mother, concentrating instead on what I could see of the rest of him, the muscular torso partially hidden by a tatty grey vest, the hairs in his armpit as he leaned against my car. He had a musky, animal smell – not unpleasant – and his

19

jeans looked as if they had never been through a wash, but he had something about him, the confidence of someone happy in his own skin.

'Look, I've said I'm sorry,' I began when he didn't seem in a hurry to get back to his tractor.

'You don't come from round here, do you?' he said slowly, in a West Country accent as thick as clotted cream. He paused to flick a wave of light brown, almost blond hair from his eyes. 'I can give you directions back to town, if that's where you're heading.'

'I'm fine,' I said, refusing to be helped in any-way, no matter how well intentioned the offer might have been. Since David left me, I've had to do virtually everything myself, and I don't intend for that to change. Although I doubted it at first, I've discovered that I like my independence.

'Mum!' Georgia said at the same time as Sophie aimed a kick at the back of my seat.

'I know where I'm going,' I said adamantly.

'Ah, but do you know where you are?' the man said, with a spark of humour, and in spite of my embarrassment at being caught out, driving like a maniac, I smiled back.

'Would you mind getting out of my way so we can get on?' I said, quickly sobering up. I refrained from adding that we had a house to move into.

'You'll have to reverse.' He grinned as if he could read my panic. The brambles in the hedges were touching both sides of the car, and there was the hint of a ditch, hidden by long grass and wild-flowers, running alongside the lane. 'The nearest passing place is about half a mile back,' he added.

I reversed until my neck cricked and my brain

almost melted, while the man in the tractor nodded and waved me on back condescendingly, until I reached a gateway and pulled in to let him squeeze past. I could feel myself shrinking, making myself small as if that was going to spare my paintwork, although I don't know why I was worrying about something so trivial when, with one wrong turn of those massive wheels, we could all have been crushed to death.

'Why didn't you let the man tell us how to get there?' Georgia complained when I was watching the tractor rolling on down the hill behind us. 'Why did you pretend you know where we're going?'

'Because I don't expect he knows. He's just some old country bumpkin.' I don't know why I said 'old' because I reckon he could have been a few years younger than me.

'What's one of those – a bum-kin?' asked Sophie.

I thought Adam couldn't possibly hear anything over his music, but he switched off his iPod and joined in.

'It's someone who looks like a scarecrow and goes round wearing a battered hat with a feather sticking out of it. And they usually have a piece of straw in their mouth and speak like this.' At which Adam launched into a fair imitation of a West Country accent, which made Sophie laugh, and brought a smile to Georgia's face.

I wasn't lost after all, just temporarily disorientated, I thought triumphantly as we reached the brow of the hill where the lane divided into two. The left-hand branch was signposted Uphill Farm and Uphill House, the sign itself leaning against a

churn on a stone platform by the hedge. There was a board too with 'Potatoe's' and 'Cider' chalked on it, in amongst the milkmaids, red campions and wild strawberry plants. I turned past them and bumped up the rutted track for another half a mile and here we were...

'The driver got out to speak to Mummy, and Granny, I didn't like him,' says Sophie. 'He said "bloody" and that isn't allowed, is it? I think he's a very rude person.'

'Oh, let's forget about that now,' I say. 'We're here. We made it.'

'The removal people are here too.' Mum glances towards the front door, where a lorry is drawing up. 'We'd better get the kettle on. Where is the kettle?'

'It's in the boot of my car.' It was the last thing we packed. I send Adam out to fetch it.

'Jennie,' my dad interrupts. He's seventy now, recently retired from his job as director of an engineering company. He's tall and slim, and plays golf as much as he can, although I suspect he spends just as much time at the nineteenth hole as he does on the course proper. Even today, he's wearing a burgundy polo-shirt with the golf-club logo.

'Yes, Dad?'

'The driver wants to know if he can park the lorry in the yard and take the furniture through the back door.'

'I don't see why not.' Just between the house itself and a tumbledown barn is a five-bar gate which gives access to a yard bordered by a row of three stables and a post-and-rail fence with a gate

22

on to the paddock.

'He isn't at all sure about the sofas,' Dad goes on, pulling a handkerchief from his pocket and using it to wipe his glasses.

'What do you mean? He hasn't left them behind?'

'No.' Dad slips his glasses back on. 'It's just that the doors on this house are rather narrow and your sofas are rather large.'

'Can we take a window out or something?' I seem to remember having seen this done on TV before.

'The windows are rather dinky too,' Dad says. 'I doubt we can dismantle the sofas, so the only option left is to put them in the barn, covered up, and buy another suite.'

My heart sinks. Another expense to add to all the others that I hadn't budgeted for, like paying for the Aga to be serviced and having the chimneys swept before we moved in.

'What will we sit on?' I groan.

'Our bums,' says Adam.

'Adam, that's rude,' Sophie says, wagging a finger at her big brother.

Dad grins. 'We aren't going to have much time for sitting, are we? This place is going to take a bit of work to get it sorted.' He squints towards the exposed beams above our heads. 'I hope you haven't taken on too much.'

'You do like it, though?' I say anxiously. 'You do think it'll be worth it in the end?'

'I love it, Jennie.' Mum links her arm through mine. 'I wish me and your dad had had the courage to move out of London when we were your

23

age. I'd have loved a place like this. It's so romantic, like something out of a fairytale.'

'Without the handsome prince,' I say wryly.

'You don't know that yet,' Mum says.

But I do, I think, my chest tight with regret.
With David gone, there are no princes left for
me. I still feel so let down. The princess – because
David did treat me as a princess to begin with –
was abandoned with her three children and
banished from the kingdom. Okay, it's a modern-
day fairytale without a happy ending, in which
we share joint custody and I chose to move away.

'Let me give everyone a quick tour so you know
where everything is,' I say, changing the subject.
'Let's go.' I pick up the cool bag and the cake
boxes and take them through the next room, a
kind of lobby with stairs leading up to the landing, then into the kitchen, my favourite room. It's
enormous, double aspect with views to the front
of the overgrown garden, the lane and open fields,
and yet more overgrown garden to the back. In
the stone alcove which used to house the open fire
is an ancient but, I'm assured, perfectly service-
able Aga. To the right there is a hole in the stone-
work, the access point to the original bread oven
that doesn't appear to have been used for years.

Dad walks across to the stable door on the far
side and opens the top, letting the afternoon
sunshine stream in across the stone floor.

'You'll be able to bake plenty of cakes in this
kitchen, Jennie,' he says.

'That's what I'm planning to do,' I say. *Jennie's
Cakes*. I can see it now. A vast oak table in the
centre, cooling racks piled high with all kinds of

calorie-laden goodies: cream pastries, chocolate-chip cookies, fairy cakes, tea breads, lemon drizzle cake. I picture myself flicking through an exercise book – one with a chintzy cover to go with the lifestyle, of course – filled with orders. I imagine removing three tiers of rich fruit cake, fed with brandy, from the walk-in larder, to be covered with marzipan and iced a few days before a client's special day. My mind runs riot.

'It's going to take some cleaning before you get your hygiene certificate,' Mum observes, bringing me back to earth. She scratches at the butler's sink with her fingernail. 'I reckon this is sixteenth-century grease.'

It's true. I am realistic though. It's going to be some time before I get a taste of success. Whatever. I know it'll be sweet eventually, like golden syrup.

'When did anyone last live here?' says Dad, looking up at the cobwebs which hang like rags from the ceiling.

'Mrs Barnes – the last owner – moved out a few years ago, so I've been told.' I run a finger across the wooden draining board, picking up a sheen of reddish dust and a splinter. The kitchen is going to have to be sorted out before I can set up my business – it needs a little updating.

'It doesn't look as if she looked after the place,' says Dad.

'I got the impression from the agent that she was pretty ancient.' I squeeze the splinter out and rinse it off under the tap. The water comes out with a bang and a gurgle then a rush.

'Like the house,' says Adam. 'You know, this

would make a great games room, Mum.'

'No way! This is my domain. I thought you could make yourself a den in the barn eventually. It's twice the size of this.'

'But the pony's hay will have to go in the barn,' says Georgia.

'There are three stables,' I point out. 'We aren't having three ponies so you can store pony food in one of those. Guys, we have four acres – there's more than enough room for all of us.'

'Yeah, I'll be able to get away from you lot,' Adam says, and he gives Georgia a big brotherly shove at which she flies back at him, aiming a kick at his shin, a scene repeated so many times before that I've lost count.

'Let's go upstairs,' Mum says quickly, diverting them before the scrap can escalate, but I can't help suspecting that another fight will ensue almost immediately over allocating bedrooms.

'This is a strange layout,' Mum observes when we reach the upper floor. All four bedrooms and the bathroom lead off one long corridor which runs along the rear of the house.

'It's very traditional,' I say. 'I've been doing my research, and the longhouse was built to house the family and their animals under one roof. They would have been separated by the cross passage – the hall under our feet.'

'How on earth do you get a cow upstairs, Mum?' Adam says.

'The animals didn't live upstairs,' I say, giving him a teasing nudge. 'This would have been a loft with ladders up to where the people slept and where they kept the hay.'

'Which end did the animals live in?' Georgia asks.

'Yeah, I wanna know because I'm not living in a cowshed,' says Adam, the authentic voice of a twenty-first-century teen.

'The kitchen and lobby would have been for people. The drawing-room end was the shippon, the area for the cows. That's why the floor slopes and has a drain running down the middle. It would have been for the dung.'

'That's completely disgusting.' Adam wrinkles his nose. 'No wonder it stinks in here.'

'It's a lovely countryside aroma,' Mum says, bending her knees slightly to look out of the low window where red roan and white cows are visible, grazing in the field. 'I expect it's from those cows – or are they bulls? – across the way there. Malcolm, are those cows or bulls?'

'Better find out before anyone goes out there,' Dad says.

'We can't go out there,' says Georgia. 'It's the farmer's field.'

'Yuck,' says Adam.

Ignoring him, I open the door to the first room we come across, the bathroom.

'That's a good size,' says Mum before falling silent, because that's about all you can say. The rose-patterned wallpaper is peeling away and faded to brown. The bath has lost much of its enamel and stands in the middle of the dark floorboards. The old-fashioned toilet with its high cistern, and a chain to pull, is positioned on top of three steps like a throne.

'I'd make a feature of that,' says Mum brightly,

'it's historic.'

'There's no shower,' Adam says.

'We'll get one fitted,' I assure him, quickly moving on to the next room. 'I thought this would be yours, Adam.'

He takes a quick tour of the room, opening the door to the left of the fireplace and closing it again.

'There's no en suite?' he says.

'Well, you've been spoiled up to now,' I say. Adam was lucky – at our old house, he had his own shower room attached to his bedroom. 'There is just the one bathroom.'

'It's like the Dark Ages,' he says. 'You'll be telling me there's no broadband connection next.'

'Um, actually, as far as I know, there isn't. What else did you expect, Adam? We're out in the sticks.'

'How am I going to get on Facebook? How am I going to keep in touch with my friends?'

'I'll have to contact the phone people and get them to set up some kind of internet access.' I'm being suitably vague. I haven't a clue what I'm talking about. David used to deal with all the techie stuff.

'I'll do that with you tomorrow, Adam,' Dad tells him.

'Okay,' Adam says, and I wish he'd add a 'thank you'.

'I don't like the look of that patch of damp up there,' Dad says, moving closer to the window to inspect the black mould which adorns the ceiling above. However, there isn't as much damp in Adam's room as there is in the one which is supposed to be Sophie's. Even more off-putting is the desiccated bat lying in the middle of the floor.

'I'm not sleeping in here.' Sophie squeals and runs to Mum, grabbing her around the waist. Mum strokes her hair, tangling her fingers through Sophie's curls. 'It's a horrid room.'

'It is a bit different from what you're used to,' Mum agrees.

'You'll have to share with Georgia then,' I say, repressing a memory of Sophie's delight at moving back into her old room after we had it redecorated with pink and pale lime paint, and a new carpet. This is shabby, dirty, and I can imagine a decrepit old lady – think Miss Havisham from *Great Expectations* – living here with her withered wedding dress and mouldering cake. Poor Sophie.

'I don't mind sharing,' Sophie says hopefully.

'I don't wanna share,' says Georgia.

'I think people who want ponies might have to be a bit more accommodating,' I point out gently. At least, if the girls share, it'll make decorating easier. I take Georgia's silence on the matter for a yes, and give her a hug.

'I wanna go home,' says Sophie. 'I really wanna go home now.'

Mum gives me a small, sympathetic smile.

'Let's go and make that tea, and find some squash for the removal men. Come on, Sophie. Georgia too.' She touches my shoulder and a few minutes later, I join them back in the kitchen, wondering how long it's going to take us to settle in.

There's a lot to do, but I'm confident that I can deal with everything by taking one day at a time.

The work doesn't scare me at all. What is worrying me is the children's reaction to the house. The last thing I want is for them to be unhappy living here.

Dad disappears with Adam for a while then reappears.

'About the sofas,' he begins.

'You can't get them indoors,' I say, reading his expression.

'I'm afraid we can't get them in the barn either,' Dad goes on.

'It's full of stuff already,' Adam adds.

'What kind of stuff?' I say sharply, picturing my sofas having to stand outdoors, exposed to the elements.

'Rubbish,' says Adam.

'Junk,' Dad says. 'Old lampshades, wardrobes, a roll of chicken wire...'

'Ladders, tractor tyres, even a rusty old tractor,' Adam goes on.

'Great,' I say. (I'm being sarcastic.) 'I was told everything would be cleared out before we arrived.'

'Did you get that in writing?' says Dad, smiling wryly because he already knows the answer.

'No. The agent said he'd spoken to the owner's son and he'd promised to deal with it.' I feel let down.

'Come and have a look, Mum.' Adam tugs on my arm.

'Just a minute. Are you all right there?' I ask Mum who's firing up the Aga for pizza, shop-bought ones that she brought with her.

'I'm not sure,' she says. 'Does this thing come

30

with instructions?'

'If it does, they'll be written in Mediaeval English,' Adam says, sounding more cheerful now.

'I've got a book somewhere.' Summer, my best friend, gave it to me before we left. 'It's called *How to Make Friends with Your Aga*.' I'm not sure, looking at it though, that we are going to be friends and I rather wish I'd brought my old cooker with me. The cream enamel surface is chipped and scratched, and I'll never be able to work out how to use all those ovens. It has four, and two hotplates with lids on the top.

'It's taking its time. There is some oil in the tank outside, isn't there?' Mum asks.

'There'd better be. Mr Barnes charged me for it, right down to the last litre.' He didn't give anything away, except all this stuff that Dad and Adam say is in the barn.

I join them to investigate, following them back out into the late-afternoon sunshine, then picking my way across the stone path which is obscured by long grass and apologising to the poor snail that I scrunch underfoot en route. The yard is cobbled and patched with brick where the weeds have forced their way through. We skirt around the removal lorry where the men are sitting on the tailgate, taking a break, and reach the open end of the barn which is built from cob and thatch, like the house. It's filled from floor to rafters with – well, I tend to agree with Adam – rubbish, and I'm not happy. It's been a long, hot and increasingly frustrating day, and this is the last thing I need.

'That Barnes man's been nothing but a pain in the neck,' I say, close to tears. He didn't want to

31

sell the house to me, and now it's as if he's getting back at me for paying him good money – cash, by the way – for it. His delaying tactics almost forced me to pull out when my buyers threatened to withdraw their offer if there was no prospect of moving in until the beginning of the school summer holidays, but I managed to mollify them by knocking another two thousand off the price. 'If he really didn't want to sell, he shouldn't have put it on the market in the first place.'

'I expect he has his reasons,' Dad says philosophically. 'These old Devonians are never in a hurry to do anything. Don't you remember how we used to wait hours in the tea shop for a cream tea when we were on holiday? We used to joke that they were picking the strawberries for the jam.'

'Now you tell me it was a joke?' I say, chuckling. 'I believed you, Dad.' Then I sober up again. Part of my reason for moving here was because I remember the area from happy childhood holidays when the sun always shone.

'We'd better get on,' Dad says, looking up the hill behind the house where clouds are sweeping across the sun as it sets behind the copse of trees, then back to my lovely cream sofas that sit in the yard like a modern-art installation. 'It looks like rain.'

A breeze shimmies around my ankles, dives down and lifts a swirl of dust as Adam and my father start dragging bits and pieces out of the barn. I force myself to help them, my body weighed down with worry and exhaustion, my skin gritty with dried sweat. When I told Mum about my plans to move to the country, she said

32

I'd only remembered the good bits. For the briefest moment as I look back at my beautiful new house, my throat tight with mixed emotions, I wonder if perhaps she was right.

Chapter Two

Boudoir Biscuits

The next morning, I open my eyes to cool, pale light that casts faint shadows across the fresh cotton sheets. I can hear the house waking up too: the creak of floorboards as one of the children pads across to the bathroom, the sound of my father's voice from outside the window and Adam singing. Adam's up? He's never up before me. I check my alarm clock. It's gone eleven. I must have gone back to sleep after the noise and disturbance that began at about three-thirty, before dawn.

I sit up in bed and look around me. My wardrobe is a cupboard built into the eaves to one side of the chimney breast. There's no central heating yet, but every bedroom has a fireplace. There's no carpet, just a rug I bought from IKEA. Its bright, geometric design clashes with the dark red, Regency-stripe wallpaper which someone must once have found fashionable. There are boxes, as yet unpacked, stacked in front of the window-seat.

I am, as always in the early days of a love affair, gradually discovering the flaws, but they don't matter. To me, the house already feels like home.

I breathe a sigh of contentment and calm.

Something has changed. I didn't have the dream last night, the one where I forget David and I aren't together any more. I didn't wake and reach out across the sheets, seeking the warmth of his body, only to find a cold and empty space. I didn't curl up with my knees as close to my chest as I could get them, unable to suppress the anger and shame which would well up inside me: anger at David for what he did to me, to us, to our family, and at myself for not being able to let go; shame for not being a good wife – or not good enough anyway. I didn't wake up to find my joints aching with grief, and feel sick to the pit of my stomach.

Smiling to myself, I get up, throw on some jeans and a loose shirt, and wander downstairs to the kitchen, following the smell of cooked bacon. Mum looks up from where she's putting mugs out on the worktop.

'You look a bit rough, love,' she says.

'I'm fine,' I say, running my fingers through my bed hair. I'm used to my mother's occasional lack of tact. She doesn't mean anything by it, but it can be hurtful. I remember how she responded the day after David left and I told her he'd gone for good. We were in the kitchen then, the one at the old house with its glossy black units and stainless-steel appliances.

'What makes you think he won't come back?' Mum said.

'Because–' I started to sob again '–he's "in love", whatever that means, and I can't compete with her, not with my love-handles and Buddha belly.'

'Oh, don't be ridiculous, Jennie. You've got a

34

marvellous figure.' Mum paused and then added, 'For your age.'

'For my age?' I repeated. My mother was being straight, brutally honest in fact, and it hurt. 'You see, that's just it,' I exploded. 'She – the other bloody woman – is fifteen years younger. I didn't... I don't stand a chance.' I paused. 'Look at me. My body's been ravaged by pregnancy and childbirth, I'm almost forty and on my own with three kids...'

'You aren't alone, darling,' Mum said, taking me in her arms where I broke down completely.

'I'm a complete failure...'

'It isn't you. It's him,' Mum said bitterly. 'You are a lovely young woman with three beautiful children. You're smart – you have a degree which is more than I have – and you run a home and cook the most wonderful cakes. You have absolutely nothing to be ashamed of.'

I didn't believe her then either, of course. It was too soon.

'Coffee?' she says now, offering me a mug and bringing me back to the present.

'Thanks, Mum.'

'Did you hear the cockerel this morning?'

'You could hardly miss him.'

'Your dad did – he brought his earplugs with him so he missed everything, the cows trampling along the drive outside *and* the milk tanker.' Mum grins. 'Oh, for the peace and tranquillity of the big city.'

'Don't say it.'

'I'm not saying a word.' She takes a step back, bends down and opens an oven door. 'I have tamed the beast though. Look at that – full English breakfast for six.'

'How did you do that?' I ask, surprised to see a tray of browned sausages and crispy bacon. Last night, it took an inordinately long time for the Aga to warm up. In fact, it didn't really get going so we ate lukewarm pizzas, the cheese barely melted on the top, sitting at the sleek, glass-topped table which I'd thought looked so cool when I bought it, but now looks completely out of place. We drank lemonade and champagne to toast the house, and cleared the dusty cobwebs from the ceilings above our heads before the girls would agree to go to bed. Mum and Dad slept on an airbed in the drawing room.

'It works on the principle of stored heat. We didn't give it long enough to warm up.'

'Thanks, Mum.' I put my arms around her. 'I couldn't have done this without you and Dad.'

'It's the least we could do, love. Just promise me though that this is the first and last of your harebrained schemes?'

'Where is Dad?' I say, changing the subject. 'I thought I heard him outside.'

'He's taken the girls shopping for a draining board – this one's cracked and you can't have that in a professional bakery.' Mum emphasises the word 'professional' and I can hear the pride in her voice. I'm touched that she's proud of my ambition and entrepreneurial instinct. 'We thought we'd get the kitchen sorted first since that's going to be the most important room in the house. The sooner that's done, the sooner you can get on to environmental health to register your premises.' She smiles. 'Jennie, this is so exciting.'

It is exciting, but I'm also finding it tremendously scary too. I think I can cope with the paper-work and the baking, of course. I'm just not sure how I'm going to find my customers. I look out of the window, past the drive, at the green fields stretching away down to the river. I can see cows and birds, but where are the people?

'Sit down and eat. The bread's on the table.' Mum hands me a warm plate of food, then picks up a cloth and a bottle of cleaner. 'I think I saw your new neighbour, the farmer. Or I suppose he could have been a farmhand. Anyway, I was looking out of the window, admiring the view and watching the cows go by, when he walked past. He saw me and touched his cap. Very polite.' Mum pauses. 'Come on, Jennie. Aren't you curious?'

'Not really,' I say, somewhat stubbornly because I know there's nothing Mum loves more than a good gossip. 'Oh, all right. Go on.'

'He's quite tall, about six foot, I should guess.'

'Is that it?'

'I'd say he's in his thirties, no older. Rather a hunk, if you ask me.'

'I think the term used today is fit,' I say, amused by Mum's turn of phrase.

'All right then. He was fit, and I reckon he lives on his own on that farm.'

'How do you work that one out?'

'Have you seen anyone else coming and going?' she challenges me.

I shake my head, my mouth full of bacon and egg. 'What's more, I just happened to notice him hanging out his washing this morning.'

'Mum, have you been spying?'

'You can see over the wall into his garden when

37

you're in the girls' room. It wasn't spying. It was a chance observation ... and it struck me that the clothes were all of the masculine variety.'

'So? He's a New Man. He does his own washing.' I can't help smiling. 'Mum, I know what you're trying to do, and it won't work. Farmer or farmhand, I'm not interested.'

'I'm not saying, go out and chat him up,' she says, looking hurt. 'I'm saying, you need to keep an open mind. Jennie, I want you to be happy.'

'I am happy. Funnily enough, I can be happy without a man in my life.'

'Yes, but you're still young, beautiful, bubbly...' Mum sighs. 'I don't like the idea of you living out here all alone in the middle of nowhere.'

There's a thud from upstairs. Adam?

'I'm hardly all alone,' I say, rolling my eyes.

'But when the children leave home...'

'That's ages yet.'

'Time passes more quickly than you think,' she says wistfully. 'They'll soon go.'

Time passes, but it doesn't necessarily heal, I muse as we go on to clean the kitchen, scrubbing at the years of grime that has built up on the walls. Why can't Mum see that I'm really off men? I wipe down the windowsills, clean out the row of cupboard units along the wall opposite the Aga, and start unpacking my baking utensils and recipe books.

As I pick my favourite book out of the crate it arrived in, it falls open at one particular recipe, a well-used page spattered with spots of grease. I'm not sure if it was the beating of the egg whites and sugar into stiff peaks, or the sensual pleasure of piping the mix on to baking parchment, or removing them from the oven, barely browned and still spongy under my fingertips, but I always thought there was something naughty about boudoir biscuits – until the last time I made them, as a treat for David.

It was an extraordinarily ordinary day in early spring. I remember it being particularly cold and the boiler at our old house had been playing up, so I'd been in the kitchen all day, baking to keep warm. I'd made a Simnel cake. I like to do it for my mum for Mothering Sunday – and I love having an excuse to get my cook's blowtorch out. I use it for browning the marzipan on the top. I'd also made a birthday cake for a friend's daughter – a simple round sponge cake with butter cream and jam through the middle, decorated with white fondant icing, pink ribbons and sparkly ballet shoes. It looked really sweet.

While waiting for Adam to come home from school, I slid the cooked boudoir biscuits on to a wire rack to cool, glancing out of the kitchen window where the two girls were bouncing on the trampoline under a heavy sky. The lawn, pierced here and there by clumps of battered daffodils, swept downhill beyond the trampoline to a dense hedge of beech and laurel, the boundary to the garden of our old house. Beyond that, the ground rose again, quite steeply, and if it weren't for the golfers with their buggies and brightly coloured umbrellas, and the high-rise office blocks that loomed on the horizon, I could have pretended I was in the country, not a few miles from central London.

Adam came flying into the kitchen from the hall, flung his backpack on the floor and made a grab for a biscuit.

'Hey, not so fast,' I said, intercepting him. 'They're for your dad's tea.'

'He won't miss a couple.' Adam eyed them hungrily. 'Anyway, he's on a diet, isn't he?'

David was watching his weight. He'd always been careful, but since he'd hit forty several months ago, he'd become almost obsessed. However, he hadn't been able to resist my baking so far.

'You can have two, that's all.' Adam smiled at me, revealing the tram-track braces that he wore back then. 'Just don't tell the girls.'

'What isn't Adam to tell us?' Georgia kicked off her outdoor shoes inside the back door, followed by Sophie who headed straight for the biscuits, padding across the floor in wet socks. 'Adam! What did Mum say? Why are you eating a biscuit?' Georgia turned to me, all serious. 'Mum, you said we couldn't have one.'

'It isn't fair,' Sophie began.

'All right,' I said quickly, not wishing to be drawn into a debate. 'Two each, and you'd better eat your tea,' I added as I watched the biscuits disappearing from the rack.

Georgia nibbled at hers, the picture of restraint in a long navy coat.

'They're yummy,' said Sophie, showering her school sweatshirt with crumbs. 'Mummy, what does boudoir mean?'

'It's a lady's bedroom,' I said.

Sophie frowned.

'Why does the lady have her own bedroom?' she asked, all innocence. 'Why doesn't she share it with her husband, like you and Daddy?'

'She might be divorced,' said Georgia matter-of-factly. 'Mrs Webber was in tears last week at school because her husband's left her.'

'Are you sure?' Mrs Webber, Georgia's teacher at school, had married only last term... I remembered because Georgia spent hours making her a card.

'She was so upset, she hid in the cupboard in the classroom and wouldn't come out till break-time.'

I thought of Mrs Webber's encouraging notes written in the margins of Georgia's schoolbooks. 'Well done, Georgia. Super work. You've tried very hard.' And I thought – smugly, because I reckoned I deserved to be smug after fourteen years of working at mine – that Mrs Webber obviously hadn't made that much of an effort to save her marriage.

Anyway, later that night Adam went out with a friend, the girls were sleeping upstairs and David and I were enjoying a rare evening alone together. We sat side by side on the sofa – one of the sofas that's under a tarpaulin in the barn right now – David picking at his dessert of zabaglione that I'd made to go with the biscuits. In spite of looking completely exhausted, he still managed to look as handsome as ever. Think Jude Law and you wouldn't be far wrong.

'Is there something wrong?' I asked. 'Don't you like it?' I went on.

'No. I mean, yes. It's great, Jennie. Right up to your usual standard.' David put the plate down

41

on the floor at his feet. 'It's me. I went out for lunch with a client. I'm not all that hungry.'

'Never mind,' I sighed, thinking that the children had enjoyed the biscuits at least.

'You know, you ought to be able to find a market for your baking,' he continued, his expression veiled in shadow as the tea lights burned down in the fireplace. 'You're an ace cook.'

Forgiving him for his lack of appetite, I cuddled up to him, but he didn't respond.

'I know you like being a stay-at-home mum, but perhaps you should think about setting up a business of some kind to keep you occupied and bring a little money in.'

'David, don't you think I'm occupied enough? I spend all day every day rushing about from one appointment to another, what with the school run, Sophie's ballet and Georgia's swimming, plus sorting Adam's braces which seem to break every five minutes, as if I feed him on a diet of stones.'

'You still seem to manage to fit in seeing your sister, your mum and your friends, along with trips to the hairdresser and the body shop.'

David was joking – he meant the beautician. And he wasn't really complaining. He'd have had a fit if I'd turned up in bed with whiskers and hairy legs.

'I thought we'd decided I wouldn't rush into anything until Sophie started at secondary school?' That was more than three years away. 'I don't need to. Do I?' I added, uncertain now. 'Is there some problem at work?' There had been rumours of redundancies before now. 'Are we in some kind of financial difficulty?' And then I thought how ridiculous, how demeaning, it sounded to be asking that question. I was a grown woman, an adult, and once I'd known exactly how much money we had as a couple whereas lately I'd let things slide and now had absolutely no idea, except that there always seemed to be enough. Something I'm ashamed to say I'd taken for granted.

'No, no problem,' he said quickly. 'I just thought... Well, sometimes it's good to have interests outside the home, things to talk about.'

A sense of paranoia set in. I picked up a cushion and hugged it to my chest. I should have let it go, ignored it, but I couldn't.

'Are you saying I'm boring then?'

'No, not that.'

'What then? Are you saying you're bored with me?' I looked at him, really looked at him, in a way that I hadn't recently. In a sort of narrowed-eye, what-have-you-been-up-to-this-time? kind of way. He was wearing new socks. Ben Sherman. I didn't buy them. He must have done. He never bought his own socks. Unless... My heart started to beat overly fast. 'David?'

And then it all came out. I still can't think about it now without welling up.

Anyway, when I was clearing away the remains of my marriage the next day, I noticed the biscuit broken in two on David's plate and felt sick and sad, and knew in that instant that I'd never bake boudoir biscuits again.

'Penny for them?' Mum says, interrupting my thoughts.

I snap the recipe book shut.

43

'It's nothing,' I say. 'Shall I put the kettle on again?'

'Use the one by the sink. I found it in the larder – it goes on the hotplate. The boiling not the simmering one. It's all right, I've given it a good clean.'

The kettle is whistling when Adam arrives downstairs in shorts and T-shirt for second helpings of breakfast, grumbling that as well as there being no way he can contact his friends on Facebook, there's not enough hot water to fill the bath. A few minutes later, Dad and the girls turn up with bags of provisions but no draining board. Sophie stomps in, stubs her toe on the raised edge of one of the flagstones and flies into a strop.

'I've broken my toes,' she cries.

'Well, if you will wear flip-flops,' I say. 'I bought you a pair of summer shoes, remember.'

'They're so cool. Not,' Sophie says, and I hear my mother's sharp intake of breath.

'When I was eight,' she says, 'the only pair of shoes I had was a pair of brown sandals with crepe soles which melted if you left them out in the sun. I didn't make a fuss about wearing the latest fashion, or–' she glances towards Adam who's at the table scraping his plate clean '–designer labels.'

'Were your parents very poor, Granny?' Sophie asks.

'They didn't have a lot of money,' Mum confirms.

'Luckily, my daddy's quite rich,' Sophie says. 'He and Alice take us clothes shopping when we stay with them, which is lucky for us because there aren't any clothes shops for children in

44

Talyton St George. There's not even a Primark,' she goes on, shaking her head sadly.

'Never mind,' I say lightly, wondering how I managed to bring up my children to be so materialistic. 'You won't die without one.'

'She might die of embarrassment, if we're lucky,' Georgia cuts in. When I cast her a warning glance, she continues, 'Well, she wouldn't stop snoring last night. Even when I pinched her nose.'

'You didn't, Georgia?' I say.

'She did, Mummy,' Sophie says, outraged. 'I remember now, and it really hurts.'

'It'll take your mind off your broken toes,' Adam points out. 'Which aren't broken by the way, because when I broke mine, they swelled to three times the size and I couldn't walk.'

'I can't either,' Sophie says, quickly sitting down.

'All we managed to buy were a couple of baguettes and some doughnuts from the baker's,' says Dad, talking over the squabble. 'We popped in to check out the competition, didn't we, Georgia?'

'Their cakes didn't look as nice as yours, Mum,' she says.

'Thank you, Georgia.' I'm wondering if I should be concerned about the number of outlets there are for cakes in Talyton. I've made some plans, projections of how many cakes I need to bake and sell, set against the cost of ingredients, and I reckon I can make enough money to keep us afloat. I've been realistic in my calculations and I know it'll take a while to grow the business, but I'm quietly optimistic. I'm lucky. I haven't got a mortgage, but I have spent just about every penny I have on buying the house, so I have to make a go of the business.

It isn't just about earning a living though. It's about proving something: that I'm not just a divorced mum of three and, at forty, rapidly hurtling into middle age. Okay, I admit that part of me hopes that my future success might sting David into regretting what he did, and I also want my children to be proud of me, but most of all, just for once in my life, I'm doing it for myself.

'We didn't see anywhere to buy a pony,' Georgia goes on. 'You haven't forgotten, Mum, have you?'

'How can I forget when you're always reminding me?' I say with a sigh.

'Well, Mummy, you can't say I can have one and then change your mind.' I notice Georgia's lower lip beginning to tremble.

She's right. It was a rash promise, made in the heat of the moment, soon after David threw our lives into upheaval, but now we have the paddock and stables, I have to stick by it.

'We'll look for a pony once we've settled in. Why don't you and Sophie make a start on doing whatever you have to do to prepare for it? I'm the first to admit I know nothing about ponies, but I'd guess that you need to check the fences around the paddock and make sure they're safe.'

'You said we could have a dog too,' says Adam.

'And a cat,' says Sophie.

'Now you're pushing it,' I say, smiling. I don't remember mentioning a cat.

'But that's not fair! I won't have a pet of my own.'

'How do you work that out?'

46

'Because I'm having the dog,' says Adam.

'And I'm having the pony,' says Georgia. 'And it's perfectly fair, Sophie, because I'm older than you so I must have a pet first.'

'I thought we'd have a few chickens too,' I say. 'You can look after those, Sophie. We'll have fresh eggs every day.'

She seems satisfied with that.

'What am I going to do all day, Mum?' Adam says as the girls disappear off.

'I don't know. How about use your initiative?'

'I could be down at the skate park with Josh...' Adam says mournfully. 'I hate this place. It's so boring.' Then he brightens. 'We could go and look for a dog.'

'I think that can wait for a while,' Dad says. 'I think your mum's got enough to do for now. I've found some furniture amongst the junk in the barn which might be useful for the drawing room. I could do with some extra muscle to shift it.'

I notice how Adam looks up from the table and immediately flexes his arms, checking cross-eyed on the size of his biceps which, to be honest, aren't terribly pronounced yet, although I've caught him working on them, using his friend's weights that he borrowed for a while.

'You look as if you have plenty of muscle for the job, young man,' Dad says, and I think, Flattery will get you everywhere, as Adam gets up to go and clean his teeth before going to help.

Mum and I continue cleaning and unpacking, finishing off in the kitchen then making a start on the bathroom. We break for lunch, then carry on for another couple of hours until we can take no more.

'I don't know about you, Jennie, but I fancy a lie-down,' Mum says. 'I didn't sleep too well last night.'

'Have my room,' I say, feeling guilty that she and Dad slept on an airbed while I had the bed upstairs. 'I'm going to have five minutes in the garden.'

I take a deckchair and set it up on the back lawn, sitting among the long grasses and wildflowers which seem to have taken over. I can hear Dad and Adam now and then through the open windows of the drawing room, debating over the best position for an old wicker sofa. I can hear the girls too, cantering about and whinnying as they play ponies in the paddock, and the occasional shriek of complaint as they argue over the finer points of equitation. The sun warms my skin and the birds sing high in the sky above the twisted oaks that mark the end of my property at the top of the hill. At the far end of the paddock is an area which the estate agent called the orchard. I count the apple trees that are laden with fruit. I count to eleven then close my eyes, listening to the bees nearby. I can allow myself to relax at last. This is what I've been looking for. It's perfect until...

'Mum... Mummee! Look out!' I jerk awake from my snooze on hearing the girls' frantic yells. 'They're coming to get you.'

'They? What do you mean, they?'

'The cows!'

I grab at the struts of my chair, holding on tight, as I examine the situation. I'm surrounded by red roan and white cows that have formed a semi-circle around me, and are inspecting me like a group of curious great-aunts. They stare, eyes dark and soft; their noses dripping with moisture. One belches then starts chewing, its lower jaw moving from side to side. Another stretches down, sticks out a very long tongue, wraps it around a clump of grass, tears it and swallows it straight down.

The only times I've been this close to a cow before it's either been safely on the other side of a fence at a petting farm or else on a plate. They're much bigger than I remember, quite solid, and they all look the same to me. What's most unnerving is the way they are shifting slowly towards me as more cows trudge into the garden behind them. I'm not sure whether to stay where I am, to flee or to fight.

'They are d-d-definitely vegetarian aren't they?' I stammer. I start to get up – very slowly, remembering that we haven't yet ascertained whether these are cows or bulls.

'Mum,' calls Georgia. 'It's all right. You'll be safe now. The man's coming to get them.'

'Hey, Mummy, guess what?' yells Sophie. 'It's the country bum-kin.'

'Sophie!' I say, but it's too late. The man – the tractor driver we met in the lane – cannot fail to have heard her. He strides towards me and the cows. He's an imposing figure, about six foot tall in his brown work boots, and broad-shouldered, and he's carrying a big stick. I move around behind the deckchair.

'Country bumpkin, eh?' he says, looking towards Sophie who's standing on the fence with Georgia.

'That's what Mummy said,' Sophie says, unfazed by his approach. 'Although you seem to have lost your hat and your feather and your piece of straw.'

My face burns as he goes on, 'I expect they'll turn up sometime.' He turns to me. 'We haven't been introduced,' he says, tucking his stick under one arm and retying the sleeves of his bottle-green boiler-suit around his waist.

'Jennie Copeland.' I have contemplated reverting to my maiden name but decided against it, fearing it would be too confusing for the children. I feel very much like a maiden at this moment, a modest one, trying to keep her eyes averted from this vision of manhood, his ragged vest clinging to the slabs of his pectorals, the muscles in his arms taut and clearly defined.

'Guy Barnes,' he says curtly, staring back at me, taking in, no doubt, my stained top and scruffy jeans. 'I believe we share a drive.'

The implications start to sink in. G. Barnes. The son of the previous owner of Uphill House, and current owner of Uphill Farm. My new neighbour. My only neighbour for miles around and it has to be the driver of the tractor, the old country bumpkin. I don't wish for subsidence, but right now I wouldn't mind if the ground did open and swallow me up.

'Will you get your cows off my land?' I say. 'They are cows, aren't they?' I add quickly.

'You're having me on, aren't you?' he says. 'Look at the udders on them.'

'I haven't really had a chance.'

'You can't miss them.'

'Well, I can and I have, and they're wrecking my lawn,' I add, my voice rising as one leaves her calling card in the form of a giant cowpat.

'You left the gate open,' he says.

'They're your cows.'

'And it's your land. It's down to you to secure your boundaries. That's the law.' When I don't respond, he goes on confidently, 'You can check if you like.'

'Well, whatever,' I say, sensing defeat. 'Will you get them out of here?'

'Of course, although you could borrow them to clear some of your ground, if you like? They'd soon graze this down.'

'Thank you for the offer, but no,' I say firmly. I'd only worry that they'd trample someone, and they're making such a mess.

Guy raises his stick and shouts, 'Ho, ladies! Ho!' A couple of the cows look up from where they're grazing now, but they don't move. He whacks one across its bony rump. 'Move it, Kylie.'

Kylie? This is surreal, I think. And cruel, as he gives her another whack.

'Oh, don't hit them,' I shout out, aware of Sophie's expression of horror and Georgia wincing with each blow.

'Do you want them off your property or not?' Guy says, looking slightly irritated.

'Yes, I do, but that seems too harsh.'

'I knew it. I might be a country bumpkin, but you're a right ignorant townie, aren't you?' he says, his face relaxing into a mocking smile.

'I don't like to see animals mistreated.' I fold my arms tight across my chest. I hate confrontation, but I refuse to stand by silently and watch.

'The female of the species can be very stubborn,' Guy says, lowering his stick. 'Sometimes a good smack on the rump works wonders.' And he looks at me as if he'd like to give my rump a good smack too for interfering, then he turns his attention back to the cows who decide that making a move is their best option after all. I watch them go, wandering off ahead of Guy, who pointedly latches the gate behind them as they start ambling up the drive towards the farm, presumably for milking.

'He isn't a very nice man at all, is he, Mummy?' Sophie says, skipping through the grass towards me, Georgia walking behind, deep in thought.

I have to agree with Sophie. Guy's intrusion has rather spoiled my countryside idyll. What happened to all the friendly locals I remember from my childhood? The jolly farmer, for example, who ran the caravan park on the cliff-top at Talysands? He used to take me and my sister to see the calves in his cowshed. He'd tickle the calves behind their ears and scratch their flanks, not hit them, then he'd ask my sister how many there were and she'd tell him there was one missing because she didn't want him to know she couldn't count yet, and he'd play along, pretending to look for the lost one.

If you could choose your neighbours, I wouldn't have plumped for someone like Guy. However, even though meeting him properly has confirmed my initial opinion, I wish I hadn't described him as a country bumpkin in front of the children. I have no urge to socialise with him particularly but it would have been nice to have been on good terms, because I'm not going to be able to avoid him.

Chapter Three

Sultana Cake

The day after my close encounter of the bovine kind, Mum and I do some more sorting out and putting away before I decide to put the Aga to the test, on the basis that if I can't get on with it – if we can't make friends – I have time to replace it with something else.

From the kitchen, I can see Dad strimming the long grass and brambles, and Adam hacking at the shrubs in the back garden – elder, buddleia and mallows with masses of purplish-pink flowers. Dad stops frequently to examine the end of the strimmer which really isn't up to the job. I used it to edge the lawns at the old house, that's all. The gardener used to bring his own heavy-duty gear for anything else. The strimmer was one item David and I didn't fight over – he and Alice moved into a luxury flat with views of the Thames, and no garden.

As I watch, I wonder how Adam is feeling now. In his brightly coloured clothes – orange T-shirt and check shorts – he looks like an exotic bird that's landed here by mistake on its way to warmer climes. He needs to get back to school to make

53

some friends, but that's over four weeks away yet.

'Don't fret about the children, love,' Mum says. 'They're happy enough.'

'I hope so,' I sigh.

'What are you going to bake today?'

'I thought an everyday cake – sultana, maybe. Dad's bought all the ingredients, apart from a lemon, but I can leave that out.'

'I'll find the flour and sugar.' Mum opens the door to the larder and shuffles about inside. I notice how she keeps hitching up the waist of her grey slacks.

'Mum, have you been on a diet?' I ask.

'I can't be doing with diets,' she says, emerging from the larder with various packets. 'It's all this running around after you and my grandchildren.' She gazes at me through narrowed eyes. 'Don't worry about me. I'm fighting fit.'

But I do worry, I muse, as I open various cupboard doors, looking for a cake tin and mixing bowls. And I shall worry more now that I'm living here and she's over a hundred miles away. It isn't as if we'll be able to pop in and see each other every day or two, like we used to. More sometimes.

'Can you remember where we put the tins, Mum?'

'I think it was in the cupboard to the right of the washing machine,' she says. 'And there was only one tin.'

'Oh, yes.' I take it out and put it on the worktop. 'I threw the others out – they were so battered, I thought I'd have a fresh start. I'll have to buy some more.'

'Don't you go out buying too much,' Mum says. 'I should wait and see what you really need.'

'If I'm setting up a business, I have to start with the right equipment.'

'You don't know what will sell yet. You haven't done any market research. There isn't much point in buying trays for themed fairy cakes if you end up concentrating on weddings.' She pauses. 'I'll let you get on – I'm going to check on the girls.'

'They're still in the stables.' Every now and then, I look out of the kitchen door and catch sight of them at work, moving the wood stack that's been stored in the stable nearest this end of the yard into the one at the other end, having decided that the pony must have the one that is in the best state of repair.

'I'll take them some more squash. They're ever so busy.' Mum pauses again, the vertical lines above her upper lip deepening, and wrinkles appearing in her forehead. 'Jennie, are you sure about this pony business? You have to admit, you aren't really an animal lover. You're scared of spiders, and you haven't been terribly lucky with hamsters in the past. It's a huge commitment, especially on top of keeping this house habitable, looking after three kids and setting up a business. I'm not interfering, love,' she adds firmly. 'But I'm worried that you're taking on too much.'

'Granny! Granny!' Sophie's voice interrupts us. 'Come and see what we've found.'

Mum looks at me, head tipped slightly to one side.

'You'd better go,' I say, smiling. She isn't so much worried that I'll overdo it as concerned I won't have time to socialise and meet someone else.

Mum's convinced I'll find myself another man one day, but I can't imagine being with anyone but David, and I can't contemplate the trauma of falling in and out of love all over again. It might sound old-fashioned, but when I married I really believed it was for life. My parents had made it work, so why shouldn't I?

There were a couple of occasions when I was tempted to stray, but I didn't go through with it. Why? Because of David. Because I loved my husband. Some people might say, Why not when he did it to you? Why not do it to get back at him? But I'm not like that. I can hold my head up high because I did the right thing. I kept my self-respect and hurt no one, and I don't regret that.

Although I'm still angry and upset after months of bitter wrangling and analysis, I'm beginning to be able to talk about the situation without dissolving into tears. At Christmas, I cried because Sophie no longer believes in Father Christmas just as I no longer believe in love, and by that I mean romantic love between a man and a woman.

I take the scales from the windowsill and stand them on the worktop beside the tin. I don't need the recipe for sultana cake. I know it by heart. I weigh out butter – naughtier but nicer than margarine – and caster sugar into a mixing bowl, then stand it in the warming oven of the Aga for a few minutes while I weigh out some self-raising flour. I don't sieve – life's too short for that – but I do consider the question of adding salt. I check the butter wrapper and realise Dad's bought salted, so I don't add any, although, in my view, it's probably not worth angsting over a pinch of salt when you're serving up a rich combination of artery-clogging fats and refined sugar.

Having lined the cake tin, I grab an oven glove to take the mixing bowl out of the Aga, finding the butter perfectly softened so I can easily cream it into the sugar. Then I crack an egg into the mix, add a spoonful of self-raising flour, and mix again. I repeat the last step two more times, then add the rest of the flour, some plump sultanas and aromatic mixed spice before stirring it all together until it makes a soft, shiny mixture. I lift the spoon and let the mixture slide off again, checking the consistency, part of the ritual I learned from helping my grandmother when I was about ten years old. Perfect.

I grab a spatula from the drawer and scrape the mixture into the cake tin, open one of the doors to the Aga, hoping I've got the right one, then slide the tin on to the rack before setting the timer for fifty minutes. It's a novelty timer, Humpty Dumpty. One of the children gave it to me for Christmas one year. I put it on the windowsill and get on with some washing up. There's no plumbing for a dishwasher. Not yet. Another job.

I start thinking about Mum's comment about taking on too much. I'm talking about taking on a pony, a dog and a few chickens. That's nothing compared with the number of cows Guy has to look after. Adam's tried counting them in the field, and he says there are at least ninety in the herd. I've been mulling over what I saw when they came into the garden yesterday, and I think

57

I might have overreacted. Guy was a bit mean to those cows, but he didn't exactly beat the one he called Kylie. It was more of a tap and the cow didn't appear afraid of him. She didn't flinch or run away.

It's made me think about my own attitude to animals. I like to think that I respect them as sentient beings. I believe they have a right to a decent life and humane treatment, but I love the smell of bacon too much ever to be a vegetarian, and when it comes down to it, I've never seen the appeal of keeping pets. It all seems a bit pointless because you can talk to them, but they can't talk to you. However, the children have set their hearts on having them. I only hope they last longer than the hamsters.

The last hamster, the third one, known only as The Hamster, came to an unfortunate end the day after I found out my marriage was over. I remember it as if it was yesterday. Adam found The Hamster on the drive, of all places, and called me out to take a look. He was lying on his back with his little feet sticking up, cold and stiff, and a bead of blood drying around his mouth. I held him, cupped in my palms, and I felt my heart breaking all over again.

'Are you going to tell Georgia and Sophie?' Adam asked, his eyes red and watery. He was either upset or else hadn't had much sleep.

'They'll have to know,' I said.

'They'll be gutted.'

'I know...' I started to sob again. I couldn't help it. Without David. All this. The home I'd created for us. Our family. Well, it was meaningless. I was

58

utterly, completely devastated.

'Mum,' Adam said, stroking my back, a gesture which made me cry more, 'it's only a hamster.'

'I know, but...' I wasn't all that fond of it, but this death hit me harder than I'd expected.

'How do you think he got here?'

I knew exactly.

'I shooed that black cat out of the house this morning, the one that stole what was left of the turkey at Christmas. And The Hamster's cage was never terribly secure, something else I always meant to sort out, but never did. And now it's too late.' I tried to collect myself. 'I hope he died of fright, quickly.'

'We don't have to tell the girls exactly what happened,' Adam went on. 'We'll just say he snuffed it in his bed. That he died in his sleep, not that he was brutally murdered.'

'Oh, Adam,' I sighed. 'Thank you.'

He was trying to comfort me but it was making the pain worse, because at that time I was still hiding the truth from him. His dad and I were divorcing. This life we'd led together was over. I was already on a journey that I hadn't anticipated – just like The Hamster when the neighbour's cat came to grab him out of his cage.

'Poor thing,' Georgia said when we broke the news to her and Sophie. 'Why did you have to go and die on us? Why did he die, Mum?'

'He didn't suffer,' I said. Not like I was suffering. 'He died in his sleep.'

'Like Grandma Copeland?' said Sophie, calming down after an initial burst of wailing and breast beating.

'Like Grandma Copeland,' I said. She was David's mother. Neither of the girls had met her, but Adam had retold and elaborated upon the story of her demise and subsequent cremation so many times that the girls talked about her as if they had.

'Are we going to burn him like they did Grandma Copeland?' Georgia said.

'I don't wanna burn him,' Sophie wailed again.

'We can bury him in the garden,' Adam contributed.

'I think that's a very good idea,' I quickly put in.

'I wish we'd buried Grandma Copeland in the garden,' said Georgia.

Privately, I couldn't agree with that sentiment. She'd haunted me while she was alive. I didn't want her haunting me in death as well. Divorced from David's father for many years, she made it her mission to come and live with us. She kept trying. She came to stay for a couple of months when she broke her wrist, slipping on ice, and for almost a year when a pipe burst, which necessitated major repairs to both her house and, ultimately, my sanity. She was a chain smoker with an obsession with sun-beds and an aversion to fruit and veg, who undermined all my efforts to encourage Adam to live a healthy lifestyle.

Why did I do it? For love, of course. Because it was what David wanted. He was devastated when she died, wizened and prematurely aged by cancer. That was when he'd had his first affair. The first one I knew about anyway.

'Can we fetch Grandma Copeland's ashes and put them with The Hamster?' said Georgia, continuing with the subject as I wrapped The Hamster's mortal remains in kitchen roll and fastened it with sticky tape.

I wasn't sure where her ashes were. She had a plaque on the wall at the crematorium – David made sure hers was at the top of the memorial, which would have pleased her as a woman with delusions of grandeur.

'That way, she'll have a pet in Heaven,' said Sophie.

'You don't know that,' said Adam.

'There's no such thing as Heaven,' said Georgia.

'Then why in assembly at school do we pray to "our father which art in Heaven", then?' Sophie challenged.

'I don't.' Georgia folded her arms across her chest. 'And anyway, we've got Daddy. You can't have two fathers. It's scientifically impossible.'

'You can if they're gay,' said Adam.

'Whatever. It's a load of bollocks.'

'Georgia!' I exclaimed. 'I don't want to hear you use that word.'

'Adam does,' she said. 'All the time.'

Sophie looked at me, tipping her head ever so slightly to one side. 'Mummy, what's bollocks?'

'What Georgia is trying to say is that she doesn't believe in God.' I heard myself expel a deep sigh. How did I end up with one devout Christian child and one raving atheist? I glanced towards Adam, the voice of reason, an agnostic like myself.

'We must pray for The Hamster,' said Sophie.

'I don't see why,' said Georgia. 'He didn't ever go to church.'

'That's because we never took him,' said

Sophie, scowling accusations of neglect for The Hamster's psychological welfare.

Aware that World War Three was about to break out between them, I made a move.

'Let's go and dig this hole,' I said, picking up the white parcel.

Adam frowned. 'Aren't you going to wait for Dad to come home?'

'I don't think he'll worry about missing the funeral, do you?' That sounded bitter. I couldn't help it. I knew what Adam didn't, that there was no point waiting for David because he wasn't coming home today, or tomorrow, or for the foreseeable future. 'I don't suppose he's even noticed we've got a hamster. Now, let's get out there while it isn't raining.'

I grabbed a spade from the shed, chose a spot in the flowerbed furthest from the house, and got digging. I dug for England. Fired up with repressed rage and anguish, I drove my shovel through mud and flint and chalk. The children looked at me oddly, as if they thought I was going mad, which I was.

'That's a very big hole for one very small hamster,' Adam observed.

'Mummy, you're almost in Australia,' commented Georgia as Sophie dug out a couple of larger flints from the heap I'd created to put on top of the grave.

I laid the white parcel of The Hamster in the bottom of the hole, together with a piece of paper from Georgia with 'I love you, The Hamster' on it, and some sunflower seeds from Sophie to keep him going on the trip to Heaven. Then I surreptitiously slipped my wedding ring off my finger and dropped it in too. I hesitated before throwing the first shovelful of earth and stone on to The Hamster's body, in case I should hurt him, but soon got going. I buried the remains of my marriage in the bottom of that hole. I could quite cheerfully have buried David in there too. I hated him. I found my knuckles blanching on the handle of the spade, more tears dripping on to the back of my hand. I couldn't believe how much I hated him...

Back in the present, in the kitchen at Uphill House, I straighten up at the sink. I still hate him, but the sensation is milder now, more like the tingling you get when you've had some local anaesthetic at the dentist, not like having your heart torn out of your ribcage without any anaesthetic at all. Am I over him? Humpty Dumpty makes a burring sound from the windowsill.

I open the door to the oven to check on the cake, and the scent of baking fills the kitchen. I feel a sense of peace. Yes, I am over David at last.

The sultana cake is still cooling on the rack on the worktop an hour or so later – at least, that's what I've been telling the children who keep popping back into the kitchen to see if it's ready. I probably should have made two.

At seven, as I'm about to decide what to do for tea, there's a knocking at the front door.

'You'd better go and see who that is, Jennie,' Mum says from where she's sitting at the table, dividing pot pourri between a couple of glass dishes, homely touches for the bathroom upstairs.

'I'm not expecting anyone.' Dad's having a snooze in front of the telly in the drawing room and Adam is playing hide and seek with the girls. Sibling harmony reigns, but – I smile to myself – it won't last. There's another knock, this one heavier, more insistent, than the first. I wipe my hands and head through the lobby and into the hall. I turn the key in the door and unfasten the bolt, then tug the door open to find Guy on my doorstep.

'Still locking your doors, I see,' he says, smiling. 'There's no need, but I guess old habits die hard.'

I bite back the words, What on earth are you doing here?

'Hello...' He holds out a plastic container. 'A peace offering.'

'Oh? Thank you,' I say, surprised. It's a long time since a man's beaten a path to my door, which he's had to do, literally, because Dad and Adam haven't made a start on the front garden yet. He pushes aside a few prickly stems that hang from the porch. The roses are past their best, the summer flush gone. A bit like mine, I reflect ruefully. I take the container from him and examine the label: Uphill Farm Scrumpy.

'It's last year's,' Guy says. 'It was a good vintage.'

He hovers on the doorstep and I wonder if he's really expecting me to invite him in. I can't imagine that we have anything more to say to each other after the invasion of the cows.

'Come on in,' Mum calls from behind me. Reluctantly, I open the door wider.

'It's Guy,' I say.

'Come to make amends,' he says, and ducks down to undo the laces on his trainers. He slips

64

them off and leaves them on the step before moving past me into the hall and following Mum back into the kitchen. I catch the scent of chemicals on his skin and mint on his breath. He's clean this time, freshly shaven with a nick at his throat, his hair still damp, much darker with deep gold highlights. He's wearing blue jeans, a faded polo-shirt and odd socks.

'I thought I could smell baking from outside.' He takes a moment to look around him. 'You've made it nice,' he adds, then his voice catches slightly as if with regret. 'This was our favourite room, the hub of the house. Cool in summer and the Aga keeps it warm in winter. You're using the Aga?'

'Of course,' says Mum. 'It's all part of the country lifestyle, isn't it?'

'I thought you might want to replace it. I expect you'll want to make a few changes to the old place,' he says in a challenging tone.

'Actually, I intend to preserve it as it is – with some sympathetic updating,' I say firmly. He might say he's here to apologise for his cows, but I can't help thinking that what he's really here for is to check out what I'm doing to his old place, and to make fun of my townie beliefs. Is there really so much difference between us? What preconceived ideas does he hold about me?

'I expect you're planning to grow your own veg too,' Guy says.

'I am. I'm going to turn over the old vegetable plot.'

'It'll need some manure on it.'

'I have grown plants before,' I say. 'I'm not that ignorant.'

'I didn't say you were,' he says, reddening. He might deny it, I muse, but it's what he meant.

'Would you like a piece of cake?' Mum asks. 'Jennie's been baking.'

'You can have it with tea or we can open the scrumpy?' I suggest.

'I wouldn't say no to tea and cake,' Guy says, eyeing the sultana cake hopefully.

'Jennie's planning to run a business selling her cakes. Her carrot cake is to die for. You'll never taste anything like it,' Mum says. Pushy parents – I didn't think I had them! I can't believe that I'm forty and they're still embarrassing me.

'Did someone say "cakes"?' Adam turns up at the stable door, his sisters behind him.

'Yes, they did,' says Mum. 'Adam, will you find some plates, please? And, Sophie, go and wake your granddad.'

Guy's presence seems to fill the room. He leans back against the cupboards, his back to the sink, watching me as I fill the kettle and slice the cake.

'It could be difficult to make a business out of baking cakes around here. Most people bake their own.'

'Do you do much baking then?' I have to ask.

'Me? No way. Mum used to,' he adds, sombre now. 'She always had two kinds of cake on the table after afternoon milking. I've got all her old recipes up at the farm. But if I fancy a cake, I can go to the Co-op or the baker's, or the Copper Kettle, or the garden centre. In Talyton, we're spoiled for choice.'

'Oh, Jennie's cakes aren't your ordinary every-day ones,' Mum says, handing Guy a plate of

66

cake. 'They're for special occasions – weddings, anniversaries, special birthdays.'

'All birthdays are special, Granny,' Sophie says worriedly.

'Some birthdays are more special than others, especially when you get to my age.' Mum smiles.

I can't smile with her. Is Guy deliberately trying to discourage me from setting up my business? Or is he just straight talking, telling the truth? I have to confess, I'm slightly concerned now. It sounds as though there is far too much competition.

I watch as he raises a slice of sultana cake to his lips and takes a big bite.

'That's delicious,' he says when he's eaten the lot and licked the crumbs from his lips, and I feel quite gratified that he enjoyed it. 'Did you find the old table?' he asks, as the children crowd around the glass-topped table I brought with me, the one I was so pleased with back in the London house but which looks hopelessly out of proportion here. 'The one we used to use? I put it at the back of the barn.'

'Along with all the rest of your rubbish,' I say.

'Rubbish?' Guy looks at me, rather hurt, and I wish I'd been more tactful.

'All the stuff you left behind. The estate agent said you'd promised to chuck it out.'

'I had to move my mother into a nursing home – she couldn't take very much with her. I thought you'd like to go through it beforehand. There are some bits and pieces that might come in useful.' He smiles. 'Waste not, want not. I thought everyone was into recycling and sustainable living these days, or is that a fad that's gone out of fashion already? With townies, I mean.'

Why do I feel like he's mocking me?

'What you don't want, I'll shift,' he goes on.

'You do that,' I say, aware that Mum's casting me a glance to warn me to tone it down. Just because we're neighbours, we don't have to be friends.

'There you are, Malcolm,' Mum says as my father strolls into the kitchen, with his glasses in one hand and handkerchief in the other. 'This is Guy from the farm. He's brought Jennie some scrumpy.' She glances around the table. 'Now, where's Granddad's piece of cake?'

'Um, I've eaten it,' Adam says, his cheeks pink. 'I thought it was going spare.'

'Adam!' I say.

'It's all right. There's some left,' Mum says, pouring scrumpy into glasses.

I try some of the rich golden liquid, coughing as it catches the back of my throat.

'That's lethal,' I gasp.

'It's pretty strong stuff. I should have warned you,' Guy observes, but I suspect from his expression that he's pleased that he didn't, that he's revelling in my discomfort.

I try a smaller sip, sieving the bits through my teeth. It's sharp and desert dry with an apple tang. Do I like it? I believe it might be an acquired taste.

'Can I try some, Mum?' Adam asks.

'No, definitely not.'

Everyone falls silent for a moment, savouring the cake. I don't know what to say to Guy, this man who seems completely at home in my kitchen. It is as I expected. We have absolutely

68

nothing in common.

'I hope you'll let me have your apples in the autumn,' he begins. 'I need them for next year's cider. That's where this came from.' He points to the container.

'I didn't realise they were cider apples,' I say, looking in the direction of the orchard.

'You've got one Bramley – that's a cooker.'

'I know what a Bramley is.'

'You've also got some of the good old cider varieties – Hangy Down, Slack Ma Girdle and Tremlett's Bitter.'

'Hangy Down?' says Sophie. 'That sounds rude, doesn't it, Mummy?'

Georgia giggles.

'Slack Ma what?' says Adam.

'Girdle,' says Guy, straight-faced. 'Of course, I'll understand if you want to make your own cider...'

'No, I can't imagine I'll have the time,' I say. 'You're welcome to them.'

'I'll pay you in kind. I'll give you a proportion of what I make. You can sell it on, or drink it yourself.'

It sounds like a good deal to me, I muse, cider from our own apples.

Sophie breaks the silence which descends over the kitchen.

'Do you have any children, Guy?' she pipes up. 'Only I'd like someone to play with who isn't my sister because all she wants to do is play ponies, which is really boring.'

'I don't, I'm afraid,' he says.

'Do you live on your own then?'

'Sophie, why don't you...' I begin, but Sophie's

in full flood when Guy affirms that he does indeed live alone.

'Do you have a girlfriend?' she says. 'A boyfriend then?' she runs on, not giving Guy a chance to respond. 'You might have a boyfriend if you're gay.'

'I don't have a boyfriend, and I'm not that way inclined,' Guy says stiffly.

I cringe. I wish Sophie and Georgia weren't so fascinated by other people's domestic arrangements.

'Our daddy lives with Alice who's his girlfriend. Daddy isn't gay,' Sophie twitters on, and I observe how Guy concentrates on his tea and sincerely hope he doesn't think that I put them up to it.

When we've finished eating and drinking, and I'm feeling a little lightheaded, Guy offers to help move the table out of the barn so I can take a look at it. He's a man of tremendous energy, seemingly unwilling or unable to sit down and relax, which is how we all end up in the yard as dusk is falling and the bats are beginning to flit in and out of the stables.

'It would have taken us half the time if you'd been here yesterday,' Adam says, and I see him regarding Guy's muscles with envy. Guy has strong hands too, I notice, with lightly tanned and roughened skin, and nails blunt-cut and clean.

My dad drags open the door at the front of the barn, revealing my lovely sofas covered with tarpaulin.

'We'll have to get these out of the way again,' he says, but it's no problem with Guy there. I lug one of the last packing cases out of the way.

'Here, let me have that,' Guy says, moving to-

70

wards me.

'I can do it,' I say in no uncertain terms.

'I've been eating your cake.' He stands right in front of me, his hands on the case. 'It's the least I can do in return.'

'Oh, all right then,' I say, mollified. 'Thank you.'

'It's a pleasure.' His mouth curves into a wry smile as he takes the load from me. 'I think.'

'We'll have to move the old tractor,' says Adam hopefully.

'Does it still go?' says my dad.

'Why do men go weak at the knees at pieces of old machinery?' I ask Mum, as the two of them are looking at it with Guy. I can see nothing attractive about this unprepossessing grey vehicle that stands in the way of the solid oak table lying on its side at the back of the barn. It's a third of the size of the one Guy was driving when we met him in the lane, it looks a bit rusty and, for some reason – to keep the water out maybe – it has a tin can over the end of its vertical exhaust pipe.

'I reckon she'll go all right, although she hasn't been started for months.' He scrambles on to the seat – this tractor doesn't have an enclosed cab – and turns the key that's been left in the ignition. He glances at me. 'We don't have much crime out here. Besides, I can't think anyone would want to steal this thing.' He turns the key again. The engine coughs, sending the tin can shooting up and hitting the roof of the barn, before it falls down and rolls clattering across the floor.

Adam can't stop laughing. Neither can I, partly because of the tin can, partly because Adam is creased up with tears in his eyes.

71

'I should have taken that off first.' Guy grins. 'I always forget.' He turns the key again, and the engine chunters into life. He rolls the tractor out into the yard, crushing the can on the way. 'You'll need to hang on to this, Jennie.'

'Um, why? What on earth am I going to do with a tractor?'

'Use it to take care of your land, of course.'

'I thought it took care of itself?'

'You can't leave it to its own devices – you'll get all kinds of weeds.' He smiles again. 'Your neighbour won't like that.'

'I see.' Actually, I don't, because all this about having to drive a tractor and control weeds is a bit of a surprise to me.

'If you aren't going to graze it, you'll need to harrow and cut the grass in the paddock and under the apple trees. As for the weeds, you'll have to dig out any ragwort because I won't have any of that growing next door to me. I cut hay to sell and my horsey people won't buy it if it has any ragwort in it.'

'Ragwort's poisonous,' says Georgia, interrupting.

'And how do you know that, young lady?' Guy says.

'I'm going to have a pony and I've been reading books to make sure I know how to look after it.'

I feel a rare surge of maternal pride.

'Do you think your mum knows how to drive a tractor?' he asks Georgia.

'I expect she could learn how to, if she got a book about it from the library,' Georgia says optimistically.

Guy turns to me as he jumps down from the tractor. 'I don't suppose it'll go fast enough for you, Jennie.'

In spite of determining not to, I blush. How does this man manage to disarm me? I put it down to the cider, I think, walking past him to look at the table. Adam and Guy drag it out on to the cobbles. It's dusty and scratched, and I'm not entirely sure I want it, but Guy's convinced that it's just what I need.

'A bit of sanding down and it'll be as good as new,' he says, then shows Adam how to reverse the tractor back inside before saying he's got to get back to the farm.

'So soon?' says Mum. 'It's only half-past nine.'

'I've got an early start – as always. The milking,' he adds in explanation. 'Cows don't milk them-selves, more's the pity.'

'The cow you were mean to ... the one you were hitting with the stick,' Georgia begins.

'Kylie?' Guy says. 'I didn't hit her hard. She knows I wouldn't hurt her.'

Georgia doesn't appear to be convinced.

'She wouldn't let down her milk if she was unhappy.'

'No, I suppose she wouldn't,' Georgia says, apparently softening towards him. 'Do all your cows have names?'

'They do. It's been shown scientifically that cows give more milk when they have names. They aren't sure though if it happens because they have names, or because the farmers give the named animals more attention.'

'How do you get the milk out of the cow and

73

into the carton?' Georgia asks.

And I think, He's going to make another cutting remark about ignorant townies. But instead he goes on, 'Why don't you all come and watch a milking sometime and find out?' He smiles. 'I'd recommend the afternoon session rather than the five a.m. start – then you can get your beauty sleep.' I wonder why he's looking at me when he says that?

'Why don't we leave it a few days, until we've settled in?' I say. 'Granny and Granddad go home later in the week. We'll come then.'

'I look forward to that,' Guy says formally. 'Is there anything else you'd like to know about the place?'

I ask about buses for Adam.

'Oh, yes, there are buses that go into the city. Two a week.'

'Where we were in London, often two buses came at once,' says Georgia.

'I'd say there's zero chance of that happening here,' Guy says. 'There are no trains either – Talyton doesn't have a station.'

'I'll be able to drive soon,' says Adam.

'Not that soon – you're fourteen.' You'll be forty before you start driving if I have my way, I think, although I can see that he'll need a car out here eventually. I can also see that I've not been a good role model where driving is concerned, too impatient, and I resolve to change that.

'Thank you for the cake.' Guy shakes my father's hand and kisses my mother's cheek. I stay well back.

'Thanks for the cider,' I say.

'I'll see myself out,' he says, but I accompany him to the gate anyway, making sure I fasten it securely behind him. He hesitates on the drive. 'I admire your optimism, Jennie, but I wouldn't mind betting that you'll sell up and go back where you came from within the year.'

He doesn't know me so how can he say that? I think.

'I'm sorry to disappoint you but I have no intention of moving again. This is now my home.'

'Goodnight then,' he says, turning on his heel and strolling away.

'Goodnight,' I say curtly.

'He's very frank,' I say, when I'm discussing Guy's visit with Mum later on, after the children have gone to bed.

'So are your children, darling.'

'He speaks his mind.'

'There's nothing wrong in that,' Mum says. 'Better that than a man who doesn't mean what he says or say what he means.' She's referring to David, of course.

'I think I'll go on up.' I can't stop yawning. 'I can't tell if it's the cider or the floor that's giving me this strange, tilting feeling.'

'Goodnight, love,' Mum says.

I head upstairs. My parents might be smitten with Guy next door, but I am not, and never will be.

In my room, I look out of the window towards the house at Uphill Farm. There are no lights on. A cow bellows from the darkness, breaking the silence. I reach out and touch the cob wall beside me. It's cool and bumpy, yet solid beneath my fingertips. The walls – as well as leaning in all directions so that none of my furniture will stand flush against them – are two to three feet thick, but nothing can be as thick as the defences I've built around my heart this past year.

Mum dreams of me finding happiness with another man, and I reckon she already thinks Guy fits the bill, but no man can touch me. I've made quite sure of that.

Chapter Four

Jam Tarts

Today is the day I wave goodbye to my parents. I feel utterly bereft.

When they leave, Mum has tears in her eyes, and my heart clenches with a grief I didn't expect. At least though she has come round to my crazy plans at last, and I feel fully supported. She had a good go at changing my mind before I committed to the move, giving me a thorough reality check. She told me to pull my socks up and stop thinking up mad schemes to distract myself from the divorce. She told me to stop wallowing and get on with my life. She also thought I was insane to think I could make a living out of baking cakes.

'Jennie, it'll never work.' That's what she said. And I said, 'What about Mr Kipling then?' and she burst into tears, and I realised that this wasn't about me. It was about her, how she was scared of losing regular contact with her grandchildren and missing out on them growing up.

'Malcolm,' she says, 'when you're packing the car, fetch those other things in.'

Dad heads outside. I reckon he's itching to get back to the golf club.

He returns with three carrier bags and places them on Guy's oak table which has come up well with a bit of work. Adam did it – for a small fee.

'They're for you, Jennie,' Mum says, 'our moving-in gift.'

I look inside the bags. They're full of baking tins and colourful silicone spatulas and spoons.

'Oh, thank you.' I'm overwhelmed. 'You shouldn't have...'

'We see it as a modest investment in your future,' says Dad. 'Of course, we could do more if you were prepared to accept it.'

We've had this discussion before and I refused. My parents mean well, but I am not a charity.

'If I ever need investment,' I say, 'I'll enter the den with the Dragons.'

'It's all suitable for use in the Aga,' Mum says, 'and most of it's dishwasher-safe.'

'I haven't got a dishwasher though,' I say, smiling.

'You have three,' says Dad. 'You make sure those children help you out.' He checks his watch. 'We'd better make a move.'

'I'll see you soon, Mum,' I say, my voice wavering as the impact of what I've done hits me like a train. I'm going to miss her popping in for a quick coffee and cake. I'm going to miss her offers of babysitting and Sunday lunches with Mum, Dad

77

and my sister.

'You take care, love.' She gives me a tearful smile. 'Make sure you get out and about.'

I know what she's getting at. Get out and meet people.

'It's going to be quiet for you, you being a city girl, born and bred, but at least we know you've got someone to turn to in an emergency. Guy seems like a good neighbour to have. Capable.'

I dismiss any talk of turning to him. It would have to be the direst of emergencies for me to call on him.

'And, just remember, me and your dad are at the end of the phone, and if you should decide that you've made a terrible mistake moving here, you can come home. You'll always be welcome there, whatever happens.'

'Thanks, Mum,' I say, choking up with emotion.

'We'll be back to visit. Soon.'

Before they leave, they call the children to say goodbye. I stand on the front lawn, watching the children run up the drive behind my parents' car, laughing and waving, through a veil of tears. I turn and look back at the house and I think, Oh, no, what have I done? Have I just made the second biggest mistake of my life, buying this house out in the sticks with its temperamental Aga and varied wildlife?

Talking of wildlife, when I planned to get closer to nature I didn't mean this close, I muse, as I watch the inexorable march of a column of ants through my kitchen and under the larder door, when I go back inside.

'Mum, I'm bored,' Adam says, within half an

hour of my parents leaving.

'You're always bored.'

'Yes, but I've never been as bored as I am now.'

'Why don't you find something to do then?' I say, slightly exasperated as I always have too much to do. 'Do you want to cook us lunch?'

'Boring,' Adam says, hands thrust into the pockets of his long shorts.

'You can clean my car – for pocket money.'

'Boring,' he says, but I can see from the twist of his lips that he's trying not to smile.

'How about – with your artistic skills – designing the logo for Jennie's Cakes?' I've already toyed with various ideas, but none of them are outstanding.

'What's the brief?' he asks, sounding more interested.

'It needs to have some reference to cakes, obviously. And I'd like it to have some colour, but natural colours which link with the idea of healthy ingredients.'

'No electric blues then?' Adam says, slightly disappointed.

'Probably not. There's a pad of paper in the drawer over there – but not on the table in here, please. I'm baking.'

Adam disappears off to his room with pens and paper, then Sophie and Georgia turn up, forced to endure each other's company in the absence of other children.

'I miss Granny already.' Sophie is clutching her favourite teddy. I thought she had abandoned him but he's back, one ear falling off and his red waistcoat all raggedy. 'I wish Daddy was here.'

'You know he can't be, darling.' They have spoken to David on the phone and via Adam's Facebook a few times now that we've sorted out internet access. The connection is slow, more snail trail than information superhighway, but it will do for now. The children haven't mentioned the possibility of their dad living with us for a while. I guess my parents' leaving has unsettled them again.

'Why not?' says Sophie.

'Because. Because... You know why. He lives with Alice now.'

'Why can't they live with us? We've got lots of space.'

'He and Alice can stay in the spare room,' says Georgia hopefully.

If it were that simple... If I could be that magnanimous!

'Daddy needs to live near his work,' I say. And it just wouldn't work. Imagine the scandal. A commune in the respectable market town of Talyton St George. A ménage à trois. I wonder what the staid Guy Barnes would make of that. At least the girls have accepted that there is no prospect of David and me getting back together. 'Have you finished clearing that stable?' I say, changing the subject.

'Yes,' says Georgia. 'All it needs now is some straw and a pony.'

'Okay then, why don't you take a couple of plastic boxes and see how many blackberries you can find?' There are some – they've ripened early this summer. 'And don't eat them all on the way back this time, like you did with Granddad the other day.'

Once the girls have gone, armed with boxes and sticks to beat the prickliest of the brambles out of their way, I turn my attention to baking. Maybe it's the mention of blackberries that triggers images of sticky jam tarts and apple pies. I haven't checked to see how the Aga handles pastry yet. Now seems a good time to try. It will take my mind off how empty the house seems without my parents here.

I wash and dry the new utensils they bought, then weigh out flour with a pinch of salt and tip it into a mixing bowl – my favourite, which has a creamy, rustic glaze, one of the few things I have which suits the house. My fingers are covered in fat and flour as I rub them together, lifting and separating to let the crumbs fall through and back into the bowl, when I hear a knock and a voice, an adult voice, and my heart lifts. They're back! My parents have forgotten something, or they've decided to stay on a few more days.

'Hi,' I call, as the sound of footsteps comes ringing through from the lobby.

'Good morning.'

I look up to find a strange woman in my kitchen, and when I say strange, she's dressed up to the nines, as if she's on her way to a wedding. She wears a hound's tooth-patterned grey and cream silk dress with a jacket and heels to match. On her head she wears a fascinator, silvery feathers secured around a bead with three longer feathers curling out from the top. Her hair, cut short and dyed auburn, looks as if it's set hard.

'I think you must be in the wrong place,' I say.

'Oh, no, no, no, I know exactly where I am.

Welcome–' she holds out her arms '–to our lovely town, Talyton St George.'

'You can't just wander in here,' I say, wondering who this is. She seems a bit too conspicuous to be a distraction burglar and she certainly isn't selling tarmac for the drive in that get-up. 'This is my home. It isn't open to all and sundry.'

'The door was open. I let myself in so as not to disturb you. I could see through the window that you were busy. Oh, you're making pastry...' She peers at the mixing bowl. I snatch it to my chest, and she looks at me then smiles sweetly. 'I'm sorry. I haven't introduced myself. What must you think, someone fresh from the big city, finding a complete stranger in her house? I'm Fifi, Fifi Green, and today I'm acting as your representative on the Talyton St George Meet and Greet Committee.'

'Oh, I see.' I put the bowl back on the table. 'I'm Jennie Copeland.' I hold out a hand, then realise it's coated with fat and flour.

'Don't let me stop you,' Fifi says. 'You'll spoil that pastry if you let the fat get too warm. Now, Jennie, was that Mrs Copeland or...?'

'Ex-Mrs Copeland,' I say, distracted by my pastry-making. I grab a jug of chilled water from the fridge and sprinkle some over the top of my breadcrumb-like mix. I pick up my small palette knife and use it to bind the ingredients together gradually, adding more water as I go.

'I hope you don't mind me asking these questions, only I have to report back.'

I can feel my forehead tighten into a frown.

'Is this a formal interview or something? Only...'

'Don't worry.' Fifi smiles. 'I only meant that

people will ask. If I say that you wanted me to keep all the gossip to myself then they'll assume you have lots of juicy secrets to hide, which will only make them all the more determined to winkle them out of you.'

'I haven't got any secrets,' I say, amused now that this woman is apparently so interested in the minutiae of my life. I suppose I should feel honoured by her visit – nothing like this would ever have happened to me back in London where even our nearest neighbours kept themselves to themselves. 'I'm sorry to disappoint you. I'm just an ordinary person.'

'Ah, that's not what Guy said.'

'Guy?'

'Oh, yes. He said you were the most extra-ordinary woman.'

Now it's my turn to be curious.

'I've been in to see him this morning. I promised his mother – before she entirely forgot who I am – that I'd look out for him.' Fifi shakes her head. 'It's the least I could do. Poor Mary.'

Fifi hoists her handbag on to the other end of the table, and extracts a sheaf of papers.

'I can leave these for you if you're busy,' she says. 'They're a selection of leaflets on the various services available locally. If you need an introduction to the vicar or the Baptist minister, I can organise that for you. Here's the contact number for our local doctors' surgery – I can't recommend Dr Mackie highly enough. He's done wonders with my bunions.'

I notice how Fifi moves around the kitchen, as if making an inventory of my belongings. She stops at the kitchen sink and looks out of the window towards the back garden.

'There are numbers for the vets' surgeries too. Have you got any livestock?'

'Not yet,' I say, and then it occurs to me that her visit might be useful after all. 'We're looking for a dog, a pony and some chickens, but I haven't a clue where to start.'

'The best people to talk to about ponies are the Pony Club. I'm not really au fait with chickens, but I can certainly help you find a dog. I'm a founder member of Talyton Animal Rescue, and although we haven't got our own kennels any longer, all our rescue dogs are housed with our network of approved foster carers.'

'Thanks,' I say, as she shows me the number to call.

'So many people move down here now. They take on all kinds of animals and set up these little cottage industries, find it's harder work than they imagined, then up sticks and go home. It's disruptive to the local community. Hence the idea of the Meet and Greet Committee to set you on the right track.' She runs a finger – I watch her do it – along the crossbar of the window frame and checks it for dust. 'I can recommend a cleaner, if you like.'

'I don't need a cleaner, thank you,' I say through gritted teeth. It's a nice thought, being welcomed into the bosom of the community, but the advice – which feels like criticism – is most unwelcome.

'I hope you're going to join the WI,' she goes on. 'We're very much in need of new blood.'

'Um, I'll see,' I say, then catch sight of the girls

84

who, apparently bored with picking blackberries, are sitting on the gate into the paddock, chatting. 'Actually, I'm going to find it difficult, getting out and about. The children.'

'Oh, but that's no problem. We have an excellent babysitting circle.'

Fifi Green is one of those people it's impossible to argue with because she has an answer for everything. I decide to listen, nod and inwardly disagree. The pastry mixture is coming together now into a ball of dough. I scoop it up and wrap it in clingfilm before putting it in the fridge to rest.

'Would you like a coffee?' I say.

'Oh, that's very kind of you. Thank you.'

I wash my hands, then put the kettle to boil on the Aga, at the same time as Guy rattles down the drive in his tractor.

'I hope Guy's making an effort,' Fifi says. 'He didn't want to sell Uphill House. It's been in his family for several generations, but circumstances forced his hand.'

'What happened?' I ask.

'It's a long story,' Fifi says, settling on a chair at the table while I pour coffee. I can't offer her any cake. There's none left. Then I remember I have a couple of shortbread slices in a tin in the larder, but Fifi declines. 'Guy doesn't like to talk about it – he's a very private man. Anyway, soon after his father died, his mother – Mary – was diagnosed with dementia. Because he wanted her to remember the wedding, Guy decided to go ahead and marry his fiancée. It was a beautiful wedding.' Fifi pauses. 'The happy couple lived with Mary while the house at Uphill Farm was being built for them. They moved in about a year later, but only had a few months on their own. Mary's condition deteriorated quite quickly and Guy, being the kind-hearted soul that he is, moved her in with him and his wife, Tasha.'

'That doesn't seem terribly kind to his wife,' I say, remembering how stressful it was sharing my house with my mother-in-law.

'Guy's wife wasn't terribly kind to anyone,' Fifi says. 'It was Guy who did all the caring – as well as looking after the farm. It was so bad, he had to call his brother in to help, and that's when it all went wrong. While Guy was keeping watch on his mother – because she was a liability – Tasha had her eyes on Oliver, the brother. Are you keeping up?' she adds.

'Yes. Yes, I am,' I say. 'Go on.'

'The upshot was that Guy caught Tasha in bed – in the marital bed – with Oliver. I've heard that it was almost the end of all of them because he went to get his shotgun out of the cabinet, but couldn't find the key, which gave Tasha and Oliver time to get away. Tasha called the police, but they couldn't prove anything.' Fifi smiles at me. 'Oh, don't worry. He isn't normally a violent man.'

I am concerned though. I was moving to the country to get away from guns, and now I find the neighbour's got one.

'Tasha was a striking girl and Oliver was the family's golden boy. Guy had to buy his brother out – he had a half share in the farm – so when his mother went into the nursing home, he could only find the money to keep her there by selling Uphill House. It was a dreadful scandal when it all came out.'

'How long ago did it happen?' I ask.

'It must be three years now. Guy was heart-broken. At first I thought he'd never get over it, but recently ... well, I've begun to hope that he'll be happy once more, settle down and have a family, an heir for the farm.' I wonder if Fifi is a little in love with Guy herself because she continues, 'I should hate to see him hurt again.' She takes one last sip of coffee, thanks me for my hospitality and prepares to leave, but she isn't quite finished yet. 'Guy's found it hard to accept that he'll never bring his mother home – still feels guilty about putting her away. She set fire to the barn – the one at the farm – and then he realised he could no longer cope.'

'Thanks for all the info,' I say.

'I've just remembered ... we have a voucher deal for second-hand school uniforms for single-parent families, like yours. No offence, but people are usually too proud to ask.'

'I can afford to dress my children,' I say stiffly.

'Just one more thing,' she says. 'If you're not used to an Aga – you don't need to bake pastry blind. Just put your tin straight on the floor of the roasting oven.'

'I'll try that,' I confirm. 'Thanks again.'

'I'll see myself out.'

I watch Fifi walk smartly across the lawn to her Mercedes. Why do I get the impression I've just been warned off?

I remove the dough from the fridge, unwrap it and let it warm up before kneading it gently and rolling it out. I have strawberry jam – made locally

– but I'm short of apples, in spite of the huge crop on the trees which isn't ready to harvest yet – so I make jam tarts and a cheese and onion quiche. While I'm waiting for them to bake, I ring Talyton Animal Rescue and find myself speaking to ... guess who? Fifi.

'Guess what? I've rung someone about a dog,' I tell Adam when he and his sisters come in for lunch – hot quiche and a green salad, followed by three blackberries each, and as many jam tarts as they can eat. 'I've made an appointment to see a couple, but it isn't until Saturday.'

'But that's ages, Mum,' Adam says, and I have to agree with him. Although I'm not into dogs, Adam's excitement is infectious and Saturday does seem like a long time to wait.

'Do you want to show me your ideas for this logo?' I ask.

'Um, I haven't finished them yet,' he says.

'That's because you were on Facebook,' says Georgia. 'You're always on Facebook.'

'It's the only way I have of keeping in touch with my friends.'

'Oh, never mind. I wondered if we might go and watch the milking this afternoon.' I'm thinking that it might make the time pass more quickly, which is how we find ourselves outside the parlour at Uphill Farm at three o'clock.

'I hope you don't mind us dropping by now?' I say, as Guy shoos the last stragglers of the herd into the collecting yard. I notice how he's wearing green wellies, boiler-suit and a faded blue cap, turned back to front.

'Not at all,' he says, smiling. 'It'll be nice to have company for a change.'

'I'm sorry about the inquisition the other evening. I've made them promise it won't happen again.'

'Well, you know everything now Fifi's been to see you. I'm sure she didn't hold back.' He sighs. 'I saw her car outside the house. Scandalmonger. What did she say about me?'

'Who says she said anything about you?' I say, teasing him for his arrogance in presuming he was the subject of conversation.

'Of course she did. She can't keep a secret.'

'Do you have secrets then?' I ask him.

He shakes his head. 'I'm afraid I'm not that mysterious. What you see is what you get. Go on in. That way, past the tank and through the doorway. There's a balcony you can watch from safely. I'll be with you in a minute.'

We go inside the building, past an enormous stainless-steel tank, and through a door into the milking parlour itself. There's a radio on, Radio 1, which surprises me. I thought Guy's taste would be more Radio 4. There's also the hum of machinery, and the intermittent mooing of a cow. It's noisier than I expected, more intense, and the air is thick with the scent of chemicals and cow dung.

'The cows are coming in,' says Sophie, excitedly.

'Stay behind the rail, Sophie,' says Adam, holding her back, his hands on her shoulders.

On the same level as the balcony, on each side is a platform for five cows. In the centre is a pit where Guy is walking about, making sure the cows move right up to the end. When he has five cows on each side, he pulls a lever and the doors from the yard slide shut.

'Do the cows mind being milked?' Georgia calls out.

'They look forward to it because they get fed then,' Guy calls back. He pulls more levers, releasing feed into the mangers in front of each cow.

'They're very dirty,' says Sophie, wrinkling her nose. '*Yuck.*'

It's true. The cows have muddy knees and mucky tails which they flick across their backsides now and then.

'Their udders are huge – some of them can hardly walk,' I observe.

'They tend to be the older cows,' says Guy. 'They lose their figures.'

I can empathise. At a certain age everything starts heading south.

'As for the dirt,' Guy goes on, 'we dip and dry all the teats to disinfect them. If we get bacteria in the milk, we have to throw it away. Ho, Kylie!'

The cow's udder is low-slung and I can see a network of swollen veins across the mottled skin. She has four huge teats, like a man's fingers, leaking milk.

'I'm attaching her to the milking machine now with this cluster of teat cups,' Guy explains as he slips this claw-shaped contraption with four tubes to the cow's udder. 'Then the vacuum pump sucks the milk from the teat in pulses, like a calf would suck the milk from her. That's what you can hear, the pulsations of the machine.'

It's like a regular beat and I find it hypnotic. Guy moves on to the next cow in the row.

'What's that one called?' says Georgia.

'This one's Rihanna. The next one along is Amy. Adam, if you'd like you can come down here – if you don't mind getting those city clothes dirty,' Guy says. 'You can flick this switch to let Kylie's milk into the bulk tank from the chamber here. It'll go through to the dairy via that pipe that's fixed to the ceiling.'

Adam goes down and flicks the switch. I notice how he hangs on to Guy's every word, how he watches and learns from him, and I remember, my chest aching with nostalgia for those days now long gone, how he used to help David clean the car or set up the new TV, when he was little.

'When you're in the pit here, you have to remember to watch their tails.' Guy smiles. 'If they lift them, stand well back, but keep half an eye on the cow behind you. Cows are messy creatures, but then what goes in must come out, and they have to eat a huge amount of grass to make milk every day and grow a calf inside them each year. It's a miracle. Well, I think it is.'

'I don't believe in miracles,' says Georgia.

'I like to keep an open mind,' Guy says, and he takes off the last set of clusters from the cows on the left side of the parlour and lets them out before letting the next five in. There's a rhythm to it, and an end product and, it turns out, a mess to clear up at the end, a bit like baking.

I look at Guy in a new light. Underneath the quiet exterior, he is a man of passion. He must be if he was roused to go and get his gun. He's been hurt, which might go some way to explaining his sometimes brusque manner. I can understand – I

91

know how it feels to be betrayed. David didn't run off with my sister, but it still hurt. Good grief... I pull myself together. I'll be feeling sorry for him next.

Adam and Guy drive the cows out to the field at the end, then come back to sweep and hose down so that the parlour's ready for the next morning, while the girls and I meet Napoleon – that's what Guy calls the cockerel – and the long-legged red chickens who are wandering around the farmyard, pecking and scratching at the dirt.

'Come and have a look at all the milk in the tank,' Adam calls eventually, and we head back into the dairy where Guy lifts the lid of the stainless-steel tank.

'This is what keeps the milk cool until the driver collects it in the morning.'

I've never seen so much milk, I think, watching it froth at the surface.

'It looks like one of those coffees at the coffee shop,' Adam says.

'You mean a cappuccino,' I say.

'Yeah, that.'

'Where are the cartons, Guy?' Georgia asks.

'Oh, I don't put the milk into the carton,' he says. 'It goes off to a central depot, a big commercial dairy, to be packaged. Some of this goes for organic yoghurt as well.'

'Are you an organic farmer then?' asks Adam.

'I've converted the farm to organic, hence the red-and-white cows. My father used to keep the black-and-white Friesian-Holsteins, but these Dairy Shorthorns are better suited for the purpose. They have lower milk yields and last longer

92

in the herd, and the bull calves can be reared for meat, not culled.'

I glance towards the girls. I don't think they understood and I'm glad. I don't want to have to explain the concept of the culling of cute boy calves to them, not that I knew much about dairy farming until today.

'Why did you decide to go organic?' I ask. 'Isn't it more expensive?'

'Yes, so the product attracts a premium, but that isn't the point. I don't use inorganic fertilisers on the land, or antibiotics as routine. I believe that's better for the cattle, the farm, and ultimately for mankind.'

I didn't realise milk production was so involved, and I'm surprised to find Guy is a modern, progressive kind of farmer with strong views on intensive food production and the environment. I confess, he's impressed me today.

'How much milk can a cow produce in a day?' asks Adam.

'Up to forty litres, but that would depend on where she is in the milking cycle, what she's being fed on, and her breeding.'

'How long do cows live for?' asks Georgia. 'Only we had three hamsters and they didn't live for very long.'

'It wasn't all our fault. The neighbour's cat got the last one.' As soon as the words come out of my mouth, I have to backtrack very fast, but it's too late. The damage is done, and I'm mortified.

'You told a lie, Mum. You told a big fat lie and now you won't get to Heaven when you die and I'll miss you,' says Sophie through tears.

I reach for her, but she backs away.

'I was trying to protect you.'

'If you wanted to protect someone,' Georgia joins in, 'you could have bought The Hamster a new cage that the cat couldn't get into, instead of telling us to stick the old one together with Sellotape. I told you it wouldn't work.'

Now the subject of The Hamster has been raised, Sophie remembers that we left him behind at our old house, which upsets her even more.

'You said, Mummy, that we'd dig up his skellingbones and bring him with us, but you forgot and now he's all alone.'

'You forgot too,' Adam points out. 'You can't heap all the blame on Mum.' But Sophie can and does, in no uncertain terms. I am the worst mother in the world.

I glance towards Guy. He's looking at me, his expression one of amusement. He's actually all right. Far from what I assumed at the beginning, Guy is no simpleton, no country bumpkin, but a far more complex – and, dare I say, intriguing – character than I'd thought.

'I think we'd better go,' I say apologetically. 'Thank you for showing us the parlour, Guy.'

'It's a pleasure,' he says. 'You're welcome any time.'

''Bye,' I say, getting away as fast as possible. Georgia apparently decides to keep her options open regarding the pony by letting the subject of The Hamster drop, while Sophie refuses to communicate with me again until she's forced to by circumstance later the same evening.

'Mummy, Mummy!' I hear her screaming from

94

the bathroom and immediately assume the worst: that she's taken a tumble off the throne or fallen in a bath of scalding hot water. I charge upstairs and open the bathroom door.

'What's wrong?' I say, hardly able to catch my breath.

Sophie screams again when she sees me, stamping her foot, her towel wrapped around her narrow shoulders.

'Sophie, that's enough. Now, calm down.'

'Mummy!' She's running on the spot, pounding the floorboards, as she points to the bath. 'There's a spider!'

I am overwhelmed by a skin-crawling mix of relief and fear. Of all the many consequences of the divorce, I never thought of this one. That I'd have to take on the role of removing spiders from the bath.

'Go and wait outside,' I say, my palms moist. 'I'll deal with it.' I'm not sure how. I lean over the bath to assess what I'm dealing with and suppress a scream of my own. This is no money spider. It's enormous with black hairy legs. And it's just sitting there on the rusty circumference of the plughole. I toy with the idea of turning the tap on then, feeling that would be cruel, wonder if I should suggest Sophie delays her bath-time.

'Mummy, has it gone yet?' she asks from behind the door in a voice that trembles.

'Not yet, darling.' My voice emerges as a high-pitched squeak. It's only a spider. What can it do to me? Summoning all my courage, I grab a towel and dangle the end of it into the bath, hoping the spider will hitch a ride. It doesn't, of course, doesn't move. In fact, when I dare to look more closely, it drifts in the draught that I create with the towel. Gradually, the hammering in my chest subsides, and I can breathe again. It's dead. There's nothing to fear. I pick up the delicate corpse in the towel.

'I've got it, Sophie,' I call softly.

'Have you killed it, Mum?'

'I'm going to put it out on the windowsill and release it back into the wild.'

Sophie is impressed. Later, she tells Adam and Georgia that Mummy loves spiders now and she'll never be scared of them ever again. Best of all, later when I'm printing leaflets for Jennie's Cakes from the computer, I overhear her telling their dad on the phone.

David always complained that I didn't do anything to surprise him.

'She actually held the spider in her bare hands,' Sophie adds, exaggerating as usual, and I sense with relief that she's forgiven me for the hamster revelation this afternoon. 'I saw it with my own eyes.'

It's funny, I think, while I'm gazing in the bathroom mirror, cleaning my teeth. My hair has grown longer since the divorce, falling in waves around my cheekbones which have re-emerged after my brief comfort-eating stage. I suppose I should thank my ex-husband for giving me the opportunity to discover new strengths.

I wonder if Alice is any good at spiders. Secretly, I hope she isn't.

Chapter Five

Fruity Flapjack

'You're up early.' I rub my eyes, wondering what I've done to deserve breakfast in bed. Georgia sits on the window-seat, picking the peeling paint off the woodwork. Sophie slides under the duvet beside me.

'I'm too excited to stay in bed,' says Adam, placing a tray on the bedside table. He's brought toast, cereal and a mug of tea, most of which has slopped out. 'I couldn't get back to sleep after Napoleon started crowing.'

'Well, thank you. I wasn't expecting this. It isn't Mother's Day.' I am welling up. 'I feel like a princess.'

'Mum, you're too old for that. You'll have to be the Queen,' says Georgia.

'I think you look like a princess, Mummy,' says Sophie. 'I'm going to look in the pond to find you a frog so you can kiss it and see if it turns into a prince.'

'I'm not kissing any frogs, even if they should turn out to be far–' I stop abruptly. 'I mean, princes.' Not farmers. I hope that wasn't a Freudian slip.

'If you can pick up a spider, you can definitely kiss a frog,' Sophie says.

'Eat up.' Adam plants himself on the end of the

97

bed. 'I can't wait.'

'Ah, did I mention we have a few things to do in town first?'

'Oh, Mum...'

'I need to pick up a few bits and pieces, and ask some of the shops if they'll put leaflets up in their windows.' I don't tell them the other part – my plan to tout for business for half an hour or so in Market Square. The skin at the back of my neck prickles uncomfortably at the thought of exposing myself in such a brazen way. At least, it seems brazen to me, promoting my business in public like that. I've never been good at self-promotion.

'But we are still going to choose a dog?' Adam persists. 'You haven't changed your mind?'

'Of course I haven't.' I pause. 'How do you go about choosing a dog, do you think?' Is it a bit like speed dating? I picture various dogs of different colours and sizes, sitting on cushions while being interviewed by potential owners over gravy and a bone. 'What kind of dog are you looking for, Adam?' I say, realising this is something I should perhaps have asked him before.

'A proper dog, one that'll play ball.'

'All I ask is that it isn't a big one. It has to fit in the car with our luggage for when we want to visit family and friends.'

'That rules out a Great Dane then,' he says ruefully.

'We'll have to see what Talyton Animal Rescue has available.'

'What's your idea of the perfect dog, Mum?' Adam asks.

'It's like that one in Georgia's pet hospital set,' I

say, smiling. 'Small, undemanding and inanimate.'

'Oh, Mum. Spoilsport.' Adam stretches out on his back across the bed at my feet.

'I think you should imagine you're a dog,' says Georgia, obviously finding it much easier to picture herself with fluffy ears and a tail than I do, 'and think, Would I want to live with this family? Then the dog can choose.'

'Give me ten minutes,' I tell the children, wondering how many self-respecting dogs would choose to come and live with my little monsters. 'Then we'll go. Adam, would you pick up the leaflets I printed off last night? I think they're still in the printer. And, Georgia and Sophie, there are two boxes of fruity flapjacks and mini-muffins in the larder. They need to go in the car. Don't eat them though – on pain of death,' I add, laughing.

I went with my idea for the logo for Jennie's Cakes, a naïve hand drawing of a butterfly cake – it had to be simple because I can't draw to save my life. Last night, I made up a leaflet on the computer and printed off a hundred copies on pale pink paper.

Eventually, we're ready to drive into town. I negotiate the maze of narrow streets and park behind the Co-op. Compared with where we came from in London, it's another world. We pass a tiny prefab building which houses the library. Sophie reads from the posters on the notice board outside, some of which are rather faded.

'We've missed the Duck Race,' she announces. 'That was in April. And we've missed the Country Show.'

'We'll be able to go to everything next year,' I

say, swept along with enthusiasm and nostalgia. Everything is as I remember it from childhood holidays, even down to the bunting which flutters between the lampposts. It makes me feel better about the task ahead. I've been visualising how I'm going to swan into each shop with a positive mental attitude, but that 'can do' feeling wanes as I approach the first destination, the green-grocer's, so much so that I walk straight past.

'Mum, you've missed it,' Georgia hisses.

'Oh, so I have. Silly me,' I say brightly, although my heart is pounding nineteen to the baker's dozen. Jennie, you have to do this, I murmur under my breath. Summoning my courage, I turn back and step past the fruit and veg on the pavement and into the shop. I hesitate, wondering if I should buy something to help start the conversation, but Sophie's ahead of me, already introducing herself to the man behind the till. He's about fifty-five, short and chubby with a whiskery moustache and a crown of thick dark hair around a shiny bald spot.

'My name's Sophie and my mummy's got something to show you,' she announces.

'I'm Peter,' he says. 'Nice to meet you.' He looks towards me and smiles. 'If it's cucumbers, the answer is no, I'm afraid. I'm inundated. People bring me the extras from their greenhouses to sell and there's been a glut this year.'

Adam pushes me forward, a bit like I do to him when we're at parents' evenings.

'This is about Mum's cakes.' Georgia opens one of the boxes of samples with a flourish and holds them in front of Peter, saying, 'Take one or two. They're the best cakes in the world.'

In the time it takes him to sample a flapjack and a mini-muffin, Peter agrees to put a leaflet in his window for me. I buy some apples and lettuce in return, and we move on.

The half an hour in Market Square is a doddle, and the trip into town is officially a success. The boxes are empty, there are leaflets in four shop windows – the ladies' boutique, the wine shop, greengrocer's and ironmonger's. What's even better is that I picked up a regular order for a weekly chocolate cake from the ironmonger himself, Mr Victor, who keeps a parrot in his shop. I did have to agree though for him to pay me 'in kind', seeing that it made sense for me to pick up a few 'bits and bobs' such as light bulbs and washers in exchange.

The bells on the church, a rather grand affair for a small market town, with both a spire and a tower, strike twelve.

'Can we go and choose a dog now?' Adam sighs. 'Please, Mum.'

We return to the car, pile in and make our way – using the SatNav who is talking to us today – to St Martin's Park, a road in the older part of town. I pull up on the drive of number ten, an impressive pebble-dashed Edwardian house. When we get out of the car, our ears are assailed by the sound of barking. It sounds like a choir of dogs, alto, soprano, tenor and bass. The different parts for different voices seem to mingle then merge into a crescendo of howling.

'Do you think there's a wolf in there?' Georgia says worriedly.

'No,' I say, trying to mask my uncertainty as Sophie clutches my hand tight.

We don't need to ring the doorbell. The front door opens a mere couple of centimetres, so that I'm talking to a disembodied voice.

'Hello,' it says. 'Are you here about a dog?'

'Yes.' I force a small smile. 'It seems we've come to the right place.'

'Get back, dogs. Oh, do please be quiet! How many times do I have to tell you, it isn't the postman?' The door closes again then, just as I'm feeling rather affronted, re-opens, revealing a stout middle-aged woman with short grey hair and a ruddy complexion. She wears horn-rimmed glasses, a navy and white crew-necked sweater, dark trousers and moccasin slippers. 'You must be the Copelands. I'm Wendy. Do come in.'

She shows us through to her living room at the front of the house. It's decidedly shabby, and an odour of wet dog and bad eggs pervades the air. Sophie looks at me as if she's about to pass comment, but I silence her with a frown. There are dogs everywhere – a greyhound on the rug in front of the fireplace, a row of four terrier types sitting up, watching us from the sofa, a Labrador, I think, and another large brown dog of indeterminate breed, perched on the two armchairs. There are throws draped over the furniture and various rubber toys and bones scattered across the threadbare carpet.

'Take a pew,' Wendy says. Then, smiling, 'If you can find one. Off, dogs. Off!' She flaps her arms, sending a couple of them jumping down and trotting over to investigate us. She picks up one terrier under each arm and plonks them on the floor. One makes to jump back up. 'No, Scruffy,' she booms.

Sophie's eyes widen with new-found respect.

'You have to let them know who's boss,' Wendy says more gently. 'I'm sorry, they do rather take over. Now, sit,' she adds. 'Sit,' she repeats, and suddenly I realise she's talking to us. 'If you don't sit down quick, you'll lose your places.'

I sit down on the sofa. Georgia leans against the arm and Sophie perches on my lap. Adam takes one of the chairs, Wendy the other.

'Right, I have to ask you a few questions first, then I'll introduce you to the dogs that might suit. We take great care to match our dogs with the right people.'

It's how I imagine being cross-examined in court would be, I muse as Wendy asks about our home life, our family routines, even our holiday arrangements. It's almost as if she doesn't want us to have one of her dogs at all. 'Our dogs have already been through hard times,' she explains when she notices me wilting under the pressure. 'We want them going to permanent, loving homes.'

She decides that she has three being fostered with her who might fit the bill.

'Donald,' she calls, and the large brown dog hauls himself up from where he's taken himself off into the corner of the room. He pads across to Wendy, ignoring us. He fixes his eyes on her and stands with his mouth open, tongue lolling out. Long strings of drool start to drip from his mouth.

'He's lovely,' says Georgia. 'He's just like Scooby Doo.'

103

'Is he friendly?' asks Adam.

'He's rather shy,' says Wendy.

'He's too big and I wouldn't like all that dribble around the house,' I say, and Wendy looks offended, as if I've criticised one of her children. 'I'm sure he's a very nice dog,' I go on. 'But I was thinking of something smaller.'

Wendy proceeds to show us the Labrador who's five and quite staid. The girls like her, but Adam is noncommittal.

'I want to take them all,' says Georgia. 'I can't choose – it's too hard.'

'That's just how I feel,' says Wendy. 'Now, I have one left to show you. I'll go and get him – he's gone and got himself locked out in the garden again.' She returns with a dog about the size of a Jack Russell in her arms. Dark eyes peer out through a fringe of grizzled grey and then the stringy tail starts wagging. 'Meet Lucky,' Wendy says, placing him on the floor.

For some reason, Lucky makes a beeline for Adam, jumps up on to his lap, stretches up, tail still wagging and licks Adam's face.

'Hi, Lucky,' he says, beaming, and my heart melts.

'What's his story?' I ask.

'We know very little about him. We guess he's about three years old and he's been castrated.'

'What's that?' says Sophie.

'He's had his nuts off,' Adam says casually, 'so he can't be a dad.'

'I'll explain later,' I tell Sophie as Wendy goes on, 'He likes children – we've found out that much, but the rest of his history is unknown. He came in

104

a couple of months ago – the police picked him up from the hard shoulder of the motorway. A driver reported seeing a dog being thrown out of a van.'

'Why would someone do that?' I say, appalled.

'People do the most awful things.' I notice Wendy's eyes briefly shimmering with tears before she recovers her composure. 'I can understand the reasons why people have to give up their dogs – redundancy, family break-ups – but I wish they'd come straight to us.'

I'm aware that Sophie reacts to the mention of family break-ups, reminding me that she is still feeling the pain of ours.

'We'll be all right then,' says Adam, cuddling the dog. 'Our family's already broken up and Mum can't be made redundant because she's just set up her own business, selling cakes.'

'Oh, that's great,' says Wendy, turning to me. 'About the cakes ... not the break-up, of course. I wonder if you'd be willing to donate one of your cakes to our cake sale – Talyton Animal Rescue are raising funds to maintain our existing rescues, and buy land where we can build a centre to house all our animals. Our last one burned down.'

'Yes, of course,' I say. 'Just let me know when you need it.'

'Poor thing, was he hurt?' asks Georgia, returning to the subject of Lucky's history.

'He was lucky – hence his name. He had a few cuts and bruises, that's all. And he brought a few fleas with him, which we've treated him for.' Wendy smiles. 'He isn't much of a looker, but he has a kind nature.'

There's no question of us not having Lucky

now. I fill in the adoption form, pay the donation and Lucky is ours.

'You'll need to get his vaccinations updated and have him microchipped,' Wendy says, and I'm thinking that that sounds expensive. 'That's the best way to choose a dog,' she adds as we're leaving. 'Let him choose you.'

'That's what I said this morning, wasn't it?' says Georgia.

'You're always so predictably, insufferably right, little sister,' says Adam, clutching the dog to his chest.

'I want you to remember that he's a dog,' I tell Adam, 'so he doesn't sleep on chairs or on your bed. Is that understood?'

'Yes, Mother.' Adam sighs and rolls his eyes.

In the car on the way home via Overdown Farmers, a store selling country items for country people, to pick up dog food, a collar and tag, special shampoo and all the other paraphernalia a dog needs, I notice how Adam, every now and then, when he thinks no one is looking, presses his lips lovingly to the top of the dog's head.

'What do you call that?' Guy calls through the kitchen window as the dog goes berserk, barking and jumping up and down.

'Lucky,' says Adam, getting up from his chair. He's been Googling how to bathe a dog on his computer at the kitchen table while I wash up the empty cake boxes and make cheese and ham sandwiches for a very late lunch.

Guy grins. 'What I mean is, what is it?'

'It's my new dog,' says Adam. 'Come here,

Lucky.' But Lucky isn't listening. He dashes off across the kitchen floor, claws skittering across the stone and starts barking at the front door.

'It looks more like some kind of rodent.' Guy retreats. 'I think I'll use the back door.'

If you don't mind, Jennie? I think wryly. I don't recall inviting him in.

'You'd better grab the dog, Adam,' I say.

'I'm going to take him upstairs and put him in the bath,' he says, heading out of the room.

'Our bath?'

'Where else?'

'Well, you could use a bucket in the garden or dunk him in the pond…' I begin, but Adam's gone and I can hear the tread of his feet on the stairs.

'Is it safe to come in now?' Guy looks over the bottom part of the stable door, a rolled-up paper under his arm.

'I didn't think someone like you would be worried about a little dog,' I say, smiling.

'Once bitten, twice shy. We had a collie on the farm when I was a kid. It pinned me to the ground and bit me through the lip.' He touches his mouth. 'There.'

'Where?' I say, moving closer and catching sight of a tiny silvery scar that I haven't noticed before above his upper lip.

'It put me off dogs, large ones and small,' Guy says. 'I'm sorry you had to dash off after milking,' he goes on, apparently summoning the courage to make his way indoors. 'I'd forgotten I was going to show you this. I had a think about you starting up your cake business and wondered if you'd contacted the local rag, the *Chronicle*. It isn't much of

107

a newspaper – not a lot goes on around here, at least not that's printable – but they do run a regular feature on local business people, and a half-page ad might be a good investment. I don't know anything about the cake business, but your cakes should speak for themselves.'

'Flattery will get you anywhere,' I say. 'Tea and cake?' (I managed to hide some from the kids.)

'I wouldn't say no,' he says, a twinkle in his eye.

'Coffee cake or flapjack? Which do you fancy?' Fancy? I feel the heat rising to my cheeks. Guy? It's irrational. I hardly know him, yet ... there is something about him, to look at anyway. He's enigmatic and – butterflies are dancing in my belly – utterly beautiful, especially when his lips curve into that slow smile. The sensation is instantaneous and short-lived, brought to an end by the equivalent of a cold shower when Lucky comes into the kitchen, bedraggled and wet, stands right next to me and gives himself a good shake. Guy stands well back.

'Thanks, Lucky,' I say, looking for Adam who appears in the doorway with a towel. My towel. 'I didn't need a bath. By the way, Adam, why didn't you use your own towel?'

'Because it was dirty,' he says shamelessly.

Although I'm ready to grab the dog in case he starts bothering our visitor, Lucky ignores Guy and Guy takes no notice of him, which is a relief – having once heard Lucky bark, I did worry that he might make himself a nuisance.

'Now you've got a dog to look after, you'll be looking for a part-time job, young man,' Guy says.

'Me?' Adam glances towards me.

'You were going to apply for a paper round before we came down here,' I remind him.

'You can come and work for me,' Guy says. 'I could do with some help with the milking now and again.'

I can see Adam isn't sure.

'There aren't many other jobs for teenagers in Talyton St George,' Guy continues. 'And when I was your age, I could always do with the money.'

'I thought I might work for you, Mum,' Adam says.

'One day maybe, but I can't afford to pay you yet.'

'You might get a cashier position at the Co-op, or waiting at the garden centre in the summer months,' Guy says.

'Waiting for what?' Sophie says.

'Waiting tables,' Guy says, smiling. 'Oh, and sometimes the chicken farm needs egg collectors on a casual basis. Milking would be regular, once or twice a week, depending on when you're free. You'll have to show some commitment – the cows need to get to know you so they trust you. They aren't machines. They have feelings.'

'What sort of feelings does a cow have?' Adam asks sceptically.

'Same as us, pretty much, I'd say. Happiness, sadness. They stay indoors in the winter – otherwise the fields would turn to mud and there'd be no grass in the spring. When they're first turned back out, they go bananas, kicking up their heels and gambolling about like little kids being let out of school.'

'I wouldn't do that,' Sophie says, confirming

her status as 'not a little kid any more'.

'So, what do you think, Adam?' Guy says finally. He'll never do it, I think. All that muck and those early starts. But Adam surprises me.

'I'll give it a go,' he says, and he and Guy shake on it.

Between Guy and the children, all the cake has gone, and it reminds me that I need more eggs, which leads me on to the subject of where to start acquiring a flock of chickens.

'How many do you want for this enterprise?' Guy says.

'Oh, I don't know – three to start with?'

'Three? A flock?' Guy chuckles. 'Let's start at the beginning – how many eggs do you need, say, for a week?'

'How many eggs does a chicken lay in a week?' I ask, because I haven't a clue. My best friend, Summer, once had chickens in her back garden in London, but they didn't get to lay any eggs. An urban fox had them within a week.

'You can expect one a day when they get going,' Guy says. 'So three chickens...'

'That's twenty-one eggs,' Georgia cuts in. 'That's a lot of eggs.'

'You must use more than that in a week, although you'll need to check the legislation regarding using your own eggs in cakes that you sell to the public,' Guy says.

'More red tape.'

'So, if I can get hold of ten or twelve hens... It's all right – I'll get them from the same place I got mine.'

'You don't have to,' I say, unwilling to be under

110

further obligation to him.

'I'll see what they've got next time I'm passing. It'll probably be next weekend.'

'But we'll be at Daddy's then,' wails Sophie. 'That isn't fair.'

'Guy's doing us a favour,' I point out.

'Never look a gift chicken in the mouth,' says Adam, laughing.

'Is it fair,' Georgia begins, 'to chickens to take their eggs away from them?'

I can see Guy looking at me as if to say, Do your children get their strange ideas from you?

'Do chickens have feelings?' Adam asks.

'You'll have to watch yours and decide,' Guy says, his eyes glinting with gentle humour.

'Lucky has feelings,' Adam goes on. 'He loves it here already, although he doesn't like having a bath.'

When Guy leaves, I thank him for bringing the paper.

'I'm glad we've been able to settle our differences. It was very thoughtful of you.'

'Yeah,' he says, gazing at me. 'You and your family aren't quite what I expected.'

'Well, thanks for selling me the house – I love it.'

'To be honest, I didn't want you to have it,' he says gruffly. 'I didn't like the idea of selling it to some wealthy townie who hasn't a clue how things are done around here. Local houses for local people – that's how I feel about it. The trouble is that the people who were born here can't afford to buy houses like this.' He hesitates. 'There was one other person interested in buying Uphill House, a builder who wanted to develop the barn and sell it on. There was no way I was letting him get his hands on it. You and your family were the lesser of two evils.'

I'm not sure what to say, I think. I've not been called an 'evil' before.

Guy smiles again, but I find I can't smile back. 'Thanks for the cake.'

I don't expect him to lie to me, but he could have been more tactful. I feel quite hurt, and for a moment, I wish I was back in my old house, near my friends. I recall though what Fifi said about Guy having to sell Uphill House and I begin to understand why he's been so difficult about the whole thing. I don't think it was just a business decision: it was an emotional one too.

Chapter Six

Marmalade Cake

The photo of me in the kitchen in an apron that has 'Jennie's Cakes' emblazoned across the front, in this week's edition of the *Chronicle*, is decidedly cheesy, but I hope the ad will attract some interest. I leave it open at the relevant page on the kitchen table in the hope that David might see it.

'It's about getting your name out there,' Mum keeps saying over the phone, but I beg to differ. It's about getting some orders. For the first time in my life, I'm fearful of opening my credit-card statement. In fact, I half hoped that Lucky might turn out to attack the post as well as the postman so I could blame my ignorance of my level of personal debt on him.

We've been here two and a half weeks, it's Friday evening and David's on his way to collect the children, to take them back for their first weekend away in London with him and Alice. I've had a burst of baking to take my mind off it all, sending them away with a box of chocolate crunch. I can't bear the thought of being alone here for the first time. I adore my house and love whistling for Lucky and taking him for a stroll around what we jokingly call 'the estate' at dusk, but I can foresee a long two days stretching out in front of me.

When they were at their father's while we were still living in London, I could at least pop by to see my parents, or visit my sister, or go shopping with Summer, but here... I take a deep breath. I'll have to get used to it.

I've finished feeding the children when David turns up still dressed in a suit and tie. He parks his car outside and arrives on the doorstep. Lucky's barking again, so I put him out in the back garden before I open the door. David feels the same way about dogs as he does about baggage allowances and speed cameras. He doesn't like them.

I did suggest that we should start as we meant to go on and meet halfway, but David had insisted on coming all the way to Talyton to collect the children on this first occasion.

'That's a bloody long drive on a Friday night,' he mutters. 'The traffic...'

'Hi, David. Lovely to see you,' I say cheerfully.

'Hi.'

'How was the holiday?' I ask. He and Alice spent the week before last on Kefalonia, but David appears pale beneath his tan.

'Great,' he says, then hesitates before going on. 'The children would have loved the beach...'

I refrain from commenting that he could have taken them with him. I suspect that he's often torn between spending quality time with Adam, Georgia and Sophie, and pleasing Alice.

I notice the dark shadows around his eyes and stubble on his cheeks as he looks me up and down. 'My God, Jennie. You look a fright. What have you been doing?'

Glancing down at my work clothes, jeans and a vest, I wipe my forehead with the back of my hand. 'Baking, gardening and pulling weed out of the pond.'

'How cerebral,' he says with sarcasm. 'Look at the muscles in your arms.'

I hadn't noticed before, but they are more defined and my skin, although I do remember to slap on the sunscreen, has become lightly tanned. David might not like it, but I feel very healthy. 'At least I don't have to pay out for a subscription for the gym.'

'I haven't been to the gym for a while either.'

I can tell, I think. He's put on some weight.

'Are they ready? The kids?'

'Daddy, Daddy!' Sophie's been ready since this morning, her clothes neatly packed into a pink suitcase with wheels. My throat tightens with regret when I see her clinging on to David, her arms around his neck. 'I've missed you.' She gives him a kiss on the cheek then giggles with delight,

114

her curls dancing around her shoulders.

'I've missed you too, darling,' he says, letting her down on to the step. 'Do you want to stick your bag in the car?'

'I'll just find Georgia and Adam for you,' Sophie says. Daddy's pet.

Adam isn't far away. He comes tramping through from the lobby with his rucksack, clothes and electrical cables flowing from the open top, the straps unfastened.

'Where's Georgia?' David asks.

I'm pretty sure she's still packing, deliberately stalling, so she can spend as little time away from Uphill House as possible, because of the three of them, she's the only one who's settled in, so far. So far. You see, I'm still optimistic. It's early days.

'Come in, David,' I say. 'I'll show you around.' I reckon that's why he was so keen to drive all the way down here tonight – to see Uphill House for himself. When he and Alice bought their flat, I didn't get to have a peek until the fourth or fifth time I dropped the children off. I'd thought about asking Georgia to take some video clips on her mobile, but decided that it would probably be against her ethical principles, and then I had a bit of luck: Adam left his iPod inside – it was the perfect excuse.

I went back to get it, sidling past David at the door. Alice was reclining on one of a pair of sofas, identical to the ones that David and I had when we were married. She had a copy of *Hello!* in her lap, and I recall thinking, How shallow. And how young... And how badly David had betrayed me.

I never did get to have a good look around the

flat. I had to get out of there as quickly as I could.

'There's marmalade cake in the larder,' I say.

'Thanks, Jennie, but I can't stop long. I've had a hard week. All this travelling isn't going to help.'

'Tough,' I say. He made his choice, Alice over me and the kids.

'There's no need to be arsey with me.' David pauses. 'You should be grateful that this arrangement you've thoughtlessly imposed on everyone else didn't drive me to go for full custody.'

He doesn't scare me. I feel quite secure. I know he and the girlfriend are planning to travel the world, so he can look upon these weekend trips as practice. Okay, I'm resentful, but is it surprising when David swans about, advertising his mid-life crisis, as if he's the only person in the universe who's ever had one?

'I've already offered to meet you halfway,' I say. What else can I do? I'm not moving back, that's for certain. 'If it's really such a pain, you don't have to see them every other weekend. You can make it once a month, if that's more convenient for you.' I don't mean it. I have no intention of stopping our children seeing their father.

'I want to see them,' David says, looking hurt, and for a moment I feel sorry for him, because although it's self-inflicted, he appears to be missing them – which is ironic, because he was hardly ever around before when we were married. He had a knack of timing his return home for just after I'd fed and bathed the kids, and read them a bed-time story. I used to find myself looking for hidden cameras in case he was spying on me.

'Does Alice want to come in too?' I add, although I've already noticed that she isn't in the car.

'Alice? Oh, no, she's gone off with friends for a hen weekend at some spa.'

'Is she getting fed up with you already?'

'Really, Jennie, you can be so childish,' David sighs, as he makes to step into the hall.

'You'd better take your shoes off. The muck,' I explain. I show David around – correction, Sophie shows him around and I tag along, hoping he's impressed. However, he's horrified.

'Jennie, I knew it!' he says when Sophie's showing him the throne in the bathroom and the site of the infamous spider removal. 'You're completely insane. Do you really expect our children to live here? It's dirty, damp, and it'll take you years to get it straight. You'll have Sophie down with another chest infection...'

'Rubbish. She only had those because of the traffic fumes ... the pollution. The country air will clear her lungs.'

'And why are the girls sharing?'

'Because they wanted to.'

'They told me on the phone about the dead bat. And the cattle stampede.'

'It was hardly a stampede. The cows wandered into the garden because we'd left the gate open. Sophie, go and help Georgia finish packing.' I check to see if Adam's listening in, but I can hear his voice in the garden, saying goodbye to his dog.

I'm tempted not to offer David cake, after all, but then I think that would be petty, and it wouldn't hurt to remind him what he's missing: his family, my cooking.

'Come through.' Dad and I did a lot of work on the kitchen – I don't think there's anything for David to criticise in here, although I'm sure he'll try. I set the kettle to boil on the Aga while David sits down and picks up the *Chronicle*. He casts a glance across the ad for Jennie's Cakes, then turns to the piece of marmalade cake I've put in front of him. He examines it, checking for hairs maybe. He does have this tendency towards OCD.

'That was ... very nice,' he says eventually.

'I don't suppose Alice has time to do much baking.' She works full-time.

'No, she doesn't cook,' he says wistfully, then as if he believes he's being disloyal, goes on, 'I've told her, though, she doesn't need to.' He looks at his watch. 'I'd better be getting back. The roads should be emptier by now.'

Reluctantly, I call the children together. It's tough because Sophie wants to go with David, Georgia wants to stay with me, and Adam is torn between seeing his friends in London and being with his dog. But within half an hour they're in David's car, waving goodbye, and, biting back my tears as I don't want them to see I'm upset, I almost say, 'I'll come with you and stay at Mum and Dad's.'

'I'll meet you at the McDonald's at four on Sunday,' David says, climbing into the driver's seat. 'Don't be late. I'm flying to Brussels on Monday so I'll have a very early start.'

I watch them all go, my family, the car disappearing down the lane, tyres scrunching into the potholes and dust rising in its wake. I check my watch. Forty-four hours to go. As I turn away,

118

arms folded, head down, towards the house, there's a whine from beside me. It's Lucky.

'It looks like it's just me and you, dog,' I say.

He gazes at me with mournful eyes and whips his tail once from side to side, then accompanies me indoors where I head for the drawing room and light a row of tea lights in the fireplace. Lucky settles on my lap, his head in the crook of my elbow, as I watch the flickering flames, and after all these years, I think I might have discovered the point of having a dog as a pet. 'You're such a sweetie,' I tell him, and he makes this sound, like a cat's purr, in his throat.

Seeing David must have stirred old memories in my brain because although it's been eighteen months since he revealed Alice's existence, it all comes flooding back. I considered myself a modern woman with traditional values. I gave up a good job for our family. I washed David's socks, ironed his shirts and looked after his children. I cooked for him, I muse, recalling the night I made boudoir biscuits for the very last time.

'I can't understand why you've stuck with it,' David said, as we sat on the sofa side by side that evening. 'Till now, I mean,' he added.

'What do you mean, till now?' Something was different this time. David didn't usually volunteer the information he was having an affair. He tended to confess when it was all over, or when I found out. A pulse of doubt throbbed in the back of my mind. 'You have finished with her?'

David gazed at me, his expression remorseful, and very slowly shook his head.

'I'm really sorry, Jennie.'

'You're still seeing her?' The light flickered above us. 'Oh my God, it's serious.'

David nodded, as if he'd lost the power of speech. I could smell alcohol and acrid sweat. He was as nervous as hell, and so he should have been because he wasn't telling me all this to beg my forgiveness. He was telling me because he wanted out.

Bile and the ire of betrayal rose in my throat. Before, I'd fought to save my marriage, but this was one step too far. As far as I was concerned, he could have 'out'. There was no way I was letting him come near me again.

'Who is she, this old slag?' I said sharply.

'It doesn't really matter.'

'Of course it bloody matters.' My hands were balled into fists. I wanted – needed – to know all about her. What she looked like, sounded like, what perfume she wore. What exactly David admired in her. What exactly she had that I hadn't.

'Well, for your information, she isn't some old slag, and I'm very much in love with her,' he said in a low, somewhat sheepish tone.

'That's a bit of a sudden change of heart,' I said, standing up. 'Last week you said you loved me!' It had been a spontaneous gesture, David moving up behind me as I melted chocolate over a bain-marie in the kitchen, resting one hand on the curve of my waist and saying 'I love you' out loud. Now I understood that he'd been testing his feelings for me, making his choice.

'Yeah, I said I loved you, not that I'm *in* love with you. There is a difference.'

I could feel the heat of my tears running down

120

my face, taste salt and eggs and marsala wine, as I broke down completely.

'Jennie,' David said, and I could hear the desperation in his voice. 'Please, don't cry...' He cocked his head towards the ceiling. 'Don't make a scene. The children.'

'The children?' His sudden concern for our children inflamed me. 'It's a pity you didn't think about the children when you were shagging–'

'Shhh! It wasn't like that.' David frowned. 'God, Jennie, you're making it sound so tawdry.'

'It is! It's tawdry, cheap and disgusting.' I flashed him a furious stare. *You're* disgusting. You're married to me ... have been for fourteen years, remember?' I hesitated as a single coherent thought unscrambled itself from the chaos in my brain. 'Is she married?'

'No. She's...' David picked at an imaginary piece of fluff on his sweater, then looked up at me again with something akin to a smirk on his face. At least, that's how it seemed to me. As if he was proud of himself. 'She's single. And new to the company.'

'I could have guessed you met her at work, seeing you spend most of your life there,' I cut in.

'She's also quite young.'

'Quite young?' I stepped towards him. 'What do you mean by *quite* young?'

'Will you put that thing down?' David was looking towards my hand. I glanced down, finding a bottle of Merlot in my grip. 'You're spilling it.'

I couldn't believe that all he was worried about was his precious wine, when I was so angry and upset I could have hit him about the head with it, because when he said young, he meant she was a whole heap younger than me.

'How young?' I growled.

'Twenty-four.'

At first I thought I'd misheard him.

'Thirty-four?'

'Twenty-four,' David confirmed.

'But that's–' I made a quick calculation and came to a dreadful conclusion. 'She's sixteen years younger than you, fifteen younger than me.' She's younger than me, her flesh firmer, her boobs still pert, no wrinkles, no grey hairs. 'You'll be a laughing stock, one of those sad old men being pushed around in a wheelchair by a vapid blonde. She is blonde, isn't she? I know she is.'

'Jennie, that's irrelevant.'

It was. For a millisecond, I agreed with him. He was leaving me for a younger woman. There was nothing I could do or say to prevent it, even if I wanted to. I could see that it was hopeless, and after all I'd done for him, the ungrateful ... slug. I wondered at myself sometimes. All that education and that was the best I could come up with: slug.

I was suddenly exhausted, drained, and irreversibly changed. I was not the same person. My whole existence, my identity, was based on my marriage first, family second. Life as I knew it was over, and somehow I had to find the energy and inner strength to move forward and become my own person again.

I take Lucky to the vet on Saturday morning, walking into Talyton along the lanes then through fields, passing the Talymill Inn, a country pub, and following the river valley into town. Arriving at the vet's, I greet the receptionist, a woman in her sixties or so, wearing a wig and rainbow-framed glasses.

'Hi,' I say. 'Jennie Copeland with Lucky. I rang yesterday.'

'Good morning, Jennie,' the receptionist says, revealing smudges of lipstick on her teeth as she smiles. 'What a lovely little dog,' she goes on, looking over the desk. 'Now, just to confirm, Lucky isn't registered with another vet? We don't want to go treading on anyone else's paws, so to speak.'

'Wendy from Talyton Animal Rescue said you would already have him on your books, here at Otter House – Lucky would have come in to be checked over before he was placed with her.'

'Oh, yes, of course.'

'He's the dog who was dumped on the motorway.'

'Maz saw him – she'll remember,' the receptionist says, reading from her computer screen. 'Take a seat.'

I'm not sure that I want to, considering the size of the dog that occupies the waiting area at the moment. He's a big blue-grey creature, standing up, lashing his tail against the display of toys and pet food.

'Sit!' barks his owner, a woman dressed in a nylon blouse, floral skirt and flat sandals. She tries pressing him down with one large hand flat on his back, but he remains standing. The woman smiles in my direction.

'Don't worry about Nero,' she says. 'He's the softest hound in the world. He's scared of his

123

own shadow.'

I head for a free seat, towing Lucky behind me. As I pass Nero, Lucky makes a leap for him, snapping and barking, at which Nero leaps backwards, plonking his bottom on to his owner's capacious lap.

'Oh, you silly boy,' she says, laughing. 'Mummy's baby.'

And I think, How embarrassing, and pray that I never start talking to our dog like that.

'You're new around here,' she goes on, turning to me. 'Are you from the new estate?'

'No, Jennie's bought Uphill House,' the receptionist joins in, 'Mary's old place.'

So much for client confidentiality, I sigh inwardly, but the receptionist goes on to reveal that some of her information – quite extensive information, at that – about my life and home furnishings has come from that woman, Fifi Green.

'We haven't introduced ourselves,' the receptionist says. 'I'm Frances and this is Mrs Dyer from the butcher's just down the road.'

'You can call me Avril. Frances does when we're outside the practice. Here, she likes to keep everything very professional,' she says. 'Have you tried our prizewinning local sausages yet? They've been voted the best in the South West for the fifth year running.'

'I'll buy some,' I say. 'Thank you.' I rummage about in my shoulderbag and pull out a leaflet. 'I bake cakes. Feel free to call me if you have a special occasion coming up.'

'You know, Jennie,' Frances cuts in, 'it might have been tactful to have had a chat with the

124

people who run the other outlets for cakes in Talyton, to see if your business could fit in rather than impose it upon everyone else. Cheryl who owns the Copper Kettle is most upset at the thought of someone like you entering into direct competition with her. It's rather unfair.'

'What do you mean ... someone like me?' I say, my face warm with mounting annoyance.

'You have to be pretty well off already if you can afford to buy Uphill House,' Frances points out.

'I still have to support my children,' I say.

'You could have done that where you came from. Cheryl has worked seven days a week, all year round, to keep her business afloat. The last thing she needs is competition.'

'And don't forget about Fifi,' Avril says. 'She sells cakes in the café at the garden centre.'

'She has people to bake and sell them on her behalf, you mean,' Frances says, correcting her. 'Fifi makes out that she bakes at home, but I know for a fact that she buys for herself and her husband from Marks and Spencer.'

'Well, I can't change my plans because baking's what I do,' I say, feeling very much the outsider in this conversation. 'We'll just have to hope that there's room for all of us.'

'We'll see,' says Frances. 'The people of Talyton St George are very loyal to their local businesses. I think you're going to find it incredibly hard to get yourself established.'

'Frances,' says Avril, 'give poor Jennie a break.' She flashes me a sympathetic smile. 'I wish you luck with your new venture.'

I fear that I'm going to need it.

'Lucky Copeland,' the vet calls from the door leading into the consulting room. 'Would you like to come through now?'

Lucky makes it perfectly clear that he wouldn't like to at all, and I have to drag him through. The vet is tall, pale blonde and in her early thirties. She's wearing a scrub top, like a surgeon might wear, but this one is covered with navy pawprints.

Now, I've never actually been into a vet's before, and I can only go on what I remember from watching the film *All Creatures Great and Small* years ago.

'Do you want him up on the table?' I ask.

'Yes, pop him up there.' The vet smiles. 'My name's Maz, by the way. I've met Lucky before...' She checks her records. 'What can I do for him today?'

'He needs an injection and a microchip.'

'Have you had any problems with him?'

'He's been fine. We've only had him a week though.'

The vet checks him over, then having given him an injection and a microchip with a broad needle that makes me feel faint to look at it, kisses him. A vet who kisses her patients? I don't remember James Herriot ever doing that.

Lucky lets me pick him up, but refuses to let me put him back down on the floor, so I carry him out to reception where I settle what seems like an enormous bill for a very small dog, and wonder if the vets charge pro rata according to the size of the patient. Still carrying Lucky, I take him to the butcher's shop where I have to leave him tied to a hook placed in the wall outside and next to a bowl of water that someone's thoughtfully provided for the canine residents of Talyton St George. Having been unable to hand Avril the leaflet for Jennie's Cakes in the vet's because her dog was in the way, I leave it for her in the shop and buy some sausages.

Later, I eat three for tea, give one to Lucky for being a good boy at the vet's, and freeze the rest. Then, as dusk falls, I sit amongst my tea lights and scented candles for the second evening running, with Lucky at my feet chewing on a stick of rawhide. I review the day and my encounter with Frances and Avril and wonder if I've bitten off more than I can chew.

Think positive, I tell myself. The locals are bound to be concerned about my business venture. I would be too, in their position.

Lucky growls. I tense and listen. There's a knock at the front door. Lucky jumps up and runs through to the hallway, barking. I follow, unbolting the front door and holding Lucky by the collar as I open it. Guy is standing in the porch carrying a lantern.

'You locked the door,' he says.

'Force of habit,' I say, smiling.

'I happened to notice you were in darkness. The candles. It's probably a fuse... I thought I might be able to help.'

'Oh, no. There's no powercut.' I release my grip on Lucky's collar. 'I like candles,' I say, to fill the awkward silence. 'There's something really romantic about a naked flame.' Why did I say that? It's my turn to be embarrassed. I hope he doesn't think I'm hinting at anything.

'I've always found candles rather inconvenient and outmoded,' Guy says, his tone lightly teasing. 'I've disturbed you then, Jennie. I'm sorry.' He backs away into the shadows.

'Don't apologise. Come on in. If you'd like to, I mean.'

'I thought...' He hesitates. 'Well, I knew you were on your own, apart from the rodent anyway.'

'Yes. Go away, Lucky.' I shoo him from where he's sat down on my foot, but he doesn't go far.

Guy moves into the light once more, and smiles shyly. 'I'm sorry about what I said the other day – about you being the lesser of two evils. I've been thinking about it and it didn't come out as I intended.'

'Oh, don't worry,' I say, gratified to discover that he didn't mean it and pleased to have some human company. 'I've got a bottle of wine. Would you like a glass?'

'Don't open it especially for me.'

'It's already open,' I confess.

'A small glass then.'

'I remember. You'll be up at the crack of dawn.'

'Yeah,' he says.

I switch on the lights and blow out the candles and tea lights and take Guy through to the kitchen where I pour two glasses of wine. He sits at the table. I lean against the Aga, wondering how to start the conversation.

'I took Lucky to the vet today,' I begin. 'Fifi had obviously been gossiping with the receptionist there... What's her name?'

'Frances.' Guy smiles. 'Both Fifi and Frances are very generous spirits, but they're also terribly

128

bossy and interfering. They've lived in Talyton for years and think they own the place.

'Since Mum's been ill, Fifi's taken responsibility for my welfare. She keeps telling me to be careful ... that you aren't the kind of woman I should be associating with,' he goes on lightly.

'What does she mean by *that?*' I exclaim, more amused than offended. 'And you needn't "associate" with me, as you so delicately put it, if you don't want to.'

'I'm talking about what Fifi thinks, Jennie, not what I think.'

'What exactly does she think? You have to tell me now.'

Guy tilts his head, his cheeks flushed. 'She says you're a scarlet woman.'

I find myself laughing. How quaint.

'I've never been called one of those before.'

'Fifi is inclined to make things overly dramatic.' Guy smiles. 'She's a gossip. That's how she is.'

'But I'm not like that. I've been married once and had one other serious partner before that.' I shut up quickly. Too much information. It's me who's blushing now.

'Fifi's rather prone to making snap judgements. I told her she can't make that kind of assumption just because you're single and you dress young.'

'Dress young?' I glance down at my tunic over leggings.

'Meaning that you don't go around in a twinset and pearls,' Guy chuckles.

'Well, thanks for standing up for my honour.'

'It's a pleasure.' Guy pauses. 'I expect you're missing the children.'

'Being alone has made me realise how very quiet it is around here,' I say mournfully.

'I thought that's why you moved to the country?' he says with a grin. 'You aren't really in a position to complain that it's too quiet.'

'I know.' I sit down and take a sip of wine. It's a red and tastes of liquorice and blackcurrants, an odd contrast, a bit like city versus country life. 'I miss the children terribly, but I miss my mum, sister and friends too.'

'You'll soon make friends here,' Guy says reassuringly.

'I hope so.'

'You've got me,' he says, looking me straight in the eye.

'Thank you, Guy,' I say as calmly as I can, because my heart is racing and my thoughts are in tumult, like the water in the race at the Talymill Inn was today when I walked past it with Lucky. Here I am alone in the house with a man I hardly know, but find extraordinarily attractive, physically at least, and he's telling me I've 'got him', presumably in an 'as a friend' kind of way, but how can I be sure? I'm certainly not going to make a fool of myself by asking.

Guy picks up the copy of the *Chronicle* that's been on the table since David left.

'Have you had any response to your ad?' he asks.

'Not yet,' I say, still optimistic.

'Your cakes speak for themselves,' he says. 'I don't think you need to worry unduly. Have you thought about selling at the Farmers' Market? There's one on the first and the third Saturday of the month. You could rent a pitch for the next one.'

I register that as a good idea.

'When's Adam going to start work with me then?'

'I thought Monday. I hope he does a good job.'

'Don't worry. He'll be under close supervision for a while. There's a lot to take in.' Guy pauses. 'I like Adam. He seems very bright.'

'Yes, but I'm afraid he doesn't always apply himself.'

'I always imagined having a son – or a daughter – by now,' Guy says thoughtfully. 'I used to help my father with the milking, as he helped his father before him. The farm's been passed down through three generations of Barneses, and I'd hoped I'd pass it to my own offspring, but I can't see that happening now.'

'You aren't that old, are you?' I say lightly.

'I'm thirty-five.'

'So you have plenty of time left.' I'm glad Guy doesn't ask me my age in return, although he must guess that I'm older than him. 'What's the record for the oldest man to have become a father? Seventy? Eighty?'

'I'd want to last long enough to bring them up,' Guy says rather indignantly. 'I'd want to be there for them. Tasha didn't want children, or so she said,' he begins awkwardly, 'but it turned out that she meant she didn't want them with me. She's on her second now.'

I assume he means her second child.

'I'm sorry,' I say, unsure how to react. I can't imagine not having children.

131

'I expect Fifi's told you how my wife left me for my brother,' he goes on bitterly. 'I felt completely betrayed. I loved her ... and I thought she felt the same way about me. I'd have done anything for her.'

It appears from the sadness in his voice that Guy's loss is still very raw.

'David left me for a work colleague,' I say, wanting to let him know that I'm here for him as a neighbour and a friend. 'I know where you're coming from.'

'Did you know her – before, I mean?' Guy asks.

'David's lover? I knew of her. She wasn't the first.' I smile darkly. 'The first one I excused because he was in a state over the death of his mother. The second one was married. David thought she was going to leave her husband, but she changed her mind the night he was all packed and ready. Why did I take him back?' I rest my chin on my cupped hands. 'I sound like a complete doormat.'

'Or a fighter,' Guy says, looking at me with those hypnotic grey-blue eyes.

'He took me for such a fool. That was one of the hardest parts to deal with – the duplicity, and how public it all was.'

'Tell me about it. I felt so humiliated. It turned out that half of Talyton knew Tasha had been with my brother the night before our wedding. One of my then friends even saw them together in a car down by the river, but couldn't bring themself to mention it to me...' Guy's voice grows husky as he stares into the bottom of his wineglass. 'I would have been gutted, but I wouldn't have spent the next three years living what turned out to be a complete lie.'

'You poor thing. I'm so sorry.'

'Don't worry about me,' he sighs. 'I'm big enough and ugly enough to look after myself. I should have been able to read the signs, but Tasha could do no wrong in my eyes. I was infatuated.'

'I don't know how long David was lying to me,' I say, 'but I recall the night he came clean all too clearly... We were together on the sofa when he told me he was sorry, he was seeing someone else. I was livid. In fact, I lost it and threw a wineglass at him.'

'Did you hit him?' Guy asks.

'I missed, unfortunately. It smashed into one of our wedding photos which I suppose was symbolic. I never did like it – I was holding the bouquet strategically across my bump, and David looked like a ghost because no amount of airbrushing could hide the fact he'd been out on the lash three days running before the wedding.'

'You were pregnant before you married?' Guy says.

'Are you really that old-fashioned? It's almost normal, being pregnant out of wedlock nowadays.' I'm amused to see that he's blushing.

'How long were you together then?' he asks.

'We were a couple for seventeen years, married for fourteen. We met at university. David was studying for a maths degree. I was doing English lit.'

'So we have more in common than I expected,' Guy says. 'I'm not talking about English lit, although I do have a degree in agriculture and land management. No, I'm referring to a broken marriage.'

'It's hardly something to shout about, is it?' I say. 'Why didn't your ex marry your brother in the first place then?'

'Because Oliver – my brother – isn't, or wasn't, the marrying kind. Everyone loved him. He was the golden boy of the family … sociable and funny, irresistible to women, better looking than me–'

I almost blurt out, But how can he be?

'He was also irresponsible. He left a sixteen-year-old girlfriend to bring up his baby when he was seventeen. And then he carried on with my wife behind my back.' Guy hesitates before going on, 'As the elder brother, I was always going to inherit the farm. Oliver would have received his fair share financially, but I think Tasha fancied herself as a farmer's wife. She wanted the farm – as a status symbol, or just somewhere she could keep her horses for nothing. I don't know.' He shrugs.

'Unfortunately she was a townie – I met her when she came to a Young Farmers' do – and didn't understand what was expected. What I mean is, I didn't expect her to muck in with the farm work and cook and run the house like my mother used to, but with her deciding to pack in her job – she was a nurse – we couldn't afford to hire help in. When Mum was diagnosed, I looked after her, and Oliver came to help run the farm…' His voice fades, then returns. 'It's all been so bloody upsetting.'

'You don't have to talk about it, if you don't want to,' I say, pleased that he feels able to confide in me, yet sad for him too. Up until now, Guy's seemed quite cool and self-contained. Tonight, he's revealed another side of his character: deeply caring and compassionate.

'I don't normally mention it,' he says, 'but somehow you make it easy. I don't feel as if you're judging me. And you're not like Fifi – telling me to snap out of it and get on with my life.' A shadow of sorrow darkens his eyes. 'She can say what she likes, I'll never get over it. I'll never trust anyone again.'

That wasn't how Fifi put it, I muse as Guy drains his glass and places it back on the table.

'I'm sorry,' he says. 'I'm sure you've heard enough of me going on for one day.'

'It's fine,' I say, finding that I'd be more than happy to listen to him talking for as long as he wanted. I like listening to the warm tones of his voice. I like sitting here with him, and not because there is no one else.

I go on to tell Guy how I'd expected – no, wanted – to grow old with David; for us to celebrate our Golden Anniversary, surrounded by our children and grandchildren. I'd dreamed of retiring with him to a place like Uphill House, in the country, with honeysuckle and roses growing outside the front door.

'That's exactly how I felt about Tasha,' says Guy, and for a while we're both lost in our own separate worlds.

Eventually, I try to pour him more wine, but he puts his hand over the glass.

'No, thanks, Jennie,' he says. 'I should get going,' he adds, but I notice that he doesn't seem to be in any hurry to leave my cosy kitchen. I'm aware that his gaze lingers on my face for a little longer than necessary before he eventually stands up and says that he really must go now.

I accompany him back through the snug to the hallway.

'Thanks for dropping by,' I say, when he hesitates with his hand on the front door. I can hear a pulse beating in my head. Am I reading more into the situation than I should? Is he...?

'Thanks for the wine, and your company, Jennie.'

I tilt my face towards Guy's. It's the slightest move but he responds, leaning towards me and touching his lips to mine, before muttering, 'Goodnight,' and disappearing into the darkness as if he's running away.

What does it mean? How am I supposed to feel? Flattered? Over the moon? As it is, Guy leaves me feeling elated and more than a little confused.

Chapter Seven

Lemon Drizzle Cake

It's Sunday morning and the children are still with David. Sharing a breakfast of toast and honey with Lucky, I wonder what they're doing. Guy goes past – the cows are going out again after milking. He raises his stick and waves. Touching my lips where he kissed me last night, I wave back and watch him stroll down the drive. I see him return, then go out again in his Land Rover about an hour later.

I'm not being nosy. I happen to have a great view of the shared drive from the kitchen, and Lucky barks at anything that moves.

Where does Guy go on these expeditions of his? To visit his mother? To see a girlfriend? He didn't answer when Sophie asked him that question, and I find it hard to believe he isn't romantically involved. He's obviously still upset about his wife running away with his brother, but that was some time ago now and I know for a fact that time really does heal. He kissed me last night – clearly intended it as a kiss too because he almost ran away afterwards, as if he'd suddenly realised what he'd done. Was it an impulse he instantly regretted because he's going out with someone else?

I use the time to cook a cottage pie and bake a lemon drizzle cake – Adam and the girls will want something when they get home. I whizz up a sponge mix, add the fragrant zest of a lemon, and spoon it all into a loaf tin before sticking it in the Aga.

Lucky hears the Land Rover returning before I do. Instead of passing by, it stops outside the house. Guy gets out in his smart trousers, brown brogues and a pale blue V-neck sweater over a white T-shirt, and comes over to knock on the kitchen window. I open it, wondering with a frisson of longing if he might kiss me again, properly this time. However, I'm disappointed – and too shy to do anything about it, especially in broad daylight and without being fortified with a glass of red wine.

'Jennie,' he says without a trace of embarrassment or any hint that he remembers our conversation last night, 'I've got you those chickens.' He sounds excited, much like Adam did when we collected the dog.

'Today? But it's Sunday.'

'I got them from a friend of mine. Ruthie's a farmer, so, like me, she works every day of the week. She's more than happy for me to turn up any time.'

'I see.' My stomach knots up with a sensation of envy. I don't know why. So what if Guy has friends? He had a life before I arrived on the scene. I probably shouldn't analyse it unduly, I know, but maybe he's not the lonesome farmer who's been let down in love that I took him for. I've even felt sorry for him, yet it seems I didn't have to be. He has longstanding links with the local community. He was born here.

'It's very kind of you to go to so much trouble,' I continue, ashamed that I read too much into Guy's confiding in me over the wine last night. I resolve to suppress my imaginings in future – he's an attractive guy and, in spite of my family and friends, I sometimes feel very alone here. These are not sound reasons to enter into a relationship, serious or otherwise.

'I was going right past her door, so I dropped in and picked them up,' Guy says. 'Where do you want them?'

'I haven't got a henhouse. Where will I put them?' I wipe my hands with a tea-towel. 'I was going to order one of those plastic henhouses. I

138

saw them in Overdown Farmers and took a fancy to a bright green one.'

'They'll have to lay an awful lot of eggs to pay for it. They're chickens. They don't need five-star accommodation. All you need is something to keep Charlie out.'

'Charlie?'

'The fox.'

'Are there a lot of foxes around here? We used to see lots where we lived before – they seemed to thrive on leftover fast food.' And chickens, I think, recalling the fate of Summer's birds.

'The odd one tries its luck now and again,' Guy says.

'Oh, now I shall worry about them all the time.'

'That's the problem with keeping animals.' He smiles. 'You never stop worrying about them. You can lock them in one of the stables at night, and let them out during the day. Like my hens. Go on – go and open the gate for me and I'll bring them into the yard.'

I shut Lucky in the house – I'm not sure how he'll react to chickens – and go round the back, through the yard where the weeds which we'd cleared are beginning to grow back up between the bricks and cobbles, and open the gate. Guy drives in and parks with the back of the Land Rover facing one of the empty stables. He jumps out and opens the tailgate with a flourish.

'There you go,' he says, revealing two open-sided crates with feathered occupants. 'Ten ladies ready to lay.'

'They look a bit...' I'm trying not to sound un-grateful '...scraggy.'

139

'Ah, they're ex-battery. They've been locked up in cages for the past eighteen months. Ruthie runs Hen Welfare – she rescues them. Don't worry, they'll soon pick up and lay eggs for a few years yet.'

Guy lifts the crates out and carries them one at a time into the stable, placing them on the floor that is covered with a layer of old straw. He shuts the lower half of the door, then lifts the lid on the first crate and takes out one of the birds.

'She's a thin one,' he says, assessing her. 'A size zero, I reckon. What do you think?' he adds, passing her over to me.

'Oh,' I say, backing off. 'I don't... I wasn't expecting to have to handle them.'

'Hold her wings against her sides, so she doesn't flap,' Guy says, his fingers brushing against mine as he lowers the hen into my hands.

'It's me who's flapping.' I relax, smiling, as the chicken grows still. 'She feels so light. And warm. And she's lost almost all her feathers, poor thing.' The feathers she does have are light brown with hints of cream. Her skin is pale, rough and pimply, and she has a red, rubbery comb on the top of her head and wattles under her beak. She's watching me warily with one eye. A round orange eye. 'What's that that keeps flickering across her eye?' I ask.

'Chickens have a third eyelid. She's blinking.' Guy smiles again. 'She's blinking lucky, too, to have found a luxury home like this. Pop her down on the floor.'

I lower her very gently to the ground and let her go.

'Watch,' he goes on. 'Remember, she's been living on wire slats all her life, sharing a cage with a couple of other hens. She'll never have seen straw or daylight before she arrived at Ruthie's.'

'Poor thing...'

The hen stands hunched for a minute or so then shakes, stretches her pathetic, bald wings and hops towards the light that comes through the top half of the door. She hesitates, tilts her head to one side and caws softly. She taps tentatively at the straw with her beak, retreats as if startled, then taps at it again. Apparently reassured, she scratches at the straw with her feet, reverses then pecks at the ground again.

'Clever, isn't she?' says Guy. 'Wait a mo'. I've got some grain in the Land Rover.' He fetches a small brown bag and throws out a couple of handfuls for the hen to peck at before I help him take the rest of the birds out of the crates. There is a lot of noisy squabbling before they settle down, the greedier ones continuing to search for grain, the quieter ones settling to sleep, lying on the straw. One perches on the edge of the crate.

'They're all quite different characters,' I observe as we back out of the stable, watching out for potential escapees. I close the bottom half of the door behind us and Guy and I stand side by side, leaning over the top, watching the hens. At least, I'm trying to watch the hens, but find my gaze repeatedly veering towards the man at my side. 'I've never thought of a chicken as having a personality.'

'I reckon you should call that bossy one Fifi,' Guy says, pointing to the hen that is pecking at

141

her neighbour's eyes.

'Guy, show some respect,' I say archly.

'Yes, I shouldn't malign her,' he agrees. 'You must let this lot get used to being in here for a couple of days, then you can let them out so they can forage around the garden and the paddock. You probably won't get any eggs for a week or two. They'll need access to water. Oh, and I'll let you have some layers mash until you get your own.' He looks at me quizzically. 'Layers mash – it's their food. They also like mealworms as a treat. Live ones.'

'Ugh, I'm not sure I can cope with that! I'm not sure Sophie will either.'

'Did you know that a chicken can catch and kill a mouse?'

'You're putting me off eating eggs now.' I'm not off chickens though. I can't stop watching them. 'Thanks, Guy,' I say eventually. 'What do I owe you?'

'Ruthie's always glad when they go to a good home, so you don't owe me anything, although I wouldn't mind a piece of cake, if there is some? I thought I could smell baking.'

'There's a lemon drizzle cake in the oven. Why don't you come in for some lunch – if you aren't in a hurry?'

He glances at his watch.

'I've got a couple of hours till milking.'

'I have to leave at two-thirty to meet David anyway,' I say. 'Don't you ever get fed up with working here? It must be such a tie.'

'To be honest, when I do manage to get away on holiday, I miss it.' He smiles again.

'The kids are going to be miffed that they missed seeing the arrival of the hens.'

'I'll bet. You know, we'll have to arrange a love match sometime,' Guy says as we head indoors. 'Between Napoleon and your hens,' he goes on, his tone laced with humour.

'So we'd end up with chicks,' I say, the leap in my pulse rate slowing now he's confirmed that the love match he's planning isn't to be between him and me. However, I'm quite excited – the idea of having chicks appeals to my maternal instincts.

'That's what usually happens.' Guy grins as he takes a seat at the end of the kitchen table. I remove the cake from the oven and leave it to cool on the rack while I make a couple of sandwiches.

'It has to be cheese and pickle,' I say, offering him a plate. 'There's no ham or hummus – Adam must have raided the fridge before he left.'

We eat and chat about Guy's plans for a new cowshed and mine for a stall at the next Farmers' Market while Lucky sits at my feet, begging for crumbs, until gone two when I tell Guy that I have to get going.

'I don't want to keep the children waiting,' I say, picking up my bag and keys.

'And I mustn't be late for the ladies,' Guy says, smiling. 'I'll see you around, no doubt.'

'Sure.' I call Lucky and let Guy out through the front door before locking it behind me. ''Bye then.' Our farewell feels awkward. Friends, or a bit more than that? I wish I knew where I stood with him.

I begin to understand why Lucky's previous

owners dropped him off on the M5. In the car, he barks all the way to the McDonald's at Sparkford, and then when I get there, I'm not sure what to do with him because there's a sticker in the window of the 4x4 I'm parked next to that reads 'Dogs Die in Hot Cars'. It's almost four but it's still pretty warm and I'm reluctant to let Lucky die, especially now that I've invested quite a lot of money in him. I take him out of the car on his lead, but the sign on the door of McDonald's reads 'No Dogs'. I stay outside.

I can't wait to see Adam, Georgia and Sophie again. If it hadn't been for Guy and Lucky, the weekend would have seemed very long. I catch sight of David's car pulling in and jog over to greet them. The girls give me a hug while Adam focuses all his attention on Lucky who jumps up, leaving muddy pawmarks on his jeans.

'Dad, I'm starving,' Adam says, looking up at his father.

'Okay, you can have a burger if you want one,' David says. 'Would you like a coffee, Jennie?'

'I'd love one, but someone will have to wait outside with Lucky.'

'I will,' Adam says.

'So will I,' says Georgia.

'And me,' says Sophie, and I smile to myself. They've missed the dog more than their mum.

David buys burgers and fries to take out for them before we sit inside with our coffee.

'Did you have a good weekend?' I ask.

'It was fun,' David responds. 'How about you? Have you managed to sort out a bit more of the house?'

'Not really, but I have been working on my business plan. I've decided to have a stall at the next Farmers' Market, to test the water locally.'

'How's the cake-baking going? What are you turning over so far?' Taking my silence for what it is, he goes on, 'I didn't think so. You know, Jennie, you just aren't hungry enough. You have to have real passion–' he hits the centre of his chest '–here. It isn't going to work, you know. You'd be better off getting a job, working for someone else.'

'I don't want to work for anyone else. I have a quality product I know I can sell. You were the one who suggested I might make a business from baking, if you remember.'

'I'd pack it in if I were you, get shot of that big old house and use the equity to buy something much more modest in the suburbs.'

'What did you say?'

'You'll never make it there on your own, without your parents at your beck and call.'

'But they never were.'

'They were always around at ours – or your mother was anyway. Helping you out with this and that. And your sister and Summer. You'll be back within a year. Why not save yourself a load of grief and come back now?'

'No way, David.'

'It makes sense, Jennie. Adam and I had a heart-to-heart this weekend. He didn't want to move to Devon in the first place, and I've been checking out your local school and it isn't great.'

'It's fine. I looked at the tables, for what they're worth, and the school's about average.'

'Average isn't good enough. And it isn't just

about exams, it's the social aspect too.'

I know what David means – he wants to expose his son to the movers and shakers of this world.

'You can't buy friends...' I say.

'But,' David interrupts, 'you *can* buy influence. I want the best for him, Jennie. For God's sake, why can't you see that? See past the divorce, see past your bias against me, and look at what's best for our son.'

'I know what's best for him,' I say stubbornly. 'I'm his mother.'

'And I'm his dad,' David says smugly. A muscle in his jaw tightens. 'So why was I the last to know about Adam's new job on the farm next door? Why didn't anyone run it past me first?'

'I didn't see any reason to.'

'We agreed – you have full custody, but we make joint decisions on behalf of the children.' He pauses strategically before the browbeating starts again, and I can feel the anger bubbling up in my belly. 'What about his schoolwork?'

'He'll do it – I'll make sure of that. And this job will give him a sense of responsibility, and the satisfaction of earning his own money – something he's worked for, not just been given.' Like me, I think. 'I don't know why you're making such a fuss about this, David.'

'What about my weekends with him? What then?'

'There's no problem. Guy's made it clear he's flexible.'

'I don't want my son thinking he's going to be a farmer either,' David says. 'He can do so much better than that.'

'There are other ways to live, David. And this has nothing to do with his future career. If he were doing a paper round, you wouldn't assume he's doing it so he can end up working in journalism. This is ridiculous.' I can't believe we're arguing again. I thought all that was supposed to stop when you got divorced. If anything, things are worse for us.

'What do you know about this Guy bloke?' David blusters on.

'Enough – he's a decent man.' My voice trails off. I thought David was a decent man once. Maybe I'm not such a good judge of character, but I like Guy and I don't like what David's implying. I'm sure I'd have heard on the grapevine if there were anything odd about him. This is about David himself, not Guy. David's problem is that he no longer has control. 'Adam will be fine,' I say firmly.

I try to talk to him and the girls on the way back to Uphill House, but Lucky will not stop barking. Not only that, but Sophie is so tired she falls asleep, Georgia suffers a bout of travel sickness in silence, and Adam concentrates on trying to distract Lucky who is perched on his lap. Nothing he says or does makes any difference to either the frequency or the volume of Lucky's protests.

'That bloody dog,' I say, exasperated.

'I expect he's afraid you're going to abandon him again,' Adam says protectively.

I don't say that I might just do that if he doesn't shut up, because expressing my feelings would only upset the children.

It's a relief when we get back and I can park the car in the yard, turn off the engine and let the dog out. Peace at last.

'Don't go inside just yet,' I tell the children. 'There's a surprise. No, there are ten surprises. Look in the stable, the one at the end.'

'Is it chickens, Mum?' says Sophie, rushing to the door and struggling with the bolt at the top. 'I do hope it's chickens.'

'Guy brought them over for us,' I say.

'Oh,' says Adam, and I wonder if I detect a note of disapproval in his voice.

'It was very kind of him,' I point out. 'He also wanted to know if you could start milking to-morrow morning.'

'And what did you tell him?'

'Yes, of course.'

'I knew you'd do that.' Adam eyes flash with resentment, an expression he's refined and per-fected over the past few months. 'You're always making decisions for me when I'm perfectly capable of making them for myself.'

'I'm sorry, but you weren't here.'

'You could've texted me.'

'Mummy!' Sophie exclaims as she disappears into the stable. 'Thank you. I love them.' There's some squawking and flapping and she reappears with a chicken in her arms. 'This is the best thing that's ever happened to me...' She beams. 'We'll be able to have eggs for breakfast.'

'You don't like eggs,' Adam says.

'I do,' Sophie says.

'Adam, leave her alone,' I say. 'Sophie, Guy says it will take the hens a while to settle down. They won't lay eggs immediately.'

'I don't mind,' she says.

148

'I think they need more straw,' says Georgia, looking into the stable.

'I'll find them some tea,' I say.

'What about mine?' says Adam.

'You've just eaten,' I say, laughing.

'That was hours ago,' he says. Then, grinning, checks his watch. 'One hour and twelve minutes to be precise.'

'Go and have some cake – I think Guy's left some.' Guy again. I notice how Adam's body stiffens slightly and I don't believe that this reaction is to hearing about the cake. I can foresee trouble ahead. When David abandoned me I couldn't imagine moving on myself, but after this weekend, when I've enjoyed the company of an attractive and attentive man, I'm beginning to think that I might be ready to change my mind.

Chapter Eight

Rich Fruit Cake

I reach out from under the duvet and hit the alarm. Five a.m. I never used to get up this early on a Monday morning when we lived in London, but I drag myself up and knock on Adam's door.

'Wakey-wakey, sleepyhead,' I call softly.

'I'm awake, Mother.'

'Are you decent?' I push the door open to find him already dressed in his jeans, kicking through the discarded clothing on the floor – a bit like the chickens searching for food – until he finds the T-shirt he wants. I notice a pair of dark eyes shining out from under Adam's bedding and smile to myself. I'd missed Lucky last night, but as soon as Adam arrived home, the dog forgot all about me and followed my son around like his shadow.

'I wish you wouldn't say that wakey-wakey stuff any more.'

I've always said it, since they were tiny babies.

'It's embarrassing, especially when Josh used to be round ours for a sleepover.' Adam pulls a white T-shirt over his head.

'He didn't mind.'

'I did. Josh thought it was hilarious.'

'Would you like some breakfast before you go?'

'I'll have something when I get back,' Adam says. 'You don't have to get up, you know. You don't have to check up on me all the time.'

'I didn't want you being late on your first day.'

'I had three alarms set for ten to five – the iPod dock, my phone and the travel clock.'

'Why ten to five?'

'Ten minutes for a lie-in.' He smiles. 'Stop fussing, Mum, and go back to bed.'

'I might just do that.' Lucky joins me, curling around my feet. I drift in and out of sleep, wondering how Guy does it, and whether Adam will be able to keep up these early starts.

I don't get up again until eight when Sophie comes pounding up the stairs and throws herself on to the bed to tell me the chickens are well, but there are no eggs yet.

'I've given them their breakfast, cleaned out their water and left them shut in. I can't wait until they go outside. Do you think they'll lay eggs then?'

'I hope so.'

'I can tell the difference between Lisa and Maggie,' Sophie says, 'but I can't tell which one's Marge.'

'You'll have to draw them all and make a key so we know which one's which.'

'That's a good idea.' She snuggles up to me and I put my arm around her.

'I missed you, you know.'

'I missed you too.' I know I asked them about what they'd done in the car last night, but they weren't in the mood for chatting then.

'So what did you get up to this weekend?' I ask her again.

'We went shopping in Oxford Street. It's funny, isn't it, that Oxford Street is in London, not in Oxford? It was just with Daddy. We saw Alice yesterday afternoon when she came back from seeing her friends – but she said she had a headache and went to lie down. Daddy wasn't very pleased.'

Sympathetic as ever, I muse.

'Have you sold any more cakes yet?' Sophie says, changing the subject.

'Not yet.'

'Oh?' She purses her lips, which in this light seem unusually glossy and red.

'Are you wearing lipstick?' I ask her.

'Daddy bought it for me.'

'It's a bit early in the morning for make-up, isn't it?' I point out. Eight, in my opinion, is also too young. What does David think he's doing? I wish he wouldn't keep taking them shopping when he's supposed to be spending quality time with them, not buying them everything they ask for. It's as if he's buying their love, which seems unfair because I'm not in the position to do the same.

Sophie ignores my comment and goes on, 'Daddy said you wouldn't have sold any.'

'Well, I wish he'd keep his opinions to himself.'

'Never mind, Mummy,' she consoles me. 'At least Adam's got a job now.'

I smile to myself – I can't see Adam handing over his hard-earned cash.

'If you can't sell your cakes, I'll get a job too.'

'That's very kind of you,' I say, touched by her thoughtfulness, 'but what will you do?'

'I'll look after people's chickens for them while they go on holiday,' she says brightly.

'I don't know how much money you'd earn from that – chickenfeed, I imagine. Most people probably ask their neighbours.'

'Will Guy look after our hens when we go on holiday?'

'I expect he would, but we won't be going on holiday for a while.' I can't foresee a time when I can afford to jet off somewhere exotic.

'We'll have to pretend,' Sophie says.

'I thought we'd have a housewarming party instead.' It's something I've wanted to do since we moved here, to have family and friends to visit and share our new home for a weekend.

The girls and I have breakfast and walk Lucky around the estate before Adam returns home. Having seen the cows coming into the field and heard Lucky's hopeful yapping, I intercept Adam at the back door.

'Wait,' I say, holding my nose. 'Get your boots

152

and overalls off. Outside!'

He opens his mouth to argue.

'You can't come in like that – you're filthy. I can tell you've been washing down the parlour – most of the muck's ended up on you. Go and get yourself straight in the bath.'

When he's back downstairs again, high with the scent of body spray, I ask him how he got on.

'It was great.' Adam stretches and yawns. 'I had breakfast with Guy – in the farmhouse.'

'What's it like inside?' I have to ask.

'It's a bit messy – not dirty, just untidy.'

'I'm surprised you noticed, considering the state of your bedroom. Is that all?'

'Why do you want to know?'

'Because I'm a nosy neighbour.'

'Sophie's gone clucky over the new hens,' Adam changes the subject as she disappears off to check for eggs for at least the tenth time this morning. 'They won't lay if you keep disturbing them,' he calls after her, but I don't think she hears.

We're interrupted by the sound of the phone, my mobile. It takes me a moment to find it under a sheaf of post on the kitchen table.

'Hi,' I say, answering it.

'Is that Jennie's Cakes?' says a female voice.

'Oh? Yes. Jennie speaking.' I'm gobsmacked. 'How can I help you?'

'I saw your advert in the paper and wondered if you'd be able to quote me for a wedding cake.'

A potential order? I start looking frantically for my pristine order book. Adam finds it for me. I grab a pen from the drawer and stand there, poised to write down the details. Name, address and an appointment for six o'clock this evening, to meet the bride and chat through the options.

'I'll see you there, at the Old Forge, Talyford,' I confirm before saying goodbye. Then I look at Adam and throw my arms up in the air.

'Bingo!' I'm ecstatic.

'It isn't an order, Mum,' he says, bringing me down to earth. 'It's more of an enquiry.'

'Yes, but it's a start,' I insist, my excitement already tinged with panic. Where do I start? I've got some photos of cakes that I've made for family and friends for their special occasions, and I can whip up a quick fruit cake and chocolate sponge to offer as samples... 'Adam, can I ask you a huge favour?'

'Will I look after the girls? I heard you arranging the appointment, and yes, I'll do it.'

'Thanks, Adam.' I'm touched that he realises how much Jennie's Cakes means to me. 'You're a star. What are your plans for the rest of the day?'

'I dunno. I wish Josh was here. Can he come and stay sometime?'

'Actually, you can ask him to our house-warming do – the last weekend in August.'

'Next weekend?' Adam's face brightens. 'We're having a party?'

'That's right – you'll have to see if he can get a lift with Karen or Summer. Oh,' I add, 'he'll have to bring overalls and a paintbrush. That's the deal. We'll provide the paint, food and drink, in return for a fun weekend spent decorating Uphill House.' I've worked out that I can buy cider from Guy and negotiate a deal on paint with Mr Victor at the ironmonger's, to keep costs down. I'll do a load of baking beforehand. 'It'll be wonderful to see everyone.'

'Auntie Karen won't do any painting,' Adam observes. 'You know what she's like – she hates getting her hands dirty.'

'Adam.' I try to discourage him from dissing my sister in case he starts doing it in front of her.

'Uncle Hugo won't do any painting either. He'll have a few drinks like he did on Granddad's birthday.'

'He did get a little merry,' I concede.

'Mum...' Adam grins. 'He fell over.'

'All right, he went a bit too far.' Not only did he fall over, but he also started pestering me again. Sober, he's affectionate and funny. Under the influence, he's embarrassing, suggestive and, since my divorce, even more pushy.

'Auntie Karen wasn't happy, was she?'

I shake my head. Everyone noticed Hugo staggering about in the hotel where my parents held the party for my dad's seventieth, but I'm not sure how many observed his attentions towards me. He can be pretty sly about it.

'Are you going to invite Guy?'

It's always a good idea to invite the neighbours if you're having a noisy party, but I don't think Guy would come anyway. Would he get on with my friends? Would they have anything in common?

'I'll see.' I postpone thinking about the party, my mind filling up with images of wedding cakes, sparkling with smooth icing and decorated with fresh flowers, or maybe crystals and pearls. And how about something different: tiers made to look like suitcases with a hat box on top? Or maybe heart-shaped ones?

Am I a terrible mother? Am I forcing my children to grow up too fast by placing too much responsibility on their young shoulders? I've left Adam home alone before, but not Georgia and Sophie. I suppose I'm reluctant to leave Sophie in particular, because she's the baby of the family, the last of my brood. I look at her standing between her brother and sister, holding their hands, and think, I never want her to grow up.

'Adam, promise me you'll ring straight away if there's a problem? I'll have my mobile switched on.'

'Yes, Mother,' he says sweetly.

'And if I hear there's been any trouble...'

'You mean fighting,' Georgia interrupts.

'I mean any misdemeanour whatsoever, you'll all be grounded for ever.' Wrong thing to say – I can't possibly carry it through.

'We won't have to go to school. Hurray!' says Sophie.

'I want to go to school,' says Georgia.

I glance at the clock. It's ten to six. I'm going to be late.

'There's chocolate cake in the larder.' I pick up my cake boxes, knife and pink paper napkins, a file of photos and a price list. 'I won't be long.' I hesitate. 'Do I look professional?' I wasn't sure what to wear and had settled on dark trousers and a white blouse.

'Mum, you look great,' Adam says. 'Good luck.' I love the fact they're so enthusiastic, that the order of a wedding cake would mean as much to them as it would to me... I just hope I don't let them down.

By six-fifteen, I'm sitting with a cup of tea in a tiny living room in the Old Forge at Talyford, a couple of miles the other side of town. There's a dog at my feet, a golden retriever who rests her nose on my thighs and gazes at me with soulful brown eyes.

'Sally, do stop begging. This is too good for you.' Penny, the bride-to-be, sits in a wheelchair opposite me, a few cake crumbs left on a napkin in her lap. She's in her mid to late thirties, I'd guess, and a colourful character – in more ways than one – with her purple bandana, multi-coloured locks of hair and smock spattered with paint. 'Jennie, that was delicious.'

There's no sign of the groom, and I'm assuming, from the wedding photos on the wall, that this is Penny's second marriage.

'If you choose the fruit cake, I'll need a fairly quick decision because it needs time to mature.' I can hear the words as I speak, coming out as if they've been over-rehearsed, which they have, on the way here in the car.

'Oh, it's impossible to decide,' Penny sighs.

'You could go for a tier of each,' I suggest.

'I couldn't try just another tiny sliver of each, could I?'

'Of course you can.'

Penny decides to go with the fruit, and then we run through the formalities: pricing, nut allergies and the decorations.

'Some brides like to have fresh flowers,' I say.

'I'd prefer something very plain and simple, marzipan and royal icing, with the bride and groom – oh, and Sally – on the top. You probably think I'm mad, but Sally means a lot to us. She's my lifeline when Declan's not here. She fetches and carries, even unloads the washing machine for me.'

'I could do with a dog like her,' I say ruefully. 'We've just adopted a rescue dog. He's lovely but more of a hindrance than a help. I caught him stealing the butter the other day. He had the whole packet.'

'He isn't worrying about his cholesterol then,' Penny chuckles.

'I don't think he worries about anything – he takes life as it comes. Look, I've done ponies, frogs and penguins, but never a dog before.' I notice that Sally's wearing a harness and a short lead. 'There are companies where you can send a photo and order personalised clay cake toppers that you can keep long after the cake's gone. I think that would be the way to go here.'

'Do people really have frogs on their wedding cakes?'

'I have been asked to put them on my "princess" range on occasion.' I feel a bit of a fraud saying this, but I know I'm going to have to 'big it up', so to speak, to sell my cakes. A 'range' sounds so much better than five or six; 'on occasion' so much better than 'once'. I have only ever made one frog, but decide not to bother Penny with this minor detail.

We continue chatting while I fill in the paperwork and decide on a deposit.

'Thank you,' I say when Penny countersigns the agreement: delivery of one wedding cake, iced

158

and decorated for the big day at the end of September; to be set up at the venue by 2 p.m.

'I read in your ad that you're new to the area,' she says. 'Do you like it?'

'It feels very quiet, which is what I thought I was looking for...'

Penny smiles.

'I'm glad I made the move down here, otherwise I'd never have met Declan. He's my carer, a few years younger than me, and – do you know Fifi Green? You must have met her.'

I nod as Penny continues, 'She calls me the cougar of Talyton, which makes me sound like the Beast of Dartmoor. I take it as a compliment. I can't be too critical of Fifi – she buys my paintings. Not because she appreciates them, but because she hopes they'll appreciate in value.'

'Can you manage to make a living from your work?' I ask, knowing it's relevant to my own business. Her response is disappointing.

'Only because I still sell in London. People who live in the city don't seem able to get enough of the Taly Valley, fortunately. I make a little money from the tourists too – I've got a line of prints which sell well as souvenirs in the gift shop and the garden centre. I get by.' Penny pauses, tipping her head to one side, a twinkle of amusement in her eyes. 'I can afford a decent cake for the wedding anyway, in case you're wondering.'

'No, of course not,' I say quickly. 'I didn't mean...'

'Declan and I want to do it properly. Neither of us has any intention of marrying again.' Penny sighs. 'I'm so lucky. When he first asked me out,

I kept thinking, "Why me? Why not a girl your own age?"'

When I'm driving home, I'm torn between feeling happy and sad – happy that I've got a substantial order at last, and sad when I remember my own wedding day, and how I miss having a partner to share everything with: from late-night chats about life, the universe and everything, to a bar of Kendal Mint Cake or a bottle of Pinot Grigio.

The only partnership I have now is between me and my Aga.

'Well?' says Adam when I draw up outside Uphill House. He's outside with Georgia and Sophie, waiting. 'Did you do it?'

'Yes! Look.' I hold the paperwork out through the open window. 'I'm going to frame this.'

'Yay!' Adam punches the air, making me smile. He might behave like a world-weary cynic at times, just like his father, but it's all an act. 'How many tiers?'

'Three,' I say.

'Three cheers for three tiers,' he says, the girls skipping around and echoing him.

I go inside. I have to get baking. The wedding's in less than four weeks, not really long enough for a fruit cake to mature, but I'm sure it will be fine. Later, when I'm curled up on the old wicker sofa in the drawing room, Lucky beside me, I start making a list of ingredients: dark muscovado sugar, sweet glacé cherries, succulent raisins, Courvoisier brandy to feed it. This is going to be the best cake I've ever baked.

I set aside a whole day for the wedding cake. I

take the children with me to buy ingredients, then return to my kitchen. All my worries disappear. This is it, I'm doing what I am good at, what I love. Am I worried about the state of my bank balance? A little. I need to get some money coming in soon. Okay, David pays maintenance for the children, but I've had what I'm owed.

I dig out Delia's recipe for The Classic Christmas Cake, the one I use every Christmas. I work out the amounts of the ingredients, scaling them up for the three tiers, and checking in with Adam that my calculations are correct. I'm going for round tins – with square ones, the corners tend to cook faster than the rest of the cake.

Firstly, I measure out currants, sultanas and raisins and throw them into a huge mixing bowl, along with most of a bottle of brandy to soak. Secondly, I stick the treacle tin in the warming oven of the Aga – it's easier to handle when it's runny. Then I find the glacé cherries. Unable to resist, I pop a cherry in my mouth, and another, relishing their sweet, sticky syrup... I slam the lid back on the pot. No more or I'll end up as big as a house.

I chop the cherries, then weigh out some mixed peel, almonds, plain flour and a pinch of salt. A few grains spill across the worktop. I take another pinch from the box and throw it over my left shoulder. Why? I'm not superstitious, but it's something I learned from my grandmother. 'Hit the Devil in the eye,' she used to say. I wish I'd managed to save her old recipes – apparently they were thrown out when her house was cleared after she died.

Next, I grate some nutmeg, and the rinds of an orange and a lemon, until the kitchen smells of Christmas.

Adam and the girls turn up, hovering. Adam takes a few raisins from the bowl and throws them down his throat, then coughs.

'Ugh, what's in that?'

'Brandy,' I say.

'That's disgusting.'

'Well, it serves you right for taking without asking,' I tell him, lightly. 'You can have the raisins that are left in the packet.' I pause. 'Georgia, will you fetch me the eggs? They're in the larder, middle shelf.'

'I wish you were using our eggs, Mummy,' says Sophie. 'Couldn't you have some of Guy's?'

'I'm afraid not – you can't use any old eggs in cakes that you're intending to sell to the public. Rules is rules.' I'm planning to get authorisation to use our own – if we ever get any. I glance out through the open door to the back garden where the hens are foraging over the lawn, pecking, scratching and leaving droppings all over the place. I didn't realise they were so messy. 'Sophie, if you'd like to help too, you can get the butter out of the fridge.'

In a large mixing bowl, I cream the dark muscovado sugar and butter together. I beat the eggs then add them a little at a time, with a spoonful of flour, to the fluffy butter-and-sugar mixture. Then I fold in the dry ingredients and stir in the rest, including the chopped almonds, until the mixture is thick and sticky, and difficult to move around the bowl, which is when Guy's face

162

appears at the window.

'Hi,' he says. 'Congratulations on the sale. Adam mentioned it this morning.'

'Oh, thank you,' I say. Adam went to help with the milking again – he seems to be enjoying it.

'You know you said you were planning to grow veg?' Guy says.

'I do, but I haven't got around to doing anything about it yet.' I'm aware that my tone is tinged with frustration. It's another of the multitude of tasks I've so far failed to address. 'As you can probably see, I'm up to my elbows in cake mix.'

'Don't let me stop you. I thought that as I've got a spare hour, I could run the rotavator over the old veg patch for you. It would be much quicker than digging it with a spade. That clay's heavy stuff.'

'Guy, you've done more than enough for us already.' I don't think he understands, but I'm beginning to feel as if I'm under some kind of obligation to him.

'I'm happy to do it.'

'Well...' I falter. 'I'll pay you.'

Guy frowns, and immediately I know I've said the wrong thing and offended him.

'I'm not some odd job man,' he says stiffly. 'I'm offering because we're neighbours.'

'Yes, but you've done so much for us ... the chickens, Adam's job...'

Guy sticks his hands in his pockets and gazes at the ground for a moment before looking up at me.

'Look, Jennie, if you think I'm being a pest, then say so and I'll leave you alone.'

'No! No, I didn't mean it like that.'

'I wouldn't offer if I didn't want to do it,' he says. 'And I'm not expecting cake or anything else in return.'

I give in. It would be great to have the garden dug over and the ground prepared for planting in the spring, but I don't want it to seem as if I'm taking advantage of him. I'm beginning to question why Guy's always here, in my house or on my property, when he has – what did he tell Adam? – a hundred and fifty acres of his own. Is it because he's lonely up at the farm, or is he happier here because this was once his home, or does he enjoy our company, even if we are townies?

'Okay, thank you,' I say.

'I'll go round the back,' he says.

'Can I help?' Adam asks.

'Of course,' Guy says, and I think how good it is for Adam to have a man around. I wish David had been more like Guy – David's idea of father–son bonding consisted of riding on roller-coasters, paint-balling and walking the high-wires, not staying quietly at home and doing real-life things together.

I turn back to the cake and give it another stir. The mix doesn't look dark enough somehow, but maybe my memory isn't what it was, which is odd because I thought I was over the mumnesia that I had for a while after the children were born. I glance out of the window over the sink and watch Adam and the girls who have decided that rotavating is more compelling than baking. Guy has set them marking out the edges of the vegetable patch with sticks and string. I smile as I watch them work, then remember I'm supposed

164

to be working too.

With a sense of pride I continue, deciding to go down the traditional route of greasing and lining the cake tins with baking parchment, before I start spooning the mix into them. Actually, it's more about guiding it as it crawls stiffly out of the bowl, like a sleepy snake. As I smooth the top of the first tin of mix, I breathe in the scents of spice, alcohol and citrus, but I'm sure now that there's something missing.

The treacle! I've left it in the Aga.

It serves me right for allowing myself to be distracted. I tip the contents of the cake tins back into the mixing bowl and stir in the treacle, then I panic and wonder if I've been too rough with the mix. If I have, I've ruined the texture of the finished cake.

I go ahead, washing and re-lining the tins before cajoling the cake mix, which is darker now, into them. To reduce the risk of burning, I tie a double layer of brown paper around the outside of each tin, then cover the tops with a circle of baking parchment with a small hole in the centre to let out any steam.

I decide after much deliberation to cook each tier separately, which means I'll be up until – I check the clock – about midnight if they each take about four hours to cook. I slide the first tier, the largest, on to the lowest set of runners in the baking oven and close the door. I set the alarm on my mobile phone, then decide to take some drinks outside rather than make a start on the washing up. That can wait.

It looks like pretty hard work, digging the vegetable patch, even with a rotavator. Now I know why most people don't grow their own. Why did I want such a big garden? Guy is operating the machine. It's noisy and the vibrations go right through me when I'm standing close by, hands resting on my girls' shoulders, eyes drawn to Guy's naked torso, his skin glistening with sweat, every sinew visible as he forces the machine through the yielding clay.

He has flung his vest around his shoulders to stop them burning in the sun. He looks ... utterly masculine. My chest grows tight with yearning – not for Guy particularly, but in general. I haven't seen a naked torso since before David told me about Alice, and I've never seen one quite like this, not in the flesh. Think Greek god meets Daniel Craig.

I turn my gaze towards the sky where the jet streams play noughts and crosses against the bright blue and a buzzard soars high over the copse. I lower my eyes towards the paddock. Beyond the fence the chickens have flocked together, afraid at first of the noise but now more confident. Lucky barks from somewhere in the yard as if he's discovered a rat. I love this place. I love my life.

The chickens may turn out to be a mixed blessing though, I think. They keep crowding into the kitchen, which doesn't do anything to help maintain hygienic conditions, and they don't take much notice of me when I grab a tea-towel to chase them out.

When I say, 'Shoo! Out, ladies,' they look at me, with heads twisted to one side, and cluck and caw. 'Go on, get your feathers out of here.'

166

They respond better to Sophie, but that's because they follow her for food. Poor Sophie comes indoors every time after feeding them, saying, 'No eggs today,' and I'm afraid that she's doomed to eternal disappointment. I check with Guy and he says to give them more time. You can't rush these things, he adds, yet I find it frustrating that I can't do anything about it, that I can't give them a pill or talk them into laying eggs.

Later, after Guy has gone with Adam to milk the cows, I take the first tier of the cake out of the oven. It's browned on top, and when I test it with a skewer, it comes out clean. Perfect. I put the next tier in to bake and then phone Summer to invite her to the housewarming. I speak to her and my mum most days.

'Of course we'll come,' she says. 'I can't wait to see you and the kids. Jade's missing Georgia.' Jade, Summer's daughter, is twelve. When David and I split up, some couples of our acquaintance shunned one or other of us. Summer and Paul, her husband, are on my side: Team Jennie. 'And this neighbour of yours? He sounds intriguing.'

'Well, he's often here, but he doesn't give any impression that he wants to be more than friends.' I have refrained from mentioning the way he brushed his lips against my mine the other evening. He hasn't mentioned it and neither have I. It's almost as if it never happened, and I think I'd prefer it to stay that way. It makes everything ... less complicated.

'Are you sure?' Summer chuckles when I don't respond. 'I'll ask him for you.'

'Promise you won't embarrass me? I'm the one

who has to live next door to him for the next however many years.' I'm expecting to spend the rest of my life at Uphill House: till death do us part.

'Have you seen him recently?' Summer says.

'He's here right now, digging up the garden and preparing the ground.'

'Preparing the ground for what exactly?' I can tell from her voice that Summer's smiling. 'Perhaps he has an ulterior motive. Perhaps he's preparing the ground for some other reason Romance, for example.'

Chapter Nine

Scones, Strawberry Jam and Clotted Cream

By two o'clock in the afternoon on a hot Saturday at the beginning of the August bank holiday weekend, I've already delivered Mr Victor's weekly chocolate cake order to his shop in town, tidied the house as best I can and baked bread and sausage rolls. I'm buzzing with excitement at the thought of seeing Summer, Karen and their families. Lucky starts barking and scampering from the front door through the lobby into the kitchen to the back door, and then back to the front door again. Whatever he's on, I'd like some of it, I think, smiling, as he skedaddles about, only giving up when Sophie opens the front door.

'Mum, there's a car outside!' she shouts. 'It's Summer and Jade. And Paul. And they've got Josh with them too.'

'Will you show them into the yard, Sophie?' I call from the kitchen. I slip my apron off, run my fingers through my hair, and perform a mental check through my recipe for a good party.

Clothes: flip-flops, shorts and loose-fitting top. Check.

Drink: gallons of scrumpy, and lemonade for those who aren't drinking. Check.

Food: plates of sausage rolls, bowls of salad – tomato and couscous, and green salad, three farmhouse bloomers – freshly baked, butter, cheese and ham, marmalade cake, brownies, cherry and almond slices, and my trademark butterfly fairy cakes: buns with their tops cut off, halved and stuck back on with butter icing, to look – with the eye of faith – like butterfly wings. Check. Oh, and there are scones, jam and clotted cream too, in case anyone's still hungry.

Adam, Josh and some of our other visitors, Guy, for example, have prodigious appetites.

'Karen's here too with Hugo and Chris,' Sophie calls, slightly less enthusiastically, I notice. My sister has that effect on people. Her eleven-year-old son, Chris, has acquired her pessimistic nature. 'Who else is supposed to be coming?'

'Guy is. Granny isn't.' My parents have had an attack of the 'olds' as I call it, deciding they're too old for this party, and leaving the younger generations to it. You might wonder if I invited David and Alice. I didn't. I'm not quite that magnanimous.

I greet everyone in the yard. The chickens scatter

169

and feathers fly.

'Sophie, remember to close the gate. The last time we left it open, the cows came in.'

My best friend – Summer by name, Summer by nature – turns up, all long legs, blonde hair down to her shoulders, blue eyes and bronzed skin. She refers to her nose as 'the hooter', being over-sensitive about its size and the freckles that adorn it. She used to use lemon juice to make them fade. It never worked.

She's wearing cut-offs, made from an old pair of jeans, and an embroidered sleeveless top which reveals her bra straps. She is artlessly bohemian.

I watch her look up at the house, her jaw dropping open in admiration.

'Wow. It's beautiful, Jennie,' she says, holding out her arms for a hug.

'Thank you,' I say. 'Oh, I've missed you.'

'I've missed you too.' She looks over my shoulder. 'I can see why you fell in love with this place though.' Then she turns to my sister who's joined us. 'It's fab, isn't it, Karen?'

My sister purses her lips. It's strange looking at her – it's like I'm looking at my own reflection, but not quite. Karen is three years older than me, fuller in the face and curvier in general. In fact, I would go so far as to say – although not to her face – that she's beginning to look matronly. It doesn't help that she looks as if she's helped herself from my mother's wardrobe – not that Mum is old-fashioned in her choice of clothes, but she does dress appropriately for her age, refusing to flaunt her upper arms and her bellybutton. Karen's gone for a stark black and cream shift dress which doesn't fit, being baggy at the bust and tight over the hips, and nude court shoes.

'It's such an amazing place,' continues Summer. 'The photos didn't do the house justice.' From her silence, I gather that Karen is less enthralled. Mind you, looking at Hugo, she never did have much taste. Actually, I'm being too harsh. He was quite good-looking in a chubby, cherubic way – as their son is now – but he's running to fat, like one of Guy's cattle that he's rearing for beef.

Hugo joins us, having previously been engaged in conversation on his BlackBerry. He slips it into the pocket of his shorts, and makes a point of giving me a kiss on the cheek.

'Hello, Jennie,' he says. 'You're looking as lovely as ever.'

'Thank you, Hugo.' I glance towards Karen. She's watching, but there's no visible reaction from her.

'Look at the chickens,' Summer goes on. 'Aren't they cute? Do they lay lots of eggs?'

'Not many yet,' I say. We're lucky if we get one or two a day at the moment.

'That one's going bald,' says Karen. 'Like my husband,' she adds, with a wicked smile, and I think, That's more like it. She's decided to enjoy the weekend, after all. 'Good grief, Jennie, look at your nails and your hair,' she adds.

'I still need to find a decent hairdresser,' I say ruefully. Fifi helpfully left me the name of the salon she uses, but I'm not ready for a wash and set just yet.

'Have you invited anyone else? Your neighbours?' Karen says.

'I only have one.'

'This farmer bloke?'

'Yes, Guy.' I hasten to add that I've invited him in exchange for finding us the chickens. 'It seems to be how it works around here. You have to barter in goods and services, not hard cash.'

'You don't have to explain, Jennie,' Summer says teasingly, touching my shoulder. 'We can guess why you asked him. I just hope he's as delicious as you've said.'

I notice the way she glances archly at Paul and how he smiles back, secure in the knowledge that Summer would never let him down. Fit, sporty and with excellent people skills, he works in retail, manager of a large branch of a well-known supermarket, but he could easily find gainful employment as a Beckham lookalike.

'Oh, a veggie patch,' Summer exclaims. 'You've really gone to town – that's an inappropriate phrase, isn't it, when you've actually gone and moved to the country?'

'But there's nothing growing in it,' says Karen.

'I haven't planted anything yet.'

'Do you remember your attempts to grow tomatoes on your windowsill?' she says. 'You lavished all that attention on them and they didn't produce a single tomato.'

'When I talked to them, I can't have talked kindly enough.' I think Karen's jealous. I remember how she tried to dissuade me when I first mentioned this project. We were sitting in a coffee shop, having met in town.

'I still can't believe you're going through with it,' she'd said, tapping her spoon against the side of

172

her cup. It was black coffee with artificial sweetener and she'd declined my offer of cake to go with it, because she was having one of her fat days. I wasn't surprised – she'd just bought another pair of trousers from Next in a size twelve when she should have known from bitter experience that she was a size fourteen. I was pretty sure she'd be taking them back tomorrow.

Karen's expression turned deeply serious and I knew I was in for a lecture.

'Are you sure you aren't doing this just to get back at David?'

I pressed my hands to my ears.

'I'm sorry if you don't want to hear this, Jennie, but it has to be said. Is it some kind of revenge?'

I couldn't answer because I didn't know for sure that there wasn't some truth in what she said. I was moving the family to Devon to follow my dream, but inevitably it would make it more difficult for David to see the children.

'It'll be a long drive for him to collect them on a Friday night and drop them off again on a Sunday,' Karen pointed out. 'He'll expect you to meet him halfway.'

'And that's what I intend to do. I have thought it through, Karen, and I don't know why you aren't happy for me.' Having been drowning in the depths of despair, I felt as if I had surfaced at long last. 'Is it really such a shock?'

'Well, yes, it is, Jennie. You're usually so sensible.'

'I'm fed up with being sensible.' If I hadn't been so rational and restrained, I might have left David before and lived a different, maybe happier, life. 'Anyway, this feels right. And if it doesn't work out, I can always come back.'

'Well, you definitely can't go with *that* attitude. That makes it sound as if you've already decided you'll end up back here ... so why go in the first place? It's a whim, Jennie. Please don't rush into it. You'll be making the biggest mistake of your life.'

Of course, I knew that it wouldn't be. I'd already made the biggest mistake of my life in marrying David.

'And what about Mum and Dad?' Karen said. 'They'll be devastated.'

That was something else I'd worried about, leaving them behind.

'They can spend their holidays with us – you know how much they love Devon,' I told her. 'Look, I'm forty and I haven't made anything of my life as yet.' I could see Karen frowning. She didn't understand. 'This is something I have to do.'

'What about the children?'

'I want them to have more freedom. I want them to be able to go out and forage for blackberries in the hedgerows.'

'You can forage through the bins at the back of Tesco if you really must,' Karen said. 'I'm sure this back to nature stuff is overrated.'

'Shall we go inside?' I ask, returning to the present. 'You can bring your things from the cars and get settled, if you like.' I ask Adam to sort out drinks and cakes for the children while I take the adults around to the front of the house so that I can show off the oak-panelled hallway.

'I imagine it's draughty in winter,' says my sister.

'I don't know about that yet.' I push the front

174

door open. 'It's lovely and cool inside now. Come on in.'

'I want to see this Aga first,' Karen says.

'I'd rather crack open a bottle,' says Hugo. 'I could do with a drink.'

'There's cider and some white wine in the fridge,' I say reluctantly. I'd love a glass of wine to get the party started, but I'd prefer Hugo to stay off the booze for as long as possible, after what happened at my dad's seventieth.

'Oh, no. I think today calls for champagne.' He grins. 'I've brought six bottles of Bolly as my–'

'*Our* contribution to the party,' my sister corrects him quickly.

'I hope you aren't planning to get too drunk tonight,' I say lightly.

'As if,' Hugo says, looking at me for a fraction of a second too long.

'The kitchen's this way,' I say, shifting away.

'I'm thinking of getting one when we have the kitchen done,' Karen says, looking at her husband as she checks out the Aga. 'It looks great, doesn't it? Really retro.'

'Retro as in retrospective or retrogressive?' Hugo says drily. 'The question is, does it cook food better than a twenty-first-century appliance?'

'Does that matter?' says Karen. 'You can always have an Aga and a contemporary oven and hob.

'What, both? That's ridiculous,' he says.

'Some people do,' I say. 'The Aga is on all the time and it can get pretty hot in summer. I can't see that it's any different from having a vintage Porsche and the current Mercedes at the same time.'

'Touché,' says Hugo.

'Forget the Aga,' Summer interrupts. 'Where's this handsome farmer? I can't wait to meet him.'

'He won't be here until later – he's milking the cows.' I change the subject away from Guy. 'I'll show you the drawing room next.'

'That sounds so grand,' says Summer.

'A drawing room, but no en suite, I gather,' says Karen.

It's gone four by the time we've finished the guided tour of the house and grounds, having spent quite a while at the pond where Hugo talked at length about a proposal he had for a trout fishery. We've shared a bottle and a half of champagne and I'm already feeling slightly sozzled.

'Tea and cakes, or scrumpy and savouries?' I ask.

'Scrumpy and cakes, I think,' says Summer, and we set up a buffet in the kitchen, keeping half an eye out for the younger children who are playing in the paddock while Hugo and Paul go and help them put up the tents where they're going to sleep – I've left the girls' bedroom free in case they should decide sleeping outside is too scary half-way through the night. Sophie and Georgia are in their element, showing off the chickens and the dog. Adam helps himself to a picnic and disappears off with Josh into the copse where he's planning to build a wigwam in which they can spend the night.

'Are you sure they'll be all right out here?' Karen says, as we help ourselves to food.

'They'll be fine. Lucky's a great watch dog – we'll soon hear if someone is creeping about who shouldn't be.' I'd never have let them sleep out-side when we lived in London.

'Well, here's to the new house, Sis.' Karen holds up her glass.

'Thanks, Karen.'

'You deserve it. If it had been me and Hugo splitting up, I'd have been in pieces.'

I was in pieces, I muse. It's just that Karen didn't have the perspicacity to notice when it happened because I put on a brave face. I had to stay strong, for the sake of the children, and to show David I could do very well without him.

I half thought that Karen might have moved down here too, seeing she's always trying to buy into my lifestyle. She's older than me yet since I was born she's always wanted to have what I have – that's why she married Hugo, one of David's friends whom she met at our wedding. She was on the PTA committee because I was on it. She's even gone out and bought the same clothes as me on occasion.

'It must get very lonely here on your own without the children when they're with David,' my sister says. 'I'm sure I'd hate it.'

Summer rolls her eyes at me. I know what she means, but you can't choose your family. You can't choose your neighbours either.

A few minutes later, there's a knock at the door.

'That'll be Guy,' I say, getting up from the table where Paul, having returned with Hugo from putting up tents, is talking to Karen about the price of grapes. I open the door to Guy.

'Hi, thanks for dropping by. I wasn't sure you'd turn up,' I say. I thought he might have been too shy to meet my friends.

'I'm a little later than I intended – one of the cows had her calf this afternoon. I wanted to make sure they were settled.'

'So you're a midwife as well as a farmer?'

'I guess so.' He smiles.

'You are coming in?' I add, when he hesitates on the step.

'My boots,' he says. My eyes follow his downward glance from his open-necked check shirt to his light brown chinos which are slightly creased about the knees, to his muddy leather boots, a size twelve or thirteen ... and I hope Summer's not going to make some tactless comment about what they say about the size of a man's feet.

'Leave them here in the hall. Come on through.'

All eyes are on Guy when he enters the kitchen, but if he notices, he handles it well. I introduce him and he greets Summer and Karen with his slow, shy smile, then shakes Paul's and Hugo's hands.

'Champers or cider?' says Hugo in a mock Devon accent.

'A small glass of cider, thank you,' Guy says, and Hugo looks at him, the hint of a sneer on his lips.

'Oh, come on. Don't be a party pooper.'

'I have to be up at five.'

'On a Sunday?' Karen raises one eyebrow.

'Every day,' Guy says.

'Crikey,' says Hugo. 'Still, you do some strange shifts, don't you, Paul?'

'Yeah, but not every day of the week.'

'Paul manages a supermarket,' I explain, then

178

remember Guy's opinion of supermarkets and their influence on the price of milk. However, ignoring Hugo, Guy soon starts chatting with Paul.

'Shall we go outside?' I suggest. 'We can keep an eye on the happy campers – the younger ones anyway.'

'What about the painting?' Paul asks.

'Tomorrow,' says Summer, already comfortably sozzled.

'I'm afraid I'll have to sit that out,' Karen says. 'It's my allergy. I can't tolerate paint fumes.'

I don't believe her. She has an allergy to physical activity, I think, smiling to myself.

We head outside again, and retrieve the deckchairs and garden furniture that Chris and the girls have taken from the lawn at the back of the house to enhance their camping experience. We sit watching the darkness that creeps across the sky and the string of solar lanterns lighting up on one of the apple trees. The air here is fresh, laced with the aroma of cow. There's no traffic, just the sound of a grasshopper in the grass at the edge of the paddock. The only irritation is Hugo who has pulled his chair up too close. He touches his lower leg against mine.

'How many new friends have you made here?' Karen asks, making it sound like a competition.

'I'm not sure about friends, apart from Guy,' I say, glancing towards him.

'You know I mean girlfriends. Men don't count–' Karen lowers her voice '–because there's always a sexual subtext.'

'In your opinion,' I say lightly. 'I've met a few

179

people from Talyton – they're friendly enough, but I couldn't call them friends, not yet.'

'Jennie's only been here four weeks,' Summer says, rescuing me from certain embarrassment. 'I expect you'll meet more people when the children start school.'

'I'm not lonely. I don't feel isolated.' I slide my foot away from Hugo's where his deck shoe is getting intimate with my flip-flop. 'I see Guy, and I've had to go out and talk to people to get the business off the ground.'

'How many cakes have you actually sold?' says my sister.

'Not many.'

'How many exactly?' Hugo cuts in.

'Two.'

Hugo chuckles. 'Which only goes to prove that woman cannot live by cake alone. I can have a look at your business plan for you, if you like.' He reaches over and presses my hand. 'Gratis.'

'Hugo, are you trying to wriggle out of the painting?' Summer asks.

'I'm just suggesting that my talents might be better used elsewhere. Business is business. As far as I'm concerned cake is just another commodity.'

'Talking of cake,' I say, getting up, 'would anyone like some more?' Summer accompanies me inside to fetch some.

'It's glorious,' she says, looking out of the kitchen window.

'I'm so pleased you like it. You can see the attraction then?'

'Mmm ... the view.' But she could be talking about Guy, and I'm glad it's dark because I can feel myself blushing.

'Guy's noticed,' she adds.

'Noticed what?'

'Hugo.'

'I wish Karen had left him behind,' I whisper. 'He's all right most of the time, but when he's drunk, well, he's all over me and it's really embarrassing as well as insulting to my sister. I don't know what to do about it.'

'You could talk to her.'

'I've tried,' I say, 'and she's in denial. She doesn't want to know.'

'I probably wouldn't either, if I was in her position,' Summer says thoughtfully.

David tackled Hugo about it once, not long after Georgia was born. Hugo behaved himself after that – at least, he did until David and I split up. 'Summer, would you mind taking these outside?' I hand her a couple of loaded plates. 'I'm just going upstairs for a minute.' I pay a visit to the bathroom, stopping on the landing to listen to the party in progress. The house is alive with people, talking and laughing. I love it. I fluff up the towels and open a new soap, honey and oatmeal. I pause when I catch my own name being uttered outside.

'Jennie's great, isn't she?' says Summer.

'You have to admire her for taking on this house and bringing up three kids,' says Guy.

'She's a tough cookie,' slurs Hugo.

'With a soft centre,' says Summer. 'She'd do anything for anyone.'

'I'm not sure that's entirely true,' Hugo says. He's really drunk now, I think, with disgust. He's being crude. 'She wouldn't for David.'

181

'Hugo,' Karen warns.

I hear someone shifting a chair, Hugo's laughter as a drink goes flying, and Karen making an executive decision to return indoors because she's being eaten to death by midges.

Feeling a little awkward, thanks to Summer's stirring and Hugo's implication that my frigidity contributed to the end of my marriage, I head back to rejoin the party.

However, before I reach the top of the stairs, Hugo appears in front of me, his expression lecherous, his face shining with sweat. I press myself against the wall, allowing him room to get by, but he stops right beside me, the scent of alcohol seemingly oozing from every pore, and I find my own skin crawling, just like it does when I see a spider close up.

'Jennie, you've done well,' he says in a low voice, and I think with relief that it's okay, he just wants to talk, nothing else. 'Forget about the cakes, this place is a great investment. You can do it up and sell it on separately from the outbuildings, then convert them. A high-spec barn conversion – you'll be minted.'

'I'm not planning to sell up,' I say, smiling to myself. Why does everyone have this idea that I'm going to sell up? I'm in love – I'm hardly going to abandon Uphill House.

'Do up the barn, sell that and keep the house then.'

'It would spoil the house, and I'm sure my neighbour would have something to say on the matter.'

'Your neighbour has opinions on everything,'

Hugo says.

'Yeah,' I say, deciding to make my escape with a quick sidestep, but Hugo catches hold of my arm, and whispers in my ear, 'How about it, Jennie? If you won't take any business advice, at least let me give you a quantum of solace.'

'No way, Hugo. Never in a million years.'

'Jennie, please...' The breath catches in his throat. 'We wouldn't be hurting anyone. No one need know.'

'Hugo, you're drunk,' I protest as he turns, pressing his palms against the wall above my shoulders and his warm belly against mine. It's too much. I feel suffocated, threatened ... and afraid that someone will catch me in a compromising position. 'Even if I did fancy you, which I don't, I would never agree to go through with this ... this fantasy of yours. You're married to my sister. You're family!'

'But you're so ... lush.'

'Leave me alone.' Hearing footsteps on the stairs, I try to push him away, but he's too big. 'Please, get off me.'

'You heard what Jennie said.'

'Guy!' I exclaim as he grabs Hugo's shoulders and pulls him away. Hugo staggers back, stumbles sideways and knocks his head against the corner of the wall at the top of the stairs. Recovering his balance, he turns round to face Guy.

'What did you do that for?' he says, grimacing as he touches the side of his head.

'The lady asked you to let her go,' Guy says coolly. 'You should learn to listen.' He moves past and heads into the bathroom, slamming the door shut so I don't have the opportunity to thank him for looking out for me.

'Are you all right up there?' Summer shouts.

'We're fine,' I call back. 'Hugo tripped on a loose floorboard, gave himself quite a whack.'

To my disappointment, Guy doesn't stay any longer. While Karen's checking Hugo's bruise and admonishing him for not being able to take his drink like he used to, Guy peers around the kitchen door, his expression slightly sheepish.

'Goodnight, all. Goodnight, Jennie. No, don't get up.' He holds out one hand. 'I'll see myself out.'

I don't go after him, but I do wonder why he's in such a hurry to leave. Is he embarrassed by what happened with Hugo? I don't see that he has any reason to be. He pulled Hugo off me, that's all. It isn't as if he hit him, or anything like that. Perhaps he's afraid of how it looks. More likely, he doesn't want to spend any more time than necessary with my obnoxious brother-in-law.

'I told you he was a party pooper,' Hugo says. He pulls Karen on to his lap and starts serenading her with the 'Combine Harvester' song.

'Oh, Hugo, really,' Karen sighs, but she slides her arm around his fat neck and pours herself another glass of scrumpy.

'That stuff's lethal,' I say.

'We don't have to dash about in the morning, do we?'

'What about the painting?' Paul repeats. 'Jennie wants us to paint and here we are getting plastered.'

Later, I'm clearing up in the kitchen, chatting

184

with Summer.

'Country living wouldn't be for me, but I can see that it has its compensations,' she says. 'You and the handsome farmer?'

'Oh, no, not after David.'

'He asked me about you. I told him to take care of you.'

'Thanks, but I can look after myself.'

'Yes, but do you want to? Jennie, it's been over a year … eighteen months … since you and David split up.'

'I'm not ready for another relationship.' It's a phrase I trot out quite regularly.

'You could go on a few dates, have some fun.'

I know I can't though. I'm not like that. For me, it's all or nothing.

'What happened up there with Hugo?' Summer keeps her voice low. 'Come on. Something did.'

'He came on to me.'

'The old lech.'

'Guy pulled him off me, Hugo tripped and hit his head.'

'Where did this happen?'

'On the landing, like Hugo said.'

'What were you all doing up there? If I'd known the party was carrying on upstairs, I'd have come up too.'

'I went up to go to the loo. When I came out of the bathroom, Hugo was there – he'd followed me upstairs. Then Guy turned up.'

'You aren't going to say anything to Karen?'

'No, you know what she's like – she only hears what she wants to hear.' Karen may be my sister and I feel protective towards her, but she's always

185

made it quite clear that she won't tolerate any criticism of Hugo, whether it's justified or not. I shrug. 'I used to do the same with David, make excuses for him. He's had too much to drink. He's a man. And the best one of all – he wouldn't have done it if the woman involved hadn't come on to him...'

'I can't imagine you doing that now though, Jennie,' Summer says, smiling. 'You're like a different woman. Another toast to your new home, and to the people of Talyton – let them eat cake, and lots of it!'

Chapter Ten

Apple and Cinnamon Muffins

I'm surprised to find myself being woken by the sound of banging in the corridor outside the bedroom. I must be used to the cockerel by now. Ever so slightly hungover, I get out of bed and pull on some scruffy trousers and a T-shirt, thinking, I'll have a bath after we've done the painting – if we do any painting.

I push the door open to find Hugo on the landing, on his knees, tapping nails into the floorboards outside the bathroom, with my sister standing over him.

'Morning, Jennie,' she says ever so sweetly, which isn't like her. She's putting on an act and I can feel the tension between us. She knows about last night. She isn't stupid. 'You look rough,' she goes on.

'Not as rough as Hugo...'

Sweaty and pale, he wipes his brow with the back of one hand, and I can't help thinking from his subdued manner that Karen must have given him a good talking-to.

'We found the hammer and nails out in the barn,' she says.

'My wife insisted that I made myself useful. There you go. All fixed.'

'Thank you very much,' I say. 'Now there's no risk of a repeat performance of last night.'

'Yes, I'm sorry,' says Hugo, 'I had a little too much to drink.'

'I think we all did,' Karen says, smiling wryly. 'Hugo darling, you can get up off your knees now.'

'I reckon we need a big fat greasy breakfast,' I say, watching him stand up very slowly. 'I'll go and get started. Free-range eggs from our own chickens, and some locally produced bacon. And bread fresh from the oven.' When I check the eggs in the larder, though, there are only two of ours, and a box of twelve that I bought from the Co-op the other day, having used all of the eggs I bought from Guy in my baking. When I check the fridge, the bacon's completely disappeared.

I call Georgia in from the garden.

'Have you seen your brother this morning?'

'Yeah. Him and Josh are cooking breakfast on a camp fire.' Her eyes shine with delight. 'They collected lots of wood for it.'

'And lots of bacon, I imagine.'

I manage to provide the rest of us with a breakfast of fried eggs on toast.

'Are these your eggs?' says Karen, picking a clean knife and fork off the draining board.

'Oh, yes,' I say, not wanting to disappoint my guests.

'You can see they're free-range,' Hugo says, showing off his knowledge of fine foods. 'Look how yellow these yolks are.'

'I didn't know hens laid them already date-stamped,' my sister says, holding up an empty shell, taken out of the composting basket that I keep on the worktop. Then she grins in a superior, big-sisterly way at having got one over on me and I can't help smiling back.

'You'd better be careful you don't get done under the Trades Descriptions Act, advertising your cakes as containing free-range eggs from your own hens,' Hugo says.

'I did so much baking yesterday I ran out,' I say. 'I wouldn't mislead anyone.'

'Only your friends and family.' He sighs and shakes his head.

I look to Summer for moral support. She's smiling.

'There go the cows,' she says, waving towards the window. I move around to look at them, ambling back down the drive after milking. I can't see Guy though. He must have gone by already to open the gate into the field. I wait, arms folded across my chest, to see him pass back towards the house. He strides past, his cap pulled down over his head, the peak obscuring his face. I make to raise my hand, but he doesn't cast even a glance in my direction.

I feel a pang of regret.

Is he deliberately keeping out of the way because Hugo is still here? Have I offended him in some way? Does he not like my townie friends?

'The jolly farmer must have done half a day's work by now,' Hugo says sarcastically.

'Talking of work,' says Paul, 'what about this painting?'

We manage to paint one room: the drawing room. In spite of the dustsheets, the paint gets everywhere. I chose a soft antique pale green for the walls and white for the ceiling, and spend a long time admiring it after everyone's gone home. Summer leaves me one more example of her handiwork: a sign for the house made from a section of plank that Paul attaches to a stick and hammers into the lawn at the front. The sign reads: Jennie's Folly.

Jennie's Folly? Summer's probably right, I muse as I look at the debris that's accumulated from the party: empty bottles of champagne; sugar soap and brush cleaner; spattered dustsheets; mounds of washing – extra sheets and towels. I feel over-whelmed. It's Tuesday morning, and all the time that I'm clearing up, I'd prefer to be baking. I fancy cooking some apple and cinnamon muffins to fill Adam up. He's always hungry, that boy, I muse fondly.

Glancing out of the window, I notice the post-man cycling along the drive.

'Lucky!' I call, but it's too late to intercept him. He races out to the hall, barking hysterically. I follow, finding him jumping up at the letterbox where he makes a grab for the post and tugs it through. It would be all right if he stopped there, but he doesn't.

'Lucky, no! Bad dog.'

Growling, he attacks the post, shaking it and ripping at it with his teeth, until it's torn to pieces and he's standing over it, panting.

'I'd really rather you waited until I'd read it before you shredded it,' I scold him. I squat down to examine what's left: it's all junk mail, apart from the dreaded credit-card statement. 'At least you chose the right day to do it.' I give Lucky a quick stroke, then pick up the pieces and stick them in a drawer.

I decide to take the bottles to the recycling centre on the Green. Sophie and Georgia come with me, Georgia hopeful that we'll see horse-riders on the old railway track – we have done when we've been down this way before, during a recce of our new surroundings.

The Green is bordered by two bridges. The Old Bridge that carries traffic from Talyton St George to the coast has recently reopened after repairs to flood damage. The New Bridge is a footbridge across the river.

'Your Auntie Karen lost her shoe from that bridge,' I tell the girls as I drive across the Old Bridge before turning into the small gravelled car park that also contains the recycling centre. 'She sat on the edge of the wall, swinging her legs, and her flip-flop fell into the river. Granny was not pleased. She said, "Karen, flip-flops don't grow on trees."'

'Fancy not knowing that,' Sophie says. 'What

happened to it?'

'I don't know. I expect a cow ate it, or it floated out to sea.' I remember being secretly pleased because Karen had chosen flip-flops identical to mine and now she'd have to have a different pair.

On the way, Sophie has counted the bottles in the boxes, and divided the number by three to work out a fair allocation for each person to dispose of. I get the green ones minus four.

It feels as though half the population of Talyton St George is out on the Green, some walking their dogs and others using the recycling facilities. However, no one else seems to have quite so many bottles to dispose of as we do, and each bottle falls into the bottle bank with an attention-seeking smash.

'Hellooo! How lovely to see the Copeland family out and about.'

It's Fifi in a long black coat with purple trim, and purple heels which match her earrings. I can't help blushing, as if I've been caught out doing something I shouldn't.

'Goodness gracious me,' Fifi exclaims very loudly, 'someone's been having a party.'

'I had a few friends down from London for the weekend.' I can see her mentally adding up the number of bottles still left in the boxes and dividing the figure by 'a few'. Perhaps I should have exaggerated and made it a much bigger party, because I believe I've gone down in Fifi's estimation. I can just hear her talking to her cronies. 'That Jennie Copeland. A waster and drunkard ... and in front of her children. Not the calibre of person we wish to encourage.'

'It was a housewarming party,' I say.

'And a painting party,' Georgia cuts in.

'How odd,' says Fifi, apparently more accustomed to getting the professionals in. 'If you're struggling to afford a painter-decorator, perhaps you shouldn't spend all that money on champagne.'

'Mum didn't buy it – Uncle Hugo brought it with him,' Georgia says. 'He said he tripped over a floorboard, but we all know he was drunk.'

'Georgia, Fifi doesn't want to know all this,' I say, watching the gleam in Fifi's eye. 'I'm sure she's very busy.'

'Oh, never too busy for a chat. I dropped by here in my official capacity as local councillor to check all's well – there've been some problems with rabble on the Green.'

'Rabble?'

'Teenagers. There was some trouble over the weekend,' she says. 'I believe it's the same everywhere. The countryside is not immune from yobbish and anti-social behaviour. It's creeping in, like a disease, from the towns and cities.'

'My son and his friends know how to behave,' I say.

'I'm not saying that they don't.'

'Adam stole the bacon,' Georgia points out helpfully.

'He took it without asking me first, that's all,' I say. 'At least I know where he was this weekend – camping in the copse at home with his friend Josh.' A slight feeling of unease creeps across the back of my neck, like a spider that I can't shake off. Wasn't one of the reasons I moved away from

London so that Adam didn't fall in with a bad crowd?

'Anyway,' Fifi starts again, 'I'm on my way home from my weekly visit to Guy's mother – I don't think she has a clue who I am any more, but I do my duty.' Fifi's mouth purses. 'I know poor Guy can't get up there as often as he'd wish, so I share the burden.'

'That's very good of you.'

'You didn't happen to invite him to your party?' she asks.

'Actually, I did. He didn't stay long ... the cows.'

'Is that what he told you?' Fifi raises both perfectly plucked and dyed eyebrows. 'I expect he was going over to Ruthie's. Oh, that's so typical of a man, isn't it?'

'I don't understand.'

Fifi lowers her voice to a conspiratorial whisper. 'Guy and Ruthie are "good" friends, if you know what I mean?'

'It's really none of my business,' I say. I know I shouldn't be, but I'm a little upset that he might not have seen fit to enlighten me over his real relationship with Ruthie of Hen Welfare. However, I'm not sure that I believe Fifi. Guy doesn't strike me as someone who is economical with the truth – economical over the use of material goods maybe, keeping all that old stuff in the barn, *my* barn, imagining that I could put it to use one day – but he seems very straightforward. He tells it how it is. Not only that, I didn't hear his Land Rover go out again after the party, and I would have noticed. My ears seem to be attuned to the throaty growl of that particular engine.

193

I don't know why, but Fifi seems determined to make it clear that Guy is out of bounds to me, and he does seem to be keeping out of my way. It's three days before he drops by again, and I find myself missing his company – for no other reason than he's another grown-up to talk to, I hasten to add, although he's also a fount of knowledge when it comes to country matters.

I wish he would turn up again – I'd like to clear the air after the other night with Hugo, if that's what's keeping him away – and I can't think of an excuse to go up to the farm.

Today, Adam has been helping with the milking again. On the way back from letting the cows out, they both stop at the house. Adam goes upstairs to run a bath.

'I thought I'd stop by to see how you were, Jennie,' Guy says.

'Have you got time for a coffee?'

'I'm a bit smelly,' he says, sniffing the sleeve of his boiler-suit.

'You can take that off and leave it with your boots,' I suggest, then it's my turn to look abashed as he kicks off his boots, and rips the front of his boiler-suit apart, the studs unpopping to reveal an indecently tight-fitting grey V-neck T-shirt. He tugs the boiler-suit down over his legs and feet. Underneath it he's wearing jeans that are torn across both knees and, when he turns to put his things out of the way, I see they are also torn across one buttock, revealing dark-coloured pants and a hint of firm flesh.

'I'm sorry – I didn't dress up,' Guy says shyly.

He can hardly look at me, although I can't stop

looking at him.

It's strangely erotic, watching him strip like this, not that he's anywhere near naked. I force myself to tear my eyes away and concentrate on something else, like baking cakes. I show Guy through to the kitchen.

'Do you mind if I get on with this cake?' I ask. 'I've got to feed it.'

'Not at all. Forgive me for interrupting.' He sits down at one end of the table. I pour two coffees and put three apple and cinnamon muffins on a plate in front of him. Then I start fetching the tiers of Penny's wedding cake from the larder, unwrapping them from their jackets of grease-proof paper, and releasing their rich, fruity scent.

'I'm sorry for what happened to your brother-in-law the other night, Jennie,' Guy begins. 'Sometimes I don't know my own strength.'

'It wasn't your fault Hugo banged his head – he tripped. What's more, there really was no reason for you to wade in like a caveman,' I say, smiling.

'I'd have done it for any woman,' Guy stammers.

'Of course.' I'm disappointed, unreasonably so, that he didn't do it especially for me.

'The man is a boor,' Guy growls.

I can't disagree. Hugo is the kind of person you can't play Scrabble with because he makes words up as he goes along.

'I apologise for saying that about one of your friends, but I couldn't stand him.'

'He isn't a friend. He's family.' I hesitate, on my way to fetch the brandy from the top shelf. 'Guy, why are you so angry?'

'I'm not.'

'You are.' I can see his fingers blanching on the coffee mug as he talks about my brother-in-law.

'I heard you say "no" to him, and he wasn't taking "no" for an answer. It was no way to treat a lady.'

I'm flattered that he thinks me a lady, and even more pleased when, gazing into my eyes, he adds hesitantly, 'You're a lovely woman, Jennie...'

I touch my throat. My pulse seems to skip a beat. A compliment, awkwardly made, but a compliment all the same.

'He reminds me of my brother. No respect for women or anyone else for that matter.' Guy goes on gruffly, 'I can't understand why every female in Talyton fell in love with him. I guess women are like that. Fickle. Tasha certainly was...' His voice trails off.

'You can't generalise,' I admonish him. 'We aren't all the same, you know.' There's no way I'd run off with someone like Hugo, or Guy's brother, or with anyone, in fact – not even Guy. Yes, I might have experienced a frisson of lust, seeing him remove his boiler-suit, and enjoyed the compliment, but there's nothing more than a growing friendship between us. Whether he's with this Ruthie woman or not, Guy still doesn't appear to be over his ex-wife. He often talks about her, which makes me think he was so badly hurt that he might never get over the break-up.

'I don't usually have such a short fuse,' he says, returning to the cause of his anger. 'Perhaps it was my father's influence. He was a control freak, always losing it when things were out of his control – my brother, the weather, rain on the hay crop. I remember him running around a field in the rain once, the hay cut and supposedly drying before we could bale it. Dad was yelling and shaking his fist at the clouds.' Guy smiles ruefully. 'It's no wonder he ended up with heart disease, he was always completely stressed out.' He pauses then says, 'I respected my father, but I never loved him. I don't want to be like him.' He gazes at me, his gaze searching. 'I don't want anyone being afraid of me.'

I'm not afraid, I muse. I feel protected by him.

Guy continues, 'Mum was scared of him. When he died, she blossomed – but then her freedom was cut short. She started forgetting silly things – it wasn't like her.'

I'm not sure what to say in the ensuing silence, so I concentrate on running a skewer repeatedly through the three tiers of wedding cake.

'I've let Mum down,' he begins again. 'She wanted to stay at home – she made me promise her she could, and I've failed her. Packing her things and moving her was the hardest thing I've ever done.'

'It must be impossible to run the farm and be a full-time carer. Couldn't you have had someone living in?'

'I tried to find someone, but live-in carers who are trained to look after dementia sufferers are few and far between, especially around here.'

'At least, from what I've heard, you can say that you did all that you could.' I take the cap off the brandy bottle and pour some out on to each tier of cake, watching it soak away through the holes left by the skewer.

'Yes, but I still wonder if I could have done more. Could I have been more patient? Could I have given her a few more months here on the farm?' He shakes his head. 'It got to the point where she was violent and abusive. She couldn't help it. Anyway one day she pushed me to the limit. She kept wandering off – people were very kind, bringing her back when they found her in town or walking the fields. Fifi tried to help, tried to make me see sense, that I wasn't coping, but I sent her packing.

'I had to lock Mum indoors while I went out. One day she escaped, made her way into the barn, lit a match and set the hay alight. I can only assume she was feeling cold. She was wearing just a tatty old nightie at the time because she refused to wear anything else. It was a miracle she didn't go up in flames. I lost most of the winter's feed for the cattle, but worst of all, I lost a cow and several calves. I realised then that I couldn't do it any more. I looked at her, this empty shell of an old woman, and thought, I want to kill her.'

'Did you?' I say apprehensively.

'I didn't hit her,' he says, 'although I came close. You won't understand, no one does until they've been in that position. It wasn't her. It was the illness I wanted to hurt ... to destroy as it had destroyed her.'

Guy buries his head in his hands, and I suppress an impulse to hold him and tell him it will be all right. He looks up again after a while. 'I had to put her in a home, and I felt like a traitor.'

'You don't have to tell me all this,' I say gently. He seems upset by raking up the past. 'But if it helps to talk...'

'I shouldn't be unloading this on you.'

'What else are friends for?'

'Thanks, Jennie.' Guy reaches across and touches my hand very briefly. 'I thought I might have gone and wrecked everything the other night, spoiled the party, so to speak.'

'Don't be silly. Let's forget it.' If anything, it's helped to improve neighbourly relations, I think. Guy is far from insensitive. He might be shy at times, but he's also passionate and caring.

I rewrap the cakes in greaseproof paper and foil, and put them away until it's feeding time again. Then, after Guy has gone back to the farm, I turn my mind to developing a signature product for my brand.

Chapter Eleven

Marbled Chocolate and Raspberry Cake

It's the first Monday in September. The branches of the trees are bowing under the weight of the ripening apples, the mist has come sweeping in from the coast and there's dew on the grass, which is brilliant green. The excitement of the party has fizzled out, the children have gone to their new schools, and I'm having a lonesome moment. I was so proud of them when I dropped them off, wearing their new uniforms. Georgia told me to make lots of cakes, Sophie shed a couple of crocodile tears and exhorted me to check on the chickens during the day, while Adam didn't look back.

I am in experimental mode in the kitchen, planning a marbled chocolate and raspberry cake. You see, I'm still looking for that unique selling point, a signature product for my brand. It should work, but I'm not sure it's quite what I'm after.

I smile as I stir the mix, thinking of Guy. I divide the finished mixture into two bowls, one for the addition of vanilla essence and raspberry jam, the other for cocoa, then combine them in the cake tin, using a fork to swirl them together, before sticking the cake into the Aga. I clear up, then decide to call Summer.

'I thought you might be finding it rather quiet now we've all gone home and the kids are at school,' she says. 'What's the gossip?'

'There isn't much to say.'

'Hasn't Guy been round?'

'Actually, he has.'

'There you go. As I said before, he has the hots for you.'

'Summer, you are incorrigible. We're friends, that's all.'

'Well, you know what I think. And your sister's the same.'

It's true that my sister can't believe that it's possible to be friends with a member of the opposite sex. 'There's always a sexual subtext', is one of her favourite phrases.

'Jennie, your radar's stopped working, that's what's happened. You wouldn't have a clue that a man fancied you – unless he came out and told you to your face.'

'And then I wouldn't believe him,' I say regret-fully.

'Are you sure he didn't give you any other clues?'

'He did say he thought I was a lovely woman–'

'There you are,' Summer interrupts.

'It isn't a great chat-up line, if that's what it was meant to be. "Lovely". It's almost a non-word, non-committal. It doesn't speak of a grand passion.'

'That's because Guy is the strong, silent type. He won't bc outside your bedroom window, serenad-ing you with *"Nessun Dorma"*, like David did when you first met,' Summer says. 'I expect it took him a lot of courage to say what he felt.'

Perturbed that I might have misread the signs, I change the subject. 'Have you managed to arr-ange any work experience yet?'

'Indeed I have. I'm going into Jade's school two mornings a week, and as soon as a teaching assis-tant post comes up, I'm going to apply. If I like it, I'll enrol on a teaching course to start next Sep-tember.'

'You'll love it.'

'I know. I'm really excited and dead nervous at the same time, but I've seen what you've done and it's inspired me to go for it, to change my life before it's too late. I don't want to wake up one morning and find it's passed me by.' She pauses. 'I'd better go – I've got to get my car in for its MOT and then I'm off to do a bit of shopping in town.'

I feel a pang of homesickness, a sudden yearn-ing to be back in London with Summer, treading pavements dotted with gum and crowded with people instead of walking the lanes with only a scruffy little dog for company. I do talk to him, but it isn't the same.

Does Lucky ever listen to me? Occasionally, in between sniffing and chasing after rabbits, he deigns to cock one ear in my direction, but I don't find him all that interactive. He has a much better relationship with Adam than with me, and thinking of Adam...

'Jennie, are you still there?' Summer says.

'Yes,' I say, forcing brightness into my reply. I don't want to worry her.

'You'll have to come and stay with us some-time,' she goes on. 'Remember, the offer's always there if you should tire of country living, or just want a trip to IKEA.'

I look around the kitchen, and out through the window where the chickens are pooping on the lawn, and realise the impossibility of getting away. Who will look after the animals? Who will bake for Jennie's Cakes?

'Keep your chin up, Jennie. I'll ring you later in the week.'

'Okay, Summer. Keep in touch.'

I check the clock. Still four hours until I go and collect the children.

I turn my attention to preparing for the Farmers' Market which is at the end of the week, on Saturday morning. Before that, though, I have to organise the children so they're ready to go to David's for their second weekend back in London since we moved away. I know some people say they love the freedom they have when their kids

202

are away with their ex-partner, but I've never looked forward to it.

'What was it like?' I say on the way home from school the same day.

'All right,' says Georgia.

'One of the boys swored at the dinner lady,' says Sophie happily.

'Adam?' I say.

He shrugs.

'Any homework?'

He shrugs again.

I don't ask any more questions. This isn't going well. Since Josh returned home, Adam's been giving me the silent treatment. I wish I knew what was going on in his head.

On Friday afternoon, Georgia is hanging around the kitchen after school, waiting to pounce on the icing bowl as soon as I've finished decorating the first batch – or should it be a group? – of ginger-bread people. I'll make a fresh lot of icing for the next ones.

'When you've had that, will you go and pack your things for the weekend, please? We've got to meet your dad at eight.' I've arranged to meet David halfway this time.

'I'm glad you're taking us some of the way. We always seem to get to places quicker when you're driving,' says Georgia. 'Can we have a McDonald's?'

'No, Georgia, you've just had your tea here, and Dad will be in a hurry to get home.'

'Camilla at school is having some friends round to her house this weekend, and she's going to show everyone her pony. I want to see Dad, but I'd like to go to the party as well.'

I am racked by guilt, hearing this. Georgia needs to fit in, to make new friends, and her parents have made that impossible this weekend. Sometimes you have to make sacrifices to get what you want, but are those sacrifices too much? I miss them all so much when they're away.

I wouldn't have chosen this for my children, but it happened and we'll have to deal with it as best we can, I tell myself.

Georgia reverts to her favourite subject.

'Mum, where are we going to get a pony from? I've asked at school and Camilla's mum bought her pony in Wales, but if that's too far for you to go and look, there's a riding school near Talysands. She says they often have ponies for sale.'

'All right. I'll ring them.'

'When?'

'Sometime. I can't do it right now – I'm in the middle of something.'

'Okay,' she says, and off she goes to pack. Or at least that's what I think until I overhear her out in the lobby, calling directory enquiries.

'Georgia, put that phone down right now,' I say, poking my head around the door, the icing bowl in one hand, piping bag in the other.

'I thought I'd save you a job.' I give her a stare, and she switches the handset off. 'You're always complaining that you have too much to do. I don't understand why, when we moved here so you didn't have to be so busy, Mum, because you're busier than ever. Now, you're always doing stuff. And when I ask you to help me find a pony, you're always baking cakes, or icing them, or shopping for ingredients. And Adam's got a dog and Sophie's got chickens. And I haven't got anything to look after.'

'I'm sorry, love.' Georgia is right. In my race to set up my business, I've been neglecting her. 'The problem is that ponies cost money. Money that comes – or will come eventually – from baking cakes.' I put my arm around her shoulder and give her a squeeze. 'It will get easier, I promise.'

'Mum, I wish you and Dad... I wish we were all still together,' she says wistfully.

I say nothing. There was a time not so long ago when I felt the same, but – my heart lifts a little – well, I must be moving on at last because I can see other possibilities opening up for me, which is probably why I've been inspired to create my gingerbread farmers with big smiles and green icing-sugar wellies.

The children are tired after their first week of school. The last thing they need is to travel to London and back to see their father this weekend. I can see that now. What's more, although I don't begrudge them this time at all, I could really do without having the two- to three-hour round trips every fortnight. I still have cakes to bake and ice before the market tomorrow morning. I'd rather have too much on the stall than too little. I don't want to sell out within half an hour.

'Georgia, how many times do I have to ask ... please will you go and do your packing? Otherwise we'll be late.'

'I haven't licked out the bowl yet, Mum.'

'Oh, all right. Be quick though.' I leave her to it

and head upstairs to find out how Adam and Sophie are getting on. Sophie is trying to squash as many soft toys as she can into her suitcase. I help her choose two, and make sure she has all the clothes she needs, then check on Adam who's in his bedroom.

'Are you ready, love?' I ask, from the door. I raise one eyebrow when I see the amount of clothing and electrical equipment he has on his bed. 'I don't think you need all that for two nights, do you?'

'I dunno.' He shrugs.

'Adam, are you okay?'

'Yeah,' he says, frowning.

'What's wrong?' I persist. 'There's something wrong. I know there is. Is it school?'

He doesn't respond.

'You know, you're bound to be a little unsettled again now Josh has gone home, but it'll pass.' I hate to admit it, but I miss my friends too. 'You're lucky – you've got a good job with Guy.'

'I like the cows,' he says, his expression brightening briefly.

'It's good money too.'

'Mother, stop going on, will you? I know what you're doing. You're trying to get me to say how much I love it here, so you don't have to feel guilty any more. Well, it's no use because I hate it. I'm saving all my money from the milking and then, as soon as I hit sixteen, I'm leaving.'

'Adam, that's...' It's a shock. 'Say what you just said again?'

'I'm leaving home.'

'What about your sisters, and Lucky?'

'I'll take Lucky with me.' The ghost of a smile crosses Adam's lips. 'You can hang on to my sisters.'

'What will you live on? Where will you live?'

'I'll find a flat, get a job...' He glares as I open my mouth to raise the obvious flaws in his plan. 'I can always go on benefits,' he adds. 'Everyone else does.'

'You won't be able to afford new iPods, and computers, and clothes.' Words fail me as I imagine Adam living alone in some tatty bedsit, surviving on cornflakes and Pot Noodles. As for the girls and me... I try to contemplate life without Adam. He was always going to leave home one day, just not so soon.

'I'll manage,' he says. 'I'm not stupid.'

'I never said that – I don't think you're stupid at all. Oh, I wish you'd come here with a more positive attitude to begin with,' I say, hurting at the idea that my own son doesn't want to spend any more time with me than he has to. I'd like to reassure myself that it's just a phase he's going through, but he seems deadly serious. 'I think you should forget about these long-term plans for now and go and enjoy the weekend with your dad.'

'Don't tell me what to think! I can think for myself,' he says angrily. He picks up his laptop from the floor and walks towards his bed, dragging the charger behind him. I grab it off the floor and hand it to him, but he doesn't thank me for it.

'I can give you a hand, if you like...'

Adam turns away, and a chill draught catches me around the ankles, making me shiver. It isn't the cold, it's the rejection.

I have a quiet word with David about it when we meet up briefly later in the evening, and the children are transferring their luggage from my car to his. I didn't bring Lucky this time.

'Is everything still rosy in the country, Jennie, or are you putting a brave face on it?' David looks at me with a wry smile. His eyes are dark with exhaustion, his complexion pale as undercooked pastry. He's dressed in his suit, jacket but no tie, and bears with him the now-alien scent of the city, a faint odour of cold chips and cigarette smoke.

'I have no complaints.'

'Well, you would say that to me, wouldn't you?'

'Think what you like,' I say with a shrug. 'About Adam... I'm worried. He's got some crazy plan to leave home when he's sixteen. Perhaps you'll have a conversation with him, man to man. He won't listen to me.'

'When have you ever listened to him?'

'Don't go there,' I say, casting him a warning glance. 'What's done is done. I can't change it. I just hoped you'd give him some extra support. I think he needs it right now.'

'I'll see what I can do,' David says with a long sigh.

'Thank you.' I notice that Alice isn't with him again. They used to be inseparable and I wonder if the first flush of romance is over. They have been together for over eighteen months; longer than that for all I'll ever know.

'What are you up to this weekend?' David asks.

'I've got a stall at the Farmers' Market, so I'll be working.'

'Oh?'

'Oh what?'

'Hugo made some suggestion that you and this neighbour of yours...'

'That's all down to Hugo's rather vivid imagination.'

'Yes, he said this chap was a bit of an oik and not your type.'

'Maybe my taste in men has changed,' I say, a little miffed that David has the temerity to suggest that he knows exactly what 'type' I prefer. No more city boys for me. An image of Guy jumps into my mind. I definitely prefer the outdoorsy type.

When I return home, I continue with my preparations for the stall.

Having done a straw poll of my party guests the other weekend, I was surprised to find that a decent home-made treacle tart was high on their wish lists when it came to buying cakes and pastries. I've made several, cooking them in foil containers. I wrap tarts and label them before checking the rest of my list. *G/bread people. Lemon drizzle cakes – need drizzling. Choc-chip muffins – better fresh, leave till last. Choc and raspberry cakes.*

The chocolate and raspberry cakes worked, but I don't think they are right for my signature cake. They don't quite say what I'm all about. I don't mind though. It gives me the opportunity to try out more recipes.

I pack the last of the gingerbread people into boxes, wash up and wipe down. I'm ready. I thought I'd feel more apprehensive about it than I do, fretting over whether or not my cakes will sell, but Adam's revelation has put everything else into perspective.

I am in bed by three, and have an hour's sleep before the cockerel wakes me. Why is that? Why is it that some days I can't hear him, and others he sounds as if he's crowing on the pillow beside me? Eventually, I decide to get up and make tea before I start taking my cake boxes and tins out of the larder and stacking them on the worktops. I'm in the larder when there's a knock on the door.

'Come on through,' I call, my heart skipping a beat at the thought of seeing Guy again.

'Are you ready then, Jennie?' he says, appearing around the door, fresh-faced and recently showered, his hair still damp and curling slightly at the ends. 'You don't want to be too late setting up – the locals like to get in and do their shopping early.' He pauses. 'What would you like me to do?'

'Well, let me see,' I say cheerfully. It seems rather early in the day for flirting but Guy is definitely in a flirtatious mood, and although I'm out of practice, I'm happy to join in. Friends, or 'could-be-more-than' friends, ex-wives and other women … it really doesn't matter. It's just a bit of fun.

'You can carry those boxes out to the car,' I go on, and Guy helps me pack everything into the boot before I drive into Talyton with him and park temporarily in Market Square, which is crowded with other traders and their vehicles.

'This is your pitch,' Guy says, pointing towards the space in front of Petals, the florist, and a couple of metres along from the tethering stone, one of Talyton's least impressive landmarks, a roughly hewn block of granite with a rusty iron ring through it, set in one corner of the square. 'I think it's okay.'

'It looks perfect,' I say, checking how far it is from the tea shop. After what the receptionist at the vet's said, I don't want to spend the day feeling that I'm under siege. 'You don't think there'll be any trouble from the owner of the Copper Kettle, do you?'

'Cheryl? She'll be too busy serving teas and coffees to worry about Jennie's Cakes. She's always run off her feet on market day,' Guy says, as he helps me unload the trestle table, cash box, price list, banner and cakes, then takes the car round to the Co-op car park. I set up the table which wobbles on the stones.

When Guy returns, he puts up the banner across the table which I've dressed with a pink cloth. 'Jennie's Cakes'. It looks amazing, and I have a tear in my eye when I arrange the last gingerbread man on the rack at the rear of the display. I slip into an apron, clip my bum-bag around my waist and wait nervously for my first customers – nervously because it's beginning to dawn on me that I've been presumptuous, assuming I will have any. I recall Summer's toast: 'To the people of Talyton, let them eat cake', and I wonder if they will.

'That,' Guy says, looking from me to the stall and back, with a twinkle in his eye, 'looks irresistible.'

'It is rather gorgeous,' I say, looking straight at him. 'Thanks, Guy. Thanks for telling me about the market, and for helping out. I really don't think I could have done it without you.'

A flush spreads across his cheeks.

'Can I be your first customer?' he says, picking up one of the chocolate and raspberry cakes.

'Yes, but I can't let you pay for it.'

'Oh, but I have to, otherwise it doesn't count...' Guy pulls a fiver from his pocket and hands it over. I give him change.

'I could get used to this,' I say happily.

'I'll see you in a couple of hours or so. I've got a few bits and pieces to do while I'm in town.' He grins suddenly. 'There's Fifi – I'll make a quick getaway.' I watch, amused, as he ducks away behind the stall beside mine, BB's Honey, as Fifi, in a red and white polka-dot dress and white jacket, hastens towards me.

'What a lovely display,' she gushes. 'I must buy one of your cakes. No...' She presses her finger to her lips, thinking. 'I'll have four of the ginger-bread men. Or are they women?'

'They're androgynous,' I say, picking up a paper bag and tongs. 'I wouldn't like to upset anyone's sensitivities by being politically incorrect. Would you like to choose?'

'No, you decide.' Once her purchase is in the bag, Fifi starts negotiating the price. 'How much are they?'

I state the price, showing her the label on the rack.

'Oh, dear,' Fifi says. 'I haven't got much cash on me today.'

I find this odd since she's clearly well-heeled.

'You couldn't see your way to do an exchange – a voucher to spend in the garden centre, perhaps...?'

'That's a bit cheeky, isn't it?'

'You can buy so many useful things with a voucher – we don't merely sell garden equipment and plants. We stock pet food for your dog, for example, Christmas cards virtually all year round, and cookware.' While I stand there, mouth gaping, Fifi goes on sternly, 'It's the way we do things around here.'

'Oh, go on then,' I say, relenting.

As I'm tucking Fifi's voucher away, she says a polite goodbye and disappears. I don't see her again for an hour, by which time I'm inundated with customers. In fact, I'm proud to say that I have a queue of them, and very soon I'm sold out.

I start to tidy up.

'Hello, Jennie.' I look up to find Wendy beside me, struggling with six dogs on leads.

'Oh, hi. How are you?'

'I'm fine. How's Lucky?' she asks. 'Donald, will you sit down!' She tugs ineffectually at the leads while the dogs mill around her legs, tangling themselves up. 'Oh, you silly things.'

'Would you like me to hold a couple for you while you sort yourself out?' I offer.

'Oh, would you? Thank you so much.' She hands me three leads, and untangles the others. 'Um, Jennie, you wouldn't mind hanging on to them for five minutes, would you? I want to buy some more dog biscuits.'

While I'm stammering a polite refusal, she shoves the leads into my hands and leaves me with six dogs. Luckily, they all line up in the same direction, straining to follow Wendy across to the pet food stall and pulling so hard when she returns across the square that I have to let go.

'Sorry!' I call, when they're jumping up at her, wagging their tails as though she's left them for months not minutes. I can't help laughing as she puts the bag of biscuits down to gather up all the leads – and the dogs fall on it like a pack of hyenas. 'It looks like you'll have to buy some more,' I say, helping her with the leads and picking up what remains of the bag.

'I really should take them along to dog training,' Wendy says, sounding breathless. 'It's lovely to see you, Jennie. Perhaps, once Lucky's settled in, you'd consider taking on another dog to keep him company?'

'Lucky's more than enough for us,' I say, admiring her determination to rehome as many waifs and strays as possible.

'It was worth a try,' she says jovially. 'I hope to see you and Lucky out and about on his walks sometime. Goodbye, Jennie.'

I return to the tidying up. I put all the rubbish in a cardboard box, fold up my cloth and take down the banner, then I remove my takings from the bum-bag and lock them in the cash box I've brought with me. There isn't much in the way of cash. After all that work I've earned a joint of beef for roasting, a jar of honey, Fifi's voucher, a bag of parsnips, a dozen eggs, three pig's ears for the dog, a mixed bag of sweets from the newsagent, and a small bunch of spray carnations from the florist. On the plus side, I have two orders for occasion cakes: one for a christening, the other for a Golden Wedding Anniversary celebration.

I'm worried though – it's all very well this bartering system, but it isn't going to keep me in the manner to which I became accustomed when I was David's wife. Not that I'm complaining. Not so long as my family is happy.

The church bell chimes midday, and I catch the sound of Fifi's voice again. She's around the other side of the honey stall, talking to BB, a woman of about my vintage, who wears her dark – almost black – hair in a beehive, aptly. She has a small bust and large hips, a loud voice and a cheerful smile.

'Guy came with her,' I hear Fifi say. 'He thought I hadn't seen him... Well, I reckon she has her claws into him already. I've spoken to him about it.'

'I'm sure you have,' BB murmurs, 'but if he's smitten with her, you won't change his mind. Guy Barnes's love life is one of the very few things you have no control over in this community.'

'That's as may be, but I'll have a good try. I don't want to see him hurt again. I promised his mother...'

Interfering busybody! I think, and for a moment, I wish for the anonymity of city life, where nobody knows anybody else and you can disappear into a crowd.

'Not only that,' Fifi goes on, 'I've dreamed for years of a match between Guy and my lovely niece. Ruthie and Guy are so well suited, and unlike this Jennie, she's still young enough to have a family.'

Ouch, I think. I have no desire to add to my brood, but the reminder that I can't have many minutes left on my biological clock makes me feel quite sore.

215

'Uphill Farm has been in the hands of the Barnes family for years and that's where it should stay,' Fifi adds. 'Guy met up with Ruthie this morning, you know. I saw him in her Land Rover, driving back into town.'

'Well, I wish you luck,' BB says.

'Hi, Jennie.' I turn at the sound of Guy's voice. 'Are you done?'

'Yes, I've been cleaned out.' I smile when I see him, walking towards me, but I can't help wondering what he's been up to.

'I didn't take much money though,' I sigh. 'Not enough to keep us in wellies.'

Guy chuckles. 'I've realised that baking is very much like farming – you do it for love, not the money. I'll go and get your car.' He holds out his hand for the keys.

On the drive back he is quiet, even by his usual standards.

'Did you get everything done?' I ask, aware of how close my hand is to his thigh, clad in navy cord, and resisting the urge to touch.

'I did, thanks,' he says.

'Where did you get to earlier?' I don't like to pry, but I'm curious after what Fifi was saying, and I'm a little confused because I thought he'd been giving me signals that he fancied me. Now I wonder if I've been mistaken.

'I did a bit of shopping to take up to Mum tomorrow, and then I met up with Ruthie to help her load some feed for the hens. She's got a bad back. I help her out every couple of weeks or so.'

'Oh,' I say.

I'm aware that Guy is smiling.

'You aren't jealous, are you?'

'No, of course not,' I say, my hands tightening on the steering wheel. Why should I be?

'How about you and your ex-husband? Do you ever...?' Guy clears his throat and keeps his eyes fixed on the road ahead.

'You aren't still worried about my driving?' I say lightly.

'A little,' he confesses. 'I wouldn't give you the keys to my brand new combine harvester, if I had one.'

'I can understand that.'

'You haven't answered my question.'

'What question?'

'Do you and David...?'

It suddenly dawns on me what he's trying to say.

'Do I have feelings for my ex-husband? *That* kind of feeling? Oh, good grief, no...' The gears grate as I change down to second to pass a horse-box that's coming down the lane in the opposite direction 'We don't ... you know, for old times' sake. Nothing like that.' I'm blushing – not at the thought of making love with David after all this time, but at the thought of making love with Guy. Where did that come from?

'I shouldn't have said anything – your private life has nothing to do with me. I'm sorry.' Then I hear his voice change tone. 'Actually, I don't know why I'm apologising – you were the one who started it,' he goes on, teasingly. 'Are you in a hurry to get back, only we could stop for a late lunch? The Talymill Inn's good for a quick ploughman's, or ham, egg and chips.'

'I probably ought to get back for the dog,' I say, and then I burst out laughing. 'What do I sound like? I'll be buying him dog gravy and a mono-grammed jacket next.'

'I doubt it somehow,' Guy chuckles. 'I can't be out too long either because of the cows.'

We eat at the Talymill Inn, watching the re-stored wheel turning in the race that diverts away from the river, and, in spite of my recurring worries about Adam, I feel content. The market stall was a success and now my friendship with Guy seems to have moved to another level, deeper and more meaningful.

Chapter Twelve

Chocolate and Beetroot Cake

After my triumph at the Farmers' Market, I'm on a roll. I book a regular slot – that's a market every fortnight. The ad in the *Chronicle* brought me two more orders, rather belated ones. I'm not sure where to go next with the business. I don't need an MBA, just drive and commonsense – and, if I'm honest with myself, a good dose of self-con-fidence. I know I can talk to people, handle selling on a market stall and give out free samples, but the thought of going into a shop to ask if they'll stock my cakes still sends me into a cold sweat.

I have to build on my success though. I'm not earning enough to keep the wolves from the door,

I muse as the dog whines from outside, asking to be let in. Perhaps it wasn't such a good time to take on another mouth to feed.

I let Lucky indoors. The girls are playing a game out in the stables. Adam is upstairs – I'd like to say he's doing his homework, but it's far more likely that he's on Facebook, chatting to his London friends. I had a long talk with David about him when the children went back to school after their weekend away. He said that Adam still had a lot of concerns about leaving his friends and trying to fit in with a new set at school, but couldn't actually offer any solutions. All he could do was continue to be supportive of our son – which, as he loves to remind me, is particularly difficult when I've moved him so far away.

The tea is in the Aga and I have an hour or so to make a start on the next step in creating Penny's wedding cake.

'Mummy, Georgia says I can't be the owner,' Sophie says, marching into the kitchen. She stops and rests her elbows on the table, stamps her foot and pouts. 'She says I have to be the pony, but that isn't fair.'

'I don't see why you can't take it in turns.'

'Would you come out and be the pony?' Sophie asks.

'I've got to do this cake,' I say, smiling at the idea of trotting around the paddock and whinnying like a horse. Guy would think I'd gone mad.

'The wedding cake?' says Sophie. 'I think it's going to be beautiful, Mummy. Can I help you?'

'You can fetch and carry for me,' I say, concerned that the cake won't be as beautiful as Sophie expects if she gets her hands on it.

'I want to decorate it,' she says, crestfallen.

'You have to practise first. And I'm not decorating it today anyway. I'm getting it ready to be decorated.'

'I see.'

'I need jam and marzipan.'

'I'll find them.' She runs to the larder and tugs the door open.

'Thank you,' I say. 'No, I'll carry the cake – I don't want it to meet with an accident.'

'The bride wouldn't like that, would she? I think she'd be rather upset.'

'It wouldn't be good for business. This cake has to be fantastic because I want everyone to think: When I get married, I'll order the cake from Jennie.'

I take out the three tiers of cake, unwrap them and line them up on boards. I roll out what Sophie describes as white marzipan worms, and use them to plug the gaps at the bottom of the cakes, smoothing the join all the way round with a palette knife.

'What next, Mummy?' Sophie says.

'We need a little bit of icing sugar for the work surface.'

'Why?'

'To stop the marzipan sticking when I roll it out.' I make three circles of marzipan, large enough to cover the tops and sides of the three cakes, with some overlap, then I paint the sides with jam. 'That helps the marzipan to stick.'

'First you don't want it to stick, then you do,'

Sophie chuckles. 'You can never make up your mind.'

Is she saying I'm indecisive? I smile to myself. I'm not sure.

I place the first circle of marzipan on to the smallest tier to begin with, sliding it slowly until it's in the right place and smoothing it gently across the top before attending to the sides. When I'm happy with it, I go on to the next two tiers, then put them back in the larder for the marzipan to dry. Twenty-four hours later, they'll be ready for the layer of fondant icing, and then it won't be long until the fun part begins: the decorations.

I'm reminded of my own wedding cake – it was beautiful (I didn't make it myself) – a square, three-tiered affair with cascades of burgundy and cream sugar roses set against pristine white icing. I recall thinking, as David held my hand, helping me guide the knife, that it was almost sacrilegious to cut it.

I ask Sophie to call Georgia and Adam in for tea.

When I've served up dinner – boiled ham, parsley sauce, roast potatoes and some carrots that I bought at the greengrocer – Adam and the girls turn up to eat. I sit down with them at our farmhouse table, thinking how funny it is that we all sit at one end. Georgia has pointed out before that if we spread out and try to make conversation, we feel as if we're talking to ourselves.

'Georgia, have you had any thoughts about what you'd like to do for your birthday? It isn't very long now.'

'I don't want a big party like last year.'

221

'We have to do something to celebrate.'

'Can I have someone round for tea?' She squirts half a bottle of tomato ketchup over her carrots.

'Who do you want to invite?'

'Camilla from school. She's in my class and she's got her own pony.' Georgia pauses. 'I'll make her an invitation, shall I?'

'That sounds like a good plan to me.'

It doesn't take Adam long to clear his plate.

'Mum, I could do with some cash,' he says, shovelling the last of his food into his mouth.

'What for?'

'I'm going to buy some more chews for Lucky, and I need to top up my account at the Bistro.'

'I wish you'd take sandwiches,' I sigh.

'I wouldn't eat them. Your sandwiches are like doorsteps.'

'Well, you could make them exactly how you want them.'

Adam gives me a winning smile and holds out his hand, palm uppermost.

'Cash, Mum...'

'There's change in the pot.' The pot being a small ceramic piggy bank that I had when I was Sophie's age, a present from a prudent and frugal great-aunt.

'I was thinking more notes than coins,' Adam says.

'Try my purse.'

'Already have.'

'Adam, you must ask me before you go through my things.' I'm not too fierce with him – he's seemed happier for a while and hasn't mentioned leaving home again recently. I don't want to

222

upset him.

'Sorry,' he says, and I decide to give him and the girls a quick lesson in economics.

'There isn't any money because I've spent our budget for this month. If I give you some money now, Adam, we'll have to cut back next month to make up for it.'

'I thought Dad paid for our keep,' he says.

'He does.' David pays me a monthly allowance to look after them and buys lots of extras I can't afford. 'However, it's for paying the bills like the electricity, water and council tax, as well as your food.'

'I'll ask him for an allowance for Lucky,' Adam says.

'I don't think that's fair. Anyway, what about all the money you've earned so far from working on the farm? Can't you use some of that?'

'I told you,' he says. 'I'm saving it.'

'I can let you have some of my money, Mum,' says Georgia, 'but not very much because I'm saving up to buy a grooming kit.'

'Yeah, your hair's a bit of a mess,' Adam teases.

'Not for me.'

'For the pony,' he finishes for her.

'Why don't you go and get some money out of the bank, Mummy?' says Sophie. 'There's a bank next to the Co-op.'

'I can't get money out of the bank if there isn't any in there,' I point out, and Sophie stares at me, appalled and surprised.

'But there's always money in the bank. That's what banks are for.'

'Sophie, you have to put money in the bank

223

before you can take it out.'

'But... Do you?'

'Daddy works to earn money which gets paid into the bank each month. It doesn't miraculously appear. If it did, we'd all be billionaires.'

'So, Lucky won't be able to have any chews this week,' Adam says, but the next day when the children are back at school, I relent and head into town where I withdraw cash from my savings account so that neither Lucky nor Adam need go without.

Passing by the newsagent, I happen to glance in the window at the ads. Mine is still there, *Jennie's Cakes*. There's another ad, more recent, beneath it which catches my eye. *Pony for Sale*. There's a photo, a rather fuzzy computer printout, of a brown pony. *Mare 13.2hh, 8 years old, snafflemouthed, sold through no fault of her own. Not a plod. POA. Contact Delphi at Leatherington Equestrian.*

I don't know if it will do, but there's only one way of finding out. I call the number from my mobile.

'How old is your daughter?' the woman asks me.

'Almost ten. She hasn't had much experience of ponies, but she's very keen.'

'Has she ridden before?'

'Oh, yes,' I say, but before I can enlighten the woman at the end of the phone that Georgia's ridden twice, once on holiday and once at a friend of a friend's, she goes on.

'What does your daughter want the pony for?' She speaks clearly and correctly.

'To ride, really,' I mumble. I'm not sure what else you can do with a pony.

'I mean, what discipline is she interested in? Dressage? Showjumping? Hunting?'

'Showjumping, I think.' I've seen Georgia and Sophie making jumps in the paddock.

'Well, you name it, this pony can do it. She's ready to go on in any sphere.'

'Great,' I say, 'thanks.' And when I've arranged a time for Georgia to go and try her and put the phone down, I realise, too late, that I've forgotten to ask how much she wants for the pony. I call her back. She wants a thousand pounds, which is about what I budgeted for – before we moved here and Dad did the work on the kitchen, and then there was the party and all the paint that I bought, that we didn't use in the end... I suppress any niggling doubts about whether or not I can afford it. Once we've bought a pony, there won't be too many overheads. I mean, they eat grass, don't they? And we have plenty of that.

I hurry home. I can't wait to tell Georgia when I fetch her from school.

Arriving at the house, I find the postman waiting on the doorstep. Lucky's barking on the other side of the front door.

'Is there a problem?' I say. 'Is it the dog?'

'The dog's your problem, not mine,' he says, handing me an envelope. 'It's for you, but the address is incorrect.'

My brow tightens. It's from Summer, a thank you note for the party probably, but she's written 'J. Copeland, Jennie's Folly' on the envelope. I can't help smiling.

'You do know you have to apply to change the name of your house, otherwise there'll be all kinds

225

of confusion?'

'It's from a friend. It's a bit of a joke,' I say, but the postman is serious-faced.

'You'll be all right while it's me, my lover, but when you get a new postman, they won't know, will 'em? We can't have that.'

'I'll sort it out,' I say. I haven't had the heart to take down the sign, and I've noticed how the children have begun to refer to the house as Jennie's Folly. Perhaps I should change its name. I'm not sure how Guy will feel about it though... To him, it will always be Uphill House.

As soon as I tell Georgia about the pony, I wish I hadn't. She's so excited that she can't sleep and, the next morning, says she doesn't want to go to school, which is so unlike her.

'I won't be able to concentrate,' she says.

'It will be better than hanging around here – the time will go faster.'

'Of course it won't, Mother,' Adam says, picking a flake of cereal off his pyjama top. 'It just seems to go faster.'

'There's no need to tell me that, Adam,' Georgia says. 'I'm not stupid.'

'You're being pretty stupid about this pony. You haven't stopped going on about it since Mum told you.'

'You're the same with Lucky.' Georgia drops her spoon back in her bowl. She hasn't eaten a thing, I notice.

'I'm not,' Adam says.

'Adam, will you go and get dressed?' I say, checking the time 'You have five minutes.'

'Or?' he says, stretching lazily.

'I'll have to leave without you.'

'I'm cool with that.'

I look at him through narrowed eyes. There was a time when I would have taken him by the arm and dragged him out to the car, but he's bigger than me now. There's no point even trying.

'Adam, get dressed,' I snap, half cross, half lauging. 'Go on.' I flap a tea-towel at him, just as I do with the chickens. Grudgingly, he gets up and does as he's told, and I breathe a sigh of relief at avoiding a confrontation. 'Georgia, if you don't go to school, there's no pony.'

After school, I take the children home to change, then drive Georgia and Sophie to the equestrian centre where Delphi, a woman of about my age with blonde hair tied back, wearing a navy jacket with Team GB on it, and tight beige jodhpurs, leads a brown pony out of one of the stables in the yard and ties it up to a rail outside.

'This is Bracken. Would you like to give her a brush and tack her up?' Delphi fetches a box of brushes and hands it over to Georgia. 'That way you'll get to see if you like her.'

I suspect that, given Georgia's obsession with horses, any pony would do.

'If there's anything you want to know, do ask,' Delphi says, looking at me.

'Is she healthy?' I ask.

'She's fit as a fiddle. She hasn't had any health problems as far as I know.'

When I am unable to think of anything else, she goes on, 'Bracken will live out all year round. She spends the daytime in the stable over the summer because she's prone to putting on weight. She's a good doer, which is great because she doesn't take much extra feeding over winter.'

'We've got a stable,' says Georgia.

'Your mother said you were interested in jumping her,' Delphi says. 'We have popped her over a few poles, but to be honest with you, we haven't had her all that long. We tend to buy ponies in for the riding school and keep them for a while to see if they're suitable.'

Does that mean Bracken's no good? I wonder.

'Bracken's turned out to be too good to be a riding school pony,' Delphi goes on, putting my mind at ease. 'I feel she deserves to have a home where she gets some one-to-one love and attention.'

'When you say she's too good, what do you mean? I thought riding school ponies would have to be well-behaved.'

'She has too much potential. She'd be wasted being used for lessons, day in, day out. She's very forward-going, and I can see her making the perfect jumping pony with a little work.' Delphi turns back to Georgia. 'Would you like to tack her up now?'

When Georgia puts the saddle on, Bracken puts her ears back and tosses her head.

'You must tell her off whenever she does that,' Delphi says, helping Georgia slip the bridle over Bracken's head. 'Now, have you got your hat?'

'I haven't got one yet,' Georgia says.

'There'll be one you can borrow in the tack room.' Delphi fetches it and Georgia rams it on to her head. 'Let's take her into the school. I thought we'd ask one of our working pupils to show her off, then you can have a go.' Emily, a girl in her late teens, rides the pony first. Georgia seems impressed. The pony walks and trots and gallops about, the rider's feet dangling level with her knees. The rider keeps the reins really tight, I notice, and the pony dances about beneath her.

When it's Georgia's turn, my heart is in my mouth. I didn't expect this, that I'd be scared for her.

'You aren't going to let Georgia gallop about, are you?' I say to Delphi.

'Of course not,' she says, clipping a lead rope to the pony's bridle. 'We're always very careful with novices.' She walks the pony up and down with Georgia hanging on to the front of the saddle. 'I think Bracken will suit you very well.'

Georgia is instantly smitten by the pony. I'll never forget the look on her face when I agree that we'll have her. So you can't buy love? I can't stop smiling, because I just have.

'We can deliver if you haven't got transport,' Delphi says. She reminds me of a horse herself, the way she utters a small whinny instead of a laugh.

I decide not to embarrass Georgia by opening a discussion about transporting ponies. A pony is for getting from A to B. Why on earth do you need a transporter for it when it's supposed to transport itself?

'So, when can you bring her over?' I ask.

'I can do tomorrow afternoon.'

'After school?'

'That'll give you time to get some tack fitted,'

229

Delphi says.

'We'll need a saddle and bridle,' says Georgia.

'And a head collar and a rug,' says Sophie knowledgeably. I think her big sister's been indoctrinating her.

'And a grooming kit, and hoof oil.' Georgia is allowed to untack Bracken and lead her back into the stable, and then I spend another thousand pounds, or very near it, on all the gear that she and her pony will need.

Twenty-four hours later, I've covered the tiers of cake for Penny's wedding with fondant icing. It's gone on smoothly, its surface completely flat, like the water in the pond at the far end of the copse, not undulating like the paddock. I've also received the personalised cake toppers of the bride and groom and a golden retriever in a harness, by courier. All I have left to do is the beading, but that can wait. The wedding is on Saturday. There's still plenty of time, but as the big day approaches, I'm becoming more and more nervous, as if I'm the bride.

I occupy myself until the school run, having another go at finding my special signature cake. Marbled chocolate and raspberry cake didn't hit the spot. I have a go at chocolate and beetroot instead. I know beetroot isn't everyone's favourite vegetable, but it's rustic and healthy, and I think that people won't easily forget the unusual combination.

I purée some cooked beetroot – not in vinegar, of course – then I put the purée through a sieve, put the deep purple juice aside, and put the pulp into my food processor. I add oil, eggs and vanilla essence, then mix it together before pouring it into a well in the centre of the dry ingredients, the flour, sugar, cocoa and a pinch of bicarb. I fold it all together, pour into a tin, then bake for almost an hour.

In the meantime, I call Camilla's mum. She sent a business card via Georgia in return for the invitation to Georgia's birthday tea. *Maria Winters. Mobile Hairdresser*. I have a quick chat with her and arrange for her to do my hair when she comes to pick Georgia up. It's for a cut only. I'm economising.

I take the cake out of the Aga. It looks good, quite light and plain, but I can't ice it until it's cooled on the rack, and I can't wait that long because it's time to collect the children. I shut Lucky out of the kitchen and go...

At four o'clock, the pony is delivered, arriving in a luxury horsebox. Georgia is beside herself with excitement and Sophie is rushing around, scattering the chickens as she goes, making sure the trough is filled with fresh water and cleared of leaves.

'Here she is, a mother's dream,' Delphi crows as she leads Bracken out down the ramp of the lorry.

I pay Delphi in cash and she gives me the pony's passport in exchange.

'You'll need that when you take her to Pony Club. I hope to see her in the showring soon. She's a super little pony with great potential.' She pauses. 'Any problems, let me know straight away.'

I watch the girls' faces, their delighted smiles. Their happiness is infectious, but I do wonder – as

I hand over my thousand pounds – if I'm buying their affection, making up for taking them away from their dad? Why is my life riddled with guilt?

Georgia leads the pony into the yard, gives her a brush, feeds her a carrot then turns her out into the paddock, slipping off the head collar, a fluorescent pink affair. Bracken seems in a hurry to go... She trots about, snorting and sniffing the air. I don't know much about ponies – correction, I don't know anything about ponies – but she seems like a cute little thing. Georgia loves her already.

'She's got an amazing tail,' I say. 'It's right down to her ankles.'

'Mum, they're called fetlocks,' Georgia says.

'Don't you have to trim it? And what about her mane? She can hardly see through her fringe.'

'That's her forelock.'

'How do you know all this stuff?' I ask her, impressed.

'I've been reading the books I got out of the library, because if you have animals, Mum, you have to know how to look after them properly.'

'I wish you'd pay as much attention to your homework.'

'I do,' she says coolly.

'I'm sorry,' I say, putting my arm around her shoulders and giving her an apologetic hug. 'I was teasing.'

Guy appears with the cows, returning from the afternoon milking. He waves and I go running over to see him, looking over the gate on to the drive.

'What have you been up to?' he asks. 'I saw the lorry.'

'You don't miss much, do you?' I say lightly. 'I'm starting to wonder if you're stalking me.'

'Jennie, I only happened to–'

'It's all right,' I cut in, laughing. 'I'm joking.' I lower my voice and go on, 'I rather like the idea you're looking out for me...'

'Right,' he says, looking embarrassed, and my chest tightens with what I can only describe as desire, a longing for him to take me in his arms and hold me... I suppress an inward sigh of regret because, even if he should feel the same way, he seems too shy ever to be able to act upon it. 'So, what have you been up to?'

'I've bought a pony.' I put my hand to my mouth. 'I can't quite believe it.'

'Now I'm sure that you're completely mad, Jennie.' Guy is smiling, but there's a serious tone to his voice. 'I hope you know what you're doing. A pony isn't like a dog. It's a big responsibility.' He hesitates. 'I'd better go. I'm going to visit my mother this evening – I don't want her to be in bed. I'll see you soon.'

'Drop by tomorrow,' I say, 'I've got a cake I'd like your opinion on.'

'Thanks. It'll have to be after five – I've got the vet coming in the morning.'

'I'll save you a piece.'

'Thanks. I'll see you then.'

I watch him go before I return to the pony. It dawns on me then as she trots up and down beside the fence exactly what kind of responsibility I've taken on.

'She looks upset,' I say, as the girls look on anxiously. 'You have to remember what you felt like when you moved house.'

'I expect she's missing her friends,' says Sophie. 'I miss mine. I miss Heather ... Amber...' And she reels off the thirty or so names of the people who were in her class at her old school.

'It's better now, isn't it?' I say.

'Yes,' says Sophie, after a pause.

Within half an hour Bracken has her head down, grazing, and all is well with the world...

...until the next afternoon when Georgia goes out to catch Bracken to take her for a ride.

'Mum, Bracken won't let me get her.' Georgia's lip trembles at the apparent rejection. 'She doesn't like me. Mum, you come and catch her.'

That wasn't part of the plan.

'She's your pony – you're supposed to be looking after her.' I'm busy, but I stick a batch of fairy cakes in the Aga and set the timer for twenty minutes before joining Georgia outside.

'Call her then,' I say, but Georgia's right. Bracken tilts one ear in our direction, then flicks a few flies off her hindquarters with her tail and continues munching the grass. Georgia takes a carrot into the paddock with her, but Bracken ignores that too. I go in and walk towards her, but she lifts her head and trots away, stopping when she's just out of reach.

'This is ridiculous.' After several attempts, I'm hot and sweaty, and Georgia's face is flushed bright red, and we aren't getting anywhere. 'I don't understand. She let Delphi catch her. What do your books say?'

Georgia dutifully goes and checks.

234

'They say let her calm down then bring her something nice in a bucket. Have we got any more carrots?'

'I was going to use them for carrot cake, but she can have one.'

However, Bracken still won't be caught.

I call Delphi, but although she had said she was keen for me to call her with any problems, it seems that she's changed her mind.

'Bracken was never any trouble to catch when she was here,' she says.

'I'm going to ask Guy when he comes,' Georgia decides eventually. 'He might know what to do.'

We head back indoors and into the kitchen. I check on the timer, but it must have gone off some time ago.

'I've burned the cakes,' I say, rushing across to open the oven door and retrieve a tray of smoking buns. 'How stupid of me.'

'You aren't a very good baker sometimes, Mum,' Georgia giggles.

'It's lucky it wasn't a special cake.' I'm laughing with her as I throw them straight in the bin.

Georgia waylays Guy before I can offer him the last slice of chocolate and beetroot cake. He comes to assess the situation, leaning over the paddock gate with us. 'Is the new pony giving you the runaround then?'

'I don't think she wants to be ridden,' Georgia says.

'It isn't surprising. She's got too much grass out there.' He pauses. 'Did you catch her when you went to try her out?'

'She was in a stable.'

'Ah, there you go.' Guy turns to me. 'Didn't that ring alarm bells, Jennie?'

'It didn't occur to me...'

'Where did the pony come from?' he asks.

'Delphi Leatherington. I saw an ad in the news-agent's.'

'What did it say? Good to catch, box and shoe?'

'It didn't say anything about catching...'

'It's a horsey thing. You have to read between the lines.' Guy chuckles. 'Delphi's a bit of a dealer. She knows all the tricks of the trade.'

'So you mean we're never going to be able to catch her?' I say, aghast.

'We'll get her. When you keep animals, you have to think like them.' Guy goes off to the farm-house, returning with two long reins, which we use to corner Bracken.

'Now you go and put the head collar on, Georgia. Then I'd leave it on with a short piece of rope attached, so you'll be able to catch her next time.'

'Thanks, Guy,' Georgia says, more cheerfully. She hangs on to the rope and walks Bracken towards us, at which the pony rolls her beady little eyes and refuses to move any further.

'Walk on, Bracken.' Georgia tugs at the rope, but no joy.

Guy walks around behind her and clicks his tongue.

'Get on, pony,' he growls, at which Bracken ambles forward and out of the paddock to the yard.

Thanks, Guy,' I say, with admiration for his talent for horse-whispering.

'She's going to get too fat out on that pasture. You'll have to pen her in a smaller area – she won't have so much to eat or so far to run.' He grins.

'How do you know so much about horses?'

'Oh, I used to ride. I used to belong to the Pony Club.'

I'm not sure I can imagine him on a horse, but I look at him with new-found respect.

'I could have helped you if you'd asked, given you a second opinion, not that you'd have listened – you're as stubborn as that pony, you are.'

I give him a gentle dig in the ribs.

'It's too late now though,' he sighs. 'You've bought the ruddy thing.'

'Yes, and Georgia would never forgive me if I sent her back.'

'Have you got a saddle and bridle for her?'

'We bought one from Delphi at the Tack 'n' Hack shop. It cost me almost as much as the pony.'

'I hope you're made of money, Jennie. Owning a pony is like standing naked under a cold shower tearing up fifty-pound notes.'

'I hope it's going to be more fun than that, for Georgia's sake.'

We walk together into the yard and stand watching her brushing the pony's sleek, gleaming coat. Sophie is allowed to paint oil on the pony's hooves.

'See those rings on her feet?' Guy says, pointing. 'That's a sign she's had laminitis in the past.'

'What on earth is that?'

'It's a disease of little fat ponies.'

'Delphi said she hadn't had any health problems in the past. I did ask her.'

'I bet she said, "as far as I know".' Guy walks around to Bracken's head and takes a look in her mouth. 'How old did she say she was?'

'Eight,' I say a little curtly.

'Eighteen more like. Did you have her vetted? No ... thought not. Never mind, I should think she's got a few more years left in her yet,' he says. 'Have you got any posts and tape anywhere?'

'What kind of posts?'

'To set up an electric fence – for the restraint of beasts.' He smiles. 'It's a book – *The Restraint of Beasts*. You see, I can read.' He's teasing, but I still blush at the memory of calling him a country bumpkin. 'I am an educated man.'

My heart sinks – I'm supposed to be baking – then rises again at the thought of a trip to Overdown Farmers where I was lusting over a pair of pink wellies and a Puffa gilet when I last went in to buy a couple of sacks of layers mash for the chickens. However, Guy says he's sure he saw a roll of tape in the barn the other day when he came out to find a ladder to change the light bulb on the landing for me, and he probably has some posts and a shrike up at the house.

The girls take turns to ride Bracken around the orchard – she stops now and then to snatch a mouthful of grass, and Guy shows them how to tie a piece of baler twine from the bit to the ring on the saddle so she can't put her head down. When Georgia grows bolder and asks Bracken to go faster, she continues to amble about at the same pace, until Guy gets behind her, waving his arms, when she suddenly wakes up, kicks up her heels and flies from one end of the paddock to the other.

'Hold on, Georgia,' I yell, my pulse racing as I watch her cling on. Then, as Bracken comes to an abrupt stop, she slides unceremoniously on to the ground on her bottom. I run towards her but she gets up, brushing herself down.

'I'm all right,' she says, gasping. 'It was my fault, not Bracken's – I didn't hold on tight enough.' She turns, takes up the reins and puts her foot in the stirrup to remount.

'You aren't getting back on her?' I say.

'She's doing the right thing,' Guy says, holding on to Bracken's head. 'You don't want to let this kind of pony get away with anything. Don't worry, Jennie. I'll walk beside her.' He looks up at Georgia and smiles encouragingly. 'I don't think we'd better run before we can walk.'

After half an hour of walking, Guy decides the pony's probably had enough.

'Put her away in the stable, Georgia, and I'll go and get the bits and pieces for the fence. We'll make a pony trap.'

He arrives back with plastic posts and white tape, and a shrike to power the fence, and he and I put up a barrier which cuts across about a third of the paddock. Guy puts the posts in and I put up the tape. He sets up the shrike, attaching it to the tape then switching it on.

'It's live now,' he says, feeling for the switch underneath it. 'Now it's off.'

'Are you sure?' I ask.

'Have a look,' he says, and I stand close beside him, trying to find the switch. 'It's right there.' Laughing, he takes my hand and shows me. 'Have you got it now?' he asks.

'I don't know.' Keeping hold of my hand, he touches the tape, pulling away almost immediately, but not before a sharp pulse of electricity passes between us.

'Ouch!' I say, jumping away from him.

'It's on,' he says. 'I didn't mean to electrocute you – I thought it was off.'

It didn't really hurt. It was the shock of it. Guy held my hand and I don't think it was merely so he could show me where the switch was on the shrike. I'm still surprised, both by his boldness and by my reaction. He isn't so shy, and I'm not dead after all.

It's as if he's brought me back to life, I muse, watching him taste the last slice of chocolate and beetroot cake while sitting at the kitchen table. I used white icing on it, cross-hatched with pink made from the beetroot juice.

'What do you think of the choc and beetroot combo?' I ask.

'Beetroot?' He stares at his plate. 'I can't stand the stuff. I'd rather feed it to the cows. I don't mean that I'd like to feed this cake to the cows,' he goes on quickly.

'So you don't like it?' I say, a little disappointed.

'I like it, but I'm afraid I don't love it.'

'At least you're honest. Thanks, Guy. I'll go back to the recipe books.' I pause, observing with a smile how he continues to eat, methodically clearing his plate.

'You did ask Delphi if Bracken has any vices?' he says, looking up again.

'Vices?' My mind is running riot, galloping away

with me. 'What kinds of vices do ponies have?'

'Bucking, rearing, biting, cribbing ... I could go on.'

'Please, don't,' I say firmly.

'Does she jump?' Guy asks me.

'Delphi said she does.'

'You didn't try jumping with her?'

'I took Delphi's word for it.'

I can see that Guy is still finding this funny.

'I think she might have taken you for a ride, so to speak,' he says.

'Well, I wish you'd stop going on about it,' I say sharply. 'I don't want you telling me I've got it wrong, even if you're right!' It's what David used to do, all the time. It rankled then and it rankles now. 'I'm sorry,' I add quietly. 'I shouldn't have snapped like that. It's just that I'm upset for Georgia and furious with myself. And I managed to burn the cakes earlier on.' To my chagrin, my eyes fill with tears. I turn away.

'I apologise too,' Guy says. 'I should have been more tactful.'

'It isn't you.' I touch my throat. 'It's me.'

I hear the scrape of a chair and Guy is on his feet beside me.

'Jennie, are you all right?'

'I'm fine.'

'That's what you always say.' Guy slides an arm around my back, resting his hand on the curve of my waist. 'You don't have to pretend to be fine all the time, not with me,' he adds tenderly, bowing his head and gazing into my eyes. My heart lurches as I read in his expression a mixture of compassion and desire. I catch his flicker of hesi-

241

tation, but make my move before he can change his mind this time, leaning up and kissing him on the mouth. He responds and we share a kiss, and I'm flying – until I pull myself back to my senses and down to earth.

'What's up?' he murmurs, frowning.

'The children,' I whisper guiltily. 'I forgot. I mean, I–'

'You don't have to explain,' Guy says. He gives me a wry smile as he straightens and steps away. 'I'd like to do that again though...'

'I'm sure it can be arranged, but Guy, I have to think about–'

'The children. I understand.'

'Perhaps, you'd like to come for dinner one night?' I say tentatively. It's been a long time since I've done this. I'm not sure how I'm coming across: making my feelings clear, or scaring him off.

'No, Jennie,' he says.

'But–'

'I won't come for dinner. I'll take you out for a meal.'

'Like a date?' I say doubtfully.

'Yes, if you want to put it that way.'

'That would be lovely. Guy, I haven't been out on a date – not since David. I'm not looking for a brief fling – it isn't my style.'

'Mine neither.'

I'm going to have to find the courage to ask him straight out, because I can't be worrying about it any longer.

'Have you dated anyone since Tasha?'

Guy looks at me, half laughing, half annoyed.

'You mean, have I been out with Ruthie? Ruthie and I are mates. She's like one of the lads. Jennie, why don't you believe me?'

'I do. I do,' I say, as if repeating 'I do' will make it fact.

'You don't trust me?'

I hesitate. When David had those affairs, he wrecked my trust in men. I know they're no more all the same than we women are, but it's difficult...

'Jennie, how can I prove it to you?'

I look at him – I mean, really look at him.

'You could always kiss me again,' I say, and he does. I'm speechless, overwhelmed, deliriously happy. My head is spinning.

'Is it next weekend that Adam and the girls are with their dad?' he says, pulling away, his breathing fast and ragged.

'Next weekend then...'

I'm looking forward to it. I'm excited and scared in equal measure. Me and Guy. Can it be possible? When I moved here, I never anticipated this, that I'd start dating again. it is just a date though, I tell myself. If – I hardly dare to hope – it goes well, then I will have to start introducing the idea of Guy becoming my boyfriend to the children. I'm not sure how they'll take it, particularly Adam. I've already detected his disapproval when I talk too much about Guy.

Later, I trawl the internet for ideas for new recipes. The children have had their tea and headed to bed, but I can't concentrate. Every now and then, I suppress a tiny quiver in my loins as I relive that kiss, and the surges of electricity, both real and imagined, that have passed between us.

Chapter Thirteen

Cupcakes

On the Friday afternoon before Penny's wedding, I collect the children from school, casting a glance towards Bracken who's eating her way through the grass in her tiny area of paddock. Georgia has been catching her twice a day, before and after school, but she hasn't ridden her again yet. I've said that I'll walk with her sometime, like Guy did. Guy? My pulse thrills each time I think of him, which, I have to confess, is unsuitably often. Tomorrow night he's taking me out for dinner, and I can hardly wait.

I leave Lucky behind because, although we've tried taking him in the car again, he barks all the way to school and back, leaving your ears with that painful thrumming sound that you get after a rock concert. Not that I've been to any recently.

When we get back home, it seems that Lucky's taken umbrage because he doesn't come running out to greet us. In fact, I can't hear him at all.

'Lucky,' Adam calls. 'Where's the dog?' He turns to me.

'I expect he's run away,' I say, but I don't believe it for one minute. He's got his paws well under the table. I watch Adam's face, his anxious frown. 'Lucky won't be far away, love.'

We go inside, Adam, Georgia and Sophie

dropping their schoolbags and leaving their shoes in a heap in the hallway.

'Do you mind?' I say, remembering how my mother used to say the same to me and my sister. We didn't mind in the slightest. We knew, as they do, that Mum will pick everything up and put it away.

'Lucky,' Adam calls again, as he disappears through to the kitchen. His tone changes to one of dismay. 'Lucky!'

'What's happened?' I say, pushing past the girls. 'Adam, what's going on?'

Adam is standing in the middle of the kitchen in front of the table, arms outstretched as if to hide something behind him.

'He didn't mean to do it, Mum,' Adam stammers. 'He must have had an attack of the munchies...'

I move closer. Adam turns, ducks down under the table and sweeps Lucky into his arms, revealing the carnage of crumbs, fruit cake and marzipan in the middle of the kitchen floor.

'Lucky's snaffled the wedding cake!' Georgia exclaims. 'You naughty dog!' She wags her finger at him, but to me that is a far from adequate response to the disaster which lies in front of me.

'I'll kill that bloody dog,' I yell, taut with fury and disappointment.

'Someone must have left the larder door open,' Adam says, his voice quavering. 'You can't blame him for that. He's a dog. He doesn't understand.'

Lucky cowers against Adam's chest as if he knows he's done wrong.

245

'Oh, get him out of my sight,' I snap, and Adam makes a quick exit out through the back door. I sink down on one of the kitchen chairs and stare at the mess. The girls tiptoe around, making their own inspection of the damage.

'It's ruined,' I say. There are the remains of two tiers of cake on the floor.

'He didn't eat the marzipan, Mummy,' Sophie points out, as if that's going to make any difference. 'He's licked the icing off.'

'Well, I can't re-ice it. He's taken great bites out of it.' Then, I think, perhaps I can salvage something. There's one tier left, the largest. I check in the larder, but that too is on the floor, shards of icing surrounding it, and a corner nibbled off. My idea of a dramatic cake rescue goes out the window. I'll have to start all over again, but the wedding's tomorrow and I can't possibly bake, marzipan and ice a fruit cake in less than twenty-four hours.

Panic surges like iced water through my veins. Tears spring to my eyes and trickle down my cheeks.

How am I going to tell Penny? I'm sorry, the cake's off. I'm sorry, the cake wasn't up to scratch. I'm sorry, the dog ate the cake. It sounds like some of the excuses Adam uses for not handing in his homework. I decide to settle on the truth, no matter how far-fetched it sounds.

I dry my tears, sweep up the remains and throw them in the bin outside, then pour myself a measure of the brandy from the larder, and phone Penny, wondering how on earth I can retrieve the situation – and my reputation.

'Hi, Penny,' I say when she answers. 'It's Jennie here.'

'Oh, hello.' Penny's voice is warm and friendly. 'I suppose you're ringing to confirm the arrangements for tomorrow. I'm in such a flap, I can tell you. Declan's been to collect his morning suit and the shop's ordered the wrong size. I wish everything wasn't so last-minute. In fact, I wish it was this time next week, and it was all over, bar the honeymoon.'

'It's about the cake, I'm afraid,' I say when I can finally get a word in.

'Is there a problem?'

'I'm so sorry, Penny.' I imagine how I would have felt if someone had told me my cake was ruined the day before the wedding. 'I can't apologise enough – I don't know how it happened – but the dog's just eaten it.'

'You don't mean that?' Penny says, rather sharply. Wincing, I await her further angry response because I'd be livid if I were her. However, after a long silence, then a chuckle, she goes on, 'The dog, you say? Oh, Jennie...'

'I feel really bad about this, Penny.'

'Please, don't be upset on my behalf,' she says. 'It's only a cake, and I completely understand. Sally's a terrible thief. Last year, she almost died because she stole the Christmas dinner. You would have thought she might have learned from the experience – she was at the vet's for some time after that – but she's incorrigible. She's supposed to help me, being an assistance dog, but she often helps herself to the food on my tray.'

'Yes, but this shouldn't have happened.' I'm

247

running a business. I'm a professional. Lucky's escapade makes me look like a complete amateur. 'The dog shouldn't have been anywhere near the kitchen, let alone in the larder.' One of the children – Adam, probably – must have left the doors open.

'Dogs are like men,' Penny says, 'you can't live with them, you can't live without them.'

Right now, I think, I could live quite happily without a dog.

'I'm not sure you can have a wedding without cake though,' she goes on thoughtfully.

'I know, so I have one or two suggestions – I can make three tiers of chocolate or plain sponge with butter-cream icing, so you end up with a traditional-style wedding cake. I won't charge you, of course, and I'll refund your deposit. Or – you may have seen them in bridal magazines – I can bake cupcakes, one for each of your guests, and decorate those in a theme of your choice. When they're displayed on a stand, which I'll get hold of before I come and set up at the venue, they can look amazing.' I pause. 'It's entirely up to you. I'll understand if you want to try someone else...'

'No, that sounds great,' Penny says. 'It'll be something different. It's a shame about not being able to cut the cake though. That won't be quite the same.'

'I'll make a small cutting cake for the top of the stand – that means you and Declan can cut the cake and we can still use your cake toppers. I'm so sorry,' I say again.

'Never mind. These things happen. You go ahead.'

'Good luck for tomorrow,' I say, relieved.

As soon as I'm off the phone to Penny, I'm calling around for a suitable stand, finding one I can collect from a supplier in Exeter the following morning, and then I get baking. I bake as if I am in fast forward and soon the sink is piled high with mixing bowls, pans, spoons and spatulas, and there's a queue of trays of cupcake mix lined up to go in the Aga. I start washing up.

'Mum, aren't we going to Daddy's tonight?' Sophie asks, coming into the kitchen clutching one of the chickens.

'Hey, get that bird out of here!' I say. First the dog, now a bird. There would be dire consequences for Jennie's Cakes if health and safety ever found out. 'I'll have the hygiene police after me.'

'Okay,' she says, letting it down right outside the back door where it turns, caws and steps across the threshold again, picking its feet up high. 'Shoo!' Sophie says, chasing her away. 'Mum, we should have let the chickens have the crumbs.'

'I'm not sure. That cake had so much brandy in it, we might have ended up with boozy eggs.'

'Mum, about going to Daddy's?' Sophie starts again.

'I know.' I run my wet Marigolds through my hair. 'I'd forgotten. I'm sorry.' I was supposed to be meeting David halfway. I check the time, hoping he hasn't left yet. I call him, and – not surprisingly – he isn't happy.

'I'd feel the same in your situation,' I say, 'but this is an emergency.'

'Jennie, you're hopeless,' he says. 'It's no good. I'm sticking to my guns. You'll have to meet me

249

halfway as we arranged.'

'I can't. I've got to bake and decorate one hundred cupcakes for a wedding by midday tomorrow.'

'What is this – Jennie's Cakes or last-minute dot com?'

'I'll explain another time. David, I have to get on.'

'It isn't me who lets the children down. It's you. Adam has plans to meet Josh and Sophie wants to go shopping with Alice.' David hesitates. 'Jennie, you need to think about whether you're getting your priorities right.'

'David, I'm running a new business – it needs nurturing.'

'And so do our kids.'

'You don't have to tell me that.' I feel guilty enough already about changing the arrangements for their weekend away. 'I'm asking you one small favour: to come here and get them tonight. I'll drive up to yours on Sunday to pick them up. Please, David.' I wait for his response. The timer's buzzing. I need to get the latest batch of cakes out before they bum. 'Either you come down and get them or we'll have to make it another weekend. Let me know what you decide.' Frustrated, I cut the call then turn to Sophie, aware that she's staring at me.

'Why do you and Daddy still argue when you're divorced?' she asks.

'I don't know, darling,' I say, taking a tray of cupcakes out of the oven and testing the springiness of the sponge with the tip of my finger. They're cooked.

'What's for tea, Mum?' Adam interrupts.

'Don't say it–' I hold up my hands '–you're starving. Well, I tell you, we'll all be starving if you don't let me get on with this. And get those boots off. No boots in my kitchen. And no dogs either!' I catch sight of Lucky sneaking his nose around Adam's knees to see if it's safe to return.

'Lucky isn't feeling very well,' Adam says.

'As he richly deserves, the ungrateful little so–' I correct myself quickly, noticing Sophie's just about to pass comment. 'Sausage. Adam, get that bloody dog out of my sight. In fact, tomorrow I'm going to ring what's her name ... Wendy ... from Talyton Animal Rescue and send him back.'

'If you do that, Mother,' Adam says coldly, 'I'll go with him.'

'Well, I'm sorry you feel like that.'

'He's my best friend. My only friend in this dump.'

I soften slightly, touched by the misery in Adam's eyes.

'We give Lucky dog food every day, and biscuits, and chews,' I say gently. 'We don't let him go hungry.'

'He couldn't help himself, Mum. The larder door must have been open so he took a look inside. How could he resist?'

'He couldn't – obviously.'

'I expect his old owners, the mean ones, didn't feed him properly so he had to take what he could find.'

'Cut the sob story, Adam.'

'You aren't going to send him away, are you?'

'The way I feel at the moment, I just might.

251

Adam, I'm up to my neck in baking. I haven't got time to think about it.' I notice a wet black nose appearing again between Adam's ankles. 'Just get him out of my sight.'

I regret speaking to him like that later. The cupcakes are out, cooling down ready for icing. Georgia and Sophie cooked beans on toast for their dinner. David, having consulted Alice, rang back and cancelled the weekend, and Adam went up to his room with the dog. I decide to take him a couple of cupcakes – yes, I've baked extra, having learned my lesson.

'Adam?' I knock on the door. 'Can I come in?'

'What's the point?' he says flatly.

'I want to have a word.'

'I think you've already done that – had words.'

I push the door open anyway. Adam's lying on the bed in the dark with his curtains pulled back, so the lights on in the farmhouse are visible. As I approach I realise Lucky's there too, panting and beating his tail against the duvet. Adam has his arm around Lucky's neck and he's stroking the dog's belly, which looks taut and swollen.

'I've brought you some food,' I say, moving his iPod, styling wax and sweet papers out of the way so I can put the plate on the bedside cabinet.

'I'm not hungry.' His tone is sullen.

'As you're not going to Dad's this weekend, you could do the milking in the morning,' I suggest, thinking that might distract him and give him something to look forward to, instead of brooding.

Adam shakes his head, his mouth turned down at the corners.

'If you're afraid I'll take Lucky back while

you're out, you shouldn't be. I can see how much you love him...' I pause. 'He can have another chance, but if he steps out of line again then he will have to go. I'm sorry, but I can't have him wrecking the business.'

'The business, Jennie's Cakes – that's all you talk about.'

'You know that isn't true,' I say, hurt.

'You don't care about *us* any more...'

'But I do.' I perch on the edge of the bed and reach for his shoulder. 'Adam, I care about you more than anything else in the world. That's why I'm so serious about the business. One day you'll want to go to university or buy a house. I want to be able to help, to give you the best start in life.' I hesitate, my heart aching as I watch him gazing fixedly towards the ceiling, tense and tight-lipped. I wish I could get through to him.

'I'm sorry about the visit to your dad's,' I begin again. 'I know you're disappointed not being able to see Josh, but I'll make up for it. I'll see if we can reorganise it for next weekend.'

'Whatever.' Adam shrugs, but I can sense his resistance melting away.

'Hug?' I ask tentatively. He answers with a sigh, turning away from the dog and putting his arms around my neck as I crane closer, inhaling his scent of deodorant and Clearasil that is soon overlaid by the pungency of Lucky's doggie breath as he scrambles into the space between us.

'Lucky wants a hug too,' I say, smiling.

'He's jealous.' Adam's teeth glint in the dusky light and I relax. I should have been more careful the way I handled the 'dog, cake and David' situation. Adam might play at being an adult, but he's still a boy – I press my lips to his forehead – my boy.

A little later, I send Georgia and Sophie to bed, then turn my attention to icing one hundred cupcakes. At number seventy-two, I find I've run out of icing sugar. It's three in the morning and I know the Co-op won't be open. I wait until four-thirty, then call Guy.

'It's your next-door neighbour, wondering if by any chance you have some icing sugar I could borrow? I haven't disturbed you, have I?'

'I'm having an early breakfast.' I hear him moving about. 'There's a bag of icing sugar at the back of the cupboard, but it would have been my mother's, so I can't guarantee it's useable.' There's a pause and a rustling of paper. 'No, it looks okay, and there's no "use-by" date. What do you want it for at this time of the morning?'

'It's a long story, but Lucky snaffled Penny's wedding cake and I've been up all night making an alternative. The wedding's tomorrow – I mean, today.' I swear under my breath.

'I'll drop the icing sugar in on my way down to get the ladies in for milking. Give me two minutes.'

'Guy, you've saved my life,' I tell him when he passes the bag through the kitchen window.

'I saw your lights were on all night. I wasn't stalking you, by the way, I was up with one of the cows.' I can't see his face clearly, but his voice is hoarse as if he's upset.

'I hope she's okay,' I say, then wish I hadn't.

'She died,' Guy says curtly.

'Oh, how awful. Which one was it?'

'Old Kylie. I know it sounds stupid, but I loved that cow. She was my first Dairy Shorthorn. She's been a real star...'

'I'm so sorry.' Before I moved here, I found it odd that anyone could get attached to an animal, but I've grown quite fond of the chickens, particularly the feisty ones. I can't say the same about the dog. However, I can understand how Guy feels about losing his favourite cow when he's cared for her and milked her twice a day for years. It must be quite a wrench. 'Why don't you come in and sit down for a minute? You look as if you've had a bit of a shock. I've got some brandy – unless you think it's too early?'

'Maybe I will.' He hesitates. 'But you're busy, Jennie.'

'I could do with a break,' I say. 'Come on in.'

Guy joins me in the kitchen and I pull two chairs up close to the Aga. I pour a slug of brandy into a mug and hand it to him.

'Thanks, Jennie,' he says, slumping on to a seat.

'I'll call Adam down to give you a hand with the milking,' I say.

'Is he here then?' Guy says, surprised. 'I thought he was off to London this weekend.'

'He was. I was supposed to be meeting David halfway, but I knew I'd never get these cakes done if I took a couple of hours out. I feel really bad about it, but what could I do? The wedding's today.'

'Don't disturb Adam.' Guy drains the mug. 'The knacker will be coming later. To pick up the body,' he adds in explanation. 'I think it would be a bit traumatic for him. I'll find it hard enough, but Adam's a sensitive young man.'

I stand up, take the mug from Guy's hands and slip my arm around his shoulders. He leans his head against my apron and I give him a comforting squeeze.

'Thanks for the sympathy – and the brandy,' he murmurs before pulling away. 'You're pretty understanding.' He stands up and a small smile crosses his lips as he adds, 'For a townie.'

'About tonight,' I begin, 'or should that be later today? I'm not sure. I'm sorry to let you down, but I can't–'

'Make dinner tonight,' he finishes for me. 'It's all right. I kind of guessed...'

'It isn't because I don't want to,' I stammer. 'Circumstances have rather overtaken me.'

'I can see that.' Guy smiles ruefully. 'Another time then?'

'Definitely.' I hesitate. 'Why don't you have supper with us tonight? I know it won't be quite the same, but...'

'I'd like that,' he says. 'Thanks, Jennie.'

Chapter Fourteen

Carrot Cake

Guy's intervention means that I can finish decorating the cupcakes and leave the icing to dry while I drive the twenty miles or so into Exeter to collect the stand. At twelve-thirty, only half an hour later than I'd planned, Adam, the girls and I are bringing the stand and boxes of cupcakes into the wedding venue, the Barnscote Hotel, not far from Talyton St George. It's another longhouse, very much like Jennie's Folly – I mean, Uphill House – on the outside, but in a better state of repair. Inside, the rooms have been knocked through to create an entrance hall which runs into a much larger function room with a galleried mezzanine floor. Above that, the roof space is open, revealing the oak trusses and beams.

However, I don't have time to dwell on my surroundings. The proprietor of the hotel shows me the table where I'm to set up the wedding cake, and I give the stand one last wipe over and start setting out the cakes. I finish by placing the figurines of Penny, Declan and Sally on top of the cutting cake, making sure they're secure. Finally I take a step back.

'What do you think, guys?' I say to the children who are looking on, their expressions weary with boredom.

'It's pretty good,' Adam says, which is high praise indeed, I think, from a fourteen-year-old boy.

'I love it,' says Georgia.

'I'm going to have one like that when I get married,' says Sophie, and I'm relieved that at least one of my children has escaped being scarred for life by the breakdown of my marriage.

Though I say it myself, I think the cupcakes look gorgeous: butter frosting dusted with glitter and topped with dusky-pink fondant hearts. I only hope that Penny feels the same. Not only do I want her to enjoy her big day, but my reputation

– the reputation of Jennie's Cakes – is at stake.

On the way back from the Barnscote Hotel, I drop in to the Co-op to pick up some more icing sugar. Much to the check-out woman's consternation, I clear the shelf.

'Can I ride Bracken when we get home?' Georgia asks as she stands there, holding the bag while Adam packs.

'Do you have to?' I say. On the one hand, I'm euphoric because I've managed, I hope, to retrieve the situation regarding Penny's wedding cake, but on the other, I feel light-headed through lack of sleep.

'Mum, it will do you good to get outdoors in the fresh air,' Georgia says.

'Oh, all right, but not for very long,' I say, caving in. It might help to make up for her missing out on her weekend with her dad, and anything for a quiet life.

Back at home, I change into my jeans and a long-sleeved top. I check my appearance in the mirror on the way downstairs. I don't know why. I look as if I've had a fright: no make-up, my hair frizzed up as if someone has attached me to the pony's shrike, and shadows around my eyes dark enough to be bruises. Escaping from the wreck that is my reflection, I hasten downstairs to find my wellies and go outside to find that Georgia has already caught Bracken and tied her up in the yard.

'How is she today?' I ask.

'Good,' Georgia says, picking up a brush from the grooming kit, which has a decidedly pink theme.

'I thought your favourite colour was blue,' I say, taking the brush as she hands it to me.

'Blue doesn't suit her,' Georgia says. 'She's going to have pink everything.'

'She doesn't need anything else, surely?' I'm really regretting what happened to Penny's wedding cake now, because that would have gone a long way towards paying for the pony.

'She needs a fly mask and lightweight raincoat.'

'Ponies don't need coats.' I touch the brush to Bracken's neck and sweep it down her shoulder, following the lie of the hair. 'They have their own.'

'It's so that when it rains and I want to ride her, she'll be dry.'

'Can't you put her in the stable?'

'S'pose, but I noticed this pink rug when we were going round Tack 'n' Hack ... and a pink wheelbarrow.' Georgia squirts some conditioning detangler on to Bracken's tail before she takes a brush to it. When she's finished that, she sprays the pony all over with fly repellent.

'I should be a bit more sparing with that in future,' I say gently. I can taste it on the back of my tongue.

Georgia fetches her hat and Bracken's tack, at which point the pony takes exception to the saddle. She snorts at it and rolls her beady little eyes as if to say, I've never seen one of those before. When Georgia lifts it up to put it on her back, she sidles away then back again, pushing Georgia out of her way. Remembering how Delphi dealt with it before, I take hold of Bracken's head collar.

'That's enough,' I growl at her. 'Stand still.'

Bracken doesn't move. 'Go on, Georgia. Put the saddle on.' Bracken doesn't even put her ears back as Georgia slides it on to her back and fastens the girth. 'You see, I'll make a horse-whisperer yet.'

'A horse-shouter, more like,' Georgia says, smiling, as she puts the bridle on.

I hang on to Bracken while Georgia mounts from an upturned bucket, then I walk with them to the paddock, through the pony trap and out the far side, my plan being to take a circular route, going up past the apple trees, along the hedge at the top, then dropping back past the pond and through the copse. Bracken has other ideas though. We reach the end of the hedge safely, but then she stops and stands there.

'Come on, Bracken,' I say.

Georgia gives her a squeeze with her legs and Bracken puts her ears back. Now, I might not know anything about ponies, but I'm surprised how easy it is to understand what they're saying. Bracken is saying 'no', and to me that seems totally out of order. Georgia loves her to bits, but Bracken doesn't seem to have any respect for her owner at all.

With growing impatience, I move around behind her – out of range of her hind legs – and click my tongue, like Guy did. Bracken doesn't budge. Her ears remain pinned back to her head and the skin around her muzzle wrinkles up. She looks decidedly cross. In fact, I'm not sure which of us is more annoyed.

'I'll get her going.' Georgia takes a stronger hold on the reins and kicks with her legs, at which Bracken leaps forwards, spins round and gallops off the way we came, leaving Georgia in a heap at my feet, my heart in my mouth and all kinds of worst-case scenarios running through my head.

Groaning, Georgia tries to sit up.

'Georgia! Keep still.' I'm down beside her in the mud, holding her. 'Where does it hurt?'

'My arm,' she says, pointing to just above her wrist.

'I think you've broken it,' I say gently. 'Does it hurt anywhere else? Your back? Your neck?'

'No...' she says, uncertain.

'Do you think you can stand up?'

'I think so.' I help her up. She's trying to be brave, but every so often a small sob escapes her. 'Try to hold your arm close to your chest. We're going to have to get you to hospital.'

'What about Bracken? We can't leave her in the field with her tack on.'

I don't say anything. I'll only upset her further, because as far as I'm concerned I don't care what happens to Bracken when she clearly doesn't care what happens to my precious daughter. She's a liability, and I wish I'd never set eyes on her. I bite back tears of regret and exhaustion. I've been up all night and had a stressful day. The last thing I needed was this.

On the way down through the paddock, I check the time on my mobile. It's two-thirty. With a bit of luck Guy won't have started the milking yet. I call him, my fingers trembling as I dial his number.

'Guy, I'm really sorry to bother you again, especially on such a difficult day, but I have another favour to ask you...'

261

By the time I've explained, he's walking down the drive towards the yard gate.

'There's a minor injuries unit in Talyton,' he says, looking anxious. 'It's open all day, including weekends. I'll get Adam to help me see to the pony. You get going.'

I glance at Georgia – she looks as if she's about to faint, so I get her straight into the car, then call for Sophie to bring a book to read and come with us. We spend three hours at the minor injuries unit, having Georgia's arm X-rayed and put in a cast and being given an appointment to see a consultant at the hospital in a week's time.

'You won't be riding for a while,' the nurse says, smiling, and I have to admit to myself that I'm relieved to hear it. I don't think I could bear to see her on that pony – on any pony – again. Georgia apparently feels otherwise.

'When can I ride again?' she asks.

'It'll be another six to eight weeks, I'm afraid.'

'I've only just got a pony, and now I can't ride her,' Georgia says, her voice quavering. 'It's such a shame,' she goes on, sobbing into a tissue.

I hold her in my arms, unable to console her. I don't tell her my decision – it'd be too traumatic. However, I have made up my mind. Bracken goes.

Back at home, I let Georgia call David. Now that her arm isn't hurting so much, she's quite cheerful. I overhear her speaking. How proud she is when she says, 'I fell off my pony, Bracken.' The conversation is brief, then she tries to hand the phone over to me.

'Dad wants a word,' she says as I back away, miming that I don't want to talk to him, but

262

Georgia doesn't get what I mean and thrusts the phone into my hand.

'What did you think were you doing, Jennie?' He starts talking at me.

'I couldn't have been any more careful, David.'

'You're unbelievably stupid sometimes ... so irresponsible.'

'I was walking with her,' I say, hurt by his accusation. 'The pony ran away.'

'You could have stopped it.'

'I don't know how.'

'Pulled on its reins, jumped in front of it, anything.'

'David, you know nothing about horses.'

'Neither do you.'

I hold the phone at arm's length. Then, when he runs out of steam, put it back to my ear.

'You don't have to go on at me – I feel guilty enough about it already,' I mutter. 'David, I've had a really crappy twenty-four hours and I haven't got the energy for this.' Feeling completely drained, I cut him off.

'Dad wasn't very pleased, was he?' Georgia says beside me. 'Can you help me find a jumper that will fit over my plaster?'

'When's tea?' Adam interrupts.

'Guy's coming for dinner,' I say as I check through the pile of clean laundry that's made its way as far as the chair in the snug. 'In fact, he's bringing dinner.'

'Why?' Adam looks at me. Am I imagining that his eyes are narrowed and his mouth pursed with suspicion?

'Because I asked him.'

263

'I don't mean that,' Adam says quickly – so quickly that I know he's lying. 'I mean, why call it dinner when it's tea?'

'I don't know. Perhaps it's an attempt to raise the tone of this establishment.'

'Now you're talking posh.'

'I'm joking,' I say.

'It isn't funny.' Adam stuffs the rest of a cupcake into his mouth. 'What time's tea? I mean, dinner.' He says it in a mocking way. Sometimes I wonder if I'm too soft on him.

It's seven when Guy arrives with fish and chips from Mr Rock's in Talyton. He lets himself in and joins us in the kitchen where I have Sophie laying the table, and Georgia finding clean glasses for five. Adam is standing at the sink, supposedly washing up but more occupied with surreptitiously flicking the soapsuds at his sisters.

'Wine or bitter?' I ask the new arrival.

'A glass of wine, thanks.'

'Red or white?'

'Whatever you're having.'

I open the red, glancing at Guy as I remove the cork. I fancy something complex and full-bodied.

We sit down to eat and, as far as I can tell, dinner is a success. Adam is polite when we're eating, but when we retire to the drawing room for carrot cake and coffee – decaff because Guy has to get up for milking – he disappears off upstairs. Georgia and Sophie hand round, and eat chocolate before I send them off to change into their pyjamas. Once they've gone, there's a long silence. Guy gazes at me from the rocking chair, while I sit with my legs curled up on the wicker sofa.

'I'm surprised you haven't made up the fire yet,' he begins.

'Are you cold?' I say quickly.

'I'm warm enough.'

'I'm a bit nervous about the thatch,' I confess.

'Don't worry about that – it doesn't catch fire easily because it's so compacted.'

We go on to chat about my plans for the vegetable patch, nothing deep and meaningful, but it doesn't seem to matter.

Half an hour or so after the girls have gone to bed, Adam's music comes shuddering down from above.

'Ads, turn that down,' I yell.

'Mummy.' Sophie appears on the landing, wrapped in a duvet like the hungry caterpillar. 'Adam woke me up.'

I shout again.

'It's no use,' says Guy, a smile playing on his lips. 'He won't hear you.'

I run upstairs and shove his door open. He looks up, hot and angry.

'Adam, what is your problem?' I don't know why I ask. He doesn't like to see me with Guy, and I feel as if I have to justify myself, like when I was a teenager in front of my parents. 'We weren't doing anything. We are only talking.' When he doesn't respond, I go on, 'Turn that music down.'

'Why should I? You said that when we moved to the country, I could play my music as loud as I like.'

'Within reason though. This is not within reason. You've woken your sister and you're giving me a headache.'

265

'Really, Mum?' he says icily. 'Are you sure I'm not just embarrassing you in front of your new boyfriend?' There's challenge and a coolness in his voice. Just like David. He's his father's son.

'A,' I say, 'he is not my boyfriend.' On occasion I wish he was, but for the purpose of this argument, he isn't. 'He's just a friend.' Inside, I'm crying, Don't you want me to be happy?

'Yeah, yeah,' Adam sighs. 'So what's B?'

'B?'

'You've given me excuse A, so what's B?' His lip curls into a sneer. 'B for could do better?'

'Turn that down,' I repeat. 'I can't hear myself think.' When Adam refuses to move, I turn down the volume on the docking station myself.

'You know, you look really silly, making out like you're perfect to impress Guy. It's so embarrassing.' Adam jumps up and turns the volume higher again.

'Parents are supposed to be embarrassing,' I say, trying to lighten the mood. 'That's their job.'

'Do you know how ridiculous you look in those country clothes, your gilet and pink wellies and that dreadful hat? You wouldn't have been seen dead in them in London.'

'There you go then. If I was really out to impress Guy, I would have taken more care with my appearance.' I'm not being completely honest here – am I that transparent, like the wrapper on one of my cakes?

Adam is mid-strop. I can see I'm not getting through to him. My throat tightens with a yearning for years gone by when I'd put my adorable and adoring little boy to bed and read him a story.

266

It's as if he's been transformed into some alien life-form with an attitude that's out of my earthly experience and who speaks a language I can't understand. I give up trying to reason with him.

'Just turn that music down.'

'No way,' he says, so I pull out the plug from the mains. There's a spark at the socket. The old house doesn't like that – she appears to be on Adam's side because there's a click and all the lights go out. So much for lightening the mood. The house is in complete darkness.

'Jennie, are you all right up there?' I hear Guy call from downstairs.

'I've fused the lights,' I call back, unable to disguise my amusement.

'Mother, you've fused *everything*,' Adam says.

'I'll get it sorted.' I turn, feeling my way along the wall to the door.

'You'll get Guy to sort it, you mean.'

I'm grateful that he does. Downstairs, I find Georgia clinging to Sophie in the snug. Although it's grubby, Georgia's cast shows up pale in the darkness. 'Sophie is afraid of ghosts,' Georgia explains.

'I'm not. You are,' Sophie says indignantly.

'Not,' says Georgia.

'In that case, you won't mind me borrowing your mobile,' I say, taking it from her. 'Thank you.'

'Jennie, there you are,' Guy says, joining us. 'The fuse box is in the hall cupboard. This place needs rewiring.'

'It's a pity the previous owner didn't let me know before, then I could have knocked a bit off the asking price,' I say lightly. I can't afford to have the house rewired. My situation has changed. When we were married, David might have moaned that there was no money left in the current account but he'd always have some hidden in reserve that he could transfer. I didn't ever have to worry. I've lost that security with the end of my marriage. I wouldn't go back now though. I like my independence. In fact, looking back, I wonder what I was ever scared of.

I show Guy through to the hall and open the cupboard. I don't know why. He's probably more familiar with Uphill House – no, Jennie's Folly – than I am.

'Would you like the torch?' I ask him as he squats down and leans into the cupboard.

'You hold it for me.' His teeth flash in the darkness. 'You'll have to come closer...'

I stand behind him and shine the mobile's beam over his shoulder.

'Closer than that,' he whispers, and I shuffle another small step towards him, catching his heel and losing my balance. I grab his shoulder to steady myself and his hand lands on top of mine. Guy turns his face to me, his eyes gleaming. 'There's definitely some electricity here, don't you think?'

'Well, I hope so...' I relax my grip on his shoulder, but leave my hand where it is.

'We aren't talking at cross-purposes here, are we?' he asks hoarsely. 'I mean, I'm not referring to the fuse box as such.' His fingers are stroking mine, sending my pulse rate steadily higher.

I'd like to say something clever, seductive, but his mouth is on mine and I've lost the power of speech and rational thought. Until I notice the sound of footsteps behind us, and the beam of a more powerful torch bobbing up and down then sweeping across the hall.

'Is there a problem?' It's Adam and he's unusually short with Guy.

'Shine your torch in here,' I say, stepping back. 'It's impossible to see.'

'I can see perfectly well,' he says quietly.

'You keep eating your mum's carrot cake,' Guy says, as if he's trying to cover up some embarrassment.

'I don't like carrot cake,' Adam says, and I can hear the mutiny in his voice: I am not a child, so don't treat me like one. But he shines the torch into the cupboard for Guy so he can fix the fuses, and within ten minutes we have light once more.

It has been an enlightening evening all round, I think later, when Guy has gone home. I can't stop grinning. I might have ended up with a thieving dog and a psychotic pony, but I'm sure now. Guy does like me, more than like me, and I like him, and I'm ready to take the next step, whatever that may be. I'm worried though about Adam. What did he see? What does he think he saw? I resolve to talk to him as soon as I get a quiet moment. Once he's over the shock of realising that his mum's ready to enter a new relationship, I hope he'll come round to accepting the situation.

Chapter Fifteen

Victoria Sponge

To be honest, I'm nervous about speaking to Adam, afraid of his reaction because I can guess what it's going to be, which is why I still haven't said anything a few days later. Not to worry. Guy and I are taking things slowly. It feels right. So right.

A couple of mornings after, once I've taken the children to school, I get baking. I confess that I look out of the window quite often, hoping to catch a glimpse of Guy, and there he is, striding towards me. I open the window and say hi. He looks great, his hair ruffled where he's taken off his cap, fresh and wide awake, and I wonder how he manages to look so well on all this early rising. And then I think, That's very naughty, Jennie Copeland, and find I'm dusting the Victoria sponges with flour instead of icing sugar. That'll teach me to keep my mind on the job in future.

'Hi. Something smells good,' he adds, moving closer.

'I'm cooking.'

'I guessed. You've got flour on your nose.' He reaches out one hand as if he's going to wipe it off, but I'm out of reach.

'Have you got time for a coffee?' I ask.

'All the time in the world,' he says, smiling his

slow, heart-stopping smile, and soon he's ensconced in the kitchen, leaning back in a chair with his long legs stretched out in front of him.

'Jennie, I've been meaning to ask,' he says after a while. 'About Adam.'

'What's he done?'

'Nothing – he's a good worker. No, I found him up the far field the other evening.'

'I expect he was taking Lucky for a walk. The novelty of having a dog hasn't worn off yet.'

'He didn't have the dog with him.'

I feel my brow tighten into a frown. 'Did you ask him what he was doing?'

'Yeah, but one minute he said he was up there looking for mushrooms, the next that he was releasing mice back into the wild, which seemed completely far-fetched to me. I mean, who traps mice only to let them go again?'

I clear my throat.

'Um, that might have been me...'

'Jennie?'

'I've put a couple of humane traps in the barn – I can't have vermin around, you see. The chickens haven't caught any mice as far as I'm aware, but we've trapped a handful and I haven't liked to murder them, so I thought...'

'You thought you'd let them go again?' Guy laughs. 'Why didn't you knock them on the head?'

'Because it seems so cruel. They're tiny and look so defenceless. It would be murder.'

Guy is holding his sides now, tears rolling down his cheeks.

'I've told you before – you're completely mad, Jennie.'

'I read somewhere that they wouldn't come back as long as you released them at least two or three miles away,' I go on, unsure whether to be affronted or to laugh along with him. Relocating mice? It is ridiculous. Laughter wins out.

'Where have you been letting them go then?'

'In the lane on the way into Talyton.' My shoulders shake and my face begins to ache. 'I leave them in the hedge with some food and hope they'll make themselves a new home.' I don't tell Guy, but I do worry that the rest of their mouse family might miss them when they find out that they're gone.

'Only a townie could think of that,' he goes on, wiping his eyes. 'Oh, Jennie, I'm sorry. I haven't laughed like that for ages.'

'Neither have I,' I splutter.

'If Adam's really been letting mice go up in my field, they'll be straight down to set up home at mine.'

'So you don't think he was doing his bit for animal rights then?' I say, sobering up a little.

Guy looks at me, his expression turning serious. 'He seemed a bit down.'

'All teenagers can be moody. Adam's no different.'

'When I went back to see if he'd gone, I found a couple of empty lager cans in the ditch.'

'What teenager hasn't had the odd drink with their mates now and again?'

Guy is staring at me now, and I realise I'm in denial. 'He was drinking alone.'

'Alone?' I hesitate, letting this significant fact sink in. 'Why?' All kinds of questions run through

272

my mind. Is this a one-off? Is my son taking his first steps on to the slippery slope towards becoming an alcoholic? Why did he do it? Where did he get hold of it?

'What can I do?' I exclaim. 'I can't keep him under lock and key.' I can't keep him away from drink either – it's everywhere, even in Talyton St George where the good ladies of the church and WI encourage sobriety.

'Would you like me to have a word with him? Man to man.'

It's what I suggested to David, but I think man to boy is more apt. Adam's just a boy.

'Please tell me to mind my own business if you think I'm interfering, but I like Adam. He's a good boy and I'd hate to see him take the wrong path.'

It should be down to David to speak to our son, but I'm worried what he would say, especially after the way he went on at me when Georgia came off the pony. And anyway, this is probably an isolated incident. It hasn't happened before. I don't see why it should happen again.

'I don't believe it's such a problem as you're making out, Guy. I can't think of a single teenager who didn't experiment with alcohol at one time or another.'

'I didn't because my job's always depended on me being able to drive,' Guy says. 'That makes me sound like I've always been a boring old fart – unlike you with your sense of adventure and willingness to embrace new things.' He pauses expectantly, and my heart thumps in my chest, and I wonder if he's thinking of how he embraced me in the cupboard last night. 'This is where you're supposed to say, "But you're not a boring old..."' He straightens, holds up his hands, and in self-mocking tones goes on, 'No, I don't want you to feel obliged to lie on my behalf, to protect my feelings, because the truth is I'm a very dull man.'

'Oh, Guy, you're great company,' I protest. 'Does Adam really talk to you?' I go on, returning to the subject of my son. 'I mean, open up to you? He doesn't share anything with me. He blames me for moving the family here, for uprooting him from school, friends... And his dad.'

'You don't regret moving though, do you?' Guy says.

'No...'

'Adam does talk about his father. We talk about his mother too.' Guy grins and I blush. 'It's all right, I said I wouldn't hear a bad word about her.

'Now, I don't know if you still want it,' he says, changing the subject and sparing my blushes, 'but I've got a trailer-load of nicely rotted manure for the vegetable plot. I can drop it round this afternoon.' He raises one hand. 'Before you say anything, I don't want payment. It's a gift.'

Later, he returns, parking a tractor and trailer in the yard and calling me out of the kitchen.

'Leave that Aga alone for a minute,' he says. 'Come and have a go at driving the tractor – I'll see you back.'

I wipe my hands then slip my wellies on outside the back door, Bracken trotting up and down the fence alternately whinnying at me and snorting at the tractor.

Guy holds the cabin door open.

'Hop in and adjust the seat.' He pinches my bum as I clamber up into the cab. 'Then turn the key. Don't worry – it can't go much faster than thirty unless it's running downhill.' He smiles as the engine growls into life.

'Okay, put it into gear.'

'Which one?' I shout.

'You need to go forward in the lowest gear, then reverse.' Guy slams the door shut, so we have to converse through the open window.

It's noisy and throbbing in the confined space and I find it difficult to concentrate. Going forward is fine. Reversing with the trailer isn't.

'Left hand down,' Guy yells. 'Too much. Right hand down! Stop! Straighten her up again.'

Soon we're both laughing at my incompetence, but eventually I have the trailer backed on to the vegetable patch and a stinking heap of manure standing in the middle. I move the tractor forward, stop it in the yard and turn off the engine.

'That was fun,' I say. 'What a lovely present.'

I open the door and slide out, falling into Guy's waiting arms. I'm not sure exactly how it happens, but his hands end up on the curve of my waist and we're standing so close I can feel his breath on my cheek.

'Jennie?' Guy murmurs.

'We're alone,' I whisper, and he leans towards me, his eyes half closed, his lips brushing against mine. I reach up and gather the material of his sweatshirt, so it tightens across his chest. Guy's hands slide around my back, pulling me close until my body is pressed against the length of his. I can hear my heart, his heart – I'm not sure which – pounding in my ears.

Guy deepens the kiss and I respond, quaking with excitement and anticipation. I am desirable and desired, and capable of desire again.

Then, suddenly, he steps away.

'What's wrong?' I stammer. Is it me, or him?

'Get your hands off my mother!'

It's Adam. He's standing a few feet away, dressed in his school uniform and holding his backpack with one hand as if he's about to drop it on the cobbles.

'Adam, what are you doing here?' I move towards him, but he flings his backpack over one shoulder and marches past, disappearing into the house. I turn to Guy who's turned a deep shade of puce. 'I'm sorry...'

Guy's lips curve into a rueful smile. 'You'd better go after him.'

'I'll catch up with you later,' I say, touching my cheeks.

Adam hasn't gone far. He's in the larder, rifling through the cake boxes. At least seeing Guy kissing me hasn't affected his appetite, I think.

'Adam, we need to talk.' I lean against the wall just outside. 'What's the problem here, love?'

'Don't call me "love", Mother. That's sick. Actually, everything about you's pretty sick at the moment.'

'Adam!' His words hurt me, even if they are said in the heat of the moment. 'There's no need to speak to me like that.' I take a deep breath. 'I realise you've had a hard time, love–'

'I said, stop calling me "love"!' he interrupts.

'I can't help it,' I say, holding out my arms. 'It's

because I love you.'

'Yeah,' he says, but he hangs back, peering at me through his tousled fringe that's grown rather long. 'You and Guy.'

'I thought you liked Guy.'

'I do. I said the problem was you and Guy together.'

'We're both adults. Neither of us is involved with anyone else, unless you know differently. I can't see anything wrong in it.'

'You wouldn't be sneaking him in here while we're at school if there was nothing wrong with it.' Adam emerges from the larder. 'Have you told Dad?'

'It's nothing to do with him any more. I have my own life. I can see who I like.' I watch Adam's face. He won't look at me at all now. Clearly, there is a problem.

'You're a mother – mothers don't do that kind of thing.'

'You mean, fall in love?'

'Are you in love with Guy?'

'No,' I cut in quickly, which I realise from the expression on Adam's face was the wrong thing to say. 'I'm talking in general terms now. I mean, to love someone ... to be with someone again.'

'You mean to have sex with them?'

'Well, yes...'

Adam is disgusted.

'It's perfectly natural. How do you think you got here, Adam? I'm not a Vestal Virgin.'

He shudders with embarrassment.

'I'm sorry if that offends you, but it's the way it is. I thought you'd be happy for me. Guy's a good man – he's been very kind to you.' I pause. 'Me and your dad – we'll never get back together. You have to accept that, otherwise you'll never be happy.'

'I have accepted it,' he says icily. 'Dad and Alice are getting married.'

'Married?' I reach out for a chair and sit down. 'Are you sure?'

'I wasn't supposed to say anything. Don't tell Dad, will you?'

'No, no. I won't.' I'm shocked. I don't mind. It's just that I didn't expect David to marry again. 'How do you feel about that, Adam?'

'I'm cool. Dad and Alice have been together for ages. You've only just met Guy.'

'I agree that it hasn't been terribly long.' I stand up again. 'For goodness' sake, I understand that it's hard for you to see me with someone who isn't your dad, but it's bound to happen one day.' I used to think, not so long ago, that it would never happen, but Guy's changed all that. I bite my lip, watching my son turn his eyes to the floor and put his hands to his ears, blocking me out. Adam has friends, new and old, supportive grandparents, a half-decent dad, a hard-working mum ... and a dog. So why is he so deeply unhappy?

'Adam,' I continue softly, 'if you want to talk, I'm here for you. If you'd rather talk to someone else, someone outside the family, then say so... There are counsellors, people who can help you.'

'I don't need to see anyone. I'm not mad.'

'I never said you were.' I pause, giving him time to speak, but he remains silent. 'Why aren't you at school?'

278

'I walked out,' he says eventually. 'I couldn't stand Mr Hughes going on at me.'

'What did he say to you?'

'He told me I was hopeless, in front of the whole class.'

'But why?' I exclaim, feeling hurt on Adam's behalf. 'How embarrassing. And unprofessional. Is this Mr Hughes one of the younger teachers?'

'He's old,' Adam says. 'He's a sad old git.'

'Sometimes you just have to get through it, Adam. Running away is never a good option.'

'Well, I'm not going to do maths any more and that's that.' Adam's voice is brittle now and there are tears in his eyes. 'I know how to do equations. I did them at my old school, but Mr Hughes doesn't like it because I don't do them the same way as he does.'

'I think I should go into school and have a word with Mr Hughes and your tutor. I'm sure we can sort this out.'

'It won't make any difference,' Adam says. 'He's a bully.'

'We can't just leave it,' I point out.

I check my watch – there's over an hour until I have to collect the girls.

'I'll phone school and let them know where you are. Shall we take the dog out after that?' I put this as less of a question and more a statement of intent. We are going to take the dog out.

If I was expecting Adam to open up to me a bit more, I was wrong.

We end up strolling beside the river in the early-afternoon sunshine. The leaves on the trees have turned brown and orange, and some have fallen and drifted across the meadow. Lucky runs up and down the riverbank, occasionally trotting down to paddle in the water for a drink.

'Your tutor sounds nice,' I begin. 'She was worried about you. I'm going in to have a chat with her tomorrow.'

I keep trying, but Adam hardly says a word.

'You know, you can walk all the way along this footpath to the coast,' I say, for the sake of filling the silence more than anything.

'Why on earth would anyone want to do that?' says Adam, his words a painful reminder of David and his scathing remarks about country life and country people.

I think for a moment. 'To relax. To enjoy the view.'

Adam groans. 'That's sooo boring.'

Inwardly, I agree that the idea of a ramble is pretty dull, especially when I compare it with that of a kiss and maybe more with Guy.

I'm not sure what to do. I don't want Adam to be unhappy, yet I don't see why I should be unhappy either. It might sound selfish, but although Adam was deeply upset at first, he did come round to accepting David's relationship with Alice, and I don't see why he shouldn't accept that I'm entitled to move on with my life too. Okay, I wasn't bothered before I met Guy, so the situation didn't arise, but now that it has, I want to feel that I have Adam's blessing.

I didn't think he would be quite so sensitive about it. He knows Guy.

I glance towards the river, and a lump catches in my throat. The water is dazzling. If we can't be happy here, I think, then there's no hope. We'll never be happy anywhere.

'You haven't been in touch for a while,' Summer says when I call her after dinner.

'You didn't try to ring me,' I say lightly, although I'm concerned about what's happening to my friendship with her. It's changing, a consequence of the move that I didn't anticipate. 'How are you?'

'Pretty good, thanks, but what's the goss?'

'I'm not sure where to begin. The pony threw Georgia off – she's broken her arm. Then Guy came round today with a trailer-load of muck for the garden as a gift.'

'What a present,' says Summer. 'How sweet.'

'Actually, it's a bit smelly.' I bounce up and down on the balls of my feet, clutching the phone tight. 'We kissed.'

'Wow. *We* kissed? That gives the impression that it was a mutual decision. So ... go on.'

'It isn't the first time...'

'Jennie, why didn't you tell me?'

'Because I wasn't sure that it was going anywhere.'

'But you are now. Certain, I mean? Wow. You're so lucky.'

'I know, but there are complications... Adam walked in on us. Summer, he was really angry and upset.'

'I don't know why that's such a surprise to you. Adam's jealous. A teenage boy living with his single mum? He's probably worried about losing you. He's been your protector, the man of the house, and now you're letting another man muscle

281

in on his territory.'

'I hadn't looked at it like that. I thought he was being – well, difficult.'

'He'll come round,' Summer says reassuringly.

'I hope so. I thought he'd be cool about it – he likes Guy. Looks up to him.'

'Jennie, your life reads like the pages of an Aga Saga. Thwarted romance, triumph over adversity, bitter conflict between mother and son, endless toil and drudgery over a hot stove.'

'You make it sound so dramatic.'

'It is though.' I can tell from the tone of Summer's voice that she's smiling. 'Are you going to visit us soon?' she goes on.

'Maybe at Christmas. It's difficult to get away. I can't leave the animals and the build-up to the festive season is going to be a busy time for me.' I've been planning ahead. 'I'm going to sell Christmas puds and cakes on the stall at the Farmers' Market. I think they'll go down well.' I hesitate. 'You can always come here for a holiday.'

'We might be able to find a weekend sometime,' she says, 'only it's hard to fit everything in when I'm working. I plan to catch up over the hols.'

'Oh,' I say, disappointed, and although I want her to be happy and fulfilled, I almost wish that I hadn't inspired her to follow her dream after all.

'Do you remember Clare?' she says. 'Used to go to Toddler Group with us.'

'Little Clare,' I say, dredging up memories of a time when I was part of a crowd of mums, all eager to outdo each other, showing off our perfect lives. I feel a twinge of regret. It was all a sham on my part. My marriage to David was never perfect.

'Anyway,' Summer goes on, 'she teaches the Year Twos at school. She invited me to her yoga class. It's great. In fact, she's picking me up in five.'

'Have fun,' I say, my heart shrinking with regret. For the first time I sense our friendship diminishing, and it makes me sad. 'I'll let you go.' Saying goodbye, I cut the call then find Adam who's sprawled out across the sofa in the drawing room, watching the television: endless repeats of *Top Gear* and *Friends*.

'I'm popping out for a minute,' I tell him.

'To see Guy?'

'To see Guy,' I confirm. 'I won't be more than half an hour, I promise.'

'A minute or half an hour? You aren't planning to stay over, I suppose?' Adam's voice is part annoyed, part teasing, and decidedly challenging.

'I shan't be staying.' I hold out my hands. 'Look, I'm not taking my toothbrush. Keep an eye on the girls for me.' They're both in bed asleep. I don't think they'll give him any trouble.

As I leave Lucky joins me, following at my heels, and I can't help wondering, although it's ridiculous, if Adam's sent him along to act as chaperone. I walk purposefully up the drive, shining my torch to avoid the worst of the mud, then I turn left into the farmyard and walk across to the farmhouse door. It's a modern brick-and-tile house, and feels as though its been built back to front. The rear door faces the yard, the front faces the lawn on the other side. I ring the bell and wait.

Eventually, a figure appears, silhouetted against the glass in the top of the door.

'Who's there?'

'It's me, Jennie.'

The door opens and Guy's face appears.

'You could have just come on in,' he says, smiling broadly.

'Um, I wanted a word ... about earlier.'

Guy opens the door wide. Lucky invites himself in. 'You'd better come in too,' Guy says.

'Thanks.' I walk inside, straight into the utility room, and follow Guy into the kitchen. It's kind of contemporary. The units are finished in light oak, the floor tiles are terracotta and the walls willow green. It's clean but untidy, a bachelor's pad. The breakfast bar is piled up with post, and everything that I imagine Guy uses on a regular basis is out: mugs, plates, saucepans, cereal boxes, keys and wallet. There's a pot of dead and drying herbs – basil, I think – on the windowsill. The blind is up.

'Would you like a drink?' Guy shows me to one of the stools at the breakfast bar, picking up a pile of laundry and dumping it on a worktop before I can sit down.

I fancy a large gin and tonic, but I doubt Guy has any, so I settle on a mug of tea.

'I can't stay long,' I say. 'The children.'

Guy nods as he fills the kettle and plugs it in. There's no Aga here.

Lucky sits at my feet, watching Guy's every move. It's spooky.

'I don't know what the forecast is for the next couple of weeks,' Guy says, 'only your apples will soon be ready for picking, if that's still all right with you?'

'Of course it's all right.' I refrain from adding,

You can have all my apples, and more... 'Are you sure you aren't leaving it too late? I mean, the harvest festival at school has been and gone.'

'Don't worry. You can leave some of the old cider varieties on the trees until November.' Guy slides a mug of tea across the breakfast bar, diverting it around the post.

I take a sip. It's too hot, unsurprisingly.

'Would you like more milk in that?'

'I'm all right, thanks.' Actually, I think, I'm not all right. That's why I'm here, but I leave so much unsaid, fool that I am.

'How is Adam?' Guy leans against the fridge freezer. 'He seemed quite distressed.'

'I don't know what to do with him. He walked out of a lesson ... maths with Mr Hughes.'

'He used to teach me over twenty years ago,' Guy says. 'I remember him as an impatient man, prepared to explain a concept only once. If you didn't get it, tough.'

'Maths used to be Adam's favourite subject.' I tug the collar of my fleece up tight under my chin and hold it there.

'It was never mine,' Guy smiles.

'Nor mine,' I say. 'Look, I'm sorry.'

'What for?'

'I'm sorry for what happened this afternoon... It was an awkward situation.'

'It's a little–' he pauses, searching for the right word '–frustrating.'

'Adam and the girls will be off to their dad's next weekend. Perhaps we could ... meet up properly then.'

'That sounds like a good plan.' Guy grins as I

stand up. 'How about a goodnight kiss?'

'Better not,' I say quietly. 'Adam's expecting me.' Not only that, I'm not sure that once we start I'll be able to stop.

I find myself thinking about Guy like I used to think about David when we first met. I keep having these delicious dreams, one in particular in which Guy sweeps me off my feet and carries me up to the bedroom. That's where the dream ends though, strictly in his arms at the bedroom door. I can't imagine anything beyond that at the moment. I daren't. I'm too – out of practice ... and my body isn't quite what it was ... and, if I'm honest, I'm still scared at the thought of that kind of commitment. Which is why, over the next few days, I enjoy taking it slowly, the snatched kisses and Guy's romantic gestures: a gift of a basket of field mushrooms left on the doorstep, and two large bulbs of garlic for splitting into cloves and planting in the vegetable plot. They might not sound like much, but they mean everything to me.

Chapter Sixteen

Rainbow Cake

The timer rings for the second batch of ginger-bread people. This evening, I've made whole communities of them for tomorrow's Farmers' Market, along with several treacle tarts and all the other favourites. I grab the oven glove, open the oven door and tug at the tray which somehow gets caught on the rack.

'Careful,' Guy says as I pull at the tray which suddenly flies out. In a reflex action I catch it with my other hand, the one without the glove.

'Ow!' I stutter as I let go, the gingerbread men slamming on to the floor, heads and limbs breaking off. 'Oh no...' As I stand up, surveying the scene of devastation, Guy takes hold of my arm, leads me to the sink, turns on the cold water and pushes my hand under the tap. He stands behind me, slightly to one side, and I'm aware of the warmth of his breath against my scalp.

'How stupid,' I say through gritted teeth, as the pain subsides to more of an ache. Embarrassed by my stupidity and determined to show that it was nothing, I attempt to pull my hand away from the jet of cold water, but Guy exerts more pressure on my wrist to keep it there, until he deems I've had enough and turns off the tap. Using a tea-towel, he pats my fingers dry and examines them closely, and I have to confess that I rather like standing here with him pressed up against me. With my eyes closed, the sensations of touch intensify, my heartbeat quickens ... but nothing can happen.

I feel like we're teenagers in my parents' house, except that I'm the parent here and I'm trying to avoid MY teenager.

I let out a sigh of frustration. I can't wait for tomorrow night: no children, just me and Guy and dinner at the Barnscote Hotel.

'You ought to get that checked,' he says, breaking the spell.

'I've had worse,' I say.

'I'd get a bandage on it at least.'

Moving away, I check the first-aid kit, finding two empty boxes of plasters.

'Why am I not surprised?' Guy grins. He fetches some from the dairy, wraps my fingers. 'No more baking for you today.'

'I have to get these finished. The Farmers' Market's tomorrow.'

'I'll do it, but you'll have to tell me what to do.'

'You'll find out all my commercial secrets,' I say, teasing. 'I wouldn't say no to some help though...'

Guy stays for a couple of hours, talking rather than baking, but I get most of what I planned done, the incident with the baking tray giving me the inspiration to decorate the gingerbread people with bandages and stethoscopes: doctors, nurses and patients.

The girls wander in and out to ask where their dad is, and by ten-thirty I suggest that they change into their pyjamas and clean their teeth, ready for bed. Fifteen minutes later, I tuck them in and kiss them goodnight, promising to wake them as soon as David arrives. Deciding that it's too difficult to time our journeys to meet halfway at the same time to hand over the children, we've opted to do one round trip each.

'Your mum's had her first industrial accident,' Guy tells Adam when he turns up trawling for food at about eleven o'clock. 'I said I'd give her a hand.'

'Yeah, but where's Dad got to?' Adam says. 'Has he rung you, because he hasn't contacted me?'

'Have you tried his mobile?'

'He isn't answering. I've left him a message.'

Adam drums his fingers against the worktop. 'What do you think's happened?'

'I shouldn't worry, love. He's probably caught in the weekend traffic.' I hesitate. 'Would you mind printing off some more labels? I seem to have run out.'

'Do I have to?'

I tip my head to one side.

'Okay,' he says with a small smile, and disappears into the lobby to wake the printer up, giving Guy the opportunity to give me the briefest hug.

'Tomorrow...' he murmurs, brushing his lips across my cheek.

'Tomorrow,' I echo.

I walk with him – at a respectable distance – through the lobby and into the hall where he puts his boots on.

''Bye, Jennie,' he says, his voice loud as he pulls me close and plants a kiss on my lips.

'Goodbye, Guy,' I say, trying not to giggle at our attempts at deception.

As I open the door for him, Adam turns up, brandishing a couple of sheets of labels.

'Is this enough?' he says.

'Yes, thanks,' I say brightly.

'You haven't looked to see how many there are,' he says.

'I only need a few. Thanks, Adam,' I add, taking them from him. 'You can come and stick them on, if you like.'

'No. I'm going to try Dad again.' Adam turns away and disappears up to his room with his laptop and phone, and I wonder if I should be more proactive about finding out exactly what he's up to on Facebook. I did get Hugo to set me up with an account before we moved here, but Adam soon de-friended me, and despite my requests to be his friend again, he's turned me down repeatedly.

Back in the kitchen, I wrap and stick labels on the cakes that need them, then finish clearing up. There's no sign of David, and I'm beginning to feel a twinge of unease. I try his mobile and his land line, but there's no response. Where the hell is he?

At midnight, I receive the call.

'David, where are you? The kids have been waiting for you all evening. Adam's been worried sick.'

'Yeah, I should have been in touch earlier, but I've been with my solicitor.'

'All evening?' He sounds to me as if he's been drinking, and then I remember that he's quite friendly with his solicitor, a friend of his from university. 'I don't see why you couldn't have picked up the phone.'

'Well, I'll make up for it. I'm going to apply for custody – I want the children to live with me and Alice full-time.'

'You what?' I can't believe what I'm hearing. 'You can't do that... Can you?'

'I've given you a fair crack of the whip, Jennie, and this arrangement isn't working – for me or the kids. I've talked to Ross and he doesn't see why we can't reverse the current agreement, which means–'

'I know exactly what that means,' I cut in, 'and

290

it isn't fair. They're just getting settled here. You can't uproot them again.' I burst into tears. 'You can't do this, David. I'm their mum... They need me.' I need them.

'They need some stability in their lives,' David says calmly. 'Alice and I can provide that.'

'You're both out at work all day.'

'There isn't a problem. Alice is cutting her hours – we don't need two full-time salaries.'

'You mean, you think she is going to look after my children? David, what utter–' I swear out loud.

'You don't need to give me all that "I'm the only person in the world who can look after them" crap,' he says, making my fingers tighten around the handset. 'Because you haven't been making a very good job of it recently.'

'And you think you and Alice can do better?'

'There's no need to do the derisive snort,' David interrupts. 'We've got acres of floor space in the flat, we're right in the centre of civilisation, and Adam can go back to his old school. It's a no-brainer.'

'You're the one with no brain. And no heart,' I say.

'Jennie, you can't blame me for this. You've brought it on yourself. You seem oblivious to the concept of a healthy diet – the kids are always eating cake.'

'That isn't true. They have lots of fruit and veg as well.'

'It might surprise you to know that they confide in me,' David says, 'so I know what goes on in your life. I know you leave them home alone while you run your business.'

'Adam's fourteen, nearly fifteen. He's perfectly capable of keeping an eye on Georgia and Sophie for an hour here and there.'

'Well, I don't like it – three kids alone in the middle of nowhere.'

'Guy's usually around,' I say.

'The oik – I'm glad you've mentioned him. Adam says he hangs around a lot, and he's caught you and him at it. I think it's disgusting.'

'We weren't "at it",' I snap.

'So Adam was wrong? There's nothing going on between you and your neighbour?'

'It's absolutely none of your business.' I pause for a second, running over the implications of admitting any kind of relationship with Guy. 'For your information, Guy and I are merely friends.' Okay, I'm lying, but I'll lie for England if it means I'll keep my children. 'I can't see any reason why a court would give you full custody of the children over me.'

'Apart from the fact that you won't let me see them, that you keep changing the dates and giving me the runaround...'

'That's happened once!'

'That you can't stop our son playing truant...'

'I've done my best. Since the problem with Mr Hughes, I've taken him to student welfare every morning...'

'And that you put Georgia in serious danger on that pony...'

'I wasn't to know...'

'Jennie, you're an unfit mother!' With those words, David might as well have taken a knife to my heart. 'I haven't decided to do this on a whim.

I've sounded the children out – in a roundabout way, of course, because I don't want them worrying about it. I think Adam and Sophie will be perfectly amenable. I'm not so sure about Georgia...'

'The three of them will be absolutely devastated. It'll be like going through the divorce all over again.'

'Well, the sooner it's over with, the better then. I thought I'd get the ball rolling...'

'If you're expecting me to tell them, like you did with the divorce, then don't.'

'I've already thought it through. When they're next with us–'

'This weekend, you mean? They're supposed to be with you *this weekend*.'

'The one after. Alice wants me to go along to some bridal exhibition with her. It isn't my scene, but when you're in love...'

'Oh, shut up,' I interject. I can't bear it.

'I was going to say that that is when I'm going to sit the children down and talk to them face to face. You and I can talk about it some more when you're in a better frame of mind. In the meantime, you'll be hearing from Ross.' David pauses. 'I hope we can resolve this quickly and amicably, without putting the kids through the trauma of the family courts.'

'I won't give them up without a fight,' I say stubbornly.

'I was afraid you were going to say that, Jennie. Why don't you sleep on it?'

'Because nothing will change my mind. I hate you, David. All you think about is yourself.'

'Don't we all – in the long run?' he says quietly.

It must be David who cuts the call. Afterwards I stand there with the handset still pressed to my ear. On the outside, a statue. Inside, quaking with emotion.

I don't know where to turn, who to call. I can't sleep. I can't function. If I wasn't an unfit mother before, I'm one now. I sit on the window-seat in my room, watching the dawn light leak from the horizon into the sky.

I touch my chest through my sweatshirt, vaguely surprised to find that my heart is still beating, hammering lightly against my fingertips.

How did I end up in this mess?

I call David in the vain hope that he's reconsidered.

'Jennie,' he says, picking up the phone. 'I hope you're not going to make a scene. I've made my decision. I'm doing what's right for our children.'

'What you think's right for them,' I say, my voice wavering. I promised myself I'd stay calm, rational, reasonable, but with each sharp intake of breath, I'm losing it further. 'David, you can't do this. You can't take them away from me...'

'I'm not taking them away. You'll still be able to spend time with them. Quality time,' he goes on. 'That's the term you use, isn't it? Quality time.'

I put the phone down as I start to cry, thinking how most of the time I spend with my children is quality time: when Sophie comes running to me with a basket full of eggs she's collected; when Georgia shows me the smiley face she's been given for her homework: when Adam yells at me that he's taking Lucky for a walk.

I want to call Mum, to have her tell me that everything will be all right, but I really don't want to worry her. I think I've put her through enough, moving away. There isn't any point in ringing Karen because she'll only make me feel even more depressed. I contact Summer instead.

'Do you realise what time it is?' she says, eventually answering her phone.

'I'm sorry, I've lost track.' For a millisecond, I think she's going to give me the brush-off, but she says, 'What's wrong? There must be something terribly wrong for you to ring at this time of day, Jennie.'

'I had to talk to someone – David's going for custody. He wants the children to live with him and Alice.'

'The bastard!' I'd thought we were drifting apart, but Summer is there for me. 'That's such a shock. Do the children know about this?'

'I'm not telling them. David says he's going to the next time they stay with him. I was supposed to be on the stall at the market today but I can't face it, and Guy asked me out for dinner with him tonight. I'll have to cancel that too.'

'Why?'

'Because I don't want to jeopardise my chance of keeping the children. If I go out with Guy one evening, half of Talyton will know about it by breakfast. That's what it's like living here. I don't want anything getting back to David.'

'Well, it won't, will it? He doesn't know anyone there.'

'The kids might find out and let it slip.'

'Jennie, I think you need to speak to a solicitor

yourself, so you know what you're up against,' Summer says.

'You're right.'

'If there's anything I can do, if you want to talk, any time, let me know,' she says. 'You are the fittest mother I've ever met, and don't let anyone tell you otherwise. Stay strong. I'll call you tomorrow to see how you are.'

Stay strong. Summer's words remain in my head after she's rung off. What am I doing? What better way is there to prove that I'm not an unfit mother than to carry on? Jennie's Cakes will be at the market today.

I wake Adam, then Georgia and Sophie, and tell them they're spending the weekend here at home, helping out at the Farmers' Market.

'Dad couldn't make it this weekend. Something came up.' I don't go into detail and they seem to accept that this has something to do with David's work.

Adam agrees to work on the stall for a percentage of the takings, but refuses, not surprisingly, to wear an apron.

'Aw, you'd look pretty in pink, Adam,' Georgia teases. Outnumbered by female Copelands, Adam soon drifts off to chat with a couple of other boys of his age, then returns to beg three gingerbread people.

'I'll tell them they have to advertise Jennie's Cakes in return,' he says.

'Go on then...' I'm not sure I need any more advertising. I've had another expression of interest in a wedding cake, a traditional one this time, the gingerbread people are flying off the stall and

296

we're soon down to our last flapjack. I've taken more money and fewer goods in kind: a small handmade cheese, a bag of sugar mice, a jar of honey and three bottles of beer that I thought I'd give to Guy.

On our return home, I throw on my coat and wellies, and take the bottles up to the farm. I take Lucky and the kids too, determined not to give David any more ammunition for his custody battle, because that is what it will turn out to be. I *am* a fit mother.

Adam jogs up the drive, kicking a stone in front of him. The girls hold my hand, Georgia one side, Sophie the other. There's a cow bellowing in the distance, an answering call from a calf. The clouds are driving in from the south-west, bringing mist and drizzle. Guy is in the holding area outside the parlour, ankle-deep in a slush of mud and muck. He has one of the cows in a heavy-duty metal crate – I used to think a crush was a brief but passionate liking for someone who was out of reach, but I know better now. It's a trap for a cow.

Guy looks up and smiles when he sees us.

'I won't be a minute,' he says, letting the cow out again. 'I'm treating her for mastitis.'

'That's Gabrielle – she has an udder infection,' Adam explains. 'Is she any better?'

'It's clearing up,' says Guy. 'How was the market? I saw you driving out earlier on.'

'Dad's working,' Georgia says. 'That's why we were helping Mum.'

'I see.' Guy gazes towards me. 'Oh?'

'I'll tell you later.' My heart twists with regret at the thought of what I have to tell him. 'I brought

297

you some beer.'

'Thank you. Why don't you leave it in the dairy and come and give me a hand with the calves? I've got to get them fed before milking.'

The far end of one of the outbuildings is penned off with hurdles and bedded with a deep layer of straw. Inside the pen, there's a group of red roan and white calves, five of them, with knobbly knees and switching tails. When they see us, they come over to lick our hands.

'They are cute,' I say.

'They're hungry,' says Guy. He makes up milk in buckets, pours them into a tank that has rubber teats attached along one side. The calves – all except one – latch on quickly, sucking and wagging their tails. Guy climbs into the pen and shows the last calf the teat. Eventually, it gets the idea and starts drinking.

'Where are their mums?' I ask.

'They stay with them for seven days.'

'Is that all?'

'I expect you heard a cow calling from the field – she's the smallest calf's mother. I separated them this morning.'

'That seems cruel when they're so young.'

'It's the way it is,' he says. 'On many farms, the calves are taken off their mothers after twenty-four hours. It has to be done. A cow has to have a calf before she'll produce milk. It's the natural way of things. When she's given birth, she rejoins the dairy herd for milking. As for the calves, I rear them on in small groups like this. The heifers – the girls – will go back into the herd or I'll sell them on. I'll rear the bull calves for beef.'

Poor cows. Their poor babies. I think of the pain of separation, the power of the maternal bond, and of course I think of David and how he's trying to take my children away from me... I stifle a sob, then another one escapes me.

'Jennie, are you all right?' Guy asks, his voice low and gruff. 'Have I said something to upset you? Because if I did, I didn't mean it. I do care for the cows. I don't enjoy separating them from their calves. I'm not a sadist.'

'It isn't you...'

'Adam, can you make sure they finish up? Georgia, can you help Sophie wash out the buckets? There's a tap outside the parlour.' I feel the weight of Guy's arm around my shoulders as he leads me away, outside through the rain to the shelter of the overhang outside the cows' winter quarters.

'What is it?' he says.

'It's David... Guy, he's going to take my children away from me! He's determined to get them back to London to live with him. I don't know what's changed. He didn't want them before – said they'd be a tie. He said they'd be better off with me, their mother.'

Guy comforts me, holding me gently, like Sophie holds the eggs, afraid they'll break.

'I haven't told the children. They're bound to guess something's wrong, but I don't want to tell them until I have to...' Tears are pouring, hot and wet, down my cheeks.

'I guess this means we should cool it for a bit,' he says.

I nod miserably.

'For now, Jennie,' he adds. 'I can wait, you know. I will wait for as long as it takes.'

'I don't know how long that will be,' I sob. 'I've got to find a solicitor, make my case...' And I've got to get Adam on side, because the way he feels at the moment, I think he'd be happy to go and live with his father. 'It all seems so difficult. Hopeless.'

'Nothing's impossible, Jennie,' Guy reassures me. 'As my mum used to say, it'll all come out in the wash. You and your family will be all right.'

'But what about us, Guy? Will we be all right?'

He presses his lips to the top of my head. 'I'll phone and cancel dinner tonight.'

'Postpone it,' I say. 'Cancel' sounds too final.

Lucky seems to sense how I feel. Whenever I put my feet up at the end of the day, slumping back on the wicker sofa in the drawing room with an extra sweater on because it's pretty chilly in here on these autumn evenings, Lucky comes trotting in, tail in the air.

'Not now, dog. I don't want you.'

Undeterred, he comes right up to the sofa, stands on his hindlegs and rests his front paws on the edge. He nudges my thigh with his nose, as if to say, Forgive me. Forgive me for barking, or chasing the chickens, or whatever other little sin he's dreamed up for the day, because there's always something.

'All right, Lucky,' I murmur. 'I forgive you.' And he jumps up, plants his bottom on my stomach, and tips his head back, asking me to scratch his chest.

I use the evenings to reflect on my life here at Uphill House. I've found that although I pride myself on being a successful multi-tasker, I'm not as good at time management as I thought. I've also discovered that running a business isn't all that easy when you have to tackle everyday life at the same time: the twice-daily school runs – because there's no one who lives out this way to share them with – three lots of homework, and looking after the animals.

Although David's decision to pursue custody of the children is always on my mind, thoughts of Guy are there too. I love him, I'm sure of that, and all I want is to be with him, but I can't jeopardise my position with the children. If David should find out that Guy is part of my life, he'll make the most of it, especially with Hugo's character reference.

There are bright spots. I'm still feeling chuffed at the note I received from Penny when she and Declan returned from their honeymoon. She said she was very glad that our dog had seen fit to steal the fruit cake because the cupcakes were un-believable, beyond her imagination, which I take as a huge compliment. It's either that or Penny isn't such a great artist as I thought. Declan's sister is organising her wedding for next April and would very much appreciate it if I could do something similar, but different, for her.

I haven't sent the pony back. Delphi said she would take it, but she wouldn't return more than half the purchase price, on the basis that she'd done nothing wrong and had sold the pony in good faith. I haven't tried selling it on either – I don't want to inflict it on another poor child. The outcome is that Bracken is still in the paddock – I've taken the electric fence down – keeping the grass trim. She isn't a mother's dream, she's a nightmare, and the most expensive lawnmower I've ever seen, but she's here now and I have to deal with it.

I'm beginning to see that I could be independent here, but I have doubts that I'll be able to stay. I really can't contemplate living here if my children are in London. I'd want to be close to them, would mean leaving Uphill House, and Guy, and the new life I've been creating for my family here in Talyton St George.

I don't know what will happen next. What I do know is that I'm going to keep strong for the children's sake, and make sure everything carries on in as normal a way as possible, whatever 'normal' is.

We celebrate Georgia's birthday the following weekend.

'Happy birthday!' Adam, Sophie and I bring her cards and presents into the drawing room where Georgia is waiting, dressed in jeans and a sweat-shirt with a pony on the front. Adam has just got home from the milking – he's taken off his boiler-suit, but he still stinks because he hasn't had time to jump in the bath. (I decided that it wasn't fair to make Georgia wait any longer.) Sophie is wearing a sequinned shrug and floral dress with pink tights.

'You have to go into the yard for your present from us,' she says excitedly. 'It isn't wrapped be-cause it's–'

'Shhh, Sophie, don't give it away,' Adam says, smiling. 'It's the weirdest present I've ever seen.'

'Can we go out there now?' Georgia says.

'Let's go,' I say, and follow the children around the back of the house and into the yard. In the middle, covered with balloons and ribbons, sits a bright pink wheelbarrow. I bought it from Overdown Farmers. You won't catch me in Tack 'n' Hack again.

'Oh, that's so cool.' Georgia runs across to inspect it. Sophie jumps up and down, as pleased as if it were hers. Adam picks it up by its pink handles and pushes it around the yard, driving it like a maniac.

'Adam, it's mine!' Georgia yells.

'That's enough,' I call, and he gives it one last shove and leaves it for Georgia.

'It's just what I wanted,' she sighs. 'Thanks, everyone.'

We go back inside and watch her open the rest of her cards and presents, then she decides that she's going to do some poo-picking in Bracken's paddock, to try out the wheelbarrow.

'You'll make it dirty,' Sophie says.

'I can always hose it,' Georgia says.

'What about your cast?' I say. 'I don't think it's such a good idea...'

'I'll cover it up,' she says, heading off to put on her wellies. Adam goes upstairs to run a bath, reminding me that I really must do something about having a shower installed.

'What are you going to do, Sophie?'

'Can I make the Pass the Parcel?'

'I didn't know we were having one.'

'We always have a Pass the Parcel.'

'All right then – you do that while I make the cake. I'm sure we can find some things to put in it.' I'm hoping I haven't left it too late to bake and ice Georgia's cake.

Rainbow cakes are another family tradition. When I'd suggested that I do something more sophisticated this time – I had my eye on some free advertising, with Georgia's new friend coming for tea – the birthday girl declined.

It's a modified Victoria sponge recipe, with butter, eggs from our hens who are now each laying one a day, caster sugar, self-raising flour, and a splash of milk to adjust the resulting mixture's consistency. I line two tins. Sometimes I make a single deep cake, sometimes two shallower ones which you can sandwich together with plain icing or chocolate butter cream. I opt for the sandwich version today – Georgia has a sweet tooth.

I divide the mixture into three, adding vanilla to the first, a splash of cochineal or the equivalent to the second and cocoa powder to the third, then stir the ingredients together, ending up with three colours: cream, a virulent pink, and brown. I drop spoonfuls of each colour into the lined tins then, using a fork, gently swirl the colours together, taking care not to overdo it, to avoid muddying the mix.

I contacted Maria earlier to see if she could run some colours through my hair when she cuts it later. I'm still seeing Guy, after all. I don't want him thinking I'm letting myself go.

When I've finished, Georgia's cake isn't subtle or professional in any way. Sophie helped me decorate it, and it looks decidedly homemade with its bright colours and collar of icing which has slipped down and spread across the cake board. The layer around the bottom is too thick, the layer on top too thin.

'Never mind, Mummy, it looks like a cheerful cake,' Sophie says. 'Can I do a wedding cake now?'

'I think you need a little more practice,' I say, smiling. 'Do you want to make the jelly while I whizz up some pizza?' I've got the dough proving beside the Aga.

'Okay,' she says brightly, and soon there's sticky jelly everywhere.

The kitchen looks like a bombsite when Maria arrives with her daughter, Camilla.

'Hi,' Maria says. 'How are you?'

I take to her instantly. She's a few years younger than me, slim with pale skin and strawberry-blonde hair. She wears a turquoise and cream tunic top with leggings, and Converse shoes with sequins on them, the real thing.

Camilla is well-built with a big smile to match. She wears her hair, which is the same colour as her mother's, in a neat French plait. She's dressed in jeans and a T-shirt.

'Camilla didn't dress up,' Maria says apologetically. 'Georgia texted her to tell her not to worry – they're planning to build a muck heap.'

'I think she's already started,' I say, looking out of the kitchen window. In one corner of the paddock, there's a sizeable pile of muck and Georgia's standing on the top, rearranging it with a shovel. 'I'd better let her know you're here.'

We all go outside, and Georgia joins us.

'Happy birthday,' Camilla says, handing over a present

'Thank you,' says Georgia, opening it. 'Oh, that's great.' It's a horsey stationery set, and a book entitled *Ponies Behaving Badly*. 'I'll be able to write to Granny, and train Bracken to be good.'

'Is that your pony?' Maria points towards Bracken who's grazing on the far side of the paddock.

'That's Bracken,' Georgia says adoringly, as if she's talking about the love of her life, which I suppose she is.

'She's a nice-looking pony, but rather fat,' Maria says. 'You should bring her into the stable every day, so she can have a rest from all that grass.'

I put her bossy manner down to the fact that she's a Pony Club mum. Georgia told me that, hoping, I think, I'd see my way to becoming one too.

'I hear she's been rather naughty, though, tipping you off and breaking your arm like that, Georgia.' Maria looks at me, but I remain silent. I can't say how I really feel about that creature with its untamed mane and beady bug-eyes, not in front of Georgia, and certainly not on her birthday.

I do talk about her later, when the girls are eating cake – Adam's taken himself off – and Maria's finishing my colours.

'I'm sorry I messed you around, asking for colours on a Saturday,' I say.

'Oh, I don't mind. I need all the custom I can get. It's my hairdressing income that pays for the ponies.'

'How many have you got?'

'Three – there's Camilla's old pony, her current one and my horse.'

'And I thought I had trouble with one!'

'I wouldn't be without them.' Maria folds and sticks the last paper into my hair. 'I can help Georgia with Bracken when she's got that cast off.'

'I'm not sure,' I say.

'I like a challenge. Jennie, I'd be careful. I wouldn't put Camilla on any mount I thought was dangerous.'

'It was–' I'm breaking out into a cold sweat even talking about it '–really scary.'

'Georgia said she napped then bolted.'

'I don't know the technical terms, but we couldn't do a thing with her. I don't understand – Delphi said she was a good pony.' I try to recall the description she used. 'Forward going.'

'Ah, that's a euphemism for "pulls like a train and has no brakes".' Maria smiles. 'She'll probably turn out okay. Ponies are often a bit silly at first when they move homes.' She changes the subject. 'Seeing the cake there, Georgia says that you run your own bakery business. I wondered if I could order a cake for Camilla's birthday. It's in three weeks' time.'

While we're waiting for my colours to develop, I show Maria my leaflets and portfolio, taking her through to the lobby to be out of earshot of the girls.

'I do a "Princess" range,' I say, 'but maybe Camilla's too old for that now. Perhaps she'd

307

prefer something with a pony theme.'

'A pink pony would be perfect,' Maria says, and the deal is done. An order for a cake in part exchange for a cut and colour.

Maria rinses the papers from my hair, under the handheld shower attachment in the bath. Standing up, I wrap a towel around my head and we go back downstairs to the kitchen. I sit on one of the chairs and Maria picks her scissors and comb out of her bag.

'How do you want it?' she asks. 'Do you want a trim or a restyle?'

'Oh, I'd like a cut that makes me look ten years younger,' I say lightly.

'Wouldn't we all? How about having an inch or so off all round, and some layers put in to give you some more body?'

I agree to her suggestion, and Maria's soon tweaking and snipping at unnerving speed.

'Do you see much of Guy?' she asks suddenly.

'I did see him every day, walking up and down with the cows, but they're indoors now for the winter.' I turn away, to hide the blush that I can feel spreading up my neck. 'Do you know him then?'

'We used to go to Young Farmers together.' Although I can't see Maria's face, I know that she's smiling. 'We used to have such a laugh.'

'Guy seems quite serious to me.'

'He's taken a few knocks. He and his father had some kind of power struggle going on, then his wife ran off with his brother, and now his mum's ill. I went out with Oliver for short time – we all did. Oliver played the field, whereas Guy had one girlfriend before Tasha, and that was it.' Maria pauses, scissors hovering. 'I met my husband at Young Farmers. Neil's an agricultural engineer – he leases and repairs tractors and combines, that kind of thing.' She tugs my hair over my cheeks, checking the length. 'I think that's about the right length.' She plugs her hairdryer into the nearest socket, switches it on and continues talking while she blasts my hair.

By the time she's finished, I feel that I know everything about her and she knows almost everything about me, apart from Guy's and my secret passion.

Later, when Camilla and Maria have gone home, Georgia is sitting in the kitchen, reading her book.

'You know, Mum,' she says, looking up, 'I reckon Bracken's been mistreated in the past. She's had a bad experience and it's put her off being ridden. I don't think she was being nasty. This book says that ponies don't think like that.'

'If you say so, darling.'

'It says that most problems can be solved if you go back to basics. Bracken isn't a bad pony.'

I'm beginning to mellow towards her. She whinnies now whenever I go outside, and she'll stand at the fence to have her head rubbed. Maybe I'll let Maria do some work with her sometime.

'By the way, I like your hair, Mum.'

'Thanks.'

'In some lights it looks palomino and in others it looks chestnut.'

'Right ... I wasn't intending it to come out looking like a horse.'

'I wasn't saying you look like a horse,' Georgia says, smiling as she turns to the next page in her book. 'Do you think you'd better get Maria to colour your eyebrows next time?'

'Why would I want to do that?'

'Because your eyebrows don't match your hair any more.'

I chuckle to myself. You would have thought some of my lying ways would have rubbed off on my kids, wouldn't you? Yet they're always so frank.

'Mum,' Georgia says, her expression serious, 'you know all this about Daddy wanting us to go and live with him?'

My heart sinks. The girls know about the situation – David has talked to them at length via Adam's webcam, against my wishes because I thought it would be far kinder for him to have spoken to them in person. I was hoping that it wasn't worrying them too much.

'Yes?'

'I'm not going back to London.'

'Georgia, darling.' I kneel down beside her and slide my hands around her waist.

'I'm not going because of Bracken. I've told Daddy.'

'And what did he say?' I ask tentatively.

'He said I'd be able to see her every other weekend when I come and stay with you.' Eyes glittering, she bites at her lip then utters a wail of grief that tears me apart. 'I don't want to live with Alice! I want to live with *you*, Mummy.'

'Oh, Georgia...' I hold her tight, rubbing her back and tangling my fingers through her hair, like I used to when she was a baby. 'We'll work something out. Me and Daddy, we want you to be happy.' I close my eyes, suppressing a sob. We just have different ideas about how to go about it.

'Got anything to eat, Mum?' Adam interrupts, coming into the kitchen. He takes a chocolate brownie off the rack where they're cooling and bites into it.

'Hey, hands off!' I'm going to serve them up with ice cream and chocolate sauce. 'They're for later.'

'What's wrong with my little sister?' Adam walks up and gives her a playful pinch, entirely inappropriate, considering how upset she is, but it does have the effect of distracting her.

'Leave her alone, please,' I say. 'She's having a moment.'

'You girls are always having your moments,' Adam says scathingly.

'It's better to let it all out sometimes,' I say, gazing at him, 'to share your worries, not bottle them up inside.' Sadly, I muse as he walks away, I don't think I'm getting through to him. I bite my lip. I'm not sure if I ever will.

Chapter Seventeen

Cherry and Walnut Cake

I've been so involved with Jennie's Cakes and seeing the solicitor, a rather droll old man, Mr Tarbarrels, who has an office in Talyton, that I haven't done much about the way Adam is distancing himself even further from the family. He hates his new school. I've suggested he invites his classmates home for tea, but he's disdainful of his peers, who belong to Talyton Young Farmers and get their kicks from seeing who can throw their wellies the furthest.

Today, the last Friday before the October half term, his pastoral leader has been in touch to ask why Adam wasn't in school, something which is just as much of a surprise to me as to her because I dropped him off a short walk from the school gates this morning.

'We're worried about his attendance, Mrs Copeland. Since you last came in to see his tutor, he's had two more days' unauthorised absence and he's appeared at student welfare with various ailments clearly linked to his lessons with Mr Hughes.'

I'm worried too, and deeply disappointed and concerned for Adam's safety, because if he isn't at school, where is he? 'Where is he?' I ask.

'We were hoping you might be able to tell us,' the pastoral leader says.

'I'm sorry, but I haven't a clue, unless...' I suppose he might have gone to see the cows, but I'm sure Guy would have been in touch then to let me know he wasn't at school. It crosses my mind too that he might have decided to take off back to London to see David, or Josh. Or – I try not to think about it – he might have gone for a long walk with a few cans of lager or a bottle of spirits, to drown his sorrows.

'We appreciate it can be difficult for some pupils to adjust to a new school in a different area of the

312

country, but the law requires that your son receives an education. And, of course, we're concerned for his welfare.'

'I'll let you know as soon as he turns up.'

'Wouldn't it be better if you went out and looked for him? Just a thought.' She hangs up. I dial Adam's mobile. It's switched off. Beginning to panic, I try Guy's.

'Hi, Jennie,' he says quietly. 'What's cooking?'

Under normal circumstances I would have found that funny, but I'm worried about my son. 'Have you seen Adam today?'

'I haven't. I thought he was supposed to be at school.'

'I dropped him off, but he didn't make it into class.' I try to control the wobble in my voice, but it's too late. Guy picks up on it.

'I shouldn't worry, Jennie. Who hasn't bunked off school now and again? Why don't you phone around some of his friends?'

'Because, as far as I'm aware, he hasn't got any. What if he's gone off drinking on his own again? What if he's fallen over somewhere? What if he's lying unconscious in a ditch?'

'Do you want me to come over and help you find him? He's probably down by the river or up in the woods on East Hill. That's where I used to hang out when I was Adam's age.'

'I'll go down there myself,' I say. 'I'll take Lucky with me.'

'Let me know if I can be of assistance.'

'Thanks, Guy.' I appreciate his offer – I know he's busy on the farm. However, Adam is my son, my responsibility. And David's. I call him at work to ask him if he's heard from Adam.

'I haven't. Why?' he says, as I talk and check out the stables and the barn at the same time.

'He's skipped school again,' I say, trying to catch my breath.

'This can't go on. The sooner he joins me and Alice, the better.'

'So you say, but I've got to find him first.'

'Let me know as soon as he shows up.'

Half an hour later, by which time I'm distraught and running with sweat, I find him walking casually along the lane back towards Uphill House, hands in his pockets, listening to his iPod.

'Adam, where have you been?' I scream at him.

'Out,' he says, ducking down briefly to give Lucky a pat.

'Well, I kind of guessed that,' I snap.

'Why ask then, Mother?'

I don't like his tone, but my fury at his thoughtless behaviour is tempered with relief and I don't comment. I think it's far more difficult for a boy than a girl, living with a single mum and not being sure where he's going to end up in the future. I move up close to him, trying to work out if he's been drinking, but I can't smell alcohol on his breath and he seems perfectly co-ordinated. I contemplate asking him to walk in a straight line, but decide against winding him up any further. I take a deep breath and count to ten, telling myself to keep calm.

'Who were you with?' I say.

'Just some people.' He shrugs.

'Friends?' I ask hopefully, because he hasn't mentioned any before.

'Random people,' he confirms. He likes the word 'random'.

'And?'

'And?'

'What were you doing?'

'Hanging and stuff.'

Hanging, I can cope with, it's the 'stuff' I'm worried about.

'Adam, you can't keep missing school,' I say, my anger returning in response to his reticence. 'And I can't help you if you won't talk to me.'

'You can't help anyway,' he flashes back. 'You can't rewind my life so I can start where I left off, back with my real friends.'

'You still keep in touch with Josh and you see him every other weekend...'

'It isn't the same.' Adam stamps his foot. 'Even if we get to go and live with Dad, nothing will be the same any more.' He turns and storms off back the way he came, Lucky running along at his heels.

'Adam, stop,' I shout after him. 'Come back home! Now!'

He hesitates and looks scornfully over his shoulder. 'That isn't my home! It never will be.'

'Adam! Please...' I beg, but he won't listen.

'Leave me alone!'

I watch him striding away and my heart aches for him. He's so mixed up and out of control. I don't know what to do.

'I'll talk to him again,' David says when I call him a third time, the second to say I've found Adam and lost him again, the third to say that he's slipped back indoors, taking Lucky upstairs to his room, then returned to the kitchen ready for tea. 'Shall I have a word now?'

'I should leave it until he's in a more receptive frame of mind,' I suggest. 'Let him have something to eat first.'

I overhear Adam talking on the phone to his father later. He sounds calm and reasonable, and I'm envious. To Adam, David's the good guy, the perfect parent, the opportunity to escape from living here in Devon. I wish he'd talk to me like that.

'Why did you have to go and tell Dad?' Adam says to me once he's put the phone down. 'You didn't have to bother him.'

'We're worried about you...'

Adam swears. 'Mother, I'm fourteen! You don't have to worry about me any more.'

'All right,' I say, but he's my son, so I do.

It's five in the morning the next day when I hear Adam trip and swear softly on the landing. I refrain from calling out to him to mind his language – there's no way the girls will be awake yet. The swearing is followed by a crash from downstairs, more cursing, then the opening and closing of the fridge door followed by a slam.

I can't believe he is still managing to get up to milk the cows. I encourage it, because I think it's the only thing that stops him collapsing into a heap of misery.

Lucky whines at my feet. He must have sneaked into my room when Adam got up.

'Shhh,' I mutter, and pull the duvet up around my ears to muffle the first crow of the cockerel, heralding dawn. If it wasn't for the fact we're hoping for chicks one day, I'd wring his neck. Actually,

I wouldn't be able to do it myself. I'd have to ask Guy, but I don't see him as often as before. He isn't always walking up and down the drive with the cows because they're all off the fields and indoors now. I can understand how Guy feels. We're in limbo. Our future is uncertain, and he's right, I can't concentrate on anything much, apart from the children and the fact I might lose them...

And now I can't get back to sleep, my mind filled with recipes and timetables for fulfilling orders and the next Farmers' Market.

I stretch, yawn and close my eyes, and must have gone back to sleep because Georgia is suddenly in my room, running across to the window to pull the curtains open, letting in a bright shaft of sunlight which hurts the back of my eyes.

'Mum, Mum,' she says, urgently tugging at my duvet. 'There's something wrong with Bracken. Quickly! You've got to come down.'

I get up – it's chilly – and throw a baggy sweater over my pyjamas, run my fingers through my hair and head downstairs where I slip into my wellies and dog-walking coat and follow Georgia to the paddock.

Outside, there are cobwebs in the trees and hedges, glistening like necklaces of beads. There are spiders all around us, but my fear of them is soon overtaken by fears for the pony. Bracken is beside the gate, and I know there's something wrong because she hasn't got her head down eating. She's dark with sweat and standing with her front feet stretched out in front of her, as if she's praying.

I feel sick. There have been many times when

317

I've wished her dead, after what she did to Georgia, but she doesn't deserve this.

'I'll go and speak to Guy,' I say, happy to have an excuse to speak to him, at least. 'He knows a bit about horses.'

'Mum, forget Guy, we need to ring the vet.' Georgia's expression is a mixture of anguish and exasperation. 'I think it's an emergency, don't you?'

'Yes, darling. You're right.' I go inside and call Otter House Vets in town who say they don't do horses and give me the number for Talyton Manor instead. A woman answers there. She sounds very well-spoken, and stern.

'Where's the pony kept?' she asks.

'At home, Jennie's Folly,' I say, having grown used to the new name.

'I know it, but I'm afraid it will always be Uphill House to me,' she says. 'What is wrong with the pony?'

'I don't know. That's why I'm ringing. I need a vet to tell me.' I hand the phone to Georgia who seems to have a better grip of the situation than I have.

'She's in pain,' she says. 'I've looked in my *Manual of Horsemanship* and I think it's laminitis.' Georgia hands the phone back to me. 'The vet's coming out as soon as he can.'

'Georgia, what's laminitis?' I ask her anxiously.

'It's inflammation of the feet,' she says, 'and it's really, really serious.'

'Do you think we should move her into the stable?' I feel as if we should do something.

'Oh, no, we mustn't move her at all.' Georgia

318

fetches Bracken's head collar and puts it on without a struggle. I make a cup of tea for myself and hot chocolate for the girls when Sophie joins us, but Georgia doesn't want anything. Her face pale and pinched with worry, she decides that Bracken's ears are cold and that she needs a blanket, and fetches the duvet off her own bed. I don't say anything. Why do I have a horrible feeling this is my fault?

Half an hour is a long time to watch an animal in pain. The pony groans and rolls her eyes whenever she tries to shift her weight. For a while she stands trembling, with sweat dripping from her belly. Poor Bracken. I could cry for her, but I'm trying to be strong for the girls.

'Is it tummy-ache?' asks Sophie.

'I'm not sure,' says Georgia, frowning. 'It could be colic...'

'It's no use asking me,' I say gently. 'I haven't a clue.'

'Is that the vet?' Georgia says suddenly. 'I can hear a car.'

'I'll go and open the yard gate,' I say, but Sophie's ahead of me.

The vet is lovely, a handsome man in his late thirties, I'd guess, charming and confident and with a great pony-side manner. I feel that I could bear bad news better if someone like him was delivering it.

'Hi, I'm Alex,' he says, draping a stethoscope around his neck with one hand and carrying a black case in the other. 'Who does this pony belong to then?'

'Me,' says Georgia.

'And what can you tell me about–' he takes a quick look at Bracken from a distance '–her?' He listens to Georgia while he examines Bracken and takes her temperature.

Sophie looks at me when he puts the thermometer under her tail.

'Shhh!' I mouth at her. Don't say a word.

'Is it what I think it is?' Georgia asks him.

'It is, I'm afraid,' Alex says quietly, and I can tell from the tone of his voice that this isn't good news. 'Your pony's in a bad way. She has very sore feet. Georgia, will you hold on to her for a minute while I fetch some drugs from my car?' He looks at me and I read into his gaze that I should go with him so he can talk out of earshot of the girls. I feel as if I'm pushing through mud that's up to my neck.

'Is she going to make it?' I ask him when we're around the side of the house.

He turns to me. 'I have to be honest with you. I'd say her chances are about fifty–fifty.'

'Oh, no...'

There's a lump forming in my throat as he continues, 'We have three options. One: I refer her straight to the nearest equine hospital where she'll have access to the best care available.' He pauses, letting the facts sink into my head.

'Is that going to be terribly expensive?' I say, feeling terrible that I'm putting money before Bracken's health.

'I take it she isn't insured for vet's fees?'

I nod miserably. Another thing I didn't get round to.

'Okay, options two and three then,' he goes on.

'Option two is to get her into a stable here on a really deep bed of shavings. I'll bring the X-ray machine up and get some pictures of those feet. In some cases of laminitis, the hoof starts to separate from the rest of the foot, allowing the bone to sink. Worst-case scenario, the bone actually penetrates the sole of the foot and the outlook is very poor. If things look reasonable for this pony, then we get her on to painkillers, other drugs and corrective farriery here. You can nurse her. If things look grim, then we go ahead and put her to sleep, to save her any further suffering.'

And Georgia will be utterly devastated, I think. I wrap my arms around myself to stop my hands from shaking. She loves that pony, and even if I could afford another one, which I can't, it would never be the same.

'It'll be a long haul,' Alex says, 'and she may or may not come sound at the end of it, so I'll understand if you want to go straight for option three, euthanasia.'

'You mean, shoot her?'

'We do it by injection now.'

'I really don't know what to do,' I admit, then, playing for time, I ask how he thinks Bracken got it.

'These little fat ponies are prone to laminitis. Looking at her, I'd guess she had free access to good grazing all summer which made her border-line, and now the autumn flush of grass has tipped her over the edge.'

So it *is* my fault. I didn't listen to Guy or Maria. I thought I knew best.

'I'll give her a shot of painkiller while you're

321

deciding,' Alex says, and although he's being terribly nice, I feel as if I'm being judged.

'I'd like you to go ahead and do the X-rays,' I decide. 'That way, we'll know where we stand.'

'I'll give her a couple of shots now then, and come back in about an hour.'

Georgia looks at me questioningly when I return to the paddock gate.

'Alex is bringing a couple of injections for Bracken now, and we're going to put her in the stable until he comes back to X-ray her feet.' I don't go into any more detail. That can wait.

Alex returns within an hour with a load of equipment in the back of his 4x4.

'How's she doing, Georgia?' he says, looking over the stable door.

She rubs Bracken's neck. 'She seems to be more comfortable. She hasn't moved though.'

'Let's get a closer look at these feet, shall we?' Alex enlists Georgia's assistance with setting up the machine for the X-rays, using an extension cable to reach an electrical socket inside the house, and sending her out of the way of the radiation when he takes the pictures, which he downloads on to a laptop computer. Then he explains what he can see to me and the girls. It isn't good, but as we stand in the doorway of Bracken's stable with Alex holding the laptop away from the glare of the light outside, I discover that condemning an animal to certain death isn't as straightforward as it first appeared. Bracken isn't just a pony any more. She's part of my family.

According to Alex, the bones in Bracken's feet are showing early signs of rotation, and there's still a chance of saving her, so instead of going with my gut instinct to have her put down to save her further agony, I find myself letting him continue to treat her with more drugs, and special supports taped to the soles of her feet.

'Have you got any hay?' he asks. 'She needs a low-sugar, high-fibre diet, ideally some meadow hay that's been soaked for twenty minutes or so to get the sugar out before you feed it. She can't go back on the grass for a while.'

'I haven't...'

'Guy's probably got some – you could ask him,' Alex says. 'If you're really stuck, give me a call and I'll see if I can find you a couple of bales to tide you over.'

'Thank you.' My head is spinning. All these instructions. A recipe for looking after a sick pony. Weigh out the hay four times a day. Fresh water. Plenty of fresh air – that isn't a problem, the stable is well-ventilated, with holes in the wall under the eaves.

'She'll need lots of TLC as well,' Alex goes on. 'Oh, by the way, you have got a passport for her?'

'I'm not planning on taking her abroad or anything,' I say, bemused, before I remember that Delphi gave me one with her. 'Actually, I remember now. I have got one somewhere in the house.'

'I'll have a look at it next time I'm here. If you're concerned about anything at all, call me. Otherwise, I'll drop by on my way home tonight.'

More money, I think, my heart sinking further. Why on earth didn't I insure her?

Shortly after Alex leaves for the second time, I'm getting the cremated remains of a cherry and walnut cake out of the Aga when Guy drops by with Adam. That's one of the difficulties I have with the Aga – it's impossible to smell when something's burning unless you stand outside downwind of the flue.

'Did I see the vet's car?' Guy says, joining me in the kitchen as I'm throwing the burned offering in the bin.

'Bracken's sick.'

'Laminitis?' I nod as Guy goes on, 'I could see it coming ... too much grass and no exercise.'

'Yes,' I say, ashamed and embarrassed. Why didn't I listen to him? I feel so guilty. I can still see the pain in Bracken's eyes. 'Um, you don't happen to have some hay I could buy from you? She's got to stay in the stable.'

'How many bales do you want?'

'I don't know.'

'I'll bring you five to begin with.'

'Thanks.'

He's back within ten minutes – with Adam riding next to him in the cab, the bales on the back of the trailer that he tows, rattling down the drive. Guy makes handling the bales look very easy, but when I have a sneaky go at lifting one, it's a struggle to get it even a few inches off the ground. He stacks them in the stable next to Bracken's, standing them on a pallet he collects from the barn and making sure that they don't come into contact with the walls.

'How much do I owe you?' I ask.

'Oh, don't worry about that. We'll settle up when we've picked the apples,' Guy says. 'I'm going to get old Bill – he works on one of the farms round here – to give me a hand tomorrow. Anyone else who wants to help out is welcome. We'll make the cider next weekend when the apples have had time to mature.'

'I love this smell,' I say, picking at the hay and holding it to my nose.

'This is good stuff, this year's crop. Meadow hay, which is more suitable for a pony like Bracken than seed hay,' he says with pride. 'Making hay is like working to a recipe. You have to do it right. Too dry and the goodness goes out of it. Too damp and you get a load of mould. And you have to have the right ingredients in the first place – the right kind of grass, fertiliser, rain and sunshine.'

'I didn't realise there was so much to it.'

'Sometimes I wonder if you realise much about anything,' Guy comments dryly.

'What do you mean by that?' I respond, hurt by his cutting remark. 'I didn't intend for the pony to suffer.'

'I'm not sure that's any excuse,' he says. 'After all you said about animal welfare when we first met, about how it was cruel to hit the cows...'

My face grows hot with annoyance, not so much at him as at myself. I don't need Guy, or anyone else, to remind me of the part I played in neglecting to attend to Bracken's weight. I knew she was overweight, but I didn't understand the significance of that. I assumed she was like us; that she might develop heart disease or sore joints later on in life. I didn't believe she was in immediate danger.

'I'm sorry, Jennie,' Guy goes on, as if he's read my mind. 'How are you?' Stepping back into the shadows of the stable, he lowers his voice. 'I miss you.'

'I miss you too,' I say softly, moving closer. His eyes glint with desire and my heart twists with longing for what cannot be, for the moment at least.

'Is there any chance...?' he says, his voice breaking. Then he shakes his head, as if remonstrating with himself. 'I shouldn't have asked.'

I turn away abruptly and head back outside into the light where Adam's still waiting in the tractor. Guy follows.

'I'll leave you to it then.' Guy wipes his palms on his jeans, leaving grubby streaks. 'Are you helping out with the milking tomorrow, Adam?' he calls up to him.

'I thought I'd join you this afternoon as well.'

'No, Adam,' I say. 'You've got some catching up to do with your schoolwork.'

'But, Mum,' he moans.

'You can't bunk off school without there being some consequence. Catch up with your maths today and you can help with the milking in the morning.' I give him a scowl too, to show that I mean it. I don't like it, but I've realised that I have to be firmer with Adam and give him clear boundaries. Although it's tough on both of us, it's for his own good.

Alex is with us three more times over the weekend. Bracken isn't responding to the treatment and the bill is soaring. I don't know what to do. The pony is still unwilling to move about in her stable in spite of the painkillers, and Georgia refuses to leave her side, insisting on snoozing whilst sitting in a sleeping bag on an unopened bale of shavings.

I take a hot chocolate out to her on the Sunday evening and sit with her.

'Georgia, we need to talk,' I begin. I don't need to say any more. She turns her face to me, her eyes glinting in the half light, her mouth set in a stubborn line.

'There's no way I'm letting you have Bracken put down,' she says sharply.

'Georgia, darling–'

'Mum, it's our fault that she's sick, which means it's up to us to help her get better.'

'I don't like to see her suffer.'

'Neither do I.' Georgia tips the hot chocolate out into the shavings, as if it's poison, and thrusts the mug back into my hands. 'Now go away,' she says, getting up and moving over to Bracken, wrapping her arms around her neck and burying her face in her mane. 'I don't want to talk to you. And before you start going on at me, I am not going to school tomorrow.'

'You don't have to,' I say curtly. 'It's half term.' I retreat, eyes stinging and sore, because I can't see a way out. I can't see how I can afford any more treatment for Bracken. I'm not earning enough from the baking to pay the solicitor and pay out on a loan to cover the vet's fees. Whatever I decide, either Georgia will never forgive me or my family will end up in penury.

The following morning, a deputation consisting of Georgia and Sophie arrives in my bedroom at six-thirty. I don't know if they're aiming to exploit any possible weakness on my part caused by lack of sleep. Sophie is in her pyjamas while Georgia is in the same top and jeans as she was yesterday.

Rubbing my eyes, I sit up in bed. Outside a chicken is squawking and clucking as if she's trying to lay a football, not an egg.

'How's Bracken?' I ask.

'That's why we've come to see you, Mummy,' Sophie says.

'To tell you,' Georgia continues for her, 'that if you kill Bracken, we'll never get over it, and we'll go and live with Dad and Alice for the rest of our lives.'

'Or until we go to university,' Sophie corrects her big sister.

'I don't want to kill Bracken,' I say, 'but it's going to cost a couple of thousand pounds to treat her, and even then there's no guarantee that you'll be able to ride her again. Alex says her feet might never recover.'

'I know that, but I don't care if I can't ride her,' Georgia says. 'It's better than her being dead.' She adds great emphasis on the word 'dead', as if to punish me all the more.

'The problem is that I haven't got that kind of money going spare.'

'We have decided that we will pay the vet,' Georgia announces.

'How are you going to do that?'

'We'll get a job, like Adam.'

'I'm afraid you aren't quite old enough for that,' I say gently, a lump in my throat.

'We'll bake cakes then,' Georgia says, her voice rising with doubt. 'We'll hold a cake sale at school to raise the money.'

'That's really sweet of you both.' I pause, reluctant to disillusion them because to pay this vet's bill, we aren't talking about a few flapjacks and fairycakes. We're looking at several bespoke wedding cakes, at least. And there's the solicitor's bill as well.

I gaze at my two daughters, standing hand in hand at the end of the bed, looking back at me expectantly. I can't do it to them, can I? It's clear that they'll do anything for Bracken, just as I'm prepared to do anything for them. It occurs to me that I might ask David for half the money, or talk to the vet about paying in instalments, but pride won't let me. 'All right, let's have no more talk of putting Bracken down. We'll find the money somehow.' Like Mr Micawber in *David Copperfield*, I shall have faith that 'something will turn up'.

I bake two more cherry and walnut cakes for the apple picking.

Guy has already collected a trailer-load of apples from Fifi's orchard at the garden centre that he delivers to Uphill Farm before coming with his tractor and trailer to collect ours.

'How's the pony?' he says, parking the tractor in the paddock and jogging back to have a look over Bracken's stable door. I hang back, letting Georgia answer that question.

She and Sophie stay with Bracken. Alex drops by twice to check on her, pronouncing her condition to be stable. Guy, Adam and old Bill, an elderly man with a complexion much like the skin of a shrivelled russet, do the bulk of the picking. I keep to myself, checking that the windfalls aren't rotten, because then they can't be used for the cider, and picking the apples on the lower branches of the trees, while Guy and old Bill go up and down tall ladders, picking from the higher ones, the tops of which are over thirty feet from the ground.

Adam works from a stepladder. I thought he would get bored, but he picks all morning and into the afternoon. By then, the apple pickers and Bracken's nurses have gone through both cherry and walnut cakes, along with a dozen scones with jam and cream.

Whenever I see Guy, I'm aware of his shy smiles and yearning glances. I know we're staying 'just friends' for good reason, but I wish it didn't have to be this way.

Chapter Eighteen

Feather Cake

It's the last week of October. The few remaining apples have been blown off the trees in the orchard and the ground is turning to a sludgy orange mud that cakes everything: boots, shoes and Lucky's feet. The children are supposed to be going to David's for the weekend, but according to him there's a problem.

'I understand that the children aren't keen to visit this weekend,' he says.

I keep walking, talking to him on my mobile.

I'm down by the river with Lucky.

'There's a lot going on here at the moment,' I say.

'Yes, I realise that. Georgia refuses to leave Bracken and Adam's torn because he wants to help Guy make cider and watch the tar-barrel procession. Sophie says she doesn't want to come either because she's been invited to a Hallowe'en party, along with her whole class at school.'

'I'm sorry they aren't keen,' I say, 'but I've told them they have to spend the weekend with you.' David and I have a legal agreement over access but I can't reorganise the children's social lives. Sometimes I feel like piggy-in-the-middle.

'I've been thinking – if they're really desperate to want to do all these other things, then I'm happy for them to miss this weekend. It's a one-off though. And soon they'll be living full-time with me and Alice anyway, so I think it's only fair.'

'David, that's very good of you,' I say, pleased by this concession of his. 'They'll miss you, of course, but maybe you and Alice would like to come down for the day, if you want to see them?'

'Alice has planned to choose her dress this weekend – she'd rather hoped that the girls would help her.'

'Oh, I wondered when you were going to get around to the subject of your impending nuptials.'

'I didn't want you to think I was rubbing your nose in it.'

'In what, exactly?'

'Well, I've heard that things haven't worked out between you and the oik.'

'For goodness' sake, David...'

331

'Adam keeps me up to speed,' he cuts in. 'Anyway, if you wouldn't mind letting the kids know? I'd better get on – I've managed to get a booking at a rather exclusive little restaurant and I don't want to miss it. I'll let you know if Alice and I should decide to join you on Sunday.'

To my relief, they decide against paying us a visit, and on the Saturday morning I'm in the kitchen, enjoying the warmth of the Aga while looking out of the window at the pale sky and the frost that adorns the grass. I whizz up some feather cake as an excuse to remain where I am, and borrow Adam's laptop so I can continue Googling for that special signature recipe for Jennie's Cakes because I haven't found it yet and not for want of choice. I dismiss the exotic combination of courgette and lime, after Guy's opinion on the chocolate and beetroot. Everyone loves chocolate fudge cake, but you can buy it anywhere. It isn't exactly unique.

I give up looking when the feather cake's ready to ice. I've made double quantities of light, buttery sponge in shallow brownie tins, then turned them out on to a rack. I ice them with pure white icing sprinkled with desiccated coconut. I'll cut them into squares when the icing's set, I think before cutting myself a corner – to test, you understand. It's one of my favourites, ultra-sweet.

In fact, this morning, it goes a long way to putting me in a cheerful mood.

There's a knocking at the window at the front. It's Adam in his beanie hat. I gesture to him to come round the back, but he keeps knocking.

'What do you want?'

He mouths something back, but I can't tell what he's saying, so I have to open the window, letting the chill air inside.

'You should have come round the back,' I say lightly.

'We're about to get started on the apples. You've never seen so many,' he says, his cheeks flushed. 'Aren't you coming, Mum?'

'I don't think so...' I feel awkward. We might have fooled Adam with our 'just friends' routine, but I can't fool myself. I am not and never can remain just friends with Guy. It's one of the hardest things I've ever done.

'You have to,' Adam says. 'Guy says we need all hands on deck.'

'Oh, all right.' I have to admit, I'm curious. 'Have you got your coats, everyone?' Adam's in clean overalls – he must have changed – and looks to be verging on the obese with the number of layers he's wearing underneath. I turn to the girls. Sophie's in her pink padded jacket with her ear muffs on, and Georgia's in jeans and a jumper.

'Aren't you coming too?' I ask her.

'I'm going to stay here,' she says. 'Bracken's due a haynet in half an hour.'

'I'm sure you could pop back.'

'I haven't mucked out yet.' Georgia smiles. 'I don't need to know how to make cider. I'm not going to be a farmer. I'm going to be a vet like Alex.'

'Well, shout if you need us,' I say. 'A vet, did you say? That'll save on the bills.'

Cider-making is a messy business, I discover. Guy has one end of his modern outbuildings set

333

aside for the process so I was expecting up-to-date equipment, but when we go inside, there's a mix of old and new. It's also absolutely freezing.

'Hi, Jennie.' He greets me with one of his slow smiles, and my heart twists with pain because nothing's changed. I still feel the same way about him. I still get that melting sensation in my chest and weakening of the knees when I see him.

'Jennie, did you hear me?' he asks. 'I said, what do you think?'

'I really don't know,' I say with a sigh. Then, realising he's talking about the cider, 'It's all a bit primitive,' I go on, looking at the mountain of apples lying on a scattering of straw.

'What did you expect? Stainless-steel vats?' Guy grins. 'We do it the traditional way at Uphill Farm – it's what gives our scrumpy its unique flavour. That's why it's the best in the West.' He pauses. 'Unfortunately as you can see, I've had to replace some of the old wooden barrels with food-grade plastic tanks. I've also had to replace the old "scratcher", that crushes the apples before you can put them through the press, with a rather expensive new crusher.' He turns to Adam. 'Shall we make a start? So, what did we decide?'

'Sophie is on loading the apples into the buckets, Mum on feeding the hopper on the crusher, you on the press and me supervising.' Adam's grinning.

'You mean, you on the press and me supervising,' Guy chuckles, swipes Adam's hat and pulls it over his own head. 'I'm the gaffer. Let's go.'

It's hard labour and Sophie soon decides she's so bored she has to go back to the house to see

Georgia, which means that I have to load the apples into buckets and take them to the crusher. I drop them, bucket-load after bucket-load, into the hopper while Adam turns the hand wheel. The blades cut the apples into small pieces that are then crushed by the rollers, the pulp falling into a bigger bucket underneath. Within half an hour, sweat is dripping from Adam's brow and he's stripped down to a T-shirt.

'Shall I take a turn?' I ask.

'I'll do it,' he says, grimacing, and I smile to myself when I notice him glancing at his rippling arm muscles.

'Are you all right there?' Guy asks. He's been fiddling with the press, but now he walks over and stands right beside me, looking at the results of our work. 'That's great. Keep going. No, stop for a minute. I'll show you how the press works.' He takes the bucket of pulp and carries it over to the Heath Robinson contraption nearby. 'This is a rack and cloth press, the original from Uphill – I mean, Jennie's Folly. I've modified it as we've gone along. What you have to do is tip the pommy – that's another name for the pulp, pomace or pommy – on to this piece of sacking here.'

Guy tips a layer of pulp on to the hessian which lies across a square wooden frame raised above a plastic trough, then he folds the hessian over the pulp. 'Then you take another sheet of hessian, like so,' he says, 'and put that on top, pour on more pulp, and keep on layering it up until the frame's filled up.' He looks at me, eyes flashing with humour. 'This'll take me a while, so you can keep on with the crushing.'

Eventually, Guy shows us how to rack the press down on to the layers of hessian and pommy, and how the juice trickles out into the plastic trough.

'What happens next?' I ask.

'The pressed pommy's fed to the cows. The juice goes into a barrel to ferment for several weeks, then I'll put the bungs in and leave it to mature for a few months.'

'I'm impressed,' I say. 'Don't you have to add yeast, like you do with bread?'

'No, there are wild yeasts on the apple skins. That's why we don't wash the apples first.'

I don't know about the cider, but Guy's proximity has put me in a ferment. Tiny bubbles of desire expand and pop inside my belly, subside for a while, then bubble up again. I try to suppress them.

'Are you all right, Jennie?' The sound of his voice brings me back to the present. 'Would you like a break?'

'Not yet. Although there is freshly baked feather cake...' I look up at him across a bucket of pommy and our eyes connect. I feel myself swaying. Guy catches my arm.

'I'm feeling a bit wobbly,' I say.

'It's cold working out here. Let's go inside and warm up—'

'Your place or mine?' I mumble, not so faint that I can't joke about it.

'Yours, of course.'

I link my arm through his, and we walk back to the house. I'm acutely aware that Adam is staring at us, a frown on his face.

'Your mother and I are friends, Adam,' Guy

336

calls back. 'Did you hear that?'

'Loud and clear,' Adam says, walking with us. 'So long as there's no snogging.'

'Absolutely not,' Guy says firmly and, although he's doing the right thing, I wish his tone didn't sound so resolute.

We sit chatting over coffee and cake, Adam wandering off to watch some television briefly before we go back to continue crushing and pressing.

'Are you still looking for your special cake?' Guy says, flicking through the notes I've made during the past few weeks.

'Yes, I can't quite find what I want. I need something unusual but not too far out.'

'You mean, no beetroot.'

I smile. 'No beetroot. No courgette. No, I've been through all the versions of chocolate cake that I can find, because most people like chocolate, but none of them are right. I'd like something with a local connection, if possible.'

'How about a cider cake?' Guy says. 'My mother used to make it – with our cider, of course.'

'Now, that sounds promising.'

'I'm pretty sure the recipe's in one of her files back at the farmhouse – I stuck them on top of the units when I realised she wasn't coming back. I'll dig them out for you.'

'Do you think she'd mind me using it?'

'She won't know,' Guy says gruffly.

'I think she should,' I say. 'If I use it, I'd like to acknowledge her input. I don't mind asking her.'

'I'll ask her, of course, but she won't know what I'm talking about. She won't remember that she used to bake the best cider cake in the county.

She doesn't even remember who I am.'

'I'm so sorry.' I fight my instinct to give him a hug.

'The other day, she called me Oliver,' he goes on quietly. 'She thinks that I'm my brother, and the irony is that he never visits. She hasn't seen him in over a year.'

'That must be very...' I try to find the right word.

Guy finds it for me. 'Painful,' he says. 'It's like being kicked in the teeth.'

We sit in silence for a while.

'More cake or coffee?' I ask him eventually.

'You don't have to ask,' he says, sounding more cheerful, and I push the plate with the last piece towards him. 'What about Adam?'

'He's had four already. He doesn't need any more.' I get up and put the empty plate on the worktop. 'I can hardly keep up with him, the amount he eats.'

'It must be pretty tough, looking after three kids on your own,' Guy says. 'I don't know how you do it.'

'It can be, but I wouldn't be without them. I won't be without them.' I swallow past the constriction in my throat. 'I'll fight David all the way. I'll never give up.' I dab a tear from the corner of my eye. My skin stings. 'My children are the most important people in my life. I love them so much.'

'Sometimes I feel like I've missed out,' Guy goes on thoughtfully.

'It isn't too late for you,' I say. 'I told you before, men are lucky. They can father children until they're in their seventies.'

'You're right. Never say never, and all that.'

'The chances are that when you meet someone special, she'll be younger than you and perfectly able to have your children.'

A fresh silence falls between us.

I rest my elbows on the table, my hands clasped in front of me as I try to interpret what Guy's saying. Is he confirming, in a roundabout way, that he's given up on waiting for me because he's still hoping to have children one day? An irrational sensation of grief grips my heart at the thought that my biological clock is running down, and – yes, I'm jumping way ahead here – I'm too old to commit to Guy even if that's what we both want because that would mean denying him his desire to become a dad.

He slides his chair back and stands up. I make to stand up too.

'You stay there, Jennie. Come out later when you're feeling better – you're looking pale.'

'And interesting?'

'That goes without saying. I'll find that recipe for you – it probably won't be until Monday because it's going to be a long day, and tonight's the tar barrels.'

'Are you going then?' I ask.

'As the elder son of one of Talyton's long-standing landowners, I have the honour of being a barrel roller.'

'Really?' Adam's mentioned before that the residents of Talyton St George set wooden barrels, lined with coal tar, straw and paper, alight, and run around town with them. 'Isn't it dangerous?'

'That's the thrill of it.' Guy grins. 'Thanks for the cake.'

I help out with the cider-making for a couple more hours, and by the evening I'm feeling much better, which is lucky because there's no way Adam is going to miss the tar barrels, an annual Talytonian tradition.

'Guy says you have to walk into town,' Adam says when we're getting ready. 'You can't park anywhere near it – people travel for miles to see this. We'll have to hurry up though. They light the bonfire on the Green at six.'

Once we've fought our way through the busy streets, to the edge of Market Square, we find ourselves standing in a crowd three people deep. In the glow of a streetlight, our breath condenses like puffs of smoke. I rearrange my scarf around my neck and pull my hat down around my ears. It's colder than ever. Although Devon, part of a peninsula that's warmed by the Gulf Stream, is supposed to have something approaching a sub-tropical climate, it's been unusually cool for this time of year, and the long-term forecast is for little change.

'I can't see anything, Mummy,' Sophie says, tugging at my coat.

'I can't either,' says Georgia.

'Same here,' grumbles Adam.

'We'll have to make sure we all stick together,' I say. 'If I lose any of you, I don't think I'll ever find you again.'

Sophie's gloved hand slips into mine and gives it a squeeze.

I begin to wish we hadn't come, but it soon livens up, and I have to say that I can't believe what I'm seeing. A flood of people burst out of one

340

of the side roads, filling the centre of the square, shouting and cheering. I can smell burning tar, beer and burgers. In the middle of them, if I stand on tiptoe, I can just make out smoke and flickering orange flames, apparently emerging from a man's back. As the crowd shifts around, forcing us back, I realise that the man – a young one – is carrying a flaming tar barrel on his shoulders.

'Guy said he was a barrel roller,' I say, nudging Adam. 'Does he have to carry one of those?'

'Oh, yes,' says Adam. 'They started off rolling the barrels, then someone thought it would be more fun to carry them. They've been doing it for years.'

I'm not sure I can bear to watch.

'When does Guy carry his barrel?'

'At ten o'clock,' Adam says.

'That's ages away,' says Georgia.

'I know. Let's go down to the river and watch the bonfire for a while. We might be able to get something to eat.'

Under a clear night sky, we stand on the Green, eating burgers and watching fireworks, hissing rockets taking off in sequence then exploding with loud bangs, spreading showers of spangling stars that slowly fall and fade out across the sky: a metaphor perhaps for my relationship with Guy.

We return to the square later, struggling back through the crowds, and ending up in a better position to see the next barrel.

'This feels like Christmas shopping in Oxford Street,' I observe, 'exciting but stressful, and not an experience to repeat in a hurry.'

'There's Guy!' shouts Adam as another flood of

people swirls into the square. He's bowed under the weight of the burning barrel, which I can see, as he moves nearer to us, is padded with hessian.

'Guy!' I call out, and he glances in our direction and grimaces. I can see the sinews in his neck as he strains to support the barrel. He's covered in soot and sweat, and I see holes in his top from the falling embers as he passes close by.

I'd hoped to catch up with him afterwards, perhaps to stroll back towards Jennie's Folly with him, but we lose sight of him pretty quickly.

'He'll be going for a drink at the pub,' says Adam, as if he's reading my mind.

'Have you seen anyone you know?' I ask.

'I think I saw Will and Jack from school.'

'I saw one of my friends,' says Sophie. 'She was on her daddy's shoulders. I wish my daddy was here. I miss him sooo much.'

'You could have gone to stay with him this weekend, but you said you preferred to go to the party.'

'I said I couldn't decide, and you made me choose the party.'

'I did nothing of the sort,' I argue, but Sophie is tired and overwrought.

'You did, Mummy,' she whines back, 'and I don't think that was fair on poor Daddy because now he isn't going to see me until next week.'

'It is a shame, but that's what we decided. That's what you said you wanted, Sophie,' I say, feeling unappreciated – something I've had to learn to accept as a single parent. 'Let's go home.'

When we get back, there's no sign of Lucky. Adam finds him under his bed, quivering with fear.

'He's been sick.'

'That's all we need. What's wrong with him?'

'I think he must be scared of fireworks.'

'Great.' I clear it up, then retire to bed. I can't sleep... Lucky can't settle, wandering up and down the corridor outside the bedrooms, whining every now and again. Adam's mobile rings in the middle of the night – I recognise his ringtone – and then there are voices from the drive. I slide out of bed, wrapped in my duvet, and stand to one side of my window – I don't often bother to draw the curtains any more – and peer outside. I can make out four figures: two male, two female. One of them is Guy and he has his arm around one of the females. I think they're laughing. Envy and sadness well up in me. I sink down on to the window-seat and sit there for a long time. Who is she? What did I expect, that Guy was some kind of monk? Why does it matter?

'Where are you going?' I ask Adam when I catch him going out before dawn the following morning.

'I said I'd help Guy with the milking.' Adam's eating what looks like a piece of flapjack for breakfast. 'Do you have a problem with that?'

'Not really ... I'm not sure he'll be up yet though.'

'He's never late for the cows. He says the ladies don't like to be kept waiting.'

'I think he might have company.'

Adam raises one eyebrow. 'And?'

'He might not appreciate you turning up.'

Adam pulls his mobile out of the pocket of his jeans and presses a couple of buttons, then shows me the screen. 'Message from Guy received fifteen minutes ago. He was afraid I was going to over-sleep.'

'All right,' I say, itching to ask him to find out who Guy's friends are. 'I'll see you later.'

After milking, Guy turns up at the kitchen window, waving a file of some kind – I notice with regret that he doesn't let himself in any more, unless he's with Adam.

I beckon him to join me and he turns up in the kitchen, looking none the worse after the night before. He's wearing a shirt with the sleeves rolled up, a gilet and chinos, and bears the familiar, aphrodisiac scent of aftershave and cow, with extra notes of burned oak.

'I brought you this. I thought you'd be interested. The recipe for cider cake's in there, but there are lots of others.' He hands me a faded yellow ring-binder. 'Open it.'

I place it on the kitchen table.

'I don't know why but it seems like prying,' I say, opening it to the first page.

'I think Mum would be pleased that someone was using them.'

Uphill Cider Cake. It's handwritten neatly in italic print. The ingredients listed include cider, nutmeg and apple brandy, and there are detailed instructions for baking it.

'What do you think?' he asks.

'It looks like just what I've been searching for – I hope I can do it justice.'

'I'm sure you can.'

'Thanks, Guy.' I pause. 'I hope you haven't had to leave your friends so you can come here.'

344

His brow furrows.

'The people you had with you last night... I heard you rolling home last night, barrel roller.'

'Did we wake you? I'm sorry.'

'I couldn't sleep. Too much excitement, I expect.'

'I hope you enjoyed it – it's one of the highlights of the year here.'

'You'd better get back,' I say, 'to your friends.' I can hear my voice trail off. I'm making a mess of this, aren't I?

'You mean Ruthie and Co? I left them to sort themselves out. They had pretty sore heads this morning, but then they always do after the tar barrels.'

'What about you?'

'I had a couple of pints afterwards, nothing before. Alcohol and flaming barrels don't mix. I'm pretty careful.'

'You're mad,' I say gently.

He looks at me quizzically.

'Jennie, can you tell me what's going on here?' He lowers his voice. 'Between you and me? Forgive me, but I think we need to clear the air.'

I take a deep breath, then let it out slowly as he goes on, 'I'm getting mixed signals. It might be me, of course, reading things wrong. I know we agreed to cool it for a while, but I didn't mean for you to freeze me out completely.'

'Is that how it feels?'

'I understand that you're worried about the children being taken away from you to live with their dad, but–'

'How can you possibly understand when you

345

haven't got any children?' I interrupt. 'I'm sorry,' I say quickly, catching the shadow of regret that darkens his eyes. 'I don't think you should wait for me. Go out and find someone your own age.'

'But I don't want anyone else,' he says, frowning. 'And you aren't that much older than me.'

I close the file on the table, leave my hand on top of it, and watch as Guy places his hand on mine, inter-linking our fingers. His skin is rough, his nails dark with grime, but I don't care. I love everything about him.

I want him, all of him, but I can't have him because I have to put my family first and sacrifice this chance of happiness. I try to console myself with the thought that, if I let him go, Guy will be free to find someone else, someone younger who can give him kids of his own. He's great with children. He'll make a fantastic dad. If I let him go... I'm not sure that I can.

Chapter Nineteen

Uphill Cider Cake

I invite Guy, along with the children after school, to the cake-tasting a couple of days later. It took me that long to source the apple brandy that the recipe calls for – I found it eventually in a tiny farm shop on the way into Talymouth.

'Here it is,' I say, placing the cake on a plate on the table. 'Uphill Cider Cake.'

'It looks a bit plain, Mummy,' says Sophie. 'Aren't you going to decorate it if it's going to be your special cake?'

It's true – it does look rather nondescript, a round cake with a golden-brown crust on the outside, which gives it a rustic appearance.

'I wondered about dusting it with icing sugar, or brown sugar maybe, but I decided to leave it as it is and serve it with either clotted cream, or a small portion of apple, or both,' I explain.

'Mother used to dish it up with clotted cream,' Guy says.

'It's lucky I've got some then.' I smile, aware of the way he keeps giving me meaningful glances, as if he'd like to eat me up, and my spirits soar. I take a knife and cut through the cake, removing a substantial slice. The texture is perfect: moist but light. I cut four more slices, while Adam takes the cream from the fridge and the stewed apple from the larder.

'Shouldn't we have two pieces each?' Georgia says.

'Three, if we're to try every permutation,' says Guy.

'Four, if you include trying it on its own,' says Adam.

'You can come back for more,' I say. 'There's another one in the oven.'

'That was rather premature – what if we don't like it?' says Adam.

'I'll give it to the chickens.' I hand out plates, forks and spoons, and pass the apple and cream around the table. 'Okay, everyone, what do you think of it?'

'Would you like us to give you a full report, or is "Mmm, that's scrummy" enough?' Adam says, when he's halfway through his first slice.

'It's great, Jennie.' Guy looks at me, his expression tinged with sadness. 'Just the way Mum made it. It takes me right back...'

Georgia and Sophie enjoy it too. It is delicious and distinctive, sweet and spicy, with nutmeg and an underlying hint of apple.

'What do you think?' I ask. 'Shall we vote?'

The outcome is unanimous – Uphill Cider Cake becomes the signature product for Jennie's Cakes, and I make plans to sell it at the next Farmers' Market, and see if I can persuade any of the local outlets, including the farm shop, to stock it.

Later, when I'm sitting in front of the fire in the drawing room, working out a fair price for a cider cake, I rest my notebook and pen on the floor, sit back and take stock. I've not had the bill from the solicitor yet, and I've still got that vet's bill to pay, but Alex has offered me terms, monthly payments over the next six months, and it wasn't money wasted because Bracken is getting better.

I've certainly done my penance, caring for her while she convalesces. She's getting really grumpy now, desperate to escape the confines of her stable and get out to the paddock. Alex has told us to buy her a weigh tape so we can monitor her progress, and suggested that I lead her out for ten minutes twice a day for a mouthful of grass.

'Lead her out on the bridle,' he said, 'and be careful. She'll be a bit silly to begin with.'

Silly? She went berserk. I couldn't hold her. Luckily, the gate to the paddock was shut so she made a beeline for the lawn instead. It took me an hour to catch her, tempting her with a bowl of pony nuts, and then when I returned her to the stable, she trod on my toe, which was particularly painful as the farrier had been up to put special shoes on her: one hundred pounds' worth.

I told Georgia, '*I* don't pay that for shoes any more.'

'It is for two pairs, Mum,' she said, trying to justify the cost. 'She needs them if Maria's going to start training her. Alex says we should be able to start riding her again, and if she stays sound I'll be able to take her to Pony Club.' Georgia's eyes gleamed with anticipation.

I hope she isn't going to be disappointed because if the custody goes David's way, I've made up my mind not to stay here, and I can't take a pony back to London with me.

I gradually find myself looking forward to doing my bit towards looking after Bracken though. It's like an oasis in my day, tying up her haynet in the stable when Georgia's at school, giving her a rub or a brush. I even find myself talking to her, sharing my innermost thoughts about ex-husbands and family law, and how long it's fair to make Guy wait, just as I do with Lucky.

I make a second appointment to see the solicitor in Talyton for the following Friday. In the meantime, the kids have an inset or teacher-training day which means the Thursday off school, so I'm standing at the paddock gate, my heart in my mouth, watching Maria giving Georgia a leg up on to the pony. It's the first time Georgia's ridden

349

her since Bracken threw her off. Maria's ridden her twice and she hasn't done anything naughty – yet.

Maria steps away, holding on to the lunge line that's attached to Bracken's head collar.

'Walk on,' she says, flicking the end of a long whip towards the pony's heels. 'This is when she's most likely to throw a buck, Georgia, so remember to breathe. You can sing, if that helps you to relax.' Bracken walks a full circle. 'Whoaaa!' Bracken stops. Georgia's face lights up.

'Good girl,' she says, stroking the pony's neck.

'I can't believe it,' I call out.

'It's early days, but we're getting there.' Maria turns to me, smiling. 'We'll get her on the other rein and then we'll ask her for a trot.' She looks past me. 'Hello, Guy.'

'Hi, Maria.' Guy walks up beside me and leans on the gate. He's wearing his waxed coat with the collar turned up. It has an odd scent to it that reminds me of the mothballs my grandmother used to use. 'Are you okay?' he asks me.

'I'm bearing up.'

'I hope you don't mind, but I've had a word with Fifi about wassailing the trees in your orchard. She says she'll be in touch about the arrangements.' Guy grins as he takes in my look of total bemusement. 'You haven't a clue what I'm going on about, have you, Jennie?'

'Indeed, I haven't.'

'Wassailing is one of Talyton St George's many traditions.'

'Yet another excuse for a party and a few beers,' I cut in, with a half smile. 'Guy, I'm not sure I'm

350

really in the mood for a party.'

'I'm sorry. I thought you might like to have something to keep you occupied while the children are at their father's at the weekend... I'll tell Fifi you're indisposed.'

'And then she'll want to know why,' I say wryly. 'All right then, what's it all about?'

'It's done to increase the yield of the apple trees next year.' Guy's teasing me, I can tell. 'Fifi reinstated the tradition about fifteen years ago, for a bit of fun and to "promote community cohesiveness" as she calls it. The first time, we had the poorest harvest ever. Everyone said it was because it was the wrong time of year – Fifi chose a date in November rather than January – so our wassail didn't clash with anyone else's. As a VIP, she gets invited to them all.'

'Do I have to do anything?' I ask, assuming it's best to find out what I'm letting myself in for.

'I said I'd bring some cider and you'd bake a few of your cakes in return.'

'That was rather presumptuous of you,' I point out lightly. 'Don't get me wrong, I love baking, but occasionally I'd like to do something different in my spare time.'

'I can ask the WI,' he says anxiously.

'Don't be silly. Of course I'll do it.'

'Everyone meets at the tethering stone with torches and lanterns, then Fifi leads the procession from orchard to orchard, where the local folk sing, and pour cider on to the roots of the trees, and set off fireworks. We used to use shotguns, but they've been banned.' Guy grimaces. 'Health and safety. I'll see you later.' He hesitates.

'Can I hear a phone?'

'My mobile. I've left it in the kitchen.' Thanking him, I hasten indoors and pick my phone up from the windowsill. It's David calling me.

'I can't have the children this weekend.' His voice has an odd echo on my mobile.

'What did you say?' I tap the handset as if that's going to improve the signal and alter what he's said.

'I can't have the children.'

My heart sinks, like the cherries in my latest cake to the bottom of the sponge. There was something wrong with the mix.

'David, you have to have the children. They've missed seeing you, it's your weekend, and you have to explain to them what's going on.'

'You've changed your tune,' he says coolly. 'Only a week ago, you didn't want me to have anything to do with them.'

'Oh, do grow up. I'm being serious here.'

'I thought you'd be pleased. But then some people are never happy, are they?'

I ignore his comment. I'm perfectly happy, or could be if I weren't continually worrying about his application for custody.

'One minute you want them with you full-time, the next you don't want them at all,' I say with rancour. 'I shall be using this in court.'

'Um ... it won't be coming to court,' David says. 'I've changed my mind.'

'You've what?' My heart jumps with hope.

'I've changed my mind about going for custody,' he repeats, and a wave of relief washes through me.

'Why ... when you couldn't live without them ... when I was supposed to be an unfit mother? You've put me through hell over this, and then you turn round and say "I've changed my mind"?'

'Something's happened,' he says, in the manner of a condemned man. 'Alice is pregnant.'

'Oh?' I'm not sure how to react to the news. 'This wasn't what I was expecting at all.'

'Neither were we, to be honest,' David admits, 'but we're both very happy.'

He doesn't sound very happy, I muse. David's vision of a carefree, post-baby lifestyle has been replaced by the return of sleepless nights and dirty nappies. The only travelling he'll be doing with his nubile young girlfriend in the near future will be along the Purley Way to Mothercare and back.

'Congratulations, David. I'm very pleased.' Pleased that the custody suit is over, that he has to undergo the trials of early fatherhood yet again, and pleased that I can envisage him and Alice with a baby with equanimity.

'I thought you might be – upset.'

'After all this time? Of course not.'

'Well, I can't expect her to look after our three as well as one of her own. She's struggling to cope with the pregnancy as it is.'

'Oh? And I thought Alice was so capable.' I can't help saying it. She's turning out to be a bit of a drip, reliant on David to look after every-thing, whereas I – well, I'm Superwoman. All in all, this is the best news I've had for ages, and I can't wait to tell Georgia and Sophie. I'm not sure how Adam will take it though. My first impulse is to share it with Guy, but he's gone when I get back outside.

'Your dad called me today,' I tell the children when we're having a late lunch at the table in the kitchen. It's the only room in the house which is really warm. 'He's–' I hesitate. David is the one who should be explaining this, not me. I'm not sure how to put it without making it sound as if he's just decided that he can't be bothered and doesn't want to be a hands-on dad after all. 'You know that he's been talking about you going to live with him during the week?' I begin. 'He's suggesting now that we keep things as they are.'

'Hurray!' says Georgia, clapping her hands together. 'I couldn't have left Bracken behind.'

'We are still going to see him this weekend?' says Adam.

'Um, no. Not this weekend...'

Adam's face darkens as he shoves his chair back. 'He promised to take me go-karting. I can't bear to spend all weekend in this dump!' He stands up and leans against the back of the chair, knocking the legs repeatedly against the floor.

'Adam, do you mind?'

'When are we going to see Dad?'

'I don't know, I'm afraid.' I think it's up to David to tell them of Alice's pregnancy and the new half-sibling. 'I'm sorry.'

'Well, I'm glad,' says Georgia. 'I expect Maria will come over and help me with Bracken again.' Maria's done wonders with the pony in a very short time, getting her walking and trotting over poles in the paddock, and planning an outing to a Pony Club rally very soon.

'I wanna see my daddy,' Sophie wails.

'Oh, please don't be such a baby,' I say sharply, at which she throws down her bread and bursts into tears. 'We'll all be able to go wassailing instead,' I say, feeling guilty for upsetting her. I give her a hug.

'Will we be allowed to stay up late?' Sophie struggles to control herself.

'Till midnight?' Georgia asks.

'You can stay up all night as far as I'm concerned.' I'm so relieved the threat of losing my children is over that, right now, I'd let them get away with anything.

I cancel the appointment with the solicitor, and call Summer to give her an update.

'Summer, David's laid down his arms – he's decided not to go for custody.'

'That's brilliant news, Jennie.'

'Alice is pregnant. I'm cool about it. I just find it odd that history is repeating itself.'

'What do you mean?'

'She's gone from this ambitious young career woman to pregnant part-timer, supported by her husband-to-be. I know my career didn't ever get off the ground, but I ended up in a similar situation with him.' I pause then ask, 'How's school? Are you still enjoying it?'

'I love it. One of the boys told me all about his mum's whiskers.' Summer changes the subject back to me – and Guy. 'I guess this means you can start again where you left off?'

'I hope so.' I smile to myself. 'I'll have to consider Adam, of course. He doesn't know it yet, but his dad's just rejected him in favour of his new baby.'

355

'I suppose David thought he was doing the right thing, going for full custody,' Summer points out. 'He wanted Adam to be happy.'

She's right, I muse, but I'm not ready to forgive him yet. It's going to take time.

'Anyway,' I say, 'I'm going to a wassail. It isn't a date,' I add hastily, 'although it could be quite romantic, walking arm-in-arm under the stars.'

'Yeah, wrapped up in layers of Goretex and fleece. Very flattering.'

'Apparently it's a pagan fertility rite.'

'Be careful then, Jennie. You have three kids already. Do you really need any more?' Summer teases.

'It's for the trees.'

'It sounds completely bonkers,' she says, 'but have fun. I'll be in touch.'

It feels like a new beginning, for me and Guy, and for my friendship with Summer. She and I might not be able to chat about mutual friends in the same way as we used to, but when it comes to a crisis, we're still there for each other at the end of the phone.

I sit down with a pen and paper and start listing the ingredients for the cakes I've decided to bake for the wassail: Uphill Cider Cake and devil's food cake for the chocaholics.

'I can't understand why everyone is so excited about wandering around the countryside, hitting trees,' Adam says when we're getting ready to go out on the Saturday night for the wassail. 'As if that's going to make the trees produce more apples. It's crap. Utter crap.'

'Adam, mind your language,' I say lightly. 'If you want to stay here instead and play on the Wii or something, I don't mind.' However, as I suspected, his curiosity gets the better of him and he's in the utility room the next time I see him, hunting for his wellies.

'They're outside the back door,' I say.

'What did you put them out there for?'

'Because they were covered in cow's muck.'

'That's because we live in this shitty place,' he says.

'Adam!'

'Well, it's true. This place is full of shit and you can't deny it because you only have to look out of a window to see it.'

'There's the pony's muck heap, that's all. I thought you didn't mind.' My voice trails off. 'What about the cows? The milking?'

'Oh, I quite like that bit,' he admits. 'It's the rest of it. School. This poxy house. The fact we're miles away from civilisation.' He shudders, bites his lip and turns away, and I realise he's trying not to cry. Like David, he refuses to show weakness. 'I wanna go home, Mum. All my friends are in London and I'm stuck here.' He turns back to me, his eyes flashing. 'Why did you have to go and drag us here in the first place? And why did Dad go and change his mind about us living with him and Alice?'

'He's told you...' I hesitate.

'About the baby?' Adam nods.

'If you're really sure you want to go and live in London, I'll let you,' I say softly, my heart breaking at the thought of losing my son. 'I'll speak to your dad.'

'I can't live with him now,' Adam says miserably. 'It would be a nightmare with a baby screaming its head off all the time.'

'Oh, Adam.' I reach out and touch his shoulder, but he backs away, grabbing his coat from the hook on the wall. 'Where are you going?'

'Outside, to fetch my boots,' he says curtly.

I leave him alone. I'm not a martyr, but sometimes I wonder what foul deed I must have done in a previous life to deserve this.

What do you wear to a wassail? There's definitely no need for skimpy underwear, and, if I'm honest, I'm relieved by that. It's been a long time... I go for thermals, a pair of padded trousers which I once used for skiing, three jumpers, a fleece and coat. A hat, gloves and scarf complete my transformation to Michelin Man.

When my mobile rings, it takes me a while to find it about my person, and then it's only Fifi Green checking that everything is in place for tonight.

Guy turns up at seven, whistling from the front door. 'Are you ready, Jennie?'

'Hang on a mo'. I've mislaid my torch,' I call back.

'Don't worry about it. I'll be the light of your life.' A chuckle dies in his throat. 'Adam? I thought you'd be on your way to London with your dad.'

'Oh, he didn't want us,' my son says gruffly, and my chest tightens in sympathy. Deep down, Adam does care. He cares too much.

'In that case, you'd better come a-wassailing,' Guy says kindly.

'Didn't you get my text?' I say, joining him and

358

Adam under the porch, having checked that Lucky's shut out of the kitchen and called for the girls to hurry up.

'I've lost my mobile somewhere on the farm. Was it urgent?'

'David's changed his mind about having the children to live with him.'

'He has, has he? Does that mean... ?' Guy gazes at me, his expression beseeching, like Lucky's when he's asking for a biscuit, then his mouth curves into a broad smile of understanding.

Sophie turns up with Georgia.

'Hello, Guy. Mummy didn't know what to wear so she's wearing everything.' Sophie giggles. 'That's why she's so fat.'

'Sophie!' I gather up the spare tyre of fleece around my middle to demonstrate. 'It isn't me, it's all the layers.'

'I could have warmed you up,' Guy says quietly into my ear, and I notice how Sophie stares at us as if to say, What's going on?

'It feels like my bed-time.' Georgia stifles a yawn.

'It's way past mine. Come on, we mustn't keep Fifi waiting.' Grinning, he holds out his arm. 'Your chariot awaits.

'I thought I'd drive us into Talyton and we'd walk back,' he says. 'I'll pick the Land Rover up tomorrow.'

The procession starts out from Market Square. Fifi is at the head of it, resplendent in a purple robe, a jaunty hat and wellington boots with wedges. She holds a staff in one hand and a hand-bell in the other, and is surrounded by kids carrying torches to light her way.

'She looks like she's been promoted from Lady Mayoress to goddess,' I whisper to Guy.

'You're the goddess, Jennie,' he says gruffly.

'That's a terrible line,' I say, chuckling.

'I meant it in all seriousness,' he goes on, but he doesn't sound that serious to me

'Hello, Guy. Oh, and Jennie.' Maria joins us briefly, holding a lantern up to our faces before greeting Georgia and Sophie. 'Camilla's here – she's over there with Fifi, if you want to join her.'

The girls move away. Adam has already sloped off to join a pair of teenage boys near the tethering stone.

Maria touches my arm. 'I'll catch up with you soon. I seem to have mislaid my husband.'

'Maria has her suspicions about us,' Guy observes.

'I can't see any reason for that,' I say, although I don't think she's the only one to have caught on to the fact that he and I are acting more like a couple than mere neighbours tonight.

'I think she noticed me pinching your bum.'

'I didn't...' I can't help giggling. 'You'll have to pinch a bit harder.'

'I hope that isn't an excuse to make me do it again, Jennie Copeland,' Guy teases, but he does it again anyway.

The procession moves off, heading out of Talyton St George to wassail the apple trees. Peter the greengrocer plays a drum, Fifi rings her bell and, taking up the rear, someone starts up the bagpipes. Mr Victor is there too, but I notice that he doesn't bring his parrot. It's probably far too cold for it.

'That doesn't sound very traditional,' I observe.

'It is in Scotland,' Guy says, squeezing my hand.

We take in five orchards in all, Jennie's Folly being the last one. Just as we did at the other four, everyone surrounds the largest tree, holding their arms up towards its naked branches and singing the wassailing song, while the owner of the orchard pours cider on to its roots and Fifi beats it respectfully about the trunk with her staff. At the first orchard, I had to stuff my scarf into my mouth to stop an attack of the giggles, but by the time we reach ours, it seems quite normal.

In fact, the combination of the lanterns and torches dancing in the darkness, the babble of conversation, the feeling of being amongst friends and the mixed scents of bruised grass, mulled cider and Guy's aftershave, send shivers down my spine.

The girls watch, wide-eyed. Adam, I suspect, is pie-eyed by now.

Towards the end of the ceremony for our trees, Fifi joins us.

'Well, Jennie, thank you for your hospitality. And thank you for the cider, Guy,' she goes on, turning to him. She purses her lips as if she's deciding how to phrase what she says next. 'Far be it for me to interfere, but I hope you've thought carefully about what you're doing. No, don't try to tell me nothing's going on. I'm not blind, and neither's Ruthie.'

'Fifi, please don't meddle,' Guy says sternly. 'This has nothing to do with you. Goodnight,' he adds, taking my arm and leading me away.

'What was all that about?' I ask him. 'Why did

361

she mention Ruthie?'

'I've told you before, Ruthie and I are friends. We've known each other for years. That's all there is to it.' He pauses, whispering into my ear, 'You're the only woman for me...'

'Oh, Guy,' I sigh as I fight the impulse to throw myself into his arms and ignore the consequences. I'd love to forget about everyone else, but it isn't fair to reveal the extent of my relationship with him until the children are ready. They're only just beginning to get their heads round the fact that their father has rejected them in favour of his new baby. It isn't right that they should also have to deal with their mum turning up with a boyfriend, even though Guy isn't a stranger to them.

If I'm honest, it isn't just about the children though. A tiny niggle of doubt has crept back into my mind, and it's all Fifi's fault for making special mention of her... Ruthie. What exactly is her connection to Guy?

When the wassailers have gone, leaving only crumbs and empty mugs in their wake, Guy helps with some clearing up while I make sure Georgia and Sophie get to bed. Adam is home – his bedroom light is on – so I knock at his door.

'You okay?' I ask softly.

'G'night,' he mutters.

Relieved that he's stayed at home, rather than gone off with the boys he was talking to before, because I wouldn't have put that past him, I join Guy in the drawing room, sitting down next to him on the wicker sofa which creaks under our combined weight.

'This could be exciting,' he says, smiling.

'Oh, I hope so.' I lean against him as he slides one arm around my shoulder, the other around my waist, then rubs his nose against mine.

'It's difficult though,' I mutter. 'The children.'

'I know... I suppose they could wander in at any time.'

We sit like that for a while, the house falling silent, until all I can hear is the sound of Guy breathing, and the low thrumming of my pulse. I touch his face, following the curve of his jaw with my fingertips, his skin rough with stubble, and my chest tightens with desire.

Guy's breath catches in his throat. 'I really, really ... like you, Jennie.'

Our lips touch, and we're kissing ... and there's a load of noise upstairs: thudding; a door banging; someone being sick.

'Adam...'

'That's quite a way to ruin the moment.' Guy smiles ruefully.

'I'd better go up,' I say. 'He might need some help getting back to bed.'

Guy follows me upstairs, close behind.

'Adam?' I knock on the bathroom door, trying the handle when he doesn't answer.

'Let me try.' Guy holds on to the handle and gives the door a shove.

'He's locked it.' I knock harder, concerned for Adam's welfare.

'Don't panic, Jennie.' Guy puts his hand up to the architrave above the door and picks up a key, creating a puff of dust.

'I hadn't noticed that before.'

'We always kept the spare there. In case of emergencies...' He sticks the key into the lock and gives it a sharp jerk, at which the key on the other side hits the floor with a metallic clatter, allowing Guy to turn the spare key and unlock the door.

I push past him, finding my son lying on the floor in front of the throne.

'Adam?' I kneel down beside him but he's already on his knees, struggling to hold his head up.

'Mum? Oh, go away...'

'Adam, you're drunk.' I grab a piece of loo roll and wipe away the string of saliva that dangles from his mouth.

'I'm so tired,' he groans.

'Let's get him back to bed,' Guy decides. He bends down, and together we lift Adam to his feet and half carry, half drag him back to his room. We lie him on the bed, pulling the duvet out from underneath him and covering him up.

'I'll get him a glass of water,' Guy says. 'No, you stay there with him, Jennie.'

Once Adam has had a few sips of water, Guy says that he'll go home.

'It's nothing personal,' he says. 'It's just that I could do with a couple of hours' kip, and I don't think Adam's going to be helping with the milking, do you?'

'No, I'm sorry.'

'Don't you be sorry about anything. It isn't your fault. It's one of those things.'

'I should have kept a closer eye on him.'

'Only by keeping him in manacles.'

'Why is he so intent on drinking himself into oblivion?'

'I believe it's what some people call "having a good time". He'll soon learn.'

'Why do people say that? How many people do you know who've suffered a hangover, suddenly wake up and say, "Actually, I'm never going to drink again"? If they do, it doesn't last.'

'You're right, Jennie.' Guy smiles. 'On this occasion,' he adds slyly.

Chapter Twenty

Hummingbird Cake

I ground Adam for a week, but a couple of days after the wassail I receive a phone call from school at about two in the afternoon, from the Deputy Head this time. Adam has been making unauthorised absences again. Was I aware of this situation? I wasn't, and I'm not happy. After the last time, I took to walking him into student welfare every morning to make sure he got there, but since his behaviour seemed to improve – the embarrassment of walking into school with his mother was too much – I've relaxed my guard.

'I'll go out and look for him,' I say, sighing as I look at the racks of fairy cakes awaiting decoration. I've baked loads, intent on building on the stall's success at the Christmas market. I take off my apron and wash my hands, grab my coat, scarf and gloves, and call Lucky.

'Lucky, shall we?' He flies off the sofa, a blur of

dog, his claws clattering on the flagstones, tail wagging like crazy and a smile on his face. If you'd ever told me that dogs could smile, I would have laughed, but Lucky does, lifting his lip to reveal his teeth.

I plan a route to take in all the places Adam might be: hanging around at Uphill Farm, or at the pond in the copse, or down by the river. I doubt very much that he'll be in Talyton at this time of day – there are too many busybodies who'll be raring to report any truants.

I walk smartly up the drive, torn between worrying about Adam – not about his safety because he's more than able to look after himself, but more about his state of mind again – and being pleased to have this excuse to see Guy. Any excuse to spend any time at all with my lovely – dare I believe it now? – boyfriend.

Boyfriend? It seems so strange. It makes me feel like I'm seventeen again, not forty.

Since the cows have stopped wandering up and down here twice a day, there's more grass growing up through the middle of the drive. There's ice on the puddles. They gleam in the pale sunshine – crack under my feet. There are no leaves on the trees; their branches are bare, trunks thick with collars of ivy. When I reach the farmyard, the Land Rover's there, along with a second 4x4 that I don't recognise, but there's no sign of Adam or Guy. Napoleon the cockerel crows from his perch on the wall outside the barn that houses the cows overwinter, and a few chickens wander about, pecking fruitlessly at strands of frozen hay and grain. A cow utters a desultory moo over the distant buzz of a quad bike.

I walk around the side of the house, across the garden, then unlatch the gate into the field that rises quite steeply to a hedge at the top, and there, whizzing across the crown of the hill, is Adam on a quad bike, the hair on his head shining in the sun as he makes a sharp turn down the slope, speeding up until he's airborne. My heart seems to flutter, suspended in my throat, until he and the quad bike return to earth, together.

'Adam!' I yell at him. 'Get off that thing at once.'

He does a heart-stopping turn, brakes, and stops right in front of me. He sits staring at me, his wrists resting on the handlebars.

'What do you think you're doing?'

'Driving about, having a bit of a laugh. Unlike you, Mother.'

'Did Guy say you could take that bike?'

'He said I could use it any time I liked.'

'Does he know you're here?'

'I dunno, do I?'

'Adam, get off that machine.'

'But–'

'Get off *now*,' I snap. 'And go home.'

Adam slides off the quad bike and stands beside it. 'Can't I stay for the milking?' he says. He's acting contrite now, but I think that's all it is, an act.

'What do you think? You're supposed to be either at school or in your room, catching up with your homework. You're grounded, remember?'

'Mother, you are always ruining my life,' he mutters. 'If I can't milk the cows then I'm going back to London, and you can't stop me. I'll go and live on my own. I hate it here. I hate this poxy place.'

'I've got the message,' I say curtly.

'I hate my life. I bloody well hate *you*.'

'Adam, we're here now and we have to make the best of it. That's the last I'm going to say on the matter.'

He is coldly furious with me. I love him, but I don't like him much at the moment.

'Go home,' I tell him. 'Take Lucky with you.'

'Where are you going then?'

'To see if Guy's about.' I'm assuming that he is because the Land Rover's here. I'm curious too about the other vehicle. I smile to myself. I'm turning out to be a nosy neighbour. I check to see that Adam is heading in the right direction before I approach the farmhouse. As I reach the front door, which is ajar, I catch the sound of voices, Guy's and a woman's. I push the door gently and step inside, moving around the various obstacles, muddy boots and buckets, on the utility-room floor, my heart pounding as I go into the kitchen where Guy is embracing...

'Guy!' I utter a cry of anguish. 'What's going on?' I don't really need to ask. It's perfectly clear to me. He's holding this woman in his arms, kissing her hair. I can't see her face, and I don't care who she is. Guy, my wonderful, patient, kind and caring boyfriend, has turned out to be too good to be true.

'Jennie, this isn't what you think,' Guy says, turning to me, his expression neither surprised nor shocked. He doesn't even have the grace to act guilty, I think. 'Ruthie–'

'Ruthie! I should have guessed.' Between Guy's denials and Fifi's hints, I should have known they were involved in some way.

'Jennie.' Guy tries to extricate himself from Ruthie's clutches, or at least that's how it looks. She's clinging on to him like the ivy clings to the old oak in the copse. She isn't going to let him go. 'Let me explain...'

'There's no need,' I say coldly, although his betrayal is burning me up inside. 'I hope you're both very happy – and will have lots of children together.' I can't stand it any longer. I turn and flee, running through the yard and back down the drive, my feet spattering through the mud. I can hear Guy behind me, catching up with me at the picket gate.

'Jennie, wait,' he says, grabbing for my arm. 'Please.'

He flashes me a wary smile. I don't – I can't – smile back. I'm trembling.

'What's this about children?' he says. 'We weren't even kissing.'

'What I mean is that I can see the attraction. She's young enough to have your babies, give you an heir...'

'That's ridiculous! The last thing on my mind.'

'Is it, when it's pretty obvious it won't be very long until I'm too old to have any more children? No, you go back to her, Guy. She's a much better bet than I am.'

'Jennie, I didn't invite Ruthie to the farm,' he says. 'Fifi sent her, told her some cock-and-bull story about how I wanted to see her, to make things right.'

'What things?'

'I admit it, Jennie. I didn't tell you the whole truth, and I bitterly regret that now. I did go out with Ruthie for a while, after Tasha. I was on the rebound, though that's no excuse. I was ashamed later because I felt I'd led her on. Although I've always made it clear that it was over between us, Ruthie's never really accepted it.'

'So you did lie to me?' I say.

'I didn't think it was important. It wasn't so much a lie as a withholding of information. Jennie, I didn't mean to hurt you or Ruthie.'

'Guy, I trusted you...' I bite my lip so hard I can taste blood. 'I thought I knew you.'

'Please, don't cry.' He steps towards me, holding out his arms, but I step back, staying out of reach. It's as if Guy has turned into David. I said, Never again, yet here I am. I'm such a mug.

'Goodbye,' I say flatly.

'I'll see you tonight?' he says, nudging a tussock of grass with the toe of his boot.

'Not tonight. Not any night.'

I'm aware of the pressure of his hand on my shoulder, but I shrug it off.

'Just keep out of my sight.'

I walk away, through the gate and up to the front door, feeling a physical pain in my chest. Guy's betrayed my trust and we are over, over almost before we began. Our relationship has been fated from the start.

I tell myself it's for the best, finding out the truth before I was in too deep. Unfortunately, I was in deep enough that it's going to take me a long time to get over him and what might have been.

It's warm and cosy in the kitchen with the Aga going, and I'm reluctant to tear myself away when Maria arrives with her horsebox to collect Bracken and her tack. Maria and Camilla are travelling in the horsebox. Georgia, Sophie and I are going to follow on in the car.

I don't like leaving Adam behind, especially in the mood he's in, but he's still in bed when we leave early in the morning. Even Lucky refuses to get up.

It's taken us a long time to get ourselves organised enough to attend a Pony Club rally, and this one is the first of a series, every Saturday for four weeks. Georgia was so excited and nervous that she was sick last night. She's all right this morning, distracted by washing Bracken's tail – with warm water, I hasten to add – putting on her travel boots, and checking she's collected everything together. I can't believe how much she thinks she needs for one hour's riding: haynets, hairnets, grooming kit – for her and the pony, saddle, bridle, jodhpur clips... The list is endless.

By the time Georgia has finished, Bracken is immaculate, her feet shiny with hoof oil, and Georgia is very grubby, her face dusted with a fine powder of mud. I send her to change into her riding gear: shirt and Pony Club tie, jacket and jodhpurs. She returns downstairs at the sound of a lorry turning up the drive, going past then driving back down again to stop outside the house.

'Are you ready?' asks Maria, when we meet her in the yard. She's hardly recognisable as the fashionable woman who cuts my hair, dressed today in jeans and a bulky coat with a fur-trimmed hood, which is covered with mud and grime. Camilla has all the right clothes, including a blouson navy jacket with red lettering on it reading 'Mr Bojangles', the name of her pony. I notice how Georgia looks at it covetously.

'This is very kind of you,' I say to Maria.

'Oh, it's no problem. It's on our way.' She smiles. 'It's nice for Camilla to have someone to go with.'

'I'll fetch Bracken,' Georgia says.

'The ramp's down, so if you lead her straight in, Georgia.'

Straight in? It turns out that Bracken has other ideas. She takes one look into the box, plants her front feet on the bottom of the ramp and refuses to move, forwards, backwards or sideways. I fetch a bucket of pony nuts as instructed by Georgia, but Bracken isn't that stupid, or that hungry.

'Camilla, fetch the lunge whip,' Maria says, and Camilla returns with a long whip which Maria flicks at Bracken's rump.

'Walk on, Bracken,' says Georgia in a sing-song voice.

The pony is in her element, in full control of the situation, ears flicking back and forth, eyes rolling and tail swishing.

'Have you loaded her before?' Maria asks me.

'We haven't, but she did arrive here in a horsebox.'

'We'll try the lunge-line trick next,' Maria says, but before Camilla can find them, Guy rolls up behind us in his tractor. He stops some distance away, jumps out and approaches us, and my heart sinks and my stomach seems to screw itself up in knots. We haven't spoken since the Ruthie incident, and I'm still confused and upset over what happened. I was falling – I correct myself, I *had fallen* in love with him – and thought, although he hadn't told me as such, that he felt the same way about me...

I glance at his face. His expression when he glances back at me is guarded. He's dressed for the cold in a black beanie, scarf and dark green waxed jacket.

'Give us a hand, Guy,' calls Maria. 'You're good with horses.'

'Will do,' he says. 'I need to get out with the tractor. Is that all right with you, Jennie?'

I nod. Go ahead.

A half smile crosses his lips.

'That pony knows she can take advantage...' He walks up to Bracken and has a few words with Georgia before taking the rope. He rubs at the pony's face, jiggles the rope then leads her straight up the ramp into the lorry. Maria gets behind and closes the gates and ramp behind our naughty pony.

'Hurray!' she applauds as Guy jumps out through the groom's door near the front. Maria walks up and kisses him on the cheek, a gesture that I find quite painful to watch. 'Thanks, Guy.'

'Thank you,' I say, but he can hardly meet my gaze.

'It's nothing,' he says dismissively, and turns to the girls. 'Enjoy the rally.'

They do. Georgia can't stop grinning as she rides Bracken around the indoor school at a livery yard some way north of Talyford. There are five girls and their ponies in the ride, and an instructor called Polly with powerful thighs and a booming voice.

I sit on a broken chair on the balcony with Sophie, Maria and the other Pony Club mums, watching our budding Zara Phillipses walk, trot and canter. It's freezing. Within ten minutes, my toes are tingling and I can't feel my fingers. I've brought hot coffee and hummingbird cake to share, more as a thank-you gesture to Maria, because she's made it clear she doesn't want any payment for bringing Bracken here, than a shameless marketing ploy.

'This is wonderful,' Maria says, eating cake. 'What's in it?'

'It's like carrot cake, except that it contains pineapple and banana instead. Oh, and I use pecan nuts instead of walnuts.'

'How's business?' asks Maria.

'It's pretty good,' I say. I've been pleasantly surprised lately. In the past week, I've had two orders and three expressions of interest in wedding cakes – of the cupcake design, like Penny's. I have six birthday cakes lined up, and of course I also have my stall at the Farmers' Market. Even better, although I'm not about to jinx it by talking about it, I'm in negotiation with the gift shop in Talyton to supply them with cider cakes throughout the summer.

I shiver. I can't wait for the summer.

'I'm glad it's taking off,' says Maria. 'I think everyone's after your cupcakes for their weddings. Penny was completely overwhelmed that you managed to turn a potential disaster into something so special.' She grins. 'I know all about what the dog did, because I do her hair too. I did it for the wedding. Ah, you can't keep anything secret around here.'

'So I've noticed,' I say happily. The Pony Club mums aren't snooty as I expected them to be. I feel as if I belong here, that I'm amongst friends. I feel as if I've been accepted in Talyton St George at last, and I'm proud to be part of the community.

'There are whispers that you and Guy...?' Maria begins.

'Pure gossip,' I say, trying not to sound too abrupt.

'Weren't you with him at the wassail?'

'I was with half the population of Talyton at the same time,' I point out. 'We weren't together as such.'

'Shame. We used to think that he might end up with Ruthie – she runs Hen Welfare. Have you met her?'

'In passing, that's all.'

'Ruthie's always been there, in the background, biding her time. She went out with Guy's brother briefly. But then, didn't we all?' Maria smiles ruefully. 'I shan't go into the secrets of my misspent youth right now. Anyway, Ruthie was very supportive of Guy when his wife left him, and she told me – this was in confidence, by the way, so keep it to yourself – that she was hopeful that he'd marry her once he'd got Tasha out of his system.'

'And?' I say.

'Either he couldn't get over the break-up of his

marriage, or–' she pauses, giving me a long look '–someone else, someone more exotic, came along and sparked his interest.'

'I couldn't say – I don't know him all that well.' I thought I knew him, but I'm not so sure he's the man I believed he was.

'He'd be a good catch,' Maria goes on, and I'm thinking, I'd rather catch flu than be with Guy Barnes at the moment. I don't think I can ever forgive him.

'Mummy,' Sophie says, reminding me of her presence by getting up from her chair and perching herself on my lap, 'I'm bored.'

'It won't be for long,' I say. 'It's an hour's ride and they must have done half an hour already.'

'Can I join the Pony Club?' she asks

'I'm not sure there's any point when you haven't got a pony.'

'I'm sure that can be remedied pretty easily,' says Maria.

'Oh, no. No more ponies,' I say. 'They're far too much trouble.'

'But you've got plenty of space and it would be good for Bracken to have company,' Maria says, apparently oblivious to my fierce stare, meaning, Drop it. Change the subject. 'I've got the perfect pony standing out in the field at home. Camilla's first pony, Teddy.'

'I can't afford to buy another pony.'

'That's the thing though. You wouldn't have to buy him. You can have him on loan for Sophie until she grows out of him.'

'Please, Mummy,' says Sophie.

'I don't think so,' I say, refusing to weaken.

'Let's give your mum some time to get used to the idea,' Maria says, flashing Sophie a conspiratorial smile. 'Look, Georgia's getting ready to jump,' she adds, and I realise I haven't been concentrating because Polly the instructor has set up a jump and poles in the middle of the sand school.

'That's enormous.' I hold my hands over my face and peer out between my gloved fingers.

'Rubbish – it can't be more than two feet high,' says Maria. 'Mr Bojangles was jumping two foot nine all last summer and he's smaller than Bracken.'

I watch, my heart in my mouth, as Georgia, sitting up straight and smart, kicks Bracken into a trot, then a canter, and aims her towards the jump, the sight of which transforms the pony from lazy donkey to racehorse. She races the last two strides and takes a flying leap, clearing the jump with several inches to spare, and landing the other side with Georgia hanging on, then sliding back into the saddle.

'Oh, well done, Georgia. Come back and do it once more,' Polly yells, and Georgia trots back, grinning all over her face, to have another go, an attempt which is more flowing and elegant.

'That pony's got a jump on her,' one of the other mums says enviously, and suddenly I feel proud to be a horse owner and begin to see what Georgia sees in Bracken. I wipe a hot tear from my eye. The hours spent nursing her back to health, the vet's fees and coping with her naughty behaviour – it's all been worth it.

At the end of the rally, Polly chats briefly to me about Georgia and her riding.

'She's a talented rider,' she says. 'Very natural. I'm looking forward to seeing her progress when she goes on to horses. I imagine you're already on the lookout for something bigger with a bit more scope.' We've only just got Bracken, I want to say, but I don't in case I put my foot in it.

'It'll soon be spring – it's a good time to look for a new pony. If you need any help, call me. I've got lots of contacts and can give you some idea of whether or not a prospective mount is suitable.'

'Um, thank you. I'll bear it in mind.' It's dawning on me that I'm going to have to bake an awful lot of cakes to keep Georgia in horses.

I wish Adam could be happy like her. It's a pity he can't find solace in having a horse to look after, I think, although I can't imagine how I would afford another one. I check my watch. I hope he's okay. I wonder about phoning or texting him, but when I look at my mobile there's no signal.

When we get back it's growing dark although it's only three o'clock on this winter's afternoon. There's a bite to the air that savages exposed skin and chills me to the core. Even my bones feel cold.

'The sooner we're inside, the better,' I say.

'We have to feed and water Bracken first,' says Georgia.

'No way,' says Sophie, teeth chattering, in spite of her big coat and gloves. 'I'm going indoors. Bracken's your pony – you see to her.'

I shouldn't have dragged her out with us. I should at least have considered leaving her with Adam ... or perhaps not in the mood he's been in recently. I don't know. Why is parenting so difficult?

'Georgia, I'll give you a hand,' I offer. 'Come on, Bracken.'

Georgia ties her up outside the stable, takes off her tail bandage and travel boots, and throws on a rug before leading Bracken in through the door where a clean bed of shavings awaits.

'What else needs doing?' I ask.

'She needs her haynet.'

'How much hay?'

'Five pounds.'

'Why are ponies still in imperial measurements, not metric?' I say.

Georgia frowns.

'Oh, never mind.' I go into the stable next door, grope for the switch and turn on the light. A dim yellow glow washes over the stack of bales. I pull out a flake of hay from the open bale on the floor, squash it into a haynet and weigh it on the luggage scales that Georgia has tied to the rafter above with a piece of orange baling twine. I love the scent of the hay – it reminds me of summer.

I hang up the haynet for Bracken and Georgia fetches her a bucket of pony nuts, and we stand there, side by side, looking over the door while she munches on her food. Georgia slips her arm through mine, and looks up at me.

'Thanks, Mum,' she says, smiling. 'Thanks for arranging for me and Bracken to go to the rally.' In spite of the cold, my heart melts as she continues, 'It's been the best day of my life.'

'I'm glad,' I say, swinging her round and giving her a hug.

'I'm sooooo lucky to have you as my mum.'

'Oh, I think I'm luckier, having you for a daughter.' I slip my arm around her shoulders and we walk back across the yard to the house. 'Georgia, have you heard Lucky?' I ask, wondering if I've missed the dog barking. He always barks when anyone turns up on the drive outside the house. If he's out in the garden – although there can't be many self-respecting canines out and about in this weather – he always comes running to greet us and snuffle about at our feet.

Indoors, Sophie has already raided the larder. She's sitting at the table, eating chocolate cake. The Aga is throwing out a comforting heat.

'Adam,' I call out. 'Adam?' I turn to Sophie. 'Have you seen Adam or Lucky?' I can feel my forehead tightening into a frown. I assumed that Adam would be at home.

'No,' Sophie says with a careless shrug. 'I can hear the telly though.'

Taking off my coat and scarf, I head through the lobby and the hall into the drawing room. The television is on. Comedy Central. There's no sign of Adam or the dog. I look around the room.

'Come on, Adam. A joke's a joke, but that's enough...' Cue canned laughter. I switch the television off. 'Adam!'

'He isn't here, Mum,' Georgia says. 'He isn't in his room.'

'Where is he then?'

'He's probably taken Lucky for a walk.'

'Of course.' I try not to worry, a state of mind that I achieve for all of five minutes before ringing his mobile to check up on him. However, his phone is switched off – or, more likely, run out of battery. I check my watch – it's three-thirty. He's probably taken Lucky for his evening walk before it gets dark. I'm being silly. Adam's fourteen. He can look after himself.

I worry for another half an hour, occupying myself with peeling potatoes for tea and feeding the wedding cakes with brandy – there are two of them in the larder now. I line them up – five tiers altogether – unwrap the tops and skewer them a few times before opening the bottle of brandy and pouring the first measure. Now, it strikes me that the brandy looks unusually dark and thick as it creeps glutinously from the bottle to the measure. I run the measure past my nostrils. Instead of the sharp scent of alcohol, I can smell a meaty odour, more like gravy. In fact – I dip my finger into it and taste it – it *is* gravy. Someone, and I'll bet I know who, has been tampering with my brandy.

My heart thuds, my chest aching with disappointment. He promised me he wouldn't drink again. I thought he'd learned his lesson. Oh, Adam...

I wonder when he stole the brandy, if it was today or some time ago, then it crosses my mind that he might be outside somewhere in this freezing weather, with or without the dog, and out of his skull.

I abandon the wedding cakes and jog upstairs to Adam's bedroom, looking for clues, a note perhaps. His room is in a state of chaos, as usual, and although I thought I'd be able to work out from what's left which clothes and shoes he's wearing, it's pretty well impossible because they're strewn all over the floor. There is no note. I check his desk and shelves for clues. There's no

381

sign of his wallet, but I do find his phone.

I sit on the edge of his bed. Think, Jennie, think. Adam won't be helping Guy with the milking. I wish that he was, that he was safe in the parlour with Guy and the cows. Adam might well be walking Lucky, but would he take his wallet? I don't know. It occurs to me too that he might have taken off to London. I try to suppress the other possibilities which are crowding into my mind: that he's feeling so bad that he's gone down to the river to end it all, that he's gone out drunk and got himself run over, or...

I get up abruptly and run downstairs.

'Georgia, Sophie, I need to talk to you.' The girls gather around the Aga. Both are wide-eyed and anxious when I tell them I'm worried about Adam. They might fight and argue, but they do love their brother, after all. 'Did he say anything to either of you about what he might do today? Has he mentioned anything about going into Talyton or catching a train to London to see Dad? Or Granny and Granddad? Or Josh? Anything?'

Sophie shakes her head.

'He often talks about going back to London. He says he hates it here,' Georgia says. 'Shall we go and look for him? I can tack Bracken up and ride her down to the river to see if he's walking Lucky there.'

'I don't want the two of you going missing as well.'

'Is Adam missing then?' Sophie says, and her lip wobbles and I realise I've frightened her.

'No, I'm sure he's fine,' I say. 'He's just for-gotten to let me know where he is.' I'm sure he'll walk in that door with Lucky very soon. Lucky will bound up, wagging his tail, and Adam will smile and say, 'Hi, Mum, what's for tea?' I smile fondly, but inside I'm having panicky sensations like a bird flapping then settling, then fluttering up again in my throat.

'Mum, shall I call the police?' Georgia asks, apparently unconvinced.

'Um, not yet...' I can't imagine they'll take me seriously – I mean, Adam's fourteen and I have no idea how long ago he left the house. However, I need to talk to someone, someone who can reassure or advise me, and who else can I turn to but the person I think of first, the one who, in spite of everything, is always uppermost in my mind? Apart from my children, of course. I make up my mind. 'Let's go.' I slip into a coat and wellies and walk up the lane with the girls and a torch.

Within two minutes, we're in the parlour. I stand on the balcony, holding on to the rail. The strip lights are on, flickering almost imperceptibly but enough to give me a headache, and the lines carrying the milk are pulsating above me. Iyaz is singing on Radio 1 and a cow is bellowing from the yard beyond.

'Guy,' I call down to him. 'Guy!'

He looks up from where he's removing a cluster from one of the cows, and raises an eyebrow in question. He hangs the cluster on its hook, and walks over to us.

'Hello, Jennie. Sophie ... Georgia.'

'Guy.' My voice is breaking. 'Have you seen Adam?'

'So this isn't a social visit? No, I haven't. I

haven't seen him for a while. I was under the impression you discourage him from coming up here any more,' he goes on harshly and makes to turn away.

'Guy, please...' For a moment, I think he's going to ignore me, but something, the urgency in my voice perhaps, makes him stop. 'Adam's gone missing. He's taken Lucky and his wallet, but left his phone. I don't know what to think. I don't know where he is.'

Guy is up on the balcony beside me.

'Slow down, Jennie. Start at the beginning.' He takes my hands in his, very gently. 'Now, go on.'

'Sophie and I went to the Pony Club rally with Georgia. I left Adam at home in bed – I shouldn't have left him. He wasn't happy.'

'Shhh,' Guy says. 'This isn't the time for self-recrimination.'

'When we got back, we put Bracken to bed, then I realised Lucky hadn't barked, and when we went into the house, he and Adam weren't there.' I explain briefly about the brandy. 'There's no note, nothing. Guy, I'm at my wits' end. It's dark out there now and freezing cold.'

'Who does he hang out with? Could he be out with friends and have forgotten the time?'

'He keeps saying he hasn't got any friends, apart from the dog.'

'What about Josh? He often talks about him – or used to... Could he have decided to take off for London?'

'I don't think he had enough money on him for a ticket. He locked his card at the cashpoint the other day, and he's waiting for a new PIN. No, he can't have intended to travel very far – he would have taken his mobile.' I pause, pulling my hands away and wrapping my arms around me. 'Guy, what if he's... What if he's been drinking and he's gone out and ... hurt himself?'

'Give me two minutes,' Guy decides. 'I'll let these ladies out and then we'll go and find Adam.'

'What about the other cows?' I say.

'They'll keep. Their milk won't go off.' Guy smiles briefly, and I realise he's concerned about Adam too. 'We'll start with your property. Have you checked that barn of yours?'

'No,' I say.

'You three go ahead. I'll catch you up.'

Guy is as good as his word. He joins us as we're finished in the barn and rechecking the house in case Adam and Lucky should have strolled back in while we were out. They haven't.

'Why don't you wait indoors with the girls, Jennie, in case Adam rings on the land line?' Guy places his lantern on the ground while he pulls on his coat over his overalls. His breath is misty grey as it hits the air.

'I can't.' I won't rest until I find my son. I look up towards the stars, cold and metallic in the sky, and the jagged black limbs of the trees. My chest hurts. My throat is raw. I don't know which way to go, where to start, but Guy heads straight through the paddock and into the copse.

'Adam often talks about the den he and Josh built when he stayed that time.'

'He's never mentioned it to me.'

'He does a lot of talking when he's working with

me … when he used to work with me,' Guy says, and I envy him his closeness to my son.

'Adam! Lucky!' I yell as Guy moves away, beating a path through the undergrowth while the girls and I remain on the narrow track that divides the copse in two.

Suddenly, I'm answered by a bark close by and my heart lifts slightly.

'Lucky?'

The dog comes flying up into the beam of my torch, then darts back into the darkness.

'Lucky, come back! Here, boy,' I say desperately, and he trots back, panting and whining, before spinning away once more.

'Guy,' I call. 'This way.'

'We've found Lucky,' Georgia shouts, and within a heartbeat Guy is back by my side.

'Which way?'

I point my torch towards the pond.

'Adam! Adam!' I strain to listen, but there is no answering cry.

'Adam!' the girls join in.

Guy forges ahead, first to reach the pond, a glistening expanse of sheet ice, black and silver under the crescent moon. I see his figure in silhouette.

'Where's the dog?' Guy calls out.

'Over there, on the other side.' I can just make out something moving back and forth, and as I step forward to get a better look, I see the cracks in the silvered surface of the pond, the dark defect in its centre and the shape slumped alongside it. My heart lurches. Adam… 'Stay there!' I tell the girls. 'Don't move a muscle.'

'Yes, Mummy.' Sophie's voice is faint behind me as I break through the lines of withered rushes at the edge, and take a step – crack – on to the ice at the same time as Guy grabs my arm and pulls me back, swearing.

'Don't be so bloody stupid, Jennie. Get your phone out and dial 999. Now!'

'I'm doing it,' Georgia cuts in sharply. Then, 'Ambulance, please.'

I make to take the mobile from her, but she steps clear and keeps talking, and I'm keeping half an eye on Georgia and half on Guy who skirts the edge of the pond, then throws his coat over the ice before lying across it, gingerly testing his weight. There's an ominous crack as he stretches out one arm until his fingertips are centimetres away from the shape on the ice.

Is he ... is he alive?

Guy edges closer. His fingers touch the body, take a grip on his jacket, then very slowly he wriggles back on his belly, dragging Adam towards the bank where Lucky is whining.

There's another crack, like a gunshot.

'Oh, Guy. Please be careful,' I murmur, aware that both of them – my beloved son and darling Guy – are a hair's breadth from falling through into the freezing black water.

'Mum, Mum!' Georgia is tugging at my coat. 'We've got to go and put the lights on in the yard for the ambulance.'

I hesitate, unable to bear the thought of walking away.

'Mum, me and Sophie will go,' says Georgia.

'The torch,' I say, thrusting it towards her.

387

'You can keep it – I've got the light on my mobile.'

I keep my eyes fixed on Guy. He's almost back at the bank. There's another crack, but this time they've made it. Taking off my coat, I scramble round to join them.

'Here,' I say, but Guy has already wrapped Adam's inert body in his coat. He has his face close to Adam's and his fingers against Adam's neck. My son's skin is taut across his cheekbones, pale and blotchy, his teenage spots a purplish-blue in the moonlight.

'Is he...?' I sink down to my knees and reach for his hand. It's cold and limp. 'Adam?'

'He's breathing, and I can find a pulse, but it's slow,' Guy says.

'Adam, can you hear me?' I say, frantically squeezing his hand.

'I'm not sure that he can,' Guy says softly. 'Come on, Adam,' he goes on, 'let's get you back to the house.'

I'm wondering exactly how we're going to manage that when Guy slides his arms underneath Adam's, hoists him up and carries him over one shoulder, marching steadily a couple of paces ahead of me. Lucky follows at Guy's heels, unwilling to let his master out of his sight. I feel as if I'm trudging through a nightmare over which I have no control.

There are so many questions. What was Adam doing on the ice? How many times have I told him of the dangers? But all I can concentrate on now is willing my son to survive, to hang on in there, because I have to explain to him that, no matter how bad it seems, life is always worth living.

My stomach churns. Sick and scared, I jog to keep up with Guy's long strides until we reach the paddock where Georgia has left the gate open and head towards the flashing lights of an emergency vehicle waiting in the yard.

Within half a minute Adam is on a stretcher in the back of the ambulance, and I'm standing with my arms around the girls, and Guy's arms around me, watching and waiting and hoping, and maybe in Sophie's case praying.

'All right, Mum, you're coming with us,' says one of the paramedics.

I glance towards Guy.

'Go on,' he says. 'I'll look after the girls. Keep in touch.'

'Thank you,' I say through a veil of tears, but how can I ever properly thank Guy for what he's done, risking his life for my son? 'Will you call David for me?' I show him the number still on my phone – one of the many links that I wanted to delete, but couldn't because of the children.

In the ambulance the paramedics, a man and a woman, strip off Adam's wet clothes, peeling them away from his stiffly held arms and legs, before they wrap him in blankets then cover him in aluminium foil. One constantly checks his temperature; the other sets up a drip into a vein in his hand and an oxygen mask over his face, hiding the blue tinge on his lips. They stick electrodes to his chest and attach him to a heart monitor. All the time they're talking to Adam, to me and to each other, and I can only register half of what they're saying.

Adam is no longer shivering. His core temperature is 33 degrees, four degrees below normal. He's unconscious and his pulse is weak and irregular, not a good sign. His breathing is shallow, his condition critical.

'Oh, Adam...' I murmur. 'Please hold on...'

'All right, Jennie,' the female paramedic says, 'we're going to get your boy to hospital now.'

I realise on the journey that I've been trying to do too much. I've neglected him. I did listen to him, but I didn't act on what I heard. Now my son hovers between life and death, and it's my fault. I'm not fit to be a mother. I've been selfish, living out my dream. I wanted to prove myself after the divorce, but all I've proved is that I'm completely useless.

I gaze at my son's form, half hidden under the silvery foil.

Hang on in there, Adam. I stifle a sob. Stay with us. Please, don't die...

Chapter Twenty-one

Walnut, Date and Honey Cake

A few hours later – I've lost track of time – I'm still at Adam's side. He's been lucky. He's out of danger although he's confused, drifting in and out of sleep.

'Mum,' he says, reaching out wildly with his

hand. 'Mum...'

'It's all right.' I take his hand, but he wrenches it away. 'I'm here, love.'

What was he doing at the pond? How many times have I warned him about walking on ice? I wonder if David would have got through to him – if I'd given him a chance. Did he imagine he could skate on it, like he used to skate at the local rink a bus ride away from our old house? Did he do it out of curiosity? Or for the thrill? I try not to think of the other option, but it keeps popping up in my mind. Have I really made his life so miserable that he felt he had to end it? Or didn't he mean it to go as far as it did? Was it a cry for help?

'Oh,' he groans, 'I've got such a headache.' He looks exhausted, his eyes large and luminous in his face. The colour of his skin looks healthier though, compared with the stark white sheets.

'I'll find the nurse to see if you can have some painkillers.'

'Don't fuss,' he mutters. 'I'm so tired ... and cold...'

'Shhh,' I say. 'Don't wear yourself out talking.' There'll be plenty of time for talking later. I can smell alcohol on his breath and my relief that he's going to be all right is tinged with shame.

'I knew something like this would happen.' David's eyes are dark with anxiety. I've been dreading his arrival. He stands at Adam's bedside, having pushed me aside, and gazes at our son.

'He's sleeping,' I say, my body taut, awaiting the avalanche of anger and blame. 'He's been talking, and he's going to be all right. No lasting damage.'

'Thank goodness for that.'

I turn at the sound of a voice that is only vaguely familiar to me.

'Hello, Alice,' I say. I've met her a few times now – she's as I expected she would be, tall, blonde and not so much glamorous as so very young. Her pregnancy doesn't show yet under her pink angora sweater.

'It's no thanks to you, Jennie,' David says, turning to me.

'David!' Alice's hand flies to his arm. 'This isn't the place, is it, darling?'

He leans over Adam, cupping his cheek. 'I'm sorry I wasn't there for you, son,' he murmurs, and tears spring to my eyes.

'You can talk outside,' Alice says. 'There's a room back along the corridor. I'll stay with Adam. Go on. Go and get a coffee or something.'

David buys two coffees at the machine and hands one to me.

'What about Alice?'

'She's off coffee – she'll choose what she fancies later.' David leans back against the wail. 'Now tell me what happened.'

'Adam's being treated for hypothermia. I don't know how, but he ended up on the pond. Guy dragged him off the ice.'

'I should have known he'd be around,' David says. 'Your hanger-on.'

'Guy saved Adam's life – at great risk to himself,' I point out, angry with David for making ridiculous assumptions about my relationship with Guy.

My nonexistent relationship, I realise. Yet when I called him for help, he came without question.

David swears. 'What was he doing there anyway, Jennie? Where were you that you didn't stop him?'

'Adam wasn't in a great mood this morning when I went out with the girls and the pony. When I came back, he was missing. David, you can't blame me for this. How many times have I told him not to walk on ice or mess around near water? I can't be a full-time babysitter to him. He hates me anyway.'

'It's the kind of thing I'd have done at his age,' David says. 'It would have been a dare, a test of nerve.'

'No one dared him to do anything. He was on his own.' I pause, debating whether or not to mention the theory that has been plaguing me ever since we found Adam at the pond. 'I'm not sure it was an accident, David. When we found him, he'd been drinking.'

'You mean he was trying to–'

'No, not that,' I cut in. 'I think he was feeling down in the dumps...'

'It sounds like it was a bit more than that,' David interrupts.

'He was feeling depressed then, I don't know. He doesn't let me in, doesn't allow me access to his innermost thoughts. I think he had a bit to drink and decided to take Lucky for a walk. He ended up at the pond and hung around there for a while. And then, whatever dark thought crossed his mind, it made him decide to walk across the ice. It was a fatalistic impulse. In that instant, he didn't care whether he lived or...' I can't say it.

'He's never given me the impression that things were that bad,' David begins thoughtfully.

'I should have known. I'm his mum. He lives with me. I should have picked up on it.'

But I was so busy sorting out the new house, baking cakes and mooning over Guy, that, although I realised how miserable Adam was, I didn't take it as seriously as I should have done.

David surprises me.

'Don't blame yourself, Jennie. It's as much my fault as yours ... probably more so. I let him down, breaking my promise that he could come and live with me and Alice.'

'It's done now though,' I point out.

'Yes, so what are we going to do about it?' David says.

'I'm going to talk to Adam when he's feeling better, then I'm going to talk to the doctor to see if we can organise some professional counselling.'

'I can imagine how Adam will react to that,' David says, a brief smile crossing his face.

'We can't deal with it ourselves when we're part of the problem.' It had appeared on the surface that Adam had coped quite well with the divorce, but I wonder if he ever really accepted it. Hence the drinking and his anger when Guy kissed me... 'He needs to talk to someone else, someone outside the family.'

When we return to his bedside, Adam is half awake and I leave David to spend some time with him, just the two of them. I try to make small talk with Alice, asking her about the wedding and the baby, but she isn't very forthcoming. We have little in common, apart from David.

'They reckon he'll be coming home within twenty-four hours,' David says when he rejoins us.

'I expect you'll want to stay until then, at least,' I say. 'David, you and Alice are welcome to stay at the house. I'm sure the girls would love to see you.'

'Where are they? You haven't left them home alone, have you?'

'They're with a friend of mine, Maria. Guy texted to let me know he'd dropped them over there.' I pause. 'If I give you the address, you can collect them on the way. I expect they're worried sick.'

'Oh, all right. Thanks, Jennie.'

What else can I do? I think. David isn't a bad man. He loves Alice – I notice how he watches her, as if he can't believe his luck. I see how he takes her hand and raises it to his lips, and my stomach no longer lurches with jealousy, and I have no urge to tear out her golden tresses – or bitch about the fact that they're mainly hair extensions, or pray inwardly that one day soon they'll leave her with bald patches on her scalp.

Thirty-six hours later David collects me and Adam to take us back home, to Jennie's Folly. As soon as we get inside the front door, Lucky comes racing into the hall to greet Adam, jumping up and snuffling with delight, licking Adam's face as he kneels down to him, and nipping at his ears.

'Your master's home,' I start to say, but my throat's tight with emotion. I think I can safely say that I love that dog now.

'Daddy!' Sophie cries, as she and Georgia come running in from the kitchen in coats and muddy boots. I am just about to suggest they take them off when I think, What does it matter in the scheme of things? 'You're back. And Mummy. And Adam.'

'Have you seen Alice?' David asks, touching the tip of Sophie's nose.

'She's in the drawing room, having another sleep,' Georgia says, and I smile to myself when I glance round the door and catch her sitting with her feet up.

'There's no food in the house.' David glances at me apologetically. 'I haven't done any shopping – I took Alice and the girls to Mr Rock's, that fish and chip shop in town, for lunch.'

'Of course there's food,' I say. There's flour, sugar, cheese, butter and eggs.

'Yes, but there aren't any meals as such.'

'You mean, there are no ready meals.'

'Some woman, Fifi, turned up last night with a stew, but that's gone.'

'That was kind of her,' I say, touched by her generosity. 'I don't know how she knew about Adam.'

'She said she heard the ambulance going past her house and made some enquiries.' David smiles. 'I thought village gossips were an urban myth, so to speak.'

'I can assure you that they're alive and well here in Talyton St George.'

'She wanted to see you.'

'The feeling isn't necessarily mutual at the

moment,' I say, even though she did me a favour by exposing the extent of Guy's involvement with Ruthie.

'She said to give you the message that she's very sorry.'

Sorry for what? I muse. For Adam's mishap, or for interfering between me, Ruthie and Guy?

'One other thing – Alice has taken down the details of two orders for you, and an enquiry about supplying one of your local farm shops with your speciality cake … what was it?'

'Uphill Cider Cake,' I say. 'Wow, I'm chuffed.'

'I'm beginning to sense I'm going to have to eat my words,' David says. 'I doubted you, but it seems that the business is really taking off.'

'Thanks,' I say. 'David, could I possibly ask you to put the kettle on and make some tea? I need to pop out for half an hour or so. There's something I have to do.'

'Are you going far?'

'Next door, that's all,' I say. 'I want to thank Guy personally.'

'Would you like me to come? I mean, I have as much to thank him for as you do.'

'It's okay. I'd rather you stayed here and kept an eye on the children – don't let Adam out of your sight, and don't give him a hard time,' I say, fiercely protective of my son. 'Promise me?'

'Promise,' David responds. He seems to have mellowed. Maybe it's because of the baby.

'Are you and Guy…?'

I shake my head.

'But you'd like to be,' David persists.

'Would have liked to have been.' Inside my

heart is taut, as if something is about to snap.

'But?' says David.

'It isn't going to happen.' I don't reveal the real reason. 'I have to concentrate on the children and the business. Adam's accident has shown me that.'

'I'd like to see you happy and settled again.'

'I am happy,' I say determinedly.

'And I want you to know, even though I'm about to be a dad again, that I'll always be there for our children. Jennie...' For a moment, I think he's going to touch my arm, but he changes his mind.

When I start putting my coat on, Georgia asks me where I'm off to. When I say I'm going to the farm, she says not to bother because Guy's gone out. She's seen his Land Rover.

It's Guy who drops in to see us an hour or so later, to check that Adam is home, and although I thank him for what he did, he says it was nothing, he would have done it for anyone. There's so much more that I want to say, but everyone else is here, and I'm in the middle of cooking tea and phoning back regarding the orders because I don't want to lose them, and the moment passes.

David and Alice leave the next day. Adam is off school for a week or so, recuperating, and one morning I suggest we get outside for some fresh air. We walk along the bank, following the curve of the river as it meanders across the Taly valley, doubling back on itself and close to forming an oxbow lake. It's a clear winter's day with a weak, watery sun low in an almost colourless sky. Lucky runs up and down along the bank, alternately sniffing and cocking his leg.

'There was a time when I thought that was a disgusting habit,' I say lightly, 'but I'm prepared to forgive that dog absolutely anything.'

Adam stops, half turns and locks his eyes on mine.

'Lucky saved my life.'

'So did Guy,' I add quietly. 'He's heavier than you are – he took quite a risk.'

To my alarm, Adam's eyes fill with tears.

'I'm sorry, Mum. I d-d-didn't mean to hurt anyone.'

I reach out and touch my son's quivering shoulder, and, aching to hold him, I wait for him to decide. Head down, he steps closer until his forehead is touching my chest. 'Adam...' I murmur as I reach my arms around him. He straightens and for a heartbreaking moment I feel as if I'm going to lose him again, and this time, if I let him go, he'll be gone from me for good.

'I don't know why I did it.' His voice is harsh. 'I found the bottle in the larder and it seemed like a good idea at the time, then I spilled the gravy powder all over the place and had to clear it up. And you'd gone out with Georgia and Sophie, and I thought you were going to be home by three and you didn't turn up...'

'We were late back, I know.' I'm keeping my arms very still, no pressure. 'Bracken had to be untacked and have all her boots and bandages put back on when the rally finished.'

'Stupid ponies,' Adam says curtly.

'You don't mean that. Georgia loves Bracken,

just like you're fond of Lucky.'

'Stop telling me what I think,' he cuts in. 'I *know* what I think. I had too much of that brandy stuff, and I thought, I'll take my wallet and catch a train back to London.'

'You were running away?'

'Yeah. S'pose I was.'

'I ran away from home once,' I begin. 'I can't remember why. It was probably after some argument with Aunt Karen. I was much younger than you are now. I'd read a book about the Little Grey Men, and decided that I could survive on blackberries and peppermint creams like they did.'

'And did you?'

'I left the house with two packets of sweets, ate them, threw up and returned to find that nobody had noticed I was missing.'

'So that's why you can't stand peppermint creams?'

'That's right.' I hesitate. 'Adam, you've told me how you took your wallet. How did you end up where you did?'

'Oh, Lucky wanted to come with me and I wasn't thinking straight. I thought I'd walk him first, and headed up through the copse. Well, I could see the pond shining, so I went to have a look.'

'And?'

'I can't remember.' He shudders. 'It was so cold... Mum, I thought I was going to die...'

'Come here, love.' I don't know how long it is before he relaxes into me and rests his head on my shoulder. I twist my neck and press my face into his mop of hair that's fragrant with shampoo and Lynx. 'I love you so much.'

'Love you too, Mum.'

You don't know what that means to me, I think, stroking hot tears from his cheek.

'You're the best hugger in the world,' he goes on. 'You know exactly how hard to squeeze.'

'I'll squeeze all the breath out of you if you ever do something like that again.'

'I know. It won't happen again. I thought I was going to die.'

'Adam, if you really hate it here so very much...'

'I do,' he says simply. 'Sometimes I just want to go home.'

He wants to go back to London. This isn't a whim. He's serious.

'What about Lucky?'

'There are probably more city dogs than country ones. I don't think Lucky would be too fussy.' Adam wriggles out of my embrace and steps back. He's smiling, I notice, as if he's been relieved of a huge burden. As for me, I feel bruised and sore. I've been selfish, dragging the children away from friends and family, especially their dad and grandparents.

I gaze up the valley and catch sight of Jennie's Folly, its windows glinting in the morning sun, and a lump catches in my throat. I can't let this situation continue. Although it's tearing me apart, the idea of leaving the animals, the business and my new friends behind, the only way forward for my family is for me to sell up and go back to London.

It's the end of the love affair. My time at this

beautiful house has ended up being an all-too-brief fling.

'Adam, I want to tell you something, but first you have to promise me you won't say a word to anyone about this, not to your father or your sisters? I have to sort some stuff out before it becomes common knowledge.'

'What is it?' I says.

'We'll go back ... back to London.'

'But, Mum, this is your dream home,' he says, frowning.

'My dream, yes, not yours. I shouldn't have inflicted it on you. I should have waited until you, Georgia and Sophie were old enough to make your own way in the world.' I take a deep breath and let it out slowly. 'I'm going to put the house on the market.'

'What about school? I've started on my GCSE courses.'

'You can continue with those anywhere. I don't think that's a problem. People move all the time.'

'Have you told Guy about this?'

'I don't see that it has anything to do with him.'

'Hasn't it?' Adam says. 'I thought you liked him ... in a boyfriend–girlfriend kind of way.'

'Maybe, but it hasn't worked out.'

'Is it because of me?' Adam persists. 'Is it my fault you kind of broke up?'

'It's down to lots of things.'

'I was angry that day when I saw you by the tractor, not with you and Guy but with everything. What I'm saying is that I wouldn't have minded if you had got together.' It's a bit late to say that now, I think, as Adam continues, 'I like Guy.'

'I don't want to talk about it,' I say sharply.

'Okay, but what if Georgia and Sophie don't want to leave?'

'Adam! Remember, don't say a word.'

He and I walk home. As we reach the house, a cloud crosses the sun and the windows go dark. I look at the sign outside, the one that Summer made: Jennie's Folly. My friends and family were right about that. It is my folly, my mistake, but although I'm overwhelmed with regret for how it's turned out, I know that if I hadn't moved here and given it a go, I would always have wondered: What if...?

We go through the gate into the yard, Adam whistling for Lucky to come with us, and I look at the tumbledown barn and the stables, at the pink wheelbarrow tipped on its end against the wall, and Bracken's box of brushes that Georgia's left outside the stable door. At the sound of footsteps, Bracken comes trotting over and puts her head over the paddock gate, and whinnies. And I think, What about Bracken? What will happen to her, after all she's been through? And although I can just about convince myself that we'll be able to find her a lovely new home with another pony-mad girl to love her, I feel like a traitor – to the pony and, more importantly, to Georgia.

And how will I tell Sophie that we'll be leaving her chickens behind?

I didn't appreciate animals before we moved here because I didn't understand them. Now, I don't want to be without them.

I can bake cakes wherever I am, but Jennie's Cakes will never be the same. I doubt that I'll have another Aga and there will be no more Farmers' Markets, bartering for meat and honey, even lettuce.

There will be no more quirky community events, no more outings to see the tar barrels or wassail the trees. I walk to the paddock gate to hide my face. Bracken starts nudging my pockets through the bars, looking for mints.

'Mum, are you coming indoors?' Adam calls.

'In a minute.' I can hardly speak.

'Are you okay?'

'Yep. I'm going to get Bracken some hay.' I go into the stable where we store the hay and sit myself on a bale, bawling my eyes out. It isn't for the house, or for the children, or for the animals... If I'm brutally honest with myself, I'm crying for Guy, and what might have been.

The next morning I contact the estate agent who dealt with the sale of Jennie's Folly, when it was still Uphill House, and within an hour he has a potential buyer through the door, a silver-haired-man in his late fifties, dressed in a suit and tie, his Jaguar saloon parked outside. I leave the agent to show him around. It doesn't take long.

'He's been here before, of course,' the agent says, when he pops back in to give me an update. 'He wanted to buy the place the first time round, but Mr Barnes turned him down.'

If my heart could sink any further, then it would.

'You mean, he's the developer?'

'Yes, he can see the potential in this property. I wouldn't be surprised if I hear back from him by the end of the day. He'll snap it up.'

As the agent leaves by the front door, I hear the back door slam.

'Adam?' It must be him – he's off school for a couple more days yet. 'Lucky!' I call, but there's no answering bark. I rush out to see if I can see them, but Adam and the dog have disappeared. I'm annoyed with myself for letting him sneak out like that. I try Adam's mobile, but it's switched off.

I can't motivate myself to do anything. I can't even bring myself to bake a cake. I take myself off to the drawing room with a mug of coffee and sit on the sofa, wrapped in an old coat with my knees drawn up to my chin, staring at the ashes from last night's fire in the grate. My coffee grows cold, and I picture the old house growing cold too when we move out. It will be modernised, no doubt, its features stripped out and replaced with a soulless modern décor. The barn and stables will be converted. They'll no longer house chickens and ponies.

I dig an old tissue out of one of the coat pockets and wipe away a tear

I don't know how long I sit there before I become aware of another presence in the room. Glancing out of the corner of my eye, I confirm that it's Guy, but I knew that already from the tread of his feet and the dimensions of the shadow that he casts, standing in the light from the window.

'I believe you've been avoiding me,' he says gruffly as he walks over to the fire and stands to one side, facing me.

'What did you expect?' I straighten my legs and

405

clasp my hands in my lap.

'You've gone and done exactly as I predicted,' he goes on. 'The going gets tough so you walk away. I said you wouldn't last a year.'

'How did you find out?'

'I heard the cars, but it was Adam who came to find me.'

'Adam?'

'He told me you were planning to move and you'd already had the estate agent and a potential buyer in.'

'Yes, I have.' I pause, then continue with sarcasm, 'I didn't think you cared.'

'Of course I care,' he says.

'Well, if you want to save the house from developers, you could always buy it back.'

'Are we talking at cross-purposes here?' Guy raises one eyebrow. 'I'm talking about you, Jennie. I care about you.' He raises his hand as I open my mouth to make a minor observation on that particular point. 'I thought you cared for me...' A small smile crosses his lips. 'In fact, if you hadn't cared for me at all, I don't suppose you'd have been so upset about the other business.'

'Guy, there's no need to revisit the past,' I say.

'I have to. I keep going back, thinking, if only Ruthie hadn't come up to the farm. If only she'd taken no for an answer, we'd be together, you and me.'

'I'm not sure it works like that. I would still have had my suspicions about you – you didn't tell me the entire truth, after all.'

'I know. I was stupid. I made a mistake, and I'm prepared to go down on my knees and grovel for the rest of my life, if you'll only forgive me for it.' His expression is beseeching, his eyes caressing. I've made mistakes too, and if I can't bring myself to forgive him, I'll be making yet another one. I couldn't bear to leave without resolving our differences and at least parting as friends.

'I forgive you,' I say quietly. 'But,' I add quickly before he can jump to the wrong conclusion, 'that doesn't mean I can stay.'

'Why on earth not?' he exclaims in anguish.

'Look, this isn't easy for me.' My eyes sting and my chest aches. 'I'm not leaving because I'm running away from you.'

'Please, I should have done this before, but I'm a bit of a wuss when it comes to talking about feelings. Jennie, you have to hear me out.' Guy takes a deep breath before plunging on, 'I love you. I've loved you since ... since the day I brought the chickens over and I put that first one into your hands, and your face lit up...' He swears lightly. 'That sounds soft, doesn't it?'

'It's very romantic.' Keep strong, I tell myself. Don't show any weakness, otherwise you'll be in his arms before you know it and then you'll never leave. 'It's also rather odd, if you think about it,' I go on somewhat flippantly, 'because you were pretty antagonistic when we first met.'

'That's as may be.'

'There's no may be about it. You were angry with me for buying Uphill House.'

'Jennie's Folly, you mean,' Guy says. 'Jennie, you're easy to talk to. I found myself telling you about my marriage ... things I've never told anyone else.'

'Guy–'

'Stop right there.' He holds up one hand. 'I promised myself that I'd get this off my chest. Jennie, you are the best thing that's ever happened to me. I love and adore you.' His voice breaks and my resolve shatters. 'I would walk to the ends of the earth for you.'

'I love you too,' I whisper.

'Then, what's stopping you?'

'You can't ask me to choose between you and my son's happiness,' I say miserably.

'You don't have to choose.' Guy darts forward and goes down on his knees on the rug, resting his hands on the sofa, one to either side of me. 'That's why Adam came to see me. Because he thought I could make you listen, even if he can't.'

'What do you mean?'

'He said that he'd talked about going back to London, and you jumped in and put the house on the market.' Guy looks towards the door. 'Adam,' he calls. 'Do you want to come and explain this bit? I don't think I can.'

'Has he been outside the door all the time?'

'I didn't hear anything,' Adam says, but I'm pretty sure he's fibbing.

'What did you want to say, Adam?'

'Mum,' he begins, 'I wasn't saying that we had to move...'

'You said you hated it here,' I interrupt.

'I know, but I didn't mean it. Not like that.'

'I don't understand,' I say.

'Mum, you're the same. You don't always mean what you say.' Adam pauses. Silenced by the truth in his words, I let him go on. 'You never really listen to me – you hear something, make up your mind and that's it. Yesterday I said that sometimes I just want to go home, which doesn't mean that I want to go back in reality. It's how I feel on occasion. And I wouldn't expect you and my pesky little sisters to move away just for me. I've learned my lesson about the drinking, and Will and Jack have asked me to join them at football training to see if I can get on the team.'

My emotions are in turmoil. Joy that Guy, the man of my dreams, has declared his love for me. Surprise and delight that Adam wants to stay here, after all. I'm finding it hard to take it all in.

'Why didn't you say this before?'

'I tried to, but you disappeared off to feed Bracken and then you were in a foul temper last night...'

'Oh, Adam...' I make to get up, but he shakes his head.

'Stay where you are, Mother. I don't think Guy's finished yet.' Then he grins. 'I'm going to fetch more wood for the fire, so I won't be in your way.'

'That's some revelation,' I say aloud.

'Are there any more to come?' Guy puts his arms around my waist and rests his head against my breast.

I reach out with one arm, let my hand hover above the crown of his head. I touch his hair, then run my fingers through it, feeling for his scalp and the shape of his skull.

'Jennie darling, please don't go...' Guy straightens up and looks into my eyes. My heart is pounding with uncertainty and confusion as he continues in a low whisper, 'You belong here.'

It's now or never. Will I walk away, leaving Guy and my chance of true love behind? Will I leave Jennie's Folly to the mercy of the developers? Or will I stay?

Six months down the line, I'm still in the kitchen with my Aga at Jennie's Folly. I look out of the rear window, past the lawn and the vegetable patch with its mound of rotted manure and weeds in the middle, to the paddock where Georgia and Sophie have set up an obstacle course of a tarpaulin to walk across, a line of washing flapping in the breeze, and a scarecrow-like dummy that reminds me of the country bumpkin (it's to jump over). They are trotting round on their ponies, practising for the Pony Club show. Ponies? Yes, we have two now: Bracken and Teddy, Camilla's old pony that we have on loan from Maria. We have more chickens as well. The hens are scratching about in the gateway, the original ten having been joined by ten of Napoleon's daughters, still cute but growing fast.

To the left of the paddock, I can just make out the figures of Adam and my dad felling saplings in the copse, only small ones to allow space for the more vigorous trees to grow. Occasionally, I catch sight of Lucky running in and out of the undergrowth in his relentless search for rabbits.

'Have you finished with the turntable, Jennie?' Mum asks from beside me. 'Only I'll put it away if you have.'

'Thanks, Mum.' I put the last tier of the cake that I've just finished decorating back in the

410

larder for the piped icing to harden.

'You should be proud of that,' Mum says.

'I'm very pleased with the way it's turned out.' I've made my own crystal cake topper and horseshoes from fondant icing. It looks traditional but with a twist, and I can hardly wait to see it as the centrepiece of our reception. We were planning a small wedding, but what with family and old friends, including Summer, and then new friends, including Maria and the Pony Club mums, it's grown into one huge celebration.

Humpty Dumpty buzzes from the worktop.

'That's the next cake ready,' I say.

'Is that for us?' Mum asks.

'I thought we could eat it today.' Bending down, I take it out of the Aga, and lightly press the top with my fingers.

'Did I hear someone say today?' Guy strolls in, dressed in his work clothes, a vest and jeans, and an old sweater slung over his shoulder. 'Does that mean I can have some now?'

'When it's gone, it's gone,' I say, standing the tin on the rack to allow it to cool for a few minutes before I turn it out.

'Have you finished milking all those cows already?' Mum says.

'Yes, I'm getting quite good at it actually. I've been doing it for a while.' Guy's eyes flash with humour.

'Oh, do stop teasing me,' she says, and I can't help smiling.

'Watch out. That's my fiancé you're flirting with.'

'I know, love, and very nice he is too. Quite a hunk...' Mum giggles. 'Or should I say he's fit? I

411

can never remember.'

'I'll have a quick shower then the coffee should be just about ready,' Guy says hopefully.

When he rejoins us, Mum has the coffee on the table, and I have cut the cake. It isn't really cool enough so it crumbles across the plate.

'What is it?' Guy asks when I hand him a slice.

'Walnut, date and honey, not that I'm sure it matters when you eat it that quickly,' I observe, watching it disappear.

'It was particularly gorgeous today – almost as wonderful as my wife-to-be.' Smiling, Guy moves round the table and takes me in his arms, pulls me close and we share a kiss – we've done a lot of kissing to make up for what we might have missed during those months of muddles and misunderstandings.

'Love you,' I whisper.

'Love you too.'

'Ah, you two lovebirds. I can't wait for this wedding,' I hear Mum sigh. 'Forget about cake, Jennie. I reckon it's love that's the sweetest thing.'

Acknowledgements

I should like to thank Laura Longrigg at MBA Literary Agents, Gillian Holmes and the rest of the wonderful team at Arrow Books for their enthusiasm and support.

The publishers hope that this book has given you enjoyable reading. Large Print Books are especially designed to be as easy to see and hold as possible. If you wish a complete list of our books please ask at your local library or write directly to:

Magna Large Print Books
Magna House, Long Preston,
Skipton, North Yorkshire.
BD23 4ND

This Large Print Book for the partially sighted, who cannot read normal print, is published under the auspices of

THE ULVERSCROFT FOUNDATION